Ella Gets The D

TANVIER PEART

frenchy PRESS

The Frenchy Press

5325 Sheridan Drive, Suite 1196

Buffalo, New York 14221-9998

thefrenchypress.com

ISBNs: 979-8-9875061-2-7 (trade pbk.)

Library of Congress Control Number: 2024919025

First Edition: June 2024

Printed in the United States of America

1st Printing

Also by Tanvier Peart

Chance at Love Series

The Seven Month Itch (available as an audiobook)
Miles Apart
Tender Offer

Standalone

Ella Gets the D
Untitled Mafia Rom-Com (coming 2026)

Buffalo Steel Rugby Series

One Knight's Stand
Buffalo Rugby Romance Book 2 (coming 2026)

Author Note

Ella Gets the D is a romance novel about life and unexpected love amid divorce. This story takes place over the course of a year and is full of funny moments and *spicy* scenes with vivid descriptions of sex. It uses strong language and includes an ex (and his anus of a father) demonstrating (nonphysical) controlling behavior. It also mentions sexual harassment allegations and incarceration (off-page and not between the couple).

Have fun, but take care of yourself.

Disclaimer: Please do not attempt to stick your ding-a-ling in a light socket or bleach your eyes after accidentally walking in on a sibling doing the nasty.

Know your worth and add tax.

THE PLAYLIST—PART I

#1 – "Unloyal"—Summer Walker (ft. Ari Lennox)

#2 – "Home"—Snoh Aalegra

#3 – "You're Makin' Me High"—Toni Braxton

#4 – "Bed"—J. Holiday

#5 – "Taboo"—Sevyn Streeter

#6 – "I Want You"—Marvin Gaye

#7 – "Good & Plenty"—Alex Isley, Masego, and Jack Dine

#8 – "Summertime"—Ella Fitzgerald

THE PLAYLIST—PART II

#9 – "Comfortable"—H.E.R.

#10 – "Say Yes"—Floetry

#11 – "Fallen"—Mýa

#12 – "Float"—Amerie

#13 – "Sage"—Eric Bellinger & Ne-Yo

#14 – "Guess Who Loves You More"—Raheem DeVaughn

#15 – "Break My Soul"—Beyoncé

#16 – "Best of Me"—Anthony Hamilton

Chapter 1

Ella

I remember when he bought this house. *Our house.* That day, the glare from the sun seared the back of my neck, which struggled to crane up the ivory brick facade. Sweat dripped from my brow onto my one-year-old squirming in my arms while I chased after my three-year-old, who was determined to break an Olympic record for sprinting down the sidewalk. I was tired but couldn't get the stupid grin pasted on my face to fade.

Six bedrooms.

Six bathrooms.

A corner lot executive home, perfect for an executive and his family.

For three years, I scrubbed every floor, washed every sheet, and prepared every meal in appreciation of a house that was mine in every sense except in name. It became routine, like the birthday parties, swim lessons, and PTA fundraisers that eat through the weekend before you turn around and restart the clock on Monday.

That's the funny thing about routines. It's not hard to spot something out of place.

Take these black pumps at the foot of the staircase. They're fierce but look three sizes smaller than the size ten I wear.

And those moans ping-ponging off the walls? Not mine, either.

The likelihood that a robber—with expensive taste in shoes—waited for the perfect opportunity this Saturday morning to break in and pleasure themselves for the hell of it is slim to none.

I don't need routine to tell me my husband is upstairs exploring someone's insides with his unfaithful dick.

Today is April Fool's Day, and it looks like the joke is on me.

"God, Charles! *Yes.*" The knock of our upholstered headboard against the wall quickens.

What the hell am I supposed to do? Run upstairs with a kitchen knife? Sneak out and pretend I don't hear him rearranging someone else's guts?

I just changed those sheets.

I've seen this scenario play out in hundreds of Lifetime movies. Wealthy husband cheats on wife. This happened to three women at my son's elementary school this year alone.

And it looks like I'm joining the club.

"Oh! Ohh!"

He's close. A few more pumps and—

"*Arghhh!*"

Jack Sparrow got his booty.

Fight or flight, Ella.

I should feel something. Anger. Hurt. Betrayal. *Something.* My mind registers the indiscretion—I hear it, for crying out loud—but I'm numb. My fingers wrap around the refrigerator door handle. I pull out the uncorked wine and drink straight from the bottle.

Shock.

That's what this is. Sadness will come any minute now. Except it never does.

Huh.

Jade-green eyes I once fell in love with widen when Charles turns the corner. His steps falter. "Ella. You're home."

I tip the bottle at him. "Quite the perceptive one you are."

He scans around for our kids. *They're not here to see you for the bastard you are, dear husband.* It's bad enough Jackson heard "Daddy hurting Mommy." How do you explain the birds and the bees to a curious six-year-old, or that his father got caught pollinating another flower?

He adjusts the teal tie the kids and I bought him last Father's Day. His tailored gray suit is back in place. Not a wrinkle or an ounce of shame in sight. "Thought you had a party today."

And I deserved more respect than hearing you go to Pound Town with another woman in our home.

"I left Duke's gift," I say with a nod toward the front door. His eyes follow mine to a blue and green Minecraft bag I forgot to pack in my rush to get Jackson and Haile to their swim lessons on time. "Who's in our bedroom?"

He holds me in a stare, one meant to shrink me down a size for challenging the powerful Charles Hudson II. "No one important."

"Let me guess, you took a detour from the conference you're supposed to be at to give a personal tour of our house. She tripped and fell on your penis," I deadpan. "Hope she enjoyed the new headboard. Sounded sturdy."

Oh, look, I pissed off Charles the Cheater. He hates when anyone questions his authority.

Too bad.

I stand from the kitchen counter I spent countless hours cleaning and head to the staircase. Charles moves in front of me. His voice is low when he speaks. "You don't want to do this, El."

My eyes travel up his frame to reach his gaze. "Don't I?" I step around him and grab a heel to bang on the railing. "Oh, mistress!" I singsong. "Come out, come out, wherever you are!"

"*Ella*," Charles says through gritted teeth.

Hit a nerve, did I?

Footsteps pad down the carpeted runner. Charles and I watch the woman he propelled into our memory foam mattress descend the oak staircase.

She's shorter than me—five-five to my five-eleven, if I had to guess—and looks young. High school young. God, I hope she's at least twenty-one.

Champagne hair fans over her eyes, which refuse to meet mine. I look down at her red-painted toes to search for whatever has her attention. Her hands twist in front of her sheath dress like she's working on an imaginary Rubik's Cube.

She's nervous.

She should be.

"Look at me." Her head lifts at a snail's pace to reveal a flushed face and hazel eyes. She's pretty, the type who bites the sides of their mouth to contour the cheekbones they see in high fashion magazines. She has a narrow nose and plump lips that look like she sucked dick for two hours. If she wasn't screwing my husband, I'd ask where she gets her eyebrows done. They're thick like mine but look airbrushed. "How old are you?"

"Tw-twenty-nine."

I glare at Charles, who looks back unamused. Their twenty-one-year age gap is on brand with this cliché. Of course he picks a woman nearly half his age. I hope she can separate her whites from her lights and darks.

The twenty-niner opens her mouth to speak, but I cut her off. "Nothing you say will change the fact that you had sex with a married man. And don't insult my intelligence, because he's wearing his ring." I sigh. "You're young. You can still make better choices." Hope blooms in her eyes. I smother it. "Don't look at me like that. You're still a bitch. Go do better; I know I will."

"Enough!" A large vein strains against Charles's neck. "Go wait in the car," he says to his mistress, his eyes fixed on me.

Our gazes remain in a tug-of-war. Silence thickens the air until we hear the scurry of feet and the mud room door close.

"I'm going to the airport."

"If you think you—"

His hand raises. "I'll drop her off and come straight home. I won't go to the conference."

I scowl. "And you think *that* makes *this* better?" Reality sets in. "You were going to keep her in your hotel room." The audacity of this man. "Do you two work together?"

"It doesn't matter."

"You're right. We're done."

That felt good. Let me say it again.

"Done." I close the distance between us, my confidence building with each step. "Go to the conference, Charles. You're free to fuck whoever, whenever, as a single man."

I've questioned Charles's faithfulness over the years. Long hours. Endless business travel. I was too afraid of the answer, and now I know the truth. The tilt of his head and tick of his jaw tell me he's not just a bastard, but a liar and a cheater too.

I laugh. It's a ridiculous laugh—with snorting to top it off—that won't stop. I laugh at the white walls and beige decor that are a full-time job to keep clean with a four- and six-year-old. I laugh at the three pieces of furniture in every room because "less is more." And I laugh at the man in front of me. A man I wasted sixteen years with, who grunts like a pirate when he comes.

I walk back to the kitchen, grab my purse, and head to the front door for Duke's gift. Strong hands grab my waist to pin me back to his chest.

He's hard.

His breath is a whisper on my neck. "You drive me crazy, you know that?" I gasp when he tightens his grip. First he cheats. Now he wants to suffocate me? My life really is a Lifetime movie. "I'm not done with you," he says in a low voice.

I bite my lip to hold back a laugh and a little vomit. Money pays for lots of things, but not common sense. "You think we'll work this out?"

His hands lower to trace the curves of my hips. "Of course. We're perfect together."

I turn and grin. "And the women?"

Like the one you sent to the car like a dog. Does she fetch on command too?

He reaches around to cup my ass. "They don't matter. Only you."

It's not lost on me he said *they* and not *she*. How many are on his roster? I need to Lysol this house.

But first.

"Charles?" His breath hitches at my hands on his shirt. The bastard just had sex and is ready for round two. He really believes we'll turn a new leaf. My nails dig into his chest.

He's panting. "Yes, El?"

"Go. Fuck. Yourself."

I drive my knee into his balls. He squeals and drops to the floor. His eyes bulge at my sneaker on his wayward dick. If only I'd worn heels today. "Don't you *ever* touch me again."

He cries at the pressure.

"Let me make myself clear. I want a divorce. The kids will stay at my mother's house for spring break. I'll be back for my things after the party. You better not be here."

With that, I turn the knob and step into the sunlight at the end of a very dark tunnel. He can close the door whenever he gets up. I'm that petty.

"El!" he whines. "Come back here! You can't leave!"

Like hell I can't.

"We'll do couples therapy. I'll change." He staggers to the front door and holds it for support. I catch his pleading eyes through the passenger window. It takes a second for him to morph into the monster he is. "You'll regret this!"

I open the door and stand on the inside of my SUV. "You're making a scene, Charles. You don't want the neighbors to know how much of a bastard you are!"

His eyes roam across rolling lawns. I know people are looking at us, and the thought of shattering this picture-perfect facade widens my grin. "Don't forget about your mistress in the car! She needs to get home before the streetlights come on!"

His eyes are practically out of their sockets.

Good.

I jump into the car, blow a kiss, and peel out of the driveway. The rush gives me the assurance I need that everything will be okay.

I tell myself I'm fine, but it's a lie.

Chapter 2

Ella

My armor stayed in place during the thirteen-minute ride to Duke's birthday party. Me, myself, and I belted out an endless loop of Mary J. Blige hits to ward off the drama in my life. It didn't work. But if anyone knows how to deal with a lying, no-good, ashy man and bounce back with a shoulder shrug, it's the Queen of Hip-Hop Soul.

Morgan kept the festivities low-key with a backyard gathering for her son's first-grade class and friends. Like me, she never understood the need to rent out a ballroom or a theater to entertain an unruly group of tiny people who still struggle to tie their shoes. They have a palate for Lunchables, not seasonal hors d'oeuvres.

Blue, green, and gray streamers flowed from the lone tree in Morgan's front yard. Her Cape Cod-style home reflected the cheerfulness of spring with its white bricks and yellow shutters. A trail of pastel-colored tulips lined the paved walkway to the backyard, where laughter mixed with the sunlight.

Silver foil balloons that spelled "Duke" hung on the wooden swing set next to the shed, formerly known as Joseph Catlett's art studio. With Morgan's ex-husband out of the picture, there was no longer a need to house him or his assortment of paints. The two have been blank canvases for years but make the perfect family portrait as co-parents.

The seven-year-old of the hour sat with my son and friends at one of the picnic tables sprinkled between the Minecraft building blocks across the yard, his black frohawk and fresh fade on the sides peeking through his paper crown. Jackson stationed himself beside him in a matching green polo and jeans, consumed with the assorted party favors on the table, as evidenced by his lip between his teeth. Haile, my baby girl, watched her big brother sift through slap bracelets and crazy straws with wide eyes, a juice box dangling from her mouth, and a turkey sandwich in her hand.

I'm grateful my kids get along. Well, as much as you can hope for siblings two years apart.

The setup was perfect, the day light and full of laughter. Morgan transformed her yard into a Pinterest-worthy Minecraft realm. Between Duke's existing collection of toys and her fleet of extra tables and chairs she keeps for family get-togethers, she only needed a little for her outdoor oasis to come alive.

A small crowd of adults gathered under her cedar pergola, far from the screams of little ones racing after each other but close enough to keep a watchful eye. Morgan just installed a minibar, and luckily there was a stash of her special lemonade that contained more than just juice.

For a moment, I allowed myself to tear the weight of divorce from my shoulders for a slice of cake and the chance to hit one of the four piñatas.

The cake was tasty. The piñata triggered a beatdown of epic proportions.

Death by bludgeoning was the fate of the papier-mâché creeper. The poor guy had no chance after my stick collided with his face over and over again. Both of us were hollow on the inside—only my center lacks Starbursts and Tootsie Pops.

My life is unraveling faster than each strand of tissue paper that flew through the air with every hit to that lifeless face. In less than half an hour, I went from *Oops, I forgot Duke's gift* to *Time to leave my marriage*.

The morning was a regular Saturday, with me rushing to put breakfast in the kids' bellies and Charles kissing me on the cheek with the same mouth he used on the mistress for God knows how long after he left the house to catch a flight he clearly wasn't on.

A business trip.

Thwack.

His fifth in three months.

Of course he cheated. The signs were there. Late nights. Extended trips. He chooses the *one day* I'm sprinting from place to place with the kids to bring another woman into our home? Could he really not wait until hotel check-in to commit adultery? He had to defile our family living space?

Thwack.

You worry too much, Ella.

It's your job to take care of the house.

Thwack.

Just figure it out; you always do.

Being the only active parent in this relationship for so long forced me to think fast and ignore my need for support. It wasn't always like this, but Charles's selfishness shouldn't have been surprising. Yet, color me baffled at the new level of disrespect. I'm too fucking old for the games.

I thought about leaving, but I felt stuck, and I justified staying with excuse after excuse. Sixteen years together, fourteen married, is a long time. It's natural to question whether you'll go the distance, but the truth is, I had questions I pushed down for too long.

Years wasted trying to keep everything together for the children for an asshole who keeps a mistress on standby.

Never!

Thwack.

Again!

Thwack, thwack, thwack.

Dark brown eyes widened when my fists pounded into the lifeless form. Minus the slow headshake and raised brow, Morgan was every bit the model for suburbia. Her green and white tweed blazer paired perfectly with the distressed mom jeans we bought at Target. Tortoiseshell glasses framed her rich chocolate skin.

It's unclear if she wanted to laugh or call a crisis team for a wellness check.

A high-pitched scream snapped me out of my trance. It took a while to register that said scream came from me, until I took in the gathered crowd and my best friend sizing me up for a straitjacket. It was then I knew I would be responsible for the nightmares of small children if I didn't get it together.

I blew out a breath to move a strand of hair off my face and stood with the biggest smile I could fake. "Darn! No Snickers!" I said with a laugh. "Oh well. Here's your candy, kids!"

Little hands dove for the trail of sweet guts spilling from the creeper, buying me enough time to check on my kids again and make small talk with parents. All while dodging Morgan.

Jackson's curious stare lifted his tiny brows. The sharpness in his light brown eyes was too heavy for a six-year-old to wear. His sister reached over to show him a party favor, pulling his focus back to the picnic table and away from the crime scene his mother created.

I dodged questions about everything from how I'm doing—the breakdown no one knows about aside—to Jackson's sports schedule. How could I think about baseball when Charles was likely sliding into a twenty-nine-year-old at that very moment? I also dodged Morgan through a game of tag that put distance between us for fifteen minutes before I made up an excuse to leave.

I was a live wire, and I didn't want another outburst to happen at a child's birthday party, of all places.

So I grabbed my kids and ran—kidding. It was more of a frantic speed walk, but it got us to the car in record time. I was clueless about where to go, but I needed to get out of Falls Church, far away from the gossiping bloodhounds who only care about the drama and not the devastation to my family.

I owe Morgan an apology and an explanation, but the wounds of my husband's betrayal were waiting to crush my chest once the adrenaline wore off.

I had to leave.

There was no way I was going back home, so I hopped on 495 and drove the beltway loop around DC in a daze—twice.

Jackson was silent the entire trip, stealing glances through the rearview mirror that forced me to smear on the mask of a smile I've had mastered for years. Haile narrated the highs and lows of the party the entire ride, pausing to ask, "Are we there yet?" every other exit. Her guess was as good as mine. Then the one place no one in Falls Church would find me popped into my mind. Somewhere I could process my life with free childcare.

IKEA.

So that's where I've been for the last forty-five minutes, consumed with endless room possibilities on a budget while freaking out about my reality at home. My kids, however, are having the time of their lives in the play area.

My phone buzzes with a call from Morgan. *Shit.* There's no privacy in this maze of do-it-yourself furnishings, and against my better judgment, I squeeze into a children's circus play tent and close the fabric.

If this isn't rock bottom, I'm as close to it as my ass is from sticking out the side of this tent.

I take a deep breath and answer, but I don't get the chance to speak.

"Is someone dead?"

Not yet.

"No."

"Are you dying?"

"Aren't we all?"

She pauses. "Fair. Are you and the kids safe?"

"We are."

"Okay," Morgan says with a sigh. "Want to tell me why you went UFC on the piñata? All of that wasn't necessary for a Snickers. You know I keep a special stash."

"It's over."

"Yes, it is. The party was great, by the way."

My voice drops to a whisper. "Not that." I need to make this up to Duke. I would offer to take him for the weekend, but guess who doesn't have a house?

She mimics my tone. "Why are we whispering?"

"Because I'm in a tent."

"You—left to go camping?" Her frown trumpets through the phone.

"A circus tent, for kids."

"You left Duke's party to sit in a *play tent*?"

"Yes—no!" I rub my temple. Believe me when I say Jackson and Haile weren't at all happy to leave early. My four-year-old kindly scolded me for ruining her Saturday plans. She was her brother's plus-one, by the way. "I needed to clear my head. So I drove around and ended up at IKEA."

"But Charles only likes impractical furniture made from the hairs of a goat's sack. Why are you shopping there, and what's wrong with your head?"

"He cheated!" The rest spills out in a rush. "I heard him having sex. In our bed. He didn't even have the decency to take her to a hotel."

Decency would have been to not jackhammer into anyone other than his wife, but we're past that. It's the point of no return.

"No."

"Yes."

"*No.*"

"*Yes!*"

"The actual nerve of that no-good dick!" Morgan loses it. *Join the club*. "You were too good for him, El. That man couldn't get from his ass to his face without a map." There's a long exhale. "What do you want to do?"

"I don't know! What survival guide do you use after you catch your spouse with a woman ten years younger than you, a woman who still has perky breasts?" My heart pounds in my ears. "I haven't worked in eleven years, Morgan. I have no job, a small savings that won't buy a shoebox in Falls Church, and two kids in tow."

I could stay in a motel for a month before I run out of money, and there are short-term rentals around the DMV, but who will put out a welcome mat for a mom with no income?

Charles would take all the furniture and cut off the water before he left the house willingly, and going back isn't an option. Neither is his parents' house, or my mother's in Ohio. I wouldn't put it past Charles Sr. to conveniently lock me out and keep my children when he finds out I'm leaving his son. Charles inherited many things from his father, and spitefulness is right up there with generational wealth and a prenup that leaves me with the same thing I came in with: nothing.

Sweat prickles between my bra and the oversized blouse now clinging to my skin like a magnet. I squeeze my eyes shut and grasp the side of the tent, which almost topples over against my weight. Every decision I need to make hits me at once.

Tears turn into an uncomfortable sob. Leave it to Charles to break our marriage and force me to deal with the mess.

"You're coming to stay with me." Morgan's tone is final. "We'll figure this out together. After we burn down that morgue you called a home with him in it."

I sob harder at her offer—the temporary housing part. Not the arson and murder. That part is tempting.

"Morgan, I can't—"

"You *will* bring your butt and those babies over here. You'd do the same for me, so don't even think about telling me no."

"Just—thank you. I don't know what I'd do without you." The hiccup lodged in my throat becomes another sob, this one encased in fury at the man who's turning my world upside down. "I was loyal to that asshole for sixteen years! I cooked. I cleaned. I took care of our kids, stroked his ego whenever he had a bad day at work, had sex when I was too tired to fake it. And what do I get for honoring our vows?" I punch the side of the tent and scream, "*He* cheats on me, and *I'm* inside a kiddie tent in the middle of IKEA, losing my shit?"

I jump at the outline of a figure at my side. The voice is faint when the person crouches near the tent flap. "Hello? Are you okay?"

My chest tightens. Please don't let me open this tent and find people recording me on their phones. I won't survive The Shade Room or *Good Morning America*.

The pain in the back of my throat from screaming makes it hard to swallow. My fingers fumble with the ties to open the tent. I hesitate to stick my head out but meet a sad pair of eyes when I do.

A woman with white-gray hair looks at me with a smile that makes my shoulders drop. Even though she's crouching, I can tell she's chest height. "Hello there," she says in a gentle voice. "I'm Thelma. I work here, and it's good to see you."

Ms. Thelma reminds me of one of my Sunday school teachers, which is why I will not call her by her first name. She has soft curls pressed back into a bun and plump cheeks that have held a lifetime of smiles. The aroma of fresh cinnamon buns surrounds her like a halo.

I bet she gives wonderful hugs.

I need one.

"Hi." I wipe the snot from my face in a desperate attempt to not reflect roadkill run over twice.

"Sounds like you're having a day, sweetie."

I nod.

"What do you say we go sit in that bedroom display"—she points behind her—"and talk? I roped it off, and it has a partition, so no one will see us."

I'd camp out at IKEA all night if my kids weren't with me. There are beds, food, and snacks. Add wine, and it's a treatment center for scorned women. One that doesn't require assembly.

I do need a new bed set.

And furniture.

A new place to live.

A job.

A *divorce*.

Ms. Thelma stands and stretches out her hand. When I don't budge, she says, "No one is around, sweetie. It's just you and me."

Morgan and her fifty-two questions rattle through the other end of the phone I forgot I was holding. "I'll call you back," I say without breaking eye contact with the woman who has me on the verge of tears again.

One quick call later, we're on top of a plush bed with our shoes off and a tray of tasty food samples. Ms. Thelma got Jackson and Haile's time in childcare extended, which has me wondering if the seventy-four-year-old next to me is the fairy godmother of this IKEA or the boss of an underground crime syndicate in blue and yellow shirts.

The cinnamon bun scent now makes sense.

I lean into a cloud of bed pillows and sigh. My life is circling the drain, but this vanilla soft-serve cone makes the journey delicious. Every day should end with dessert.

My divorce sounds sweeter with each lick. The logistics of it do not. Leaving Charles doesn't require a second thought. Uprooting my kids is a different story.

"Here you go, dear." Ms. Thelma hands me a napkin from the pine nightstand beside her.

Potted plants hang from beams above us through a curtain of string lights. The showroom casts an enchanting glow absent of the usual fluorescent lighting. There's peace here among the neutral paradise of blush and sage. I could sleep for two days straight in this stillness.

My soul is tired and has been for some time.

"Thank you." I smile at Ms. Thelma. It's weak and reflects the exhaustion etched into my features. "I feel horrible for taking so much of your time. I'm sure you have other things to do."

Ms. Thelma waves off my concern. "Nonsense. This place will do fine without me." She touches my knee. "Do you feel a little better? I'll order up some hot tea."

My tears well back up at her kindness. In the short time since she found me hollering in the tent, Ms. Thelma picked me up, dusted me off, and filled me with ice cream. This woman is a loving grandmother in every way possible.

"I'm good right now, but thank you. I really should get out of your hair and take care of my kids." My voice cracks as I turn to the woman who gave me sympathy in a time of chaos. "I don't know how—"

"Shh." She pulls me into a hug. "I'm thankful our paths crossed. You have my number now. Take care of yourself and your family."

"Yes, ma'am."

"You're strong, Ella. You got a stubborn streak in ya, like my granddaughter. The child is heading to college but acts like she's on the Supreme Court." She snickers. "Serves her mother right after what she put me through. You'll call Grier Monday?"

"I sure will."

Grier is Ms. Thelma's youngest child, with a whip for a tongue, as she says. She also happens to be a family law attorney. Turns out losing my shit inside of an IKEA comes with perks.

Ms. Thelma isn't just a fairy godmother; she's a guardian angel.

"Wonderful!" She claps her hands and stands. "Grier is every bit of her namesake. Like Pam Grier, she's a whole lotta woman! You two are close in age and should have a good time."

My brows narrow. "I don't think divorce will be fun, Ms. Thelma." Charles is bull-headed and won't go down without a fight.

Her lips curl into a grin. I take it back—Ms. Thelma might be the boss of an underground crime syndicate after all. "Sit back and enjoy the ride to your freedom, dear."

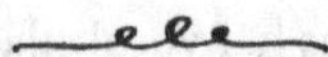

"Pass the sauce please." Haile's hand reaches to the front seat.

"Please roll up your sleeves so you don't make a mess." I have zero interest in battling another stain on that pink sweater she insists on wearing once a week.

Her button nose wrinkles at the implication. "I know, Mommy." She considers the open barbecue sauce and pushes the cotton fabric to her forearm before grabbing a nugget from the bag and dunking.

Between the cake, ice cream, IKEA playtime, and the cool points I lost pulling them out of Duke's birthday early, we should be back to normal, with normal being somewhere in the realm of doing too much. They haven't asked why we're across from our favorite park in the car with fast food and not at home with my latest failed Pinterest recipe attempt. Marry Me Chicken was a cosmic middle finger given the circumstances.

Bribes might take you far in life, especially as a parent, but my kids deserve to know why we're trading our house for my best friend's guest rooms.

"Change of plans," I say to Jackson and Haile's faces full of kids meals in the rearview mirror. "We—I—" *Shit.* "Your father and I love you."

Haile's frown deepens. "Is it terminus?"

"Huh?"

"*Terminus.*" She emphasizes the word like I didn't catch it the first time. "The health."

Oh, terminal. We spend our mornings in the library for classes and reading, which explains her vocabulary, but not why she thinks someone is dying.

"No, baby." I shake my head. "Nothing *terminal*. Our living situation is going to change. Mommy is getting us a new place soon, and your father will take care of our old house."

"What's wrong with the house?"

"Nothing, Jackson."

"Could be ghosts."

"Haile." I sigh. "There are no ghosts."

Jackson's brows draw down with a stare that mirrors his father's—only with confusion and not disappointment. "Did something happen?"

My grip on the steering wheel tightens. How do I tell a six- and four-year-old their family is splitting up, not because of ghosts or any fault of their own? Note to self: add therapy to my list of needs with money I don't have.

I take a deep breath and swallow. "You know how Duke and Aunt Morgan live in their house, and Mr. Joseph has his studio? They're still a family, but they don't live together."

Jackson fights to control the emotions playing out in his eyes. He stares out the window but eventually nods.

"For now, we'll stay at Aunt Morgan's. I called Grandma and will drop you two off to visit next week for spring break." I heard the concern in Mama's voice when I called, but I told her we'd speak more later. They need time with her, and I need child-free days to move clothes and toys.

"Grandma!" Haile cheers with raised fists. One down.

Jackson turns back to me with the shadow of a smile breaking through the corner of his cheek. "Sounds good."

It has to be, because it's all I've got for now.

Chapter 3

Julian

The faint ticks of the bronze table clock on the nightstand count away the time I should've grabbed my stuff and went upstairs. One more email, then I'll leave.

Movement from the bed steals my focus from a message about the rescheduled meeting with Tokyo. A wide hip flares out from the twisted bedsheet. Chloe stirs, shifting thick dark hair across her crinkling forehead. Her brow sinks until Tilly cradles her to her chest and presses a kiss to her cheek.

The two come over on occasion when I need a release from twelve-hour days of contract negotiations. They know what it is. They enjoy hanging out and expect nothing but good dick and a comfortable thread count.

I finish off my scotch and stuff my phone into my pants pocket, next to the wad of wrinkled toilet paper that houses our used condoms. I don't make a habit of leaving them behind or sleeping down here. The first is too risky, and the second isn't my style.

Discarded clothes and shoes form a trail to the front door. I got dressed an hour ago but grab my blazer and loafers. With one last sweep of the room and a pat to my pocket to check for my key card, I leave Tilly and Chloe sound asleep in the four-poster bed and step into an empty hall encrusted in every eighteenth-century decorative accent.

Hugh is in the lobby, reading the paper. His bushy brows peek over the top at me, the only other person wide awake at his hour. "Late night?"

"Early morning."

He nods and flips a page. "I'll have a car ready for your guests by ten." Blue-gray eyes flick to me. "Make that eleven."

"Thank you, Hugh. Please charge their breakfast and rides home to my account."

"Always do," he says without another look.

The number of "guests" has dwindled over the years, but the routine hasn't. I pay enough to this hotel for its discretion whenever I have company—that's in addition to the rate for the suite that's become my second home. It's a bitch to come down to the lobby, but it's the only way to access the car for the private floors and guarantee no one follows you up.

I like my space without strings.

It's three in the morning by the time I wash up and my head hits the pillow. Sleep is more of a nap these days. I need more—rest, obviously, but also something else. The usual vices no longer satisfy me. Not that they ever did.

My eyes finally flutter closed, then my phone rings. I hit ignore, but it rings two more times.

"Yeah?" I huff with a forearm over my face.

"Can I come up?" The familiar voice is faint and unsteady.

Only a few people can bypass my currently occupied guest room suite. It's a bad idea, a decision I would regret in the morning if morning wasn't already here.

Yet...

"I'll meet you in two."

Chapter 4

Ella

"You think you can do this to me?" Charles slams his fist into the mahogany conference table and leans over it. He has at least two more feet before he reaches my personal space, but that doesn't stop his man-child performance. His eyes darken, and his muscles coil like he'll snap any minute. If he wasn't foaming at the mouth because I moved out two weeks ago, I'd wonder if he had rabies.

I turn from the demon in front of me to the wall of floor-to-ceiling windows and the view of the waterfront park. DC is gorgeous in April. The cherry blossoms are in full bloom. The sun is out. People have hit the streets for a stroll in the spring air, void of their winter coats.

"*Ella.*" My name seeps through Charles's lips like a vile curse.

Him again.

My eyes drift back to meet his. Sitting across from my soon-to-be ex and his attorney is not at the top of my list of fun things to do on a Friday afternoon. Haile and Jackson are with his parents until tomorrow. This is my first kid-free night in the city for as long as I can remember. Charles might kill vibes and marriages, but seeing him turn a deep shade of crimson I didn't know was humanly possible makes this meeting—one *he* called—worth every second.

Turns out his unfaithfulness is my ticket to pass go and collect two hundred dollars. Did you know the State of Virginia doesn't require a waiting period to file for divorce if your spouse commits adultery? I didn't, but Grier did.

The day after I met her mother, she pushed a coffee in my hand, gave me a hug, and said, "Nice to meet you in person. Let's talk options."

I planned to call her on Monday, but she beat me to it after she got out of church and has been moving at warp speed ever since. One of her employees made the trip to Charles's office within the week, much to his disgust. Granted, she could've saved the trip by calling, but that's not Grier's style.

She shoots from her wide hips and decided that an in-person visit—on Good Friday, no less—was more appropriate. Is it her associate's fault that Charles works around the clock, which required her to leave a message with his executive assistant saying his wife is filing for divorce after his affair, or that his colleagues happened to be in earshot?

Oh, to see the smoke that erupted from his ears! I'm sure his face contorted like he was holding in gas.

Kind of like how he looks now.

Grier stands and puts a hand on her hip. Her eyes lock on Charles in a silent dare for him to keep up his tantrum. "Mr. Richardson," she says to his lawyer, her gaze still fixed on the doofus of the hour. "Would you please advise your client against his attempts to intimidate Ms. Greene? You are in my office as a courtesy, so we can come to an agreement and dissolve this marriage as swiftly as possible." She sits in her teal-on-teal power suit and steeples her hands. "I take threats very seriously and will recommend my client seek a protection order."

"*Mrs. Hudson*. Her name is Mrs. Fucking Hudson," Charles says through gritted teeth. He tries to level Grier with a stare and gets a smirk. I need to ask her who makes that cranberry lip stain. It's a good look.

"Not for long, Mr. Hudson." Her eyes move to his lawyer. "We'd like to settle this matter and avoid a trial. Adultery—"

"I said I was—"

Charles's attorney pats his hand and nods at the empty chair beside him. It's a request to sit down and shut up, one he obliges. After a brief exchange of whispers, Mr. Richardson turns to face me with a smile that doesn't match his calculated stare.

He touches the trimmed beard framing his face. "Adultery is a serious allegation that is very difficult to prove, Ella." My name comes out with a familiarity that isn't there. No "Ms. Greene" or "Mrs. Hudson." Mr. Richardson is keeping Charles in line so he doesn't look like the live wire he is. "Are you sure you want to end your marriage over a misunderstanding?"

"A *misunderstanding*? I heard my husband screwing another woman in our bed. I spoke to her. There's nothing I missed or need to understand."

He adjusts his copper-framed glasses at an unhurried pace. He's completely relaxed, as if infidelity is a pesky inconvenience, like waiting in a long line at the grocery store when you only have two items. "Adultery requires clear and convincing evidence in a divorce proceeding. Your testimony won't be enough."

"But this is."

Charles and Mr. Richardson turn to Grier. She pushes her black curls over her shoulder and hovers over her laptop at the end of the table. The flatscreen TV above the fireplace turns on. I haven't been in many conference rooms, but this one is pretty glam.

White paneled walls. White oak floors. Linen chairs. Grier Santiago is doing the damn thing with her practice.

"Mr. Hudson, would you please do me a favor and log in to your Amazon account?" The website appears on the screen behind her. Grier looks up from her laptop and smiles. She has her mother's chestnut eyes and high cheekbones. "I promise not to save your information and go on a shopping spree. The attorney fees you'll pay if this goes to court will cover that."

He scoffs but thinks better of trying to correct her again about my last name. "You wish." Charles stands and buttons his navy blazer. He reaches Grier in two strides and whacks the keyboard with his index finger to enter his password. "If you could finish whatever"—he waves a hand at the TV—"this is quickly. I didn't come to DC to shop two-day shipping deals, and I'll will charge you *my* fee if you waste more of my time."

Something flashes in Grier's eyes. "Understood. Why don't you have a seat, Mr. Hudson? This will all be over soon."

I resist the urge to look across the table at the green eyes that are burning a hole through the side of my neck. Charles wants answers, and he's about to get them.

Grier continues once he sits. "This is your account, correct?"

"I signed in to the fucking thing, didn't I?"

"Do you acknowledge your client's confirmation that this is his account, Mr. Richardson?" At his nod, she clicks on Orders and scrolls through last-minute school purchases for Jackson. It's amazing how much stuff a first-grader needs. "Does Ella have access to this account?"

"Yes," Charles says.

"Does she make most of the purchases?"

He huffs. "Does it matter?"

"Just curious."

Here comes another eye roll. "Yes. I got the account for her to buy what she needs for the house and kids."

Grier stops at a purchase from three weeks ago and clicks on it. Then she switches tabs to a website. "Want to do the honors, Ella?"

I stand and smooth out my black pencil skirt and ivory blouse. The gold bracelets on my right wrist clink with each step of these red peep-toe ankle-strap heels. Charles's eyes flick to the chunky gold choker around my neck, then drop to my feet.

Never again.

The wardrobe Charles's monthly allowance provided me belongs to someone with a corner office instead of a child-wrangler who specializes in the art of potty training and navigating elementary school curricula. Appearances have always been more important to him than comfort—which is not to say that stay-at-home parents aren't worthy of dressier clothes. I just prefer ripped jeans to a cardigan and pearls. But I heard his lectures on repeat.

I am the CFO of a multi-billion-dollar organization. What would people think if they saw my wife in mom jeans?

That I have a nice ass and don't wear pretentiousness like a uniform? I hate dressing up, but if it's for my divorce, consider this a suit of armor. My days of being his shiny plaything are over.

Grier winks when I type in the password.

Showtime.

"Ms. Greene—"

Charles snaps, "*Mrs. Hudson.*"

I avert my gaze from him so I don't fall into temptation, hop over the table, and choke what little soul he has left out of him with his tie. The nerve of this man to break up our family, look at me with *bend-over* eyes, and treat Grier with such disdain.

How is it possible to be so evil and clueless at the same time? How did I not see this side of him sooner?

"My apologies." Grier smiles at his glare. The prick has no idea he's a fly in her web. That's the problem with pride: it comes before the fall. "Ella purchased these for your home a week before your entanglement."

Mr. Richardson interjects. "My client does not acknowledge the alleged affair, Mrs. Santiago. Only that he had a colleague with him in the house as he retrieved the passport he left at home before their flight to a business conference."

Bull.

Grier laughs at the awful attempt to explain away Charles's infidelity. He might be able to expense receipts from the trip, but this crock of shit won't fly here.

Grier and I share a knowing look, one that starts with *Got* and ends with *his ass*.

In the two weeks I've known her, Grier has been a powerhouse. She's a witty, no-nonsense mama you don't want as an enemy. She puts a hand to her mouth to catch her breath. "I needed that laugh. Let's move on, though the justification for Mr. Hudson's colleague in the home is questionable at best. She did not have to enter the house—or their bedroom, for that matter—while he retrieved his passport. And, of course, it doesn't explain why your client picked up said colleague instead of meeting her at the airport."

Grier slides a folder to the middle of the table from a stack next to her computer. "Jeanine from HR was kind enough to pull the Mt. Corbel Health System travel policy. As Chief Financial Officer, you have a guaranteed car service to drive you to and from the airport." She pauses for dramatic effect. "Wonder why your client opted to drive his own vehicle to pick up this particular woman."

Charles clenches his jaw and looks away.

She switches the screen back to the purchase history. "As I was saying, my client purchased five of these cameras for the house. Can you confirm the order from your account, Mr. Hudson?"

"Yes," he says in a sharp tone.

"Did you see these around your home?"

He nods. "I helped El put them up to make sure they worked. She wanted them for the new sitter she hired."

"Yes." The corners of Grier's mouth curl. "That's right. Did you download the app that comes with this technology, Mr. Hudson?"

"I did not."

"Is there a point to these questions?" Mr. Richardson asks. "He is not on trial, and I will advise him against further interrogation outside of a court of law."

"Right." She claps the back of the chair and grins wider.

Grier paces the conference room with a gleam in her eye and glances between the men with her hands behind her back. She looks like Tegan Price from *How to Get Away With Murder*, and I can only imagine the power she wields inside a courtroom. It's direct yet subtle, the way her brow lifts and her eyes stare through her target. She's a shark circling her next meal, and they don't even know it.

"The app was a standard feature," she says after a brief pause. "What's interesting is the motion tracking these cameras provide." She stops in front of her laptop and leans in for the next part, the one neither Charles nor his lawyer anticipated. "Imagine my surprise to find that Ella signed up for the one-month free trial of cloud storage. Did you know it records video history? It defaults to motion detection. Ella forgot about that feature until I took a look at it." She switches the screen to the cloud storage site. "The videos are here."

Mr. Richardson eyes Charles, whose brows draw together. His suit doesn't hide the sweat marks puddling through overpriced fabric. He clears his throat but stays silent.

"I made sure to get to the appropriate time stamp. The two cameras downstairs pick up Charles and his coworker when they enter the mudroom."

In the video, Charles pulls her into his chest. She giggles as he grinds his pelvis into her and leans down to whisper in her ear. Her heels come off at the bottom of the steps. Charles loosens his tie, his forceful grip as evident as the desire in his eyes. Cameras in Jackson and Haile's rooms catch the pair when they're in the hall. Things take a turn once they reach our bedroom.

This isn't the first time I've watched the video, but it doesn't sting any less. Seeing the two of them traipse through my house—past my children's room—without a single care has me ready to catch a case.

"Ella put the camera in your bedroom as a precaution for future sitters," Grier says to Charles. "She didn't hide it, so my guess is you already knew but didn't bank on it recording." She turns to the TV and raises the volume.

Charles pushes the woman onto the bed with enough force for her to bounce. He removes his jacket and commands her to get on all fours. Without protection or foreplay, he hovers behind her, unzips his pants, and thrusts. He not only defiled our marriage but had no concern about my health, raw-dogging his mistress. I booked an appointment with my gynecologist faster than any worst-case scenario could play out in my mind. No STDs, thank God. I've never been so happy to have a three-month dry spell.

"That's enough." Mr. Richardson turns from the screen. He swallows hard and pinches his lips shut.

Grier chuckles. "Oh, this doesn't last long." She fast-forwards and stops when Charles pulls out and tosses his handkerchief at her. "Clean yourself up, we have to go," he says in the video. His tone is cold, void of a lover's caress. "You have five minutes." With that, he walks out the bedroom.

What a gentleman.

Charles shifts in his chair. The tremor in his voice catches me by surprise. "Ella."

Nope. Don't use that tone or those eyes on me.

Bastard Charles is easy to hate. He's arrogant, selfish, and only acts like he cares until he gets what he wants. I loathe that man. Despise him. I was comfortably miserable for too many years with him.

But this man? The one whose jade-green eyes are pleading with me? I haven't seen him in a long time, and that breaks my heart.

The day we met is etched deep into my memories and the splintered thing called my heart. I'd made it to an Ivy League for grad school. Me, a girl from Bellaire, Ohio, who got a bachelor's from a state school on a grant, was attending one of the most prestigious programs in the country for early childhood education.

I stuck out on campus like a big toe. I didn't come from money or have a million-dollar trust fund waiting for me as a graduation present. My outfits were courtesy of the thrift store. And that shiny silver spoon? More like reused plastic from the takeout meals my mom and I would order from the diner.

I worked at a tiny coffee shop with free lunch on break and access to the French press as benefits. That's where I saw him.

Time stopped when the bell over the front door chimed and his sharp eyes landed on me. My breath skipped at their intensity, which forced my gaze off the gorgeous man with neatly combed jet-black hair and back to the menus I was sorting. Charles was only a few years younger than I am now. His face was smooth, free of facial hair and the frown lines that come with a sixty-hour work week.

The corners of his eyes crinkled on his short walk to the counter. I spun in a circle twice before I crouched down to look at the pastry display. My stomach threatened to fall out of my ass that afternoon. I thought there was no way a guy like that would want a girl like me. Someone whose fanciest outfit was a vintage graphic tee with jeans and a gold belt. My attempt at one of those messy buns looked like a squirrel got caught in my hair and died. So I ducked out of sight in a sad attempt to hide behind a glass pastry display.

Those same jade-green eyes peered over the counter, and when our gazes locked, I got a half-smile and knew I was a goner.

Charles was out of my league. I should've paid attention to the warning signs and saved myself—just like I need to pay attention to the sudden urge to staple his nuts to the wall.

Grier's voice pulls me back to the conference room and my pending divorce. "Please refrain from speaking directly to my client, Mr. Hudson. I advised Ms. Greene not to comment."

He winces at Grier's words but doesn't correct her when she calls me by my maiden name. Charles is many things—proud, an asshole, and a cheater—and judging by the pained expression on his face...remorseful? That's not right. In the sixteen years we've been together, he's never apologized. But he's also never looked so sad.

Dull eyes lock with mine. Did he ever love me, or was I some DIY project he could mold to fit into his life?

Grier looks to his lawyer. "I sent a digital copy to your email."

"Thank you," he says with a sigh, unable to look at Charles or stomach the thought of smut in his inbox.

"There's additional footage of Ella and Charles's encounter in the kitchen after his entanglement." Grier closes her laptop and turns to Charles, who's still staring at me. "I'm happy to see you out and about after that knee to the genitals, Mr. Hudson." That gets her a glare. "Are we ready to discuss a separation agreement? There's no sense in denying the affair, as we have...what did you call it, Mr. Richardson? Oh yes. Clear and convincing proof."

Charles's hands tighten into fists. "No."

Come again? He can't be this spiteful.

"I messed up." He swallows and sits straighter. "I'll try couples counseling and whatever else it takes to make this work. Come home."

Home.

I lived in a showroom, a curated image of Charles's perfect family. I didn't leave a home—I freed myself from a gilded cage.

"Mr. Hudson, my client is clear in her desire to dissolve this marriage. Furthermore, her return to the property is a good defense against adultery, to make it appear she resumed the relationship after the fact. There's no condonation here."

Mr. Richardson's lips twitch. If he didn't respect Grier before, he does now. "What are your terms?"

"Ms. Greene will have primary physical custody of the children and maintain joint legal custody with Mr. Hudson. My client requests child support and temporary spousal support until she secures employment. The marital property and assets in Mr. Hudson's name will remain his. She will keep the SUV as her primary vehicle to transport the children." Grier leans forward. "Ms. Greene wants a clean break. Accept this separation agreement so we can bypass a trial."

A clean break.

Charles was making six figures before his twenty-fifth birthday. He comes from wealth, and he amassed his own fortune from different investments over the years. It's why he wanted me to be his stay-at-home trophy and stop working two years into our marriage. Well, his puppeteer days end now.

I've got no strings on me.

The seven stages of a man about to lose his shit flash through his features. The blank stare directed at no one in particular morphs into squished eyebrows and a look that says, *I can't believe this bitch doesn't want my money.*

That last part is wrong. I *do* want *some* of his money. As much as I want to dance into the street singing "You Don't Own Me" like an honorary member of The First Wives Club, it's real out here. Rent is expensive, bills laugh in your face, and the concept of savings will remain a friend with no benefits until I get a job and push the reset button on my life.

My savings will go from a few thousand to *you wish!* once I leave Morgan's house. Have you seen these home prices? They'll snatch the joy straight out of your soul.

Mr. Richardson glances at Charles. When he doesn't get a response, he moves his hand slowly in front of his face. "Charles?"

Nothing.

"Would you like to discuss these terms in private?"

Crickets.

For the most arrogant and obnoxious person in the room, you'd think a doctor told him he has two days to live. Charles has never been speechless, so this is saying something.

"Char—"

"Ninety days." He answers his lawyer with his eyes still on me. "I'll agree to the terms with the stipulation that she has ninety days to find a job and a home to live in that isn't her best friend's house."

A smirk forms.

The bastard hopes I'll fail and move back. Three months might as well be a trial separation period, one that sends me back to square freaking one. In what world is it easy to find a new job *and* a place to live in under six months? You need one to pay for the other—the security deposit, last month's rent, and the just-because rent on top of that. Charles knows it's a mission impossible.

Well, call me Tom Fucking Cruise.

I speak before Grier goes for his jugular. "Deal, but if I'm going to need to get a place within that time, I want all of my spousal support upfront."

Thin lips spread to reveal even, white teeth. Charles has what you'd call a classic look. He's a handsome man with a straight nose and a square jaw that's in perfect proportion with the rest of his features. The salt and pepper in his jet-black hair adds to his time-lessness.

I bet he thinks it's cute how assertive I'm being. The tug-of-war between wills is a routine we know well. I'd challenge whatever authority he thought he had, and he would fuck me into submission—or at least try.

I thought it was enough, that *I* was enough. Now, I'm taking back my time and my power.

And I'm just getting started.

"I want a lump sum, including for the two weeks I left after you silverbacked your coworker in our bed. Since I experienced emotional distress, let's double that amount."

Two can play this game.

His face morphs, and his eyes turn cold. "Don't push it, dear."

"You haven't begun to see me push. You're lucky I don't challenge the prenup. Don't tempt me to air your unfaithful ways throughout Falls Church. I can play the heartbroken wife, and I'd have no problem crying on the shoulders of the PTA moms who will spread our business around town. You want to treat me like *I* did something wrong? Consider this my villain origin story. Now. Sign. The. Damn. Agreement."

I sit and stare. Charles might think he has the upper hand because of his money, but I have the truth, and it will set me free.

That afternoon was the rude awakening I needed. I deserve better. My life is far from over, and I want it back.

The tic in his jaw tells me Charles feels cornered. He hates losing control. His fingers drum on the table. *Thump, thump, thump.*

All eyes are on him in anticipation of his response.

Seconds pass in our staredown until his shoulders push back and his chin lifts. "Okay, El. We'll play it your way. For now." The last part comes out in a tone that sends a chill down my spine. Charles never laid a hand on me or used his near half-a-foot height difference to intimidate me. Yelling isn't his thing, believe it or not, but the fake smile plastered on his face right now is textbook Charles.

He's up to something.

"I believe time is of the essence, gentlemen," Grier says. "While I have you two here, let's amend the separation agreement to reflect these changes."

Charles is silent for a beat but nods. "If we can get it done within the hour, I have no objections." He stands and buttons his blazer. "I need to step out and make a few calls. I trust you and my attorney will take care of this."

Mr. Richardson gathers his briefcase. If he wasn't Charles's counsel, you'd think he moonlights as Santa and spends his free time reading books to sick children in the hospital. Then again, he does look like an older version of the dad in *Get Out*. And we all know how that ended.

"Ms. Greene, it was wonderful to meet you, though I wish it were under different circumstances," Mr. Richardson says. "Take care of yourself. As for you, Ms. Santiago. I hope not to find myself on your opposing side again." He chuckles, but he's serious. Grier Santiago, attorney at law, is deadly.

The woman of the hour extends her hand with a smile. "It was nice meeting you. I'll say a prayer for your patience with that one." She nods to the glass windows that face out to the rest of the office. Charles is near the entrance, deep in conversation on his phone.

Mr. Richardson lets out a playful laugh. His eyes lift with a genuine smile. "I have years of practice, dear. I've been one of the family's attorneys since he was in preschool." *Huh.* "I'll leave the two of you to talk and will check back shortly."

The room is silent after the door clicks shut. Grier and I stare at each other before we erupt into a cheer. I hug her with everything I have. I'm so happy, I could cry.

"You were amazing," I say with a finger snap. "Your mom told me you're not to be messed with, but damn."

"Thank you, thank you." She bows with a giggle. "What about you, Ms. Run Me My Check Now?" She laughs. "You were brilliant."

"What's next?"

"All parties sign off on the separation agreement. Since Charles isn't contesting it, we'll avoid trial."

Right, a year.

Staying another hour in this marriage is a special kind of torture, but letting a court decide if Charles committed adultery is not an option. Well, it is. A costly one that will end in hundreds of thousands in legal fees I don't have and risk a judge siding with my ex and his bullshit defense. I'll be in debt and back to waiting for the one-year minimum separation requirement before I could even file for divorce since we have kids—assuming his courtroom victory wouldn't inspire him to drag things out until I get nothing and have nothing left.

Grier was smart to threaten legal action to force Charles to sign a separation agreement. If I have to wait a year until I can file for divorce, I'd rather have guardrails in place.

There's a tap on the conference room door before it opens. A head peeks around it, a head with a beautiful face and haunting brown eyes. "Is everything okay? I heard screaming," the head says in a faint accent.

His eyes move from me to Grier. The lines on his forehead deepen, drawing his thick brows together. A strong Adam's apple bobs with a swallow, and down my eyes go on a journey from pursed full lips to a short boxed beard.

Did he come with the office?

Grier's gaze lingers on the mystery man.

One second.

Two seconds.

Three seconds pass.

My fingers trail over the pulse in my neck, which is doing back flips. For Grier's sake, I hope she's not his superior the way she's humping him with her eyes. The sexual tension between them is *thick*.

If this happens when he shows his face, what's her reaction when more of his body comes into view?

"We're okay, thank you," she says, like she's playing out different fantasies in her head. *Don't blame you, girl.* "Mateo, this is Ella. Ella, meet my husband and business partner."

Oh.

Ohh.

That explains the bedroom eyes. I'm sure the photocopier and the windows in this office have seen some things. There's no way I could work in the same office as my spouse—one I wanted to stay married to—and be expected to, you know, do work.

Mateo's face has a rough edge to it beneath the surface. He's in a toffee-colored suit with no jacket, rolled-up sleeves, and a matching vest. His silk copper tie brings out his golden skin and cognac eyes, which are fixed on their target. Mateo is a few inches taller than me and built like he doesn't skip leg day, or any other day in the gym.

He extends a hand. "Ella. It's nice to finally meet you. Grier talks about you like you two have been friends for years."

That makes me smile. "She's an amazing woman."

"That she is."

"We're wrapping things up and going for drinks to celebrate her separation agreement," Grier says. "Where's The Tyrant tonight?"

"Staying over at Dejia's house. The international club leaves for Charlottesville bright and early tomorrow."

Grier bounces on her toes. "You mean?"

"She won't be back until late tomorrow night." A man wearing a wide grin replaces the scowler who stomped through the room minutes ago. The heat in his gaze for his wife still needs a parental advisory label, but his upturned face chips away at his don't-eff-with-me armor he wields. Mateo pulls out his wallet to give Grier a black card. "Tonight is on me, ladies." He lifts her chin again to take a kiss. "Call me when you're done. I'll pick you up." His eyes shift to me. "Ella, I look forward to seeing you again."

Grier calls to him when he reaches the door. "It might be late, and I don't want to wake you. I'll take a car home."

Mateo looks over his shoulder at Grier with enough passion in his eyes to make nuns repent. I might say two Hail Marys, and I'm not even Catholic. "Who said we were going home? I'll book us a room at your favorite hotel for the night." The corner of his mouth lifts. "Pace yourself. You'll need your energy later."

I don't know how long Grier and I stare at the door after Mateo's exit, but I can tell you it has satin finishes and the same egg-white color as the trim around the room.

They have good sex, I know they do. The sweaty kind where you keep a water bottle nearby and need Megan Thee Stallion knees for extra bounce.

Seeing Grier and Mateo reiterates how comfortably miserable I was with Charles. There was no passion, no heat. Yes, that stuff comes and goes in waves over time, but I'm not sure we liked being around each other.

These two?

They can't keep their hands off each other, even after nineteen years of marriage and a seventeen-year-old they call The Tyrant.

If I ever date again, I need to set the bar higher.

"That was...wow," I say through a breath.

"Yeah."

We're still staring at the conference room door. Neither of us has moved a step since Mateo turned this room into a sauna.

"Is he always that—"

"Intense? Yes." Her eyes flick to me. "I really am sorry for the PDA. We're usually able to contain ourselves until the clients leave."

This door is quite exquisite. It's nowhere near as entertaining as Grier and Mateo, but the thick hardwood barrier pivots. That has to be why we can't take our eyes off of it.

"Sorry, what?"

Grier laughs and breaks our trance. "We need to go. There's a rooftop bar a short walk from here that has every handcrafted cocktail your heart desires. Let's get this separation agreement signed and enjoy our Friday."

Right. Charles is still here.

"Let's do it."

Chapter 5

Ella

"When I tell you that you missed a *show*." I dodge the fleet of cocktail straws Grier hurls my way with a laugh and steal another sip of my mojito. It's my second, and it's hitting the spot.

Grier rolls her eyes and tosses the orange spiral on the side of her glass into her cosmo. "There was no show, Morgan," she says through a sigh. "The only thing you missed was a front-row seat to watching Ella take back her power. I'm a bulldog, but this one?" She points at me. "Ruthless."

"I took a page from the Santiago book of Try Me If You Want," I say with a wink. A hand curls over my mouth as I whisper-yell, "But the *show*"—I jerk my head toward Grier—"was her and her husband."

Morgan's chestnut eyes widen, the same way her son's do when he finds a Pokémon card that does "good damage."

The advantage of a round bistro table is that Morgan and Grier are close enough to hear without my having to yell. The disadvantage of a kid-free night with drinks is that you yell regardless.

Over the next ten minutes, Morgan fans herself at the play-by-play of Mateo's attempt to swallow Grier's soul through her mouth and tonight's hotel plans.

The sun's glow dips into the lavender horizon to the beat of soft jazz. The rooftop is full of patrons in their Friday best. Tea light candles twinkle along the scattered tables next to the bar.

"I don't know you well, but I wish you a lifetime of happiness and mind-numbing sex," Morgan says through a hiccup that morphs into a giggle.

"Hear, hear!" I raise my empty glass to Grier, whose face is now the same color as her blush. "Please don't be mad at us. We don't get out."

"Our kids watch videos of other kids playing Minecraft on repeat." Morgan's fingertips graze the side of her hair that's slicked over her shoulder. Between the threat of humidity in the air and our gushing over Grier and Mateo's mating ritual, it's a wonder her edges haven't curled to life. "If you told me you were having bunion surgery tomorrow, I would still come out to celebrate if it meant a moment to myself that doesn't involve a toilet." She lifts her margarita glass with a goofy grin and tries to lick off the salted rim, mimicking lazy head in slow motion.

That's it. We're cut off.

"You also have the longest relationship between the three of us," I say. "You and Mateo *like* each other after nineteen years. Teach us your ways, o' wise one."

We bow at Grier, who shakes her head and laughs. "Believe me when I say I'm no expert on love. But I will say you have to be with someone you enjoy as a person. Someone who challenges you to be the best version of yourself and loves you through your worst."

Grier tells us she and Mateo met in a law library during their second year of law school. Hours of books between them turned into an engagement by the end of the fall semester and a traditional Mexican ceremony over spring break. Mateo, who comes from a long line of Black and Indigenous Veracruzanos, lived in Mexico until he came to the States for college. He's one of four kids and sent back what he could to help his family. Mateo and Grier moved up their wedding when his grandfather got sick. He died months after the ceremony.

"Enough about me." Grier smacks my leg. "Tonight is about you, Slayer of Charles the Cheat and Lady of the DMV. We still have a journey ahead of us, but tonight"—she raises her glass—"we celebrate your separation agreement."

My thumb moves to twist the ring that's now absent from my finger. What I wouldn't give to take a girls' trip to a warm beach with no six-o-clock wake-up call to get the kids ready for a long day of activities.

"The countdown is on for me to find a new job and house." I blow out a hard breath to force down all of the pitfalls now playing in my mind like coming attractions. There's too much going on right now to focus on what I want. "Ninety days isn't long, and I don't know where to start."

Is there an app to help discarded spouses get their lives together? Can I swipe right for a reset that doesn't include sleepless nights?

The cost of living around here is enough to make me sob. I don't want to move back to Ohio, but I will if it gives my babies stability.

Morgan snaps her fuchsia-lacquered fingers. "I almost forgot!" She digs through her designer Mary Poppins bag of goodies, on a mission. She once pulled out a half-eaten grilled cheese sandwich, plastic vampire teeth, vitamins, and a soccer ball. There's a chance my next home is at the bottom of that bag.

"What are these?" I frown at the silver keys she puts in my hand. Does she want me to drive us home?

"Keys to your new house."

"My what?"

"Townhouse, to be exact."

My back hits the rattan chair with a thud. When I said my new house was at the bottom of her purse, it was a joke. I stare at the simple ring holding two keys that are an answer to my problems—and a gift I can't accept. "I don't have a house, Morgan. I share yours, remember?" Did she forget I took an eleven-year hiatus from my career? I have six suitcases between me and my kids, an SUV my ex won't fight me to keep, and a savings account that gives me the finger on the daily.

When did I have the time *or* the money to get a townhouse?

"You need a place to live, and that's a family property that's available until the end of December. It's not a year, but it will get you to the end of this one with some breathing room so you can save up. Don't look at me like that."

If Ms. Thelma is my fairy godmother with a knight in shining power suit for a daughter, Morgan is...there are no words.

I'm speechless.

We met three years ago, when Jackson and Duke were in preschool. I was new to Falls Church after Charles moved us from Boston faster than I could find the packaging tape. I had no friends and only my in-laws in the area until I met Morgan. We volunteered to decorate our sons' class for the holidays. I spent hours making construction-paper decorations to string from the ceiling. Morgan found a sad tree branch, wrapped the base in a blanket, and hung a red bulb from the dying needles. *A Charlie Brown Christmas* was the extent of her craftiness.

Morgan comes from a prominent DC family, in case that wasn't obvious with the spare house (but not the half-dead holiday decor). She flexes her Whitley Gilbert ways as the corporate art buyer for her father's international law firm. Outside of the occasional pair of jeans, she doesn't dress casually and lives the fancy life without apology.

Take tonight. Morgan came out for drinks in a high-waisted black jumpsuit with ruffled sleeves, a plunging neckline, and clear heels with rhinestones. Knowing her, they're diamonds. She never looks less than a million bucks or misses the opportunity to show off her petite Pilates curves. It's a far cry from her backyard Minecraft party look, but that's Morgan. High-end fashion all the way.

And this was a last-minute outfit, by the way.

If I didn't have to meet my cheating ex, best believe I would be in jeans, a long-sleeve shirt, and *maybe* strappy heels to look like I tried. Sweatpants, a concert tee, and a messy top knot is my outfit of choice when I'm not keeping up with this one.

Morgan and I are polar opposites, minus our ability to not take ourselves too seriously.

I reach for the check but come up short. Morgan looks at the receipt and says, "Careful, El. Your thoughts will give you a migraine as loud as they are."

"*Morgan*. I can't accept it." I hand back the keys at the same time Grier yanks at the check.

We both get a smack.

"Hey! Tonight is on Mateo." Grier rubs her knuckles.

Morgan shakes her head. "It's celebration of Ella and the gymnastics you and your man will do in that happy marriage of yours." The server takes Morgan's card at her nod. "It's not up for debate, counselor."

"No." I shake my head. "Thank you for the drinks, but this"—I point to the keys—"is too much. You took me and my kids in at one of my lowest points." My lip trembles. I will not cry at this rooftop bar. "I have to do this on my own."

I refuse to take advantage of Morgan's hospitality or her money. She already went above and beyond. I can do this. I *will* do this.

The keys come back to me. Morgan takes my hand in hers and levels me with a mom stare I know well. It's the same if-you-don't-close-your-mouth look I give my kids, and it scares me now that I'm on the receiving end. "Yes, you can." She takes a breath and softens her features. "Listen to me, El. I know you feel obligated to suffer alone, but you have family here. People who want to help and see you succeed.

"How many women do we know who suffered in silence? Women who loved their spouses and gave up their careers to handle things at home—only to have their trust betrayed and that love thrown back in their faces? I know you're scared, but I want you to hear me when I say I will not let you go through this alone."

Grier nods. "Morgan is right," she says about my friend who's waving her hand in an I-told-ya-so motion. "Take the townhouse and figure out your next steps. There's no need to struggle to prove you'll do it on your own. We know you will, and accepting help doesn't diminish that."

"What about Charles?" He'll fight this.

The corner of Morgan's lips curl. "I'm no legal expert, but you agreed not to live in *my* house. This townhouse is a Brooke property that *I* don't own."

Grier lifts a shoulder and says, "He put emphasis on Morgan's personal residence. Anything not in her name is fair game."

This is really happening. The end of the year will come in a flash, but this gives me a chance to finally exhale. "I'm in."

We hug and scream around the bistro table, earning a mix of claps and blank stares from people near the bar.

"The townhouse is here in Georgetown. It's about a fifteen-minute drive to Falls Church without traffic," Morgan says. "You'll find a job in no time. I know you will." She chuckles. "My father adores you. He would create a position for you on the spot."

"Sounds like you have options, Ella," Grier says with a wink.

Guess I do.

Chapter 6

Julian

"You alright tonight, fam? If you're knackered, go home."

"And miss your going-away party? Never."

Kendi is one of the first friends I made in London when I started coming over years ago. He put me on to one of the local rugby teams he's been captain of for years, and there are large cleats to fill now that he's leaving.

His grin widens in a slow spread of pearly whites. If I had a pound for every time someone mistook him for Daniel Kaluuya, I'd never have to work again. A VIP server already asked for a selfie.

"When you leaving us?" I nudge his shoulder from the balcony we're leaning against. Sweat and pheromones waft up from the dance floor of bodies grinding into each other to Soca beats.

His head tips from side to side. "A few months? Chi and I are still faffing around, but we need to be in Amsterdam by August."

"Big man doing big things."

He dips his head to hide a smile. "I do alright."

Kendi wears modesty with the same ease as his three-piece suits. We match tonight in black vests, blazers, and trousers.

"Bro, don't you dare downplay your contract. It's huge." I don't know all the details, but establishing systems for local renewable energy projects is a big deal. "I'm proud of you."

"Says the person who helped negotiate the contract." He laughs. "You're doing your thing out here, Julian. I'm proud of you too."

Our attention drifts back to the dance floor. Our teammates are scattered around, trying their best to pretend they have rhythm—except for Syed, who's twerking on a woman in a silver dress.

"Surprised you're not down there." Kendi lifts his chin to our group.

We're the only two tucked into the VIP section with bottle service, and that's fine by me. I take a sip from my glass. "I'm good."

Late nights and faceless sex. That's what's out there. I'd be lying if I said I haven't had my fill. Those days were good to me, and still are, whenever the work week is chaotic or I feel like letting off steam.

I won't deny the lure, but it's starting to get dull for reasons I can't explain.

Kendi whistles. "Is the bachelor ready to come off the market?" He chuckles into his glass. "Moms will be chuffed."

I groan. "Do not mention her. She probably heard you and is planning an arranged marriage as we speak."

Quiet as it's kept, this is the first time I've been out in a minute. I like staying in. Sometimes with company, but mostly without.

His snort morphs into full-on laughter. It's not that damn funny. "Relax, bruv. I was only taking the piss. Nothing wrong with wanting to stay in the house. Speaking of which." He looks at his watch. "I better crack on."

My lips twitch. Two years ago, Kendi would have been the first person on the dance floor and the last to leave—with a woman on each arm. Then he met Chi, and everything changed. "Tell the future missus I said hi."

We dap each other up. "Come over for dinner sometime," he says. "Bet."

Minutes knit into an hour of scrolling on my phone. There's no game tomorrow, which presents the rare opportunity to sleep in and not skim through pages of contracts. I'm lost in an email on the couch when a server places a bottle of water on the side table. "Thank you."

She stands between my legs. "I get off in an hour, in case you want a nightcap."

I crane my neck and lean into upholstered pillows, taking in full lips and auburn hair that frames a heart-shaped face. Her white dress cascades to cleavage she skims with her fingers. My gaze roves over rich brown eyes and prominent cheekbones. She is beautiful.

The attraction is there, but the desire isn't. I surprise the both of us when I graciously decline and take my ass home.

Chapter 7
Ella

Six hours of sleep, a pool of drool on my pillow, and a mild hangover later, I'm on my way back to my in-laws' to get Haile and Jackson.

Morgan and I hydrated with water until Mateo came to collect Grier. We fanned ourselves with cocktail napkins like school-girls before calling it a night. I still have a headache but look presentable as a woman about to visit her future ex-husband's parents after knocking back a few cocktails the night before.

Iron gates part on my approach to the last home on the long, tree-lined street. It's more like a compound, though no armed guards lurk in the shadows. The house is over-the-top on its own and sits pretty on acres of land fenced away from the rest of civilization.

Over the years, the Hudsons purchased the surrounding *five* properties. For privacy, and so Charles Sr. can play the real-estate edition of Whose Is Bigger? He never misses the chance to turn up his nose at his neighbors' single-acre plots to his six.

The annual soirees hosted here are the talk of Falls Church. People rearrange their travel plans for the chance to boast about attending an exclusive Hudson event. I could pay a full year's rent selling my access to the highest brown-nosing bidder. That's assuming Charles's parents don't electrify the fence now that we're divorcing.

My SUV rolls along the concrete to the custom-built colonial mansion. Flowers are blooming around the fountain in the middle of the circular driveway. I go to the far side of the home, as I always do, and find a spot in the guest parking area.

Yes, there are three designated spaces for us commoners to use, daughter-in-law included. Additional parking, for staff and overflow, is down the gravel trail and requires a golf cart for the return trip.

This house is obscene.

I pull down the visor to touch up my hair and add a nude lip color.

Mrs. Hudson will be ready for tea with the first family in a dress suit and pearls, even if it's eight thirty in the morning on a Saturday. The best she'll get from me today is an oversized boyfriend shirt, jeans, and black loafers.

Stone pavers guide me to the sound of laughter in the backyard. I pass the six-car garage and stairs that lead to the basement. A private patio comes into view. It lacks casual seating but has an L-shaped outdoor kitchen for the hired help who work the many parties here. There's enough room to fit a hundred people at tables on the tiled floor without disrupting the manicured lawn.

I follow the trail beyond the rose bushes and stop. Jackson and Haile run around the two-story cedar playground without a care in the world. Hints of auburn from their textured brown curls catch the sunlight above the canopy of pine trees. The sight of the cottage-style structure, which has three swings, a slide, and a fire pole, isn't what makes me gasp. Well, it did three years ago, when Katharine had it installed for Jackson when we moved to Falls Church. I expected Charles's father to tear it down with his bare hands, but my mother-in-law made sure that didn't happen.

She's full of surprises. Like how agile she is chasing after my children right now—which is what makes me gasp.

Katharine Hudson runs after her grandchildren with the biggest grin I've ever seen on her face. Golden white strands fall from her once-perfect bun as she speeds up to wrap her arms around Haile. My four-year-old squeals at the gentle hands that pull her into a hug just as Jackson changes course to run full speed at his grandmother.

No. No!

I yell, "Easy!" right before impact, but it's too late.

My six-year-old, possessed with the spirit of a linebacker, pummels into her back. The force of the blow knocks Haile out of Katharine's arms and sends the sixty-two-year-old head first into a pile of wood chips with an *oof*.

I scoop up Haile, who clings to my neck, and rush to Katharine's side. "Are you okay?" Do I shake her, check for broken bones? Both? I move to roll her over but stop when her body shakes. "Katharine?"

Jackson pulls at the sides of his hair. "I didn't mean to kill her, Mom, I swear!"

"She's dead?" Haile's lip trembles, a preview of a breakdown loading.

Katharine turns over with a muffled groan, her delicate wrists shielding her steel-blue eyes from the sun. The faint wrinkles around her mouth curve against the flush creeping up her pale cheeks. "I'm fine." She sits up and pulls wood chips from her hair. "Jackson is so strong."

He hangs his head. "I'm sorry, Grandma." My poor baby thought she was a goner. He's not the only one.

Katharine waves a hand and stretches out her arms to summon him and Haile, who practically jumps from my arms. "Nonsense. We had fun, didn't we?" The kids nod against her chest. "How about we go inside and get cleaned up? You two can have a morning snack while I talk to your mom." She stands, brushes down her maroon blazer and skirt, and shoos the kids to move.

"It's bad manners to stare." There's a playfulness in her voice.

Who is this woman, and where is the refined lady who hosts brunch for high society? The one who maintains perfect posture and never has a hair out of place?

The woman who—wait, are her shoes off?

This is the first time in sixteen years I've seen Katharine's bare feet. I expected a French tip, but to my surprise, a pink pedicure is on display. Hot pink at that.

Katharine follows my gaze down and smiles. "We had a spa night. Haile chose the paint color." She wiggles her toes. "What do you think?"

I huff out a laugh. I'm at the wrong house. Either Katharine has a concussion, or she added some rum to her Earl Grey tea. I'm grateful I never had to deal with a monster-in-law, but this carefree version of my mother-in-law is new territory.

"Should we call the family physician?" I touch her forehead with the back of my hand. No fever.

"You are as bad as the children." She swats me away with a grin. "I'm fine. They keep me young. Come." Her arm links with mine. "Let's go inside."

Minutes later, there's coffee in front of me and a spread of yogurt, granola, fresh berries, little croissants, and homemade jams on the table. It's the perfect sunroom experience.

"Do you need anything, love?"

"This is more than generous, thank you."

I thought Jackson got the concept of a second breakfast from *Lord of the Rings*, but it looks like I have his grandmother to thank for that one. It's a good thing she has millions in the bank so she can keep up with his appetite.

Katharine takes my hand. "I'm not talking about the food. Are you okay?"

Talk about a loaded question. *No, I'm not okay because the son you tried to raise with morals was balls-deep in another woman.* Not a refined conversation to have over an antique table.

My mother-in-law has been nothing but kind since the day Charles introduced us. She never judged my lack of social status or cared that I came from a town of less than four thousand people.

That's the kind of woman she is. One who leads with her heart and doesn't stand on her wallet.

Her husband and son are a different story.

"Things are still falling into place, but we'll be okay."

Her gold tea spoon swings around her hand-painted porcelain cup. It's the same color palette as Mrs. Potts and Chip in *Beauty and the Beast*, but I doubt the people in her circle notice. She considers me before reaching for the milk, an addition she only enjoys when we're alone. A slice of lemon and a sugar cube are her go-to for social gatherings. I suspect it's more acceptable for the wife of a chairman of a board of trustees.

"Do you think you'll move back to Ohio if you don't find a place here?" She stares over the rim of her cup and takes a sip. I wait for her to say more, but she doesn't. Thin lips purse, and the frown lines she tries to ward off with prayer and expensive creams deepen.

At no point did I think about Katharine's reaction to the divorce, or what she would do if I had to uproot the kids and move beyond a fifty-mile radius. She's a grandmother who has never spent more than a week apart from her grandchildren since we moved to Falls Church. A grandmother who maintains an impressive speed running barefoot and has the financial resources to bury me in court.

Charles is a pain in the ass to deal with, but I now question the woman across from me with the alert gaze. What happens to her poise once provoked?

I wouldn't put it past her to reenact *Kindergarten Cop*, going on the warpath to get to her grandchildren. She's already got the suit.

"Relax, dear." She gives my hand a shake. "I only ask to see how far I'll need to travel to visit."

My breath catches in my throat. Hell hath no fury like a grandmother kept away from her grandkids. I would never do it intentionally, but her son might force my hand. "You won't have to travel far. We're moving to Georgetown."

Her head tilts to examine the single mom of two with no job in sight who's about to relocate to the nation's capital. The question of how is in her eyes, but she resists an inquisition.

I give her enough to satisfy her curiosity. "An opportunity presented itself. One I couldn't refuse."

She nods. "I take it the rent is affordable?"

Try free.

"Yes."

"Wonderful." Her smile crinkles her eyes. "When do you move?"

"Soon. I have the keys and plan to swing by today."

"Well." She touches her throat and turns to look at the kids. They're in the kitchen at a small table with tissue paper and glue, covering the birdhouse they made out of a milk carton. Katharine is full of surprises that often come in the form of crafts she found online.

"This is all so sudden." Her voice quivers with a sadness she tries to mask. "I hope things between us don't change."

Charles might be her only child, but she's always treated me like her daughter. "Thank you."

Her son won't let this divorce happen without a battle. I need every ally I can get.

～∞～

"This place..." Jackson blows out a breath. "Is amazing!" He spins in a circle—for the fourth time in the last five minutes—and takes off for the staircase in front of us. If an exposed brick wall makes a six-year-old giddy, God knows what else he'll flip over in this house.

"No running!" I call to my son, who scurries up the steps with the grace of a rhino.

He whips around at the top in his socks to salute me, shooting my heart through my throat in the process. This kid is clueless about safety. "You got it, Mom," he says with a wave and rushes down the hall.

"Guess it's you and me," I say into Haile's curls. She giggles and gives me a pat on the leg to tone it down. My sweet girl is growing too fast. She still has the same little nose and curved brows as the day we brought her home swaddled in a hospital blanket, but now she's too big to carry.

We're still in the hallway that feeds into the living room. A black accent wall, the same color as the front door, holds a library of books and vinyl records on recessed shelves. A rectangular mirror anchors the center, reflecting the remainder of the open space. Soft burnt-sienna sofas sit in front of an oversized black trunk for a coffee table, and a cream rug covers most of the chestnut wood flooring.

"It's pretty, Mama," Haile says through an appreciative sigh. She's four going on thirty and has an eye for design that gets Morgan giddy. The two spend hours taking in art at museums or staring at samples for the Brooke family business. The kid knows her mid-century lighting like her *Sesame Street* characters.

"Yes it is, baby."

Cedar and sandalwood scent the air in an invitation to submerge into our new home.

Unlike the fancy dungeon we left, no part of this home screams *Look but don't touch*. It's huge for a townhouse, not that I've seen many. I counted four floors based on the windows. We don't have much, but we do have the space to start fresh.

There's an allure that calls to me, enticing me to recharge with some scotch from the decanter and one of the Duke Ellington records on the shelves.

This is our safe place to laugh without judgment and decorate for every holiday. It's the space to be myself.

Haile and I cross to the kitchen, which is a strip of white cabinets and counters and a white island across from a wall of windows and a black door. Cooking isn't my strong suit, but I'll give it a try with this fancy stove, farmhouse sink, and enough counter space to reenact *Chopped*.

Upstairs is just as beautiful as the main floor, with a collage of modern art lining the cream walls illuminated by a skylight in the hall.

Jackson lies across the top bunk bed in a slate blue bedroom, consumed by his tablet, which is likely playing yet another Minecraft video on YouTube. There's a nightstand and an oversized bean bag between two windows. Whoever designed this room had children in mind. Who else could enjoy the mini rock climbing wall and ball pit?

At least I'll save money on furniture until we move to wherever it is we'll go. This will do just fine until then. Morgan went above and beyond.

I gasp at the home office, which is styled straight out of a Restoration Hardware catalog. A series of black oak glass-door cabinets are behind a wood-and-cast-iron drafting table. Two metal pendant lights suspended from the ceiling hover feet above the smooth surface.

"Mommy, I found your room!" I follow my daughter's squeal to the end of the hall, past the bathroom and a series of doors. The main bedroom is a corner room through two doors of its own with panel walls dipped in charcoal gray above oak floors. A large bed sits against the wall with a headboard of oversized pillows in taupes and grays that coordinate with a linen duvet and matching sheets. There's enough room for a mini daybed for Haile. She could take the other bed in the second bedroom, but she likes to stay close.

My four-year-old sits in an oversized chair next to a large bay window. Next to her is a small bookcase that doubles as an end table alongside a metal floor lamp. Her grin is as bright as the sun reflecting off the auburn streaks in her hair.

Moving us out of the only home she and Jackson have known, with only a few suitcases and the hope of landing on my feet in one of the country's most expensive metro regions, nearly gave me an ulcer. Yet, my kids remain resilient. I've been waiting for the other shoe to drop, but it hasn't happened—at least, not yet.

I'm sure they'll have a million and one questions. But for now, we're taking things one day at a time.

Together.

Chapter 8

Ella

It takes a special form of evil to ruin brunch, and there's one person who will always rise to the occasion. Is it too much to ask to enjoy a Maryland lump crab omelet at the new spot Morgan and I waited *months* to try?

On Mother's Day?

Apparently so.

The fork coated in pillowy eggs and mouth-watering crustacean doesn't get the chance to touch my lips. My kids are out of their seats, winding through the maze of wooden tables and chairs to get to their father.

Charles wraps them in his arms and plants a kiss on their heads. His eyes never leave mine on his journey to my table, which captures the attention of every onlooker desperate to catch a glimpse of our real-life drama. Word spread around Falls Church that I took the kids and moved out, and it's a hot topic, to say the least.

The fake concern got so bad, I resigned from volunteering at Jackson's school. After the sixth *Hey, how are you? Never expected you and Charles to split. What are you doing for money?* I hit my limit with their desperate attempts to be in my business. Gossip around here spreads fast, and I, for one, am tired of the stares and pity smiles.

They can all stub a toe. This isn't *The Real Housewives*, and we're not in Potomac.

Morgan recoils into the potted plants behind her, turning her attention from the approaching threat in a tailor-fit heather blue suit. "What in the actual fuck," she mutters. She adjusts a strap on her canary two-piece jumpsuit and proceeds to cut Duke's French toast. Based on the tic in her jaw, it's a battle for her not to curse Charles, but she keeps it together.

I draw in a breath and release it. "His mother has the kids for family dinner tonight." She invited me, and I politely declined without referring to her husband and son as the dumbasses they are.

"So why is he here?"

"To make a scene."

Charles hasn't made any attempts to spend time with his children in the weeks since our split, give or take a handful of phone calls before bedtime when he's still at the office. We both agreed that me keeping the kids during the week is best, to maintain Jackson's school routine. He's yet to take them on weekends, which makes this attempt to earn sympathy points around town as pathetic as he is.

If only they knew he's not the family man he portrays, and I'm not the unappreciative wife who left him.

"Ella." Charles's tone is calm, a mask for a man with ulterior motives. Jade-green eyes travel down my neck to my gold initial charm and stall on my blue-and-white-striped shirt. The first three buttons are open, but he can't see anything.

"To what do I owe the pleasure?" Oh, how I want to say *displeasure*, but our kids are here.

Between the salt and pepper lining his jaw, his mouth curves in arrogance. Curse the bastard and his looks. "I was on the way to my parents' and thought I'd swing by to take the kids early. You deserve the day off."

I catch Morgan's eye roll out of the corner of mine and press my lips together. Who does he think he is? And since when does he care about a break or if I get one?

You know what?

"Sounds good," I say, to Morgan's surprise. I pick up my fork, meet Charles's flat gaze, and take a bite. Delicious. "You haven't spent time with them, and you can make up for it now." I shrug. "You all should get used to spending quality time *without* me."

Let him deal with Jackson's never-ending snack times and Haile's need to ask fifty-two questions about everything. He won't last a day, but he needs to do better. Our children deserve it.

His stare weighs heavy until he accepts his fate. He has to be present as a father now that I'm no longer around to carry the family.

Haile and Jackson look up at their dad like he's a hero who will never break their hearts. For a second, his eyes soften under their appraisal before his hardened shell resets.

"Very well." Charles nods at a nearby table and turns back to me with a look I can't decipher. "You look good. See you home soon."

Bastard.

"I'm throwing you a party."

"Excuse me?"

"Saturday."

Charles left with the kids forty minutes ago. Morgan and I are at our table with a coffee cake, two forks, and bottomless mimosas between us. Sunlight illuminates the open space through steel-framed floor-to-ceiling windows.

Joseph came shortly after Charles's cameo to pick up Duke at Morgan's request. Unlike my ex, hers arrived with pure intentions, a bouquet of flowers, and a card he made with their son. Morgan and Joseph divorced right before we moved to Falls Church. She never talks about it, only says they tried but couldn't make it work.

"Earth to Ella?"

What was she talking about? Oh, Saturday. "Why are we having a party?"

My liver groans at Morgan's smile. We don't get wild, but one cocktail after nine o' clock will knock us on our asses. "Your divorce party."

"Come again?"

"Hopefully you will after Saturday."

I check her temperature for a fever. "Did you forget I have a whole year before I officially file?" Damn Virginia separation requirement. "I haven't left your house yet, and you want to throw a party?"

Morgan's lips paint the rim of her glass pink. Pineapple mimosas are now mandatory at Sunday brunch. "We should celebrate your journey back to the single life."

"While we're at it, let's get a penis cake with matching candles and ceremonially burn my wedding vows."

"Great idea!" Morgan pulls her rattan clutch to the table and digs through her small collection of trinkets for her phone. "I'll take notes. What else?"

My wedge sandals hit the corner of the table when I face the wooden planter box behind me and proceed to sift through greenery. "What are you doing?" Morgan asks my jean-wrapped ass. It's a juicy booty, one she's about to kiss in two seconds.

"Searching for hidden cameras." A fork hits my butt and bounces on the table. "Wench," I say over my shoulder.

A throat clears. "Is there something I can assist you with, miss?"

I turn to face a young man in a black-and-white uniform with short cinnamon hair. He'll get an extra tip for using *miss* and not *ma'am*. "Nope. Just admiring the foliage," I say with a smile as I turn back around in my seat. "We'll take the check, thank you."

"The gentleman settled the bill before he left," the server volleys back.

Say what now?

He continues, unfazed by my blank stare. "The man who came with the flowers. He paid on his way out. Please let me know if there's anything else I can assist you with. Have a wonderful Mother's Day."

Morgan's gaze drops to the table, but not before I catch the shine in her eyes. Joseph Catlett is a special man who cares for his ex-wife. His intentions are clear through his words and actions.

Charles, on the other hand, would never. Do I think he loved me? Yes, in his own way. But in the selfless way Joseph loves Morgan? Not a chance in hell.

I want that.

"Saturday." The word leaves my mouth in a rush before common sense kicks in. Today is full of surprises. "We'll celebrate new beginnings, but nothing over the top."

She crosses her heart and lifts a hand. "Nothing over the top."

"I pick the location."

She hesitates but nods. I don't want to go toe-to-toe with her inner party planner, but if left unchecked she'll turn this into a red-carpet affair.

"And Morgan?"

"Yes."

I smile. "Wear sneakers."

Chapter 9

Ella

*T*hwack.

Our small group breaks out into a cheer at my bull's-eye, or whatever you call it when the axe hits the target dead center. I grin at my handiwork in hopes it will manifest a man-bunned Viking. One who's faithful and wields a thick sword.

"Ella is on fire tonight," says our coach, a burly, middle-aged man in red-and-black plaid and jeans that have seen better days. What he lacks in a man bun he makes up for with a trimmed wheat beard. He's serving mountain man and well.

I take a bow, careful not to let the tiara nestled in my messy updo fall. My black T-shirt, which is knotted in the back and reads *I called the lawyer*, inches up my spine. In jeans and high-tops, I'm in my superhero outfit, ready to fight crime and take on future ex-husbands.

Erica cheers with a beer in one hand and her phone on camera mode in the other.

Morgan stands between her and another friend who came out to celebrate in DC. Her aim tonight is shit, but she wins the fashion award with her silk crop top and ankle pants. Her long strands are gathered into the perfect top knot, a direct contrast to the thick, unruly mane plopped on my head. Amy, a fellow mom with the enthusiasm of a kindergarten class strung out on sugar, whistles like I won the Super Bowl.

Tonight, we laid to rest Ella Hudson and resurrected Ella Greene. It's been a minute since she and I have seen each other, and I embraced her with open arms.

Morgan and I compromised on the evening's shenanigans. We're at a spot with axe throwing to release my pent-up rage and cabanas and handcrafted cocktails to satisfy her inner bougie. She decked out our tented black-and-white space with gold foil balloons that spell *Divorced AF*. There's no dick cake, but we do have naked cakes with different divorce toppers, like *Boy, Bye* and *Finally Done*.

There are also divorce candles, mini cacti with *Little Prick* tags, and wine with custom divorce labels, because Morgan. If it wasn't clear before, now I'm sure she missed her calling as an event planner. But she makes up for it in the best way she knows how: doing the most.

"Having fun?" my soon-to-be-ex-housemate asks with a soft check to my shoulder. Perspiration dots the side of her face but doesn't dare smear her makeup. Her breath is heavy after throwing axes, a form of exercise she clearly loathes.

I'm in heaven, reenacting summers with Pap-Pap riding tractors and camping. He and I may have thrown the occasional hatchet between fishing, which is why I picked this place.

"Yeah," I say between sips of whatever this blue concoction is. I'm sure I broke some drinking code mixing my alcohol in the wrong order.

"You sure you don't want me to stay with you tonight?"

I'm spending the night in my new home for the first time while the kids are with their grandmother. Charles's father is in Palm Beach for his fifth business trip this year. Sounds like some bullshit, but it's none of my business. As for Charles, he had another work conflict. Shocker.

"I'll be fine." I pat Morgan's leg and laugh at how fast she swapped sneakers for heels now that we're back at the cabana. "Erica and I are sharing a car back. I'll be okay."

Tonight has been the break I needed.

Keeping up with two kids' schedules is no joke. I'm on from the time they wake up until the time they sleep. Haile is with me all day, and unless she takes a nap, there's rarely a chance to exhale, let alone pee in peace.

The thought of divorcing Charles scared me at first because of all the weight that would fall on my shoulders. But the truth is, I've been carrying it for years.

I'm not new to this, I'm true to this.

Reality will slap me in the face tomorrow—that bitch is relentless. For now, I raise my glass to the friends around the table who've stayed in my corner and allow myself to enjoy the moment.

Morgan's family property is a godsend, it truly is. But I still don't have a job, and time is running out. I can cower in a corner to the fear waiting to consume me or stay in the present with the people rooting for me. I choose door number two.

"I know I already said this, but thank you." The edges of Morgan's mouth curl. *Here she goes.* "You were right." I roll my eyes and sigh. "This divorce party is amazing."

Morgan pulls me in for a hug. "Of course it is. I planned it." She laughs and dodges the pillow I toss at her.

"Well!" Amy claps her hands together like she's waiting to do a cheer. "It's time for our next activity." She flips her golden-brown hair over her shoulder, reaches for her oversized purse, and pulls out a binder.

I frown at the pending homework assignment. Amy is the room parent chair of the PTA. Her idea of a good time is mapping out decorations and supplies for classroom parties months in advance. School is almost out for summer, and I refuse to do a group project during my divorce party.

My buzz toes the line between a happy place and tomorrow's reminder almost-forty is *not* the new twenty.

Erica catches me glancing at the artificial hedges that encase our tent. An Olympic high jump is still on the table if that binder is. I stand when Amy pulls an arsenal of colored gel pens from her bag.

"Is this something El could work on later?" Erica's coffee-brown eyes plead with mine to not attempt what we both know is an impossible jump given the amount of liquor sloshing through my veins.

Amy's shoulders droop, tempting a strap on her white summer dress to fall. She assesses me and pulls her bottom lip between her teeth. Shit, she's gonna cry. We only met at a bake sale a few months ago, but it's clear that Amy has a soft spot for overplanning and trying to make people feel better.

I caught her sniffling in a corner after her presentation at a PTA meeting. It included a slideshow—twenty-three slides, to be exact. Her intentions run in lock-step with her passion, even if it borders on robot behavior.

"Hey." I place a hand over hers, which is still gripping her coveted school supplies, and smile. "Thank you for being so thoughtful. What do we do?"

I'm already on thin ice with Jesus. I don't need to be placed on probation for messing with His patron saint of crafts.

Amy smooths out the nonexistent wrinkles in her tea-length dress and clears her throat. "It's simple, really," she says with a shy smile. "We go around and each add something for you to do before your divorce becomes final. Here." She hands me the white binder with *Divorce Bucket List* in a glittery gold script surrounded by faux floral stems. "I started your checklist."

I flip through the first few pages of yearbook-style pics of our crew. She really is so thoughtful.

And apparently quite the freak.

"Nipple piercings?" My eyes stall at the two-word challenge in perfect cursive.

Morgan chokes on her drink, then nearly tosses it onto the table to make a beeline for the binder. She snatches it out of my hand, and if it wasn't for her chocolate hue, my friend would look like Casper the Friendly Ghost.

Her brows long jump to her forehead. She looks at me with wide eyes before her gaze lands on Amy. "Public sex in the Lincoln Memorial? That's oddly specific."

Three sets of eyes land on the modern-day Suzy Homemaker, who leans back in her chair with a full-on grin and crosses her legs. The shy person who nearly cried has left the building. In her place is a woman with a quiet confidence and a kink that might land her in jail.

She twirls a pineapple ring on her right hand, one I thought was a summer fashion choice. "It has the best acoustics," she says with a shrug.

"What?!" the rest of us shout.

They say you never know what happens behind closed doors, but Amy just busted hers wide open. Of course the resident good girl swings from chandeliers.

I'm at a loss for words as I shake off images of Amy skeeting all over historical markers across our nation's capital. How does she have the time with raising four kids and her volunteering schedule that puts us to shame? Her husband keeps a protractor next to his wallet, for goodness' sake. He's a civil engineer who does site inspections and analyzes government regulations.

"We don't need details," I say with a hand in the air. "I appreciate the thought you put into this, but sex in a monument isn't how I get down—respectfully."

She nods.

Erica tilts her head to the side and purses her lips. "You forgot the nipple piercings."

I smile into my third cocktail of the night. "No, I didn't."

Three sets of eyes land on me.

"Stop staring!" I chuckle and drain the margarita Morgan ordered, which replaces itself when another lands on the table. It's a miracle I'm still forming complete sentences. "My titties are amazing."

It's true, I have nice ones. Are they double-Ds that would knock a man unconscious? No, but they're the roundest C-cups you'll see with rosewood areolas. Not too big or small.

Look at me, talking about my titties on a Saturday night.

"Well, okay then, Ms. Piercing." Erica huffs out a laugh and snaps. "What are we adding to the list?"

Amy hops to her feet. "A one-night stand!"

"You're done for the night." Morgan takes her glass and pats the upholstered bench for her to take a seat. "What about a haircut? A bob, maybe?"

Erica sucks the meat clean off a chicken wing in one go, then licks her thick lips to clear the excess sauce. "Hold up. Get back to the man." Her legs spread, and she rests her elbows on her knees, pressing the lime green fabric of her jumpsuit against her ebony skin. She's gorgeous without trying and has the personality to match. Fierce, piercing, and natural.

Seriously, the only makeup the woman wears is a lip stain and *maybe* blush.

She moved to Arlington from Baltimore last year to teach economics. Our chance meeting took place during one of two times I went to barre class in the city. After the warm-up, we exchanged a *fuck this* side-eye and spent the remainder of the hour at a nearby coffee shop.

Erica has zero desire for kids or a husband and spends her coins on exotic vacations and fancy skincare treatments. Hence, no makeup.

Her hands move in a language that's unique to her to emphasize why she's right. I catch the tail end of the rant: *Let her get dick*.

"So we're supposed to be okay with Charles thrusting into Goldilocks while Ella stays at home with the kids in her chastity belt? Make it make sense," Erica says with a flick of her Marley twists. She scans our friend circle for the person who will challenge her edict.

"Thanks for your concern about my vagina, but I don't plan on partaking in any one-night stands." I reach to pat her shoulder but find my hands in her twists. "I need your hair tech to bless me."

"I'll text you Monique's number." She unthreads my fingers running through the black bundles with envy. "Do not distract yourself from the matter at hand. Pass me the binder, Amy." Silver bangles create a symphony as she scribbles her next command on paper. "I'm adding a sensual self-care class." Her eyes return to mine. "As much fun as test-driving a new man can be, you don't need one. You can pleasure yourself."

Charles hated the idea of toys, which is why he never used them. Outside of a hidden vibrator I kept for when he was away, I never got myself off with my fingers. "My girl Janelle throws sex toy parties, and she makes house calls."

"Janelle Thomas?" Amy reaches for her glass and gets a smack to the hand.

Erica tilts her head. "You know Janelle? She's my soror."

Amy leans in and squeals. "Of course! She's our toy dealer. She helped outfit our sex room."

"Shut up! I have a consultation with her to put one in my closet. Do you have pictures of yours?"

The pair isolate themselves in the corner and compare notes.

It's crystal clear how much I missed out on in my marriage. A sex swing is nice, but I would've settled for a committed husband who took out the trash and picked up milk before we ran out.

Now that's sexy. No assembly or batteries required.

I took whatever was given to me for far too long. Never once did I ask for the moon. Only the bare minimum, and even that was too much.

My tongue darts to the salty rim of my margarita. "Sign me up," I say before taking a gulp. "Let's make it a sleepover at my new house."

The screams from our cabana mimic the sound of hyenas. I've never felt so alive. So free. So drunk.

I spent the greater part of yesterday getting the townhouse ready for our arrival. Nothing fancy—it's perfect the way it is, and I'm on a limited budget. Just some new bedding and summer essentials. Haile still needs a mini day-bed, but I'll cross it off the to-do list that won't go away when I get to it. It's not like she won't be in mine.

That leaves me with finding a job after an eleven-year hiatus *and* affordable childcare for Haile. Charles's child support should cover it, but separation has taught me to secure my own bag.

And not marry a dick. Well, not an asshole. "I need to get laid." Where'd that come from?

The bottom of the collection of cocktail glasses you're gathering like infinity stones.

Amy is on a quest of indecent exposure. Erica is texting her friend, one who comes with more benefits than a health savings account. And Morgan? She's staring at me like she hears my thoughts. Maybe she does.

I strain to concentrate, careful not to pee on myself, and send her message:

Why aren't you back with your ex?

The eyebrow she lifts questions my blood alcohol content and my desire to debate a dead issue.

"Alright!" I sing-song into our circle. "Tonight was *amahyzing*." The last word comes out like an attempt to sing the Negro National Anthem with the vocals of a reality show reject. The ancestors aren't pleased.

I try again, grab my coveted divorce binder, and place it over my chest. "I accept the challenge. I vow to pierce my nipples, jerk off, and buy all the sex toys."

"Get yours, sis!" A tan beauty in a floral wrap dress walks by with a wink.

"Okay, El. Come down now." Morgan extends her hand for me to take. When the hell did I stand on the bench? "I think it's time to go."

She's not wrong.

The evening ends with an exchange of hugs and *text me when you get home* reminders. I'll try my best to remember but won't make guarantees.

"Are you sure you're okay?" The Nina Simone in Erica's tone coaxes me awake. It's a battle to keep my eyes open as our car sways, nestling me into soft leather cushions.

My voice cracks, in need of water and a rewind from all the tall and plentiful cocktails. "Yeah."

"What a night."

The moon reflects off the cars parked along a tree-lined street. Leaves flutter on branches, undisturbed by the rush of nightlife from the surrounding streets. The brick walkways are quiet, with no trace of bar hoppers seeking solace.

I've made this drive a few times, but I still feel the flutter in my stomach when we reach the second-to-last house on the right next to a home covered in vines.

"Why are we here? The place you're staying at tonight is closer."

Erica shakes her head, moonlight dancing off her earrings. "I wanted to make sure you made it home safe." Her voice drops to a whisper. "And my *place* tonight is a friend's house a few streets up from you," she says with a wink.

"Lucky bitch." I nestle back against the seat. "I'm tired, but I'm not ready to go in."

"So let's stay out."

"What about your friend?"

"What about him?" Erica's tone leaves no question he'll wait up for her and leave the light on. "I still have a couple hours in me, and you are kid-free tonight. One nightcap, and then we'll go to bed."

I'm going to regret tomorrow morning. "Okay. One drink."

Chapter 10

Ella

My dream takes a turn in the middle of the night. The stress and lack of sleep are more potent than the cocktails I drank. I can't get up, and I don't want to.

"Come here." The command is a deep timbre, smooth in delivery with no room for challenge. It skates from my face down to my toes. Long fingers tilt my chin, and my lips find comfort against a plush pair in a series of probing caresses.

A hand moves over the back of my neck to draw me closer. The tip of a tongue brushes across my lips, breaking my mouth apart with an expert touch. My breath hitches at the dance of our tongues. My head angles toward the hungry possession of my mouth with a passion that sucks the air from my lungs.

This is my dream man. One chiseled in fantasies, cloaked in a powerful bare chest and strong shoulders. My hand meets smooth skin cased in hard muscles that wrap me into a protective hold.

My body quivers with longing only he can satisfy—*is* satisfying. Charles never took his time like this. He was impulsive, whereas my dream man invests in my pleasure, claiming me. Holding me.

He explores the valleys of my body, from the curves of my breasts to the dip of my hip. A low rumble rattles in his throat before I'm pressed so close to his chest, it's hard to breathe.

A thick bulge pulsates against my stomach, inviting my fingertips to trail across the swollen outline in silk fabric. He moans into my mouth and drapes my thigh over his leg. His fingers grip my ass, rocking his erection into my center.

I don't dare open my eyes in fear he'll vanish, leaving me cold and alone. He might be a fantasy wedged deep in untapped desires, but tonight, he's mine. I yearn for more and jerk in his arms as he pulls down the strap of my nightgown, revealing skin I doused in cocoa butter hours ago. To think I almost wore an oversized T-shirt and boxers to bed. Thank the panty angels I didn't. I'm not wearing any, and the thin barrier between my vagina, which is weeping for release in Mariah Carey high notes, and his dick ignites delicious friction. My skin heats at the flurry of open-mouthed kisses down my neck.

I'm panting, and I lick the sweat forming on his wide chest as he cups my exposed breast. My nipple pebbles at the swirl of his breath and the steady chill from the air conditioning. He teases my bud between his fingers, a prelude to the skim of his tongue on the tip.

I cry out and rub harder against his waist. His hands guide me up and down his shaft to quicken the pace. My essence coats the fabric of his shorts as our mouths devour each other. The slap of my pubic bone against his girth has my sex pulsating. Large hands angle my ass for an assault of piston thrusts.

My coochie will get an apology tomorrow for the pounding she's taking. For now, she better enjoy the ride.

The feeling in my legs is the first to go, which makes sense, given they're spread wide open. My thighs tremble, and my stomach contracts at the rush of heat jolting through my body. I come in a string of whispered curses that morph into a shout.

Holy shit.

The dream man's breathing picks up to match each thrust. If this bed had a headboard instead of a crown of pillows, I'd have a concussion by now.

His back muscles tighten at the same time the kickstand between his legs pulses. "*Fuck.*" Warm liquid soaks through his shorts, interlacing with my arousal and coating my thighs. He presses his nose into my neck and inhales.

We remain in each other's embrace, lost in the bliss of our bodies finding pleasure. His mouth searches for mine, dotting slow kisses until he reaches his destination. The kiss we share is a soft reclamation of the intimacy shared between two lovers in the moonlight.

This is what my body needed. It reignited and set free what was lost in the ashes. The aftershock of his touch spreads in a steady hum. I don't want the night to end, and I burrow deeper into the muscular frame that made me feel again.

Wanted.

Adored.

Cherished.

I sigh into the scent of cedar and sandalwood. When I wake, the carriage will turn back into a pumpkin. I'll be a newly single mom again, on a quest to untether herself from an ex who doesn't deserve her presence or her shadow. I love my children—*adore* them—but I can't recall a night when someone took care of me and satisfied my desires.

I'm not ready for love or a relationship, but dangit if I don't want my toes to curl while I climax like I did tonight. A man like this could only come from my dreams.

It's a manifestation.

One that doesn't disappear when I finally open my eyes.

Chapter 11

Julian

There are only a handful of times in my life when my nuts have retracted so far up, I prayed they wouldn't get stuck. None involved a woman in my dream who turned out to be real. Not until tonight.

"What the f—"

"Get off me!"

She pushes at my chest at the same time I roll off her, our screams tangling like the bedsheet between our half-naked bodies. I flip off one end of the bed and land on the floor with a thud. Her dismount is less graceful.

Arms and legs flail in the streams of moonlight that pierce the darkness from the bay window. "Did you follow me from Charly's?"

"Never heard of it, and this is *my* bed!"

The figure, a faceless apparition wrapped in Egyptian cotton, rises and takes labored breaths. My dick swells at the silhouette of heavy breasts and round hips, hips I gripped only minutes ago. My other head—the one that's watched too many horror movies—freaks the fuck out.

It takes a second and a creative string of curse words before she frees herself. I turn on a nearby light and meet dark brown eyes and narrowed brows. My dick is now at full attention. Thick black hair unfurls from the leopard print silk scarf she used to wrap her edges, which now look like she wrestled a bear.

She's breathtaking.

"Ow! What the fuck?!" Pain lances through my cheek. "Did you throw your phone at my face?" I wince. This shit is as uncomfortable as my cum-stained basketball shorts pasted to my leg.

She cups a hand to her mouth like her own audacity surprised her and takes a step back toward the bathroom. Her eyes land on the vinyl records on top of the dresser, and I catch a glimpse of the debate to chuck them at my head. For her sake, she better not. I'll sue her ass for messing with Duke Ellington and John Coltrane. We're already at breaking and entering and battery as it is.

I open my mouth, but the words still at the sight of her honey-tan breast hanging out of her lopsided nightgown. Damn, she's gorgeous. So is her breast, one I teased with my tongue.

Her mouth moves at lightning speed, but I don't hear a word because of the titty. She's so caught up in trying to land a plane with her hand gestures, she misses my motioning to said titty.

"I'm waiting!" Her hand finds a home on the curve of her hip.

"Could you"—I drop my eyes and point in her direction—"cover up? You have amazing breasts, but—"

A crash mixes with a scream in her sprint to the bathroom. "Could this night get any worse?" Her yell travels through quick, shallow breaths.

I rub the back of my neck in a failed attempt to ease the stress radiating from my temples and the side of my face that has a phone imprint.

Why the hell did I go to Nate's bar after an eight-hour flight from London? It's a rhetorical question. No matter how the long work week—sixty hours, in this case—Swigs to visit bro is the first stop when I get back to the States.

Exhaustion and wings doused in Mumbo sauce sums up last night. The bar, a neighborhood spot in the quiet part of Georgetown, had a steady flow of customers but a calm vibe. I kept Nate company with a glass of bourbon he never allowed to reach half empty and a mound of fried food he keeps on hand for my return. We caught each other up on the last several months before I realized it was two in the morning.

Cam texted me, and I talked to some brunette who clearly isn't the person losing her shit in my bathroom. Bar brunette is a blur. But this woman? Her soft moans, supple curves, and pouty lips are unforgettable.

I follow the scent of lavender to put hostage negotiation skills I don't have to use. If she has a panic attack, she's on her own. Not because I don't care, but because she locked the door.

"Um, you okay in there?"

I need to pee, and for you to leave my house.

The door muffles her words, an indication we're in for a long morning given it's now past three. So much for catching up on sleep.

"Listen, I don't know if there's someone I can call"—*a car, preferably*—"but you can't stay in there. Or here."

What is her name? Did she tell me, or did we get straight down to business?

None of my casual hookups have the code to my house, and I don't remember sharing a Lyft with anyone. Who. The. Hell. Is. She?

"You good?" I knock again. "I'll go get your phone, and I'll call a car to take you wherever you want."

Instinct sends me jerking back the moment the door swings open. My good razors are in there, and I wouldn't put it past her to try and cut me.

Her chin lifts, and her nostrils flare. She wags a finger at me. "You touched me!"

"You reached for me first!"

"You weren't supposed to be real! I was dreaming and didn't realize"—she motions at my bare chest— "*that* was real." Her eyes turn cold with an expression meant to scare, but it does the opposite. "You have two minutes to get out of my house."

The bedsheet spirals around her waist like a skirt, killing any chance for another peek at those long, thick legs.

Wait.

Back up a second.

"*Your* house?" I emphasize the first word. This is news to me.

"Yes," she says in a huff. "Tonight was obviously a mistake." She shakes her head with a hand to her cheek. "I don't hook up with random men—or anyone. Just get out before I beat you down!"

I raise a brow and roll my lips. "Like you did when you pelted your phone at my face? Spare me the replay."

"Out! I don't want to call the police, but I will."

This is a first. A one-night stand trying to kick me out of my own damn house. "And say what, exactly?"

A vein strains against the column of her neck. "That a man in..." Her eyes stall on my chest again. "A *man* entered my home and bed and..." She wets her lips and looks away.

"And?"

She bites her lip before pink blooms across her cheeks. Her throat works to swallow. *This should be good.*

"The point is—"

"We woke up between each other's legs and assumed we came home together." I'm still not sure how that happened if I left the bar alone, but one thing at a time. I'm two seconds from crashing and falling asleep, but I need to make sure we're both okay. Then she can take her own advice and get out—her and her delusions.

The frown etched onto her face tells me she can't decipher dream from reality. Or maybe she needs to shit. At what point do I call one of those mental health teams? Serious question. She can think she lives here all she wants. From her own house.

"You still don't get it." *Here we go.* "I. Live. Here." She walks to the bedroom door and opens it. Then she closes her eyes and takes a breath. "I'm sorry that I touched your dick." *Didn't mind that part.* "Please leave. I won't call the cops if you go now."

"You live here?"

"Yes."

The tired smile I've held up on the promise of sleep falters.

Is she—

I swallow and point at the oak floors I chose with the designer. "You live *here*? In this house?"

Her brows pull together. "I already told you, yes. I moved in—where are you going?"

My steps are heavy with fatigue as they take me to my walk-in closet, which is now empty. Just cream walls and bare hangers. I squeeze my eyes shut and imagine *I'm* in a dream, testing my own patience and playing hide-and-seek with every suit I own. But just as I tell myself to wake up, my palm lands on the center island, which is now clear of the cufflinks passed down through generations of my family.

It's a fight to stay upright. I've heard of people casing properties to take over. Did she get that ass from squatting?

I force air into my lungs through a ragged breath. My new house guest looks harmless, but she might drug me to harvest my organs.

"Where is my stuff?!" My voice relays for her to bring her juicy ass in here. "Whatever you took from me, I want it back. Now." She opens her mouth but thinks better of it. I close my eyes and sigh.

Staring at her is like looking directly at the sun. Even with disheveled hair and her desire to colonize my townhouse, she leaves me breathless.

How is it that I remember the taste of her lips but not meeting her at Swigs? My routine kicked in on autopilot once I got home, but it didn't register that she was in my bed until our bodies sought each other. The urge to fuck her overrode my rule that's in place to prevent me from scandal and headline. The press are vultures enough, sifting through the scraps of my life to piece together a story.

I don't bring people to my home for this reason. At least, not strangers. I'm barely here, but I don't need anyone equating sex with a marriage proposal or robbing me when my pants are down.

Today's lesson is the difference between want and need. I *want* her, but I *need* my shit back.

"How much?"

"Excuse me?"

I step closer. "You heard me." She won't get the satisfaction of hearing me repeat myself. I don't during negotiations, and I have no plans to start today.

Her gaze goes distant before it resets with a hardened stare. "I'm not a sex worker, you asshole!"

The word circles my brain until it lands with a plink. *Record scratch.* Now it's my turn to gape. "A sex worker?"

She inches forward with her hands on her hips. "If you think you can come here and try to force me out of my own place, you got another thing coming."

"*I* own this house, and I have the deed to prove it!" I storm out of the room in search of who knows what.

My sanity.

The friends of hers who are waiting in dark corners to throw hands.

How long has she been here? Did her boyfriend take my clothes? She's not wearing a wedding ring. Not that I checked. Four times.

I grab my phone off the nightstand to type out a message to Nate. I'll stay with him after I escort her out and lock up. *Escort.* Ha. My thumbs fly across the screen. "I was asking to buy back what you stole from me. *I* should call the police."

"Wait." The frown in her voice forces my eyes up. She glances around the room. "This has to be a misunderstanding. It's too late to call her now, but Morgan—"

"How the hell do you know my sister?"

The woman, whose name I still don't know, blinks slowly. "She's my best friend. She told me I could live here until the end of the year."

Fucking Morgan.

Chapter 12
Ella

Dodging a trip to the slammer is oddly satisfying when it comes with steak and eggs. After I gave him the highlight reel of the shit show that is my life, Julian grabbed his keys and wallet and took us to his Audi. Nerves tingled my anus he would toss me out in front of a police precinct until he hopped on Wisconsin Avenue and kept driving.

Seventeen minutes later, here we are, in the back corner of a twenty-four-hour spot, far away from any prying eyes at four a.m. The way I make *Walking Dead* zombies look put together, you'd think I was the one who traveled across the pond after working a thirteen-hour day.

Not Julian.

Morgan's *younger* brother.

The man sits on the other side of the checkered table, unfazed about giving a home intruder the business through his basketball shorts. He's chewing through a Paul Bunyan of a platter, loaded with every fried American breakfast staple the chef could pack on a plate.

Stuffing your face shouldn't be sexy, but Julian makes it an act of foreplay the way his thick lower lip wraps around the fork and drags it into his mouth. The same one that devoured me without hesitation.

Morgan and her family bring up Julian all the time, but the most I've seen of him are old family photos with acne and awkward smiles. We've never met, but he's certainly grown since rocking braces as a preteen.

Last I heard, Julian was overseas, running his father's office. Which begs the question why he's back.

"I take it the food was okay?" He nods to my empty plate, which I all but licked clean, and smirks.

When it comes to meals, I don't play. Life is too short to eat diet kale and do Common Core math counting calories. I don't eat junk—outside of a conservative chocolate stash and Wendy's on the occasional Fridays with the kids—and I appreciate fresh eggs and beef. Pap-Pap worked on a farm and taught me the meaning of eatin' good.

Minus chitterlings. I'll be damned if I try those ever again.

"No complaints here." I return the nod. "You gonna finish all of that?"

If I could bottle and sell Julian's smile, I'd be a millionaire with a line of customers stretched around the block for their next hit. It's laid-back, like he doesn't need to put in effort because fine is a default setting.

And he has dimples?

Oprah would ask me for a loan.

He scratches at his chest, now hidden under a white tee, and leans back against the booth. "It'll fit."

Down, Ella.

If you squint, the outline of his tattoo on his left pec, which goes over his shoulder and down to his elbow, is visible. I almost choked on the drool pooling in my mouth when the bedroom light illuminated him in all his glory. Charles kept in shape and has what you might call a swimmer's body with long, lean muscles.

Julian is in a different league.

The thick muscles in his shoulders and biceps flex without effort. They also make surprisingly soft pillows. His abs are flat, his six-pack evident of the work he puts in at the gym. Mix that all together, dip it in melanin, and you have a man who lit up my body like a utility company and scared the life out of me. After I came, of course.

"So." He wipes his mouth with a napkin and pins me with a stare. "Divorce."

Note to self: add forearm veins to his list of attractive features.

I gulp my water to extinguish the coochie tremors tightening my thighs. Julian stretches out his tree trunks for legs underneath the table. He's cool, calm, and collected in sweatpants.

The haze of my buzz has cleared, stripping me of the liquid courage to continue this discussion. I did move into the man's house, and we did hump each other like we had season passes to a sex party. If only hiding under the table was an option.

You'd catch a glimpse of that peen indent hanging to the right.

Stop.

"You okay, Ella? We don't have to talk if you're uncomfortable."

I wave him off. "I'm comfortable!" His brow furrows at the rise in my pitch. "I'm"—horny, possibly homeless, and trying to keep my shit together—"fine. I told you at the house I heard my ex having sex with another woman in our bed."

He exhales and rubs the back of his neck with an awkward nod that's half pity and half apology.

My focus drops to the empty plate in front of me. Either from exhaustion or the reality of how effed up my situation is comes crashing into me with hurricane force. I wrapped myself in armor to battle the goliath that is my husband and his social status. I'm prepared for constant questions and side-eyes in public, ready to roll up my sleeves and push through the mess. What I'm not ready for is the gentle hickory eyes of the man across from me. A total stranger, yet an extension of my second family which makes it easier to lower my guard.

My breath hitches when his hand covers mine. "I'm sorry," he says in a whisper, his thumb rubbing circles against my skin. "Not that it matters, but how long were you two together?"

"Sixteen years. We met when I was twenty-three, got engaged four months later, and said 'I do' when I was twenty-five." I frown for the old me who mistook red flags for charm. "I was young, in love, and completely ignorant of life. And also the man I was marrying."

"Jesus," he says through a heavy sigh. "What kind of man treats the woman he loves like that?"

A vindictive one.

"I have ninety days to find a job and a place to live that isn't Morgan's house." I swallow the lump lodging itself in my throat. "I haven't worked in over a decade, and if I don't fulfill my end of the separation agreement, Charles will take me to court to force me back home."

The last time he and I spoke, I came close to begging him to let me go. *Me* begging *him* to unclench his grip on our marriage after he broke our vows. Stress keeps me up night after night, and I'm tired from chasing the shadow of hope and wired from the never-ending to-do list.

Julian's eyes remain steady. A pained look passes through his features, as if he understands the stakes and what his return means. His mouth turns down in apology. We can't stay in the townhouse. "Ella."

"No need to make it plain. I'll figure it out." I pull out my hand to reach for my wallet. "This has been…" I laugh. "I should go."

He slides the check toward him and stands. "I'll take care of this. We can figure everything else out after we get some sleep."

It takes a few seconds to register that he's not kicking me out. At least, not yet. "Are you out your damn mind?" I ignore his chuckle and how it moves his Adam's apple. Add that to the list after forearm veins.

He shrugs. "Morgan promised you the house, and I won't be here long. I'm fine with it if you are."

I stare at him, puzzled by my own sense of calm. "It would be a temporary arrangement," I say to reiterate the obvious. "Now that I know you're not a serial killer, we can figure something out."

Julian laughs with enough force to rattle the table. He shakes his head with a grin and settles back into the booth. "It's really good to finally meet you. You are"—he searches my face—"unexpected."

The pull for our gazes to tangle is magnetic. We consider each other with a familiarity that makes no sense whatsoever. I lower my head to settle my breathing. Why am I so unhinged around him?

His eyes are still on me when I look up. *That's why.* I clear my throat to quiet the butterflies I shouldn't have for my best friend's brother. Her *younger* brother. "You live over in England? With the fancy tea and royal family?"

Two dimples wink next to his bemused smile. "Something like that. I come back for visits but enjoy the anonymity London brings. Less people in your personal life."

"Was that a problem here?" Had to be if he hopped continents.

"You don't follow the blogs, do you?"

"Should I?"

"Hell no." He laughs with less enthusiasm than before and scratches his goatee. "Being away from my family gets lonely, but it's nice to keep people out of my personal life."

"I deal with enough gossip to care about someone else's. No worries over here."

Silence threads with understanding and an intensity that shouldn't be here.

Change the subject.

"So, this townhouse. You're willing to live with me?"

"It's the other way around, but yes," he says with a panty-dropping smile. "Only if you're comfortable."

Am I really doing this? "I have two kids." Morgan's brother or not, leaving my husband to live with another man isn't an ideal setup while navigating a divorce. Unfortunately, my finances can't afford ideal. Without Morgan's house in play, my options are slim to none.

"The house is big enough for me to stay out of your hair. You won't see me, and I'm not here for long. I promise."

I cross my arms. "What's the catch?"

Sexual favors, maybe?

My cheeks burn at the memory of our bedroom acrobatics, and, being the perceptive person he is, Julian's smile morphs into a grin. His eyes drop to my chest and glide around the silhouette of my breasts in my BBD shirt, then back up to my throat.

BBD for Bell Biv DeVoe, by the way. Not BDE, which oozes from him.

"No catch," he says to Ricky Bell on my vintage tee. He's a deer in headlights, only it's my high beams that have him in a trance. I rushed out of the house without a bra again. A tiny detail Morgan's brother didn't miss.

As if he realizes he's staring like he has x-ray vision, Julian coughs and gives me an apologetic look, one that promises he's not a pervert. "I'll stay in the basement and use the door out back to come and go." He smiles. "The last thing you need is to explain to your kids why a strange man is living on the upper floors with you."

No lies detected. Also...

"What's above the floor with the bedrooms?" The door that I assume leads to the top level is locked.

"A renovation project I haven't finished," he says. "It's an open room, the length of the entire floor, with a bathroom. I don't take up much space, and I'm not around anymore to find use for it."

Must be nice.

"Will you be okay down there in the basement?" I ran out of time to venture around, and I hope it's not a crypt. Judging by his full-on laughter, it isn't. Nothing I said was *that* funny, but his tears say otherwise.

We need to go to bed. In different rooms, so we don't hump each other. Again.

"Care to let me in on the joke?"

He holds his side and tips his head back. His pearly white teeth and dimples are ready for their close-up. Julian is adorable. Mouth watering. Call it jet lag or this strange series of unfortunate events, but his carefree gigglefest has found its way to my end of the booth.

He swipes at his eyes. "I haven't laughed like that in a long time."

"Glad my life is so entertaining," I say with a chuckle. It's a joke that misses its landing.

"Shit, I'm sorry." He tenses with a frown. "None of this is funny. To answer your question, there's a guest bedroom downstairs, for visitors or people who are too tired to leave. The basement is pretty much its own apartment, but I'll have to come up to cook and do laundry. Other than that, the gym and home theater are down there with me, so I'm set."

How big is this townhouse? His family does well enough, but good damn. A gym and a home theater? What else did I miss? A bowling alley? Hyperbolic chamber?

Charles could swim in his generational wealth but is too cheap to install the screen doors I wanted. Julian has to be half his age, maybe younger.

"Okay, so you have a little room." A glimpse of a smile shines. "And please don't apologize. I speak fluent sarcasm. You allowing us to stay in your home is...I'm grateful."

"You're practically family, and your back is against the wall. Breathe easy, I got you." His eyes bore into mine, forcing me not to look away.

"What you thinking about over there?"

"Sex." My hands fly to my mouth a second too late.

"*What?*" Julian asks through a shaky laugh.

"I mean..." I close my eyes. "What I meant was sex with you." *Wrong again.* I open an eye to peek at a man who's just seconds from keeling over. "I'm not worried about your sex life."

Silence.

"I don't want to mess up your situation, but I also don't want my kids to hear anyone grabbing a headboard. Stop laughing!" I toss a ketchup packet at his face he catches with one hand.

"I don't have people like that in my house all the time. Besides, I wouldn't entertain with you and the kids there."

I nod. "Makes sense." *Move on, El.* "Why would you when there are random women already in your bed?"

"Let's talk about it."

My throat works double time. "Okay."

Julian shifts in his seat. "It was a mistake to touch you." *Damn. Want to call me ugly, too?* "I mean..." He looks away and sighs. "I mistook you for someone I met at the bar, but it's not an excuse. I'm sorry."

My brows pinch together. "I thought you don't bring strangers home?"

His stare holds me in place, and the side of his lip curls. "I'd break my rule for you."

I'm not fast enough to snatch back the gasp that escapes into the air around us. Heat floods my body at the memory of his fingers curled around my neck, gripping my hips. Caressing my breasts. I want to etch the blush in his cheeks and the yearning in his eyes deep into my heart as a reminder to my soul that I'm worthy of adoration.

"I'm sorry I thought you were a dream." I bite my lip at the Lance Gross look-alike. Had I met him at the bar, I might've worked up the courage to have my first one-night stand. "If it wasn't clear before, I'm out of my element here."

"Do you feel safe?"

I nod. "Yes."

"That's all that matters."

Trust shines in his eyes, which are the same shape and color as my best friend's. His gaze conveys a quiet assurance. "Okay," I say.

"Okay."

Jazz and unspoken words fill the car on the seventeen-minute ride back home.

Home.

When we get there, Julian grabs his suitcase from my room and says goodnight before heading downstairs to his new domain. It's almost seven in the morning by the time I close my eyes and my thoughts abandon any attempt to make sense of my new housemate.

Chapter 13

Ella

I had every intention of calling Morgan after I woke up, once the fog of grinding on her brother and staying up well past my bedtime wore off, but I didn't get the chance. I crack an eye open and see a figure by my side, one with crossed arms and a frightening glare.

"What the hell, Morgan?!" I clutch my chest to soothe the pressure holding my breath hostage and scurry away from this demon dressed in pink Chanel.

"Yes, *the hell*." She tosses her pocketbook on the bed. "You had me worried sick! I called and texted to make sure you got home okay." She adjusts the crewneck on her tweed blazer dress.

"So you break in? I was asleep!"

Now that I'm on my feet—shaky ones, at that—I take Morgan in. Her shoulders are stiff, her eyes damp.

My friend, ever the worrier. She's the mom who sends a second lunch to school with Duke in case one of his friends forgets theirs at home. Apparently she'll also pop up at your new place as a personal search and rescue party if you don't return her texts.

"I'm sorry." I sigh. "I had a...weird night and fell asleep a few hours ago. I stayed out for a little with Erica. Did you text her?"

Morgan plops down in the reading chair, her legs spread out in front of her to show off the white platform heels strapped around her ankles. "Erica isn't answering either."

I look ready for a potato sack race in these damn sheets. I'd untangle myself, but I don't need another member of the Brooke family seeing my titties in this bedroom.

I'm winded by the time I reach her. Jesus, I need to work out. "Her friend probably had her tied up all night."

Morgan stares down at her hands. "Must be nice."

The thunder of heavy footsteps drowns out my attempt to ask what's wrong. The door flies open, and we scream in perfect harmony at a man charging in with a war cry and a sword.

At some point during the scuffle, I hopped over Morgan. The sheet puddles at the bottom of the small end table I'm on top of like I saw a mouse and not the man running in here ready to off us. I hop down and pull the soft Egyptian cotton over my front. For the second time this morning, I find myself shouting, "What the hell?" Only this time it's because bare-chested Julian in sweatpants has my voice in a stranglehold.

Rewind. Seeing Julian panting, with steel raised over his head, switches my fear to intrigue. I felt the smooth planes of his muscles wrestling between the sheets last night. But seeing them in the sunlight should come with a warning label. The muscles in his arms flex the tattoos on his chest and bicep. He's not jacked in a heavy on-the-protein shake and questionable substances kind of way, but those pecs are the size of my cheek meat—and not the cheeks on my face.

I take the scenic route down to the valley of his abs and muscled butt, which is covered in cotton slung low on his hips. Are those two dimples in his lower back?

Horror drains from Morgan's face. In its place is an uncontrollable grin. "Juju Bean! You're home!" She leaps into his arms.

"Hey, Mac." He pulls her in and kisses the side of her slicked-back ponytail.

She smacks his broad chest in a blow only an older sister could deliver.

"Ow!"

"What are you doing here?" The question comes out in a screech.

"I heard Ella scream."

"So you sprint in here with a sword?"

He lifts a shoulder. "Are you okay?" With Morgan now a few inches taller than him on her stilts, he has to peek around her shoulder to ask me.

"Of course she's not!" Morgan's bracelets hula hoop around her wrist when she spins to face me. "The poor thing can't talk since you barreled in here with a katana sword." She points a finger in my direction. "Look at her!"

Please don't. Not when I'm imagining your brother reenacting a Jodeci video with baby oil.

"Ella."

Morgan and Julian favor each other with their rich chocolate hue and flawless skin. He might be the baby brother, but he clearly towers over her when she's not in heels.

"*Ella.*"

"Huh?"

Julian's stare eases to match his tone. "You okay?"

Not with you standing here shirtless for me to ogle in front of your sister.

The care and attention Julian has provided in less than twenty-four hours is more than I ever received from my pending ex-husband. The man ran up from the basement with a sword, ready to attack whatever entity threatened my safety.

"Yup, never better." Morgan's gaze shifts between us. "Just…" My eyes drop to the front of Julian's sweatpants before I blink my inner thot away. "Tired."

His smirk says I'm neither fast nor smooth.

Focus on your friend.

"I didn't expect to see Morgan this early," I add.

She crosses her arms and turns to her brother. "And I didn't expect you back in the States until next year. Why are you here?"

His brow rises. "Do I need a permission slip to be in my own house?"

Morgan rolls her eyes and reaches for her pocketbook. "I hope you called our mother."

"Relax, I'm swinging by later. It was too late by the time I got in."

Her eyes narrow. "Where did you sleep last night?"

Shit.

Morgan has yet to meet a mystery she couldn't solve and will piece together the sequence of last night's events like a game of Clue.

This is new territory—her protective big sister energy, not the sleuthing. Morgan the nosy friend is a person I know well. Morgan the sibling is a different story. She acts like I handed myself keys to the townhouse and waited in bed for her brother to fly home.

Forget the fact that I'm still married and have zero interest in dating right now. The only thing I am guilty of is climaxing in a dream that turned out to be real. She doesn't need to know that, though.

The headshake I give Julian is subtle enough for Morgan to miss. "Crashed on the couch." His eyes are still on me before they shift to his sister when I clear my throat. "Stopped by Swigs before I came home and couldn't make it up the stairs."

"Yeah, that makes sense." She lets out a nervous laugh. "I don't mean to—" She laughs again and motions between us. "What are the odds you'd come home early and find someone living in your home?" She winces. "Shit, I should've asked you first."

"You think?" There's no heat in Julian's stare. Only love.

"What if you stayed with our parents until the end of the year?"

"Mac."

"At least until Ella—"

"Hard pass. Ella and I already worked it out. You promised her the townhouse, and I'll stay in the basement."

Morgan glances at me for confirmation. "Works for me," I say. "We could stay at your house until Charles's ninety days are up. That would give me enough time to get everything ready without crowding Julian in his own home. Thanks, by the way, for the kid bedroom. I haven't bought a day-bed for Haile, but that room is so perfect for Jackson."

Her eyes soften and shift to her brother. "Thank Uncle Julian for that. He might wield swords at random, but he built that room for Duke when he visits."

I tell myself that the tingling in my chest is from not getting eight hours of sleep and not my heart's attempt to revive itself back to life. My focus tears away from Julian to stuff down the thoughts that pop up every time I'm in his orbit. Thoughts of exploring why my breath quickens in his presence, or the hyperawareness his deep voice spreads over my body like honey. My heartbeat skyrockets under his gaze, like the one he's casting me right now.

"Ella." A shiver circles my nipples, spreads down my belly, and lands between my legs. I swallow the pleasurable aches at my name on his lips and offer a smile that's shaky at best. It's a fight for him to suppress a grin, but he manages. "How about this? We'll do a test run on Friday and invite Duke over for a sleepover. If you and the kids feel comfortable, move in this weekend. You'll have time to work out school drop-off with your son before it ends."

It's not a bad idea.

The drive from DC to Virginia is a commute I need to figure out sooner rather than later. I'll have to change school districts by fall if it's too hectic, which will mean negotiating with an ex who wants me to fail. "Are you sure we're not putting you out?"

"You ask that question like my response will change. Stay." The corner of his lip curls. "Please."

Who am I to say no to a fine man on the verge of begging?

Our gazes catch, and we grin. You'd think he asked me to prom instead of moving in to save my own ass. "Yes." It comes out more breathless than I expected, which has Morgan's full attention on me. "I mean, it works."

Julian rolls his eyes and laughs. "I'll leave you to it." He turns to Morgan. "Where's my stuff?"

"Oh!" A flush creeps up her cheeks. "I moved most of it to that large storage closet in the basement." She waggles her brows. "The one near the bedroom you use for your fuck buddies."

Oh, really?

He winces in an attempt to downplay the accusation. "Don't start, Mac." The daggers in his stare are a warning she ignores.

"Fine, I'll finish." Morgan walks over with the excitement of an older sibling who has a journal of receipts to embarrass her little brother. "Julian likes to have 'friends' over," she says with air quotes. "Not all the time, but for game nights." She steps closer like she's going to whisper—she doesn't. "A woman or two will stay over, and that's where he keeps them."

"You make it sound like he ties them up."

"I wouldn't put it past him." She laughs, oblivious to the shift in atmosphere, which went from comfy to WTF.

I try to interject, but she cuts me off. "Not to worry, El. Julian keeps himself busy, but he doesn't *get busy* here. He hasn't messed with anyone in his bedroom since—"

"Morgan! She's got it."

I've never been more grateful to be an only child than I am right now.

Julian's sex life is not my business. Based on our first encounter, it's not surprising he's very active and probably has repeat customers. What happened between us was nothing special—another Saturday night, in his book. Did he not say he confused me with someone he met at the bar? There you have it.

So why am I so disappointed?

I offer my friend a small smile in encouragement to shut the hell up. "There are certain things I should know, and that's not one of them." I muster what little energy I have to slip my armor back in place. My gaze is expressionless when it lands on Julian. "As long as the kids and I don't see or hear it, knock yourself out."

Morgan rambles on about Sunday plans and dinner later with her parents. My mind is on getting out of this townhouse to untangle myself from the scent that's sending me into a frenzy and the owner's stare burning into my cheek.

Chapter 14

Ella

Mondays are a hustle with a capital H. Getting the kids back into the swing of their weekly routine is a special type of challenge—particularly if they have a grandmother who takes them to the National Zoo for a day of VIP access and unlimited rides.

Haile and Jackson didn't want to come back to Morgan's with me yesterday, much less wake up this morning. Even Duke whined about missing out and how his grandmother needed to "step it up" like Ms. Katharine, as if she doesn't have a bank account full of zeroes herself.

Jackson made it to the school bus on time, but he maintained his protest that learning about animals at the zoo is more educational than a book with pictures from the 1900s. *Brat*. That left me with just enough time to buckle Haile into her new booster seat for an appointment I cannot miss.

Bright Spot Academy is the only childcare facility in a fifteen-mile radius currently accepting enrollment for its preschool program. Tuition is affordable, but the location is on the southeast side of DC, which means a twenty-five-minute car ride from Falls Church *without* traffic.

I'll have to master the art of splitting myself in two or teleport between Jackson's school and Haile's future preschool, which are on opposite ends of the DMV. Those are the only two options. The townhouse is about sixteen minutes from each, which is a plus.

At least I'll be able to afford their college after adding to my swear jar for cussing in traffic. For now, this setup has to work, because I needed a job yesterday, and a job requires reliable childcare.

If it wasn't for the GPS and the finger paintings taped to the windows, I'd have missed the unsuspecting academy. It's clustered between a series of townhouses and what looks like the back of a warehouse. Yellow bricks stand tall and proud, with windows encased in white on every floor. A neighborhood bright spot for tomorrow's future leaders.

There's a parking spot a few feet away across the street. The building under construction on this side stretches half the length of the block, its modern industrial design in battle with the color-splashed homes rooted in DC's architectural history.

"Are we here?" Haile's thick brows squish together, her eyes searching for a destination that meets the expectation of a four-year-old raised in suburban extravagance.

She and Jackson have only known the best money can buy. If there's one lesson our family transition will teach them, it's that status does not equate to value or integrity.

And to know your worth—and add tax.

My eyes find her inquisitive stare in the mirror. "Yes, baby. The house in yellow across the street." I follow her gaze and watch curiosity morph into excitement.

"Oh, Mommy! I love yellow!"

The gleam in her eyes is contagious, spreading a slow grin across my face. *The kids will be alright.* "Yes, I do too. Ready to go check it out?"

"Thank you for your flexibility today, Ms. Greene."

I meet warm brown eyes that crinkle at the edges. "Of course; it's no problem at all," I say to the woman in front of me, the auntie version of Mister Rogers in black slacks and a yellow cardigan.

I'm on the floor between a large piece of butcher paper and three formerly ornery kids consumed with tracing the numbers and letters I wrote with dot markers. Haile abandoned ship in search of a doll and snacks.

I missed this.

Stepping into Bright Spot reawakened a part of me that went dormant years ago. Caring for children is nothing new for me, but to be a part of the calm and chaos that comes with early childhood centers is muscle memory coming back to life.

When we arrived twenty minutes ago, Haile and I sat on mismatched chairs with wobbly legs in a makeshift lobby until I saw a toddler make a run for the back door like he knew how to pick a lock. A young woman with braids in a loose bun was hot on his trail with *I swear it's not a circus like this* eyes the moment she registered someone was waiting in the front.

I learned a long time ago not to judge a book by its cover or an overworked and underpaid childcare provider doing their best. So I followed her down the hardwood hall and asked if I could help while I waited for Rose, the director.

A quick chat with Maressa turned into an exchange of war stories, which is how I ended up in her small room full of colorful scribble art and energetic toddlers. I'm in the midst of what was once chaos and in my element as a former employee at a daycare in Boston.

It's Maressa's second week as an intern and her first time in the field with little ones who'll charm you with their gap-toothed smile before reenacting *Prison Break* or having an Oscar-worthy meltdown.

The tiny mob wasn't happy with the snack delay, prompting a chorus of tantrums that quickly faded with fresh markers in their hands and a target in sight. Eight toddlers crowd me on the floor, eager to connect the dots and scribble out their hearts' desires.

"I apologize again for the delay," Rose says for the third time in two minutes. Her namesake tints her plump cocoa cheeks as she takes two deep exhales to school her expression. Dark circles line tired eyes that hold a smile meant to mask a world of exhaustion. But those eyes also reflect a ferocity not to fuck with her, this facility, or the kids.

My knees crack when I stand, another reminder that forty is set to arrive next year. "Please don't apologize, Ms. Laverne. It was my pleasure to spend time with Ms. Maressa. She's great with the kids." I smile at the doe-eyed intern.

"Call me Rose. 'Ms. Laverne' is too formal for my tastes." She extends a hand. "And that must be Haile."

We turn to my daughter, who's trying to teach a two-year-old how to count Cheerios. Sunlight teases mahogany streaks in curly brown pigtails that bounce at her own applause, which the little girl next to her mimics.

"She's quite the educator," Rose says with fascination.

Warmth thunders through my body and expands in my chest. My life might be a mess, but I have two of the most joyful and selfless children who grasp onto hope with their tiny hands and share it with the world.

"She's wonderful." I blink back tears.

Rose considers me with a knowing smile. "Are you ready for the tour?"

"Sounds great."

⌐ℓℓ⌐

"Okay, we can do this."

By *we*, I mean me and my self-esteem—the latter of which threw up a peace sign and made a beeline for the door weeks ago. She has yet to return.

Five applications submitted.

Four rejections.

One left on read.

I'm one rejection away from hiring a fortune-teller or a miracle worker to sprinkle good vibes on these job boards. There's always the recruiter route, but the gaps in my employment history are as wide as DC potholes. I don't want anyone laughing in my face or frowning with pity.

Staying home to raise my children was a privilege I don't take for granted, an experience I wouldn't change for the world. Watching them grow from babies and putting my early childhood development background to use allowed me to lean into my love of motherhood and my passion to cultivate the next generation.

The empty sections on my résumé don't encompass the blood, sweat, and tears it took to make my house a home. I was the COO of our residence—the event planner, personal shopper, scheduler, housekeeper, driver, and tutor. I would add chef to the list, but nuggets, eggs, and sandwiches are the extent of my culinary expertise.

I shift on the barstool at the counter and refill my wine. The house is quiet, the kids asleep and the kitchen wiped down for the night.

Rose assured me I don't need to stress. She admitted that she watched my interactions with the kids, prompting her to speak about Haile matriculating at Bright Spot—and the possibility of me becoming the new assistant director.

"She drank one too many juice boxes." I giggle into my wine, still in disbelief.

Tomorrow, I return for an interview. Haile will try out a preschool class, which gets zero objections from me.

The résumé on my laptop stares back at me, a reminder to stop slacking off and fill in the gaps. Tomorrow's interview isn't a guarantee, but it is a chance at a fresh start.

Here goes nothing.

Chapter 15

Ella

"**W**hat?!"

Morgan's shout is loud enough to carry through her open office door, down the hall, and to the ground floor of the building, where Ms. Maritza is putting the finishing touches on her lunch menu for Suegra's. It's a Panamanian restaurant she opened two months ago, and people have come from near and far to taste her *bistec picado*, fried fish with rice, and *sancocho* of the day.

Her patrons aren't here to listen to my best friend yell like she doesn't work for a prestigious law firm paying her to use her inside voice. I'm just as surprised as she is that the tour at Bright Spot Academy turned into a job interview, but you don't see me hollering, do you?

For someone so composed, she's at a twelve today.

"Want to scream it from the roof? I don't think your dad and colleagues heard you."

"Why the shouting, pumpkin?"

I stand corrected.

Langston Brooke absorbs the doorway with his tall frame in a tailored navy suit. His dark eyes acknowledge my presence in one of the button-tuft office chairs before scanning the room for the threats that caused his daughter to squeal so loud on a Tuesday afternoon. His features soften after a beat, the edges of his wide lips spreading his salt and pepper goatee at his oldest child, who shares his almond-shaped eyes and hydrated skin.

Morgan flicks her hair over her shoulder like her outburst is a daily occurrence. The specs of glitter in her black eyeshadow are no match for the sparkle in her eyes. "Haile's new daycare offered Ella a job on the spot. You're looking at the new assistant director of Bright Spot Academy!"

"Technically, I interviewed for the position today," I add for clarity. "No job offer yet."

I felt seen speaking to Rose during our hour-long conversation. I didn't realize how much I missed being in the childcare space until we discussed planning, programming, and aspirations to make Bright Spot the best for families and staff. It's clear that Rose pours her heart into the center. There's a magic there I'd love to be part of, and I'm crossing my fingers and toes everything works out.

A father's pride reflects in Langston's gaze. My dad died when I was five, in a car accident after a long shift at the factory. But I imagine his smile would mirror the man who's become an unexpected stand-in, one I inherited after Morgan and I became friends. He calls me on Mother's Day and sends gifts on my kids' birthdays. I might not share his last name, but that doesn't stop him from calling me his second daughter.

"Amazing news! You'll get it, sweetie pie." A squeeze is at the end of his hug, which is coated in expensive cologne.

Sweetie Pie.

Pumpkin.

Juju Bean.

The Brooke family has a thing for food names. It wouldn't surprise me if "Mac," Julian's nickname for Morgan, stands for mac and cheese.

Is Julian in the office today?

Langston takes the seat across from me. He's not a bulky man but keeps in shape. It's a hidden talent how he folds himself into Morgan's doll-house furniture. His ankle crosses over his knee, and he drapes a cufflink-adorned hand over the Italian loafers she bought him two Christmases ago. "When will you find out?"

My inhale is sharp. "In the next few days." I'm trying not to get my hopes up, but after multiple rejections and the clock winding down, I want this. I *need* this, or for something else to pan out soon.

I had five years at a daycare under my belt before Charles convinced me to stay home. Rose has been searching for a second-in-command, and I need to get back to the workforce. The stars are aligning, or at least appear to be. Not only would I get a decent salary, but I'd have full benefits and a tuition discount that my struggling bank account would kiss with an open mouth.

"So we can't convince you to join Brooke Law International?" Langston motions to the crown molding and the view of DC's historic U Street Corridor. "We just installed a new coffee machine," he says with a smile that makes him look ten years younger than his sixty-four years.

Job recruiters would throw office supplies at my forehead for turning down the prospect of a career at Langston Brooke's company. What they do here is still a mystery to me. Something with contracts and negotiations. Whatever it is, he's building a legacy in his community.

Brooke Law International is a majority-Black firm with internship opportunities at nearby universities. There's even a program for high schoolers from historically marginalized areas to spend a summer in one of the overseas offices, all expenses paid.

And that doesn't even begin to touch his DC footprint.

Take this office. It stretches across one of four floors inside a historic property on the corner of one of the busiest blocks on the corridor. He owns the building. All nine thousand square feet.

Between this floor and Suegra's is multifamily housing for struggling families who don't qualify for the low-income threshold in the area. This is separate from other office spaces across the city, which he rents to start-ups for next to nothing. They all have affordable housing.

Morgan and Julian come from a long line of Black excellence in the nation's capital. Their legacy has stood the test of time and survived gentrification, and now they give back to communities to preserve culture and prevent erasure.

Brooke Law is amazing, but it's not for me.

"You know I can only tolerate Morgan in small doses." I dodge a stack of sticky notes to the head and laugh. "Kids are my ministry."

It's true. Early childhood development is not for the faint of heart. Tantrums and screams come with the territory, and most days involve dealing with someone else's shit. Literally. But I wouldn't trade it for an all-white office or looking over pages and pages of contracts in legalese I don't understand. Morgan deals in corporate art, but she might as well be one of the lawyers with her arsenal of fancy suits.

Give me crayons, Converses, and cuddly little kids I get to help mold into kind adults. Ones who care about others, recycle, and remember to share their snacks.

Langston nods. "Understood. Can't blame an old man for trying." He looks at his watch and stands. "At least let us celebrate your job interview on Sunday."

My brow quirks. "Does this celebration include your famous pulled barbecue chicken?" Don't let the custom suits fool you, Langston throws down on the grill. His ribs are also phenomenal.

His eyes widen at the prospect of gassing up his favorite appliance. Grilling is one of Langston's greatest loves, behind his wife, kids, and career. He strokes his lip with his thumb and index finger. "That could work. You know," he says with a smile at no one in particular, "I've been meaning to try out my new smoker."

He's like a kid in a candy store, only rosemary lamb chops and cornbread entice him over lollipops. "Great idea, sweetie pie," he says. "We'll celebrate your interview and Julian's birthday."

That gets my attention. "Oh?" Morgan leans to her side in her chair and tilts her head at the breathlessness in my tone. The woman doesn't miss a thing. I cut my eyes at her to mind her business and pull my attention back to her dad with a mental note to keep my voice and vagina in check.

It's a harmless crush—not even a crush. More like an observation of his fineness. Nothing more, nothing less.

"Saturday is his birthday," Langston continues. "It's been a year since we could celebrate with him at home. We're happy to have him back." Multimillion-dollar deals don't come close to the love Julian's dad has for his family. The twinkle in his eye shows more love for his children than words will ever convey.

"How old is he?" I shrug off Morgan's glare. She's not mad, but based on the height of her eyebrows, she's got questions about my sudden interest in her brother.

It's not like I brought him up. She should blame her dad for that.

"He'll be thirty-one." Langston's brows draw together. "You alright, Ella?"

"Never better!" *Shoot, too much enthusiasm*. I don't know what I expected, but eight years my junior wasn't it.

Julian is an old soul. His house is pristine, a classic style with vintage vinyls and zero clutter. Minus the charge with a sword at perceived threats, you'd never guess he's thirty. *Maybe* thirty-five. Nothing about him screams young bachelor who doesn't know how to do laundry or his taxes. He probably pays a small team to do both, which speaks to his wealth and not his maturity.

"My son has been hard at work in our London office." Langston grins. "It will be good for you two to meet."

If only you knew.

He heads to a meeting across town, leaving me with his daughter, who sees through my attempts to downplay my curiosity about her brother.

What does she expect? The man is fine, and we live together, which is weird to say. It's not like we're going to start a secret affair and fuck each other senseless. I'm not sure I'd survive if last Saturday is a taste of the main event—and that was *with* clothes on.

Who's thinking about dating, anyway? I've got bills to pay, and I refuse to swap out one asshole for another pretending to be a decent man. Even if I was ready, I've been MIA for well over a decade. Julian wouldn't hook himself to a woman with two kids and no stability. I don't care how good my ass looks.

"He's not in the office." Morgan's tone has the finesse of nails on a chalkboard.

Am I that obvious?

I'm not the only one who needs to get laid. A Snickers isn't going to cure that crankiness.

The primary Brooke Law International office has a small reception area, twelve offices, open desks for interns, a kitchen, and a conference room. Morgan's office is one of the four that face U Street. Her father's is down the hall on the other side with views of the back alley, which they transformed into Suegra's outdoor patio.

Only Langston, Morgan, and four other partners and counsel come into the office. That leaves two open offices for the associates and consultants to use when they're not working remotely or from one of the other satellite offices around the DMV to be closer to clients. I've been here a handful of times for pop-in lunches with Morgan and her dad to remember the one tucked into the corner near the kitchen is never open. My guess is it's Julian's.

I tell myself that the Victorian windows and crown molding are why I'm on my feet so fast. Not to investigate an office that belongs to a man living as rent-free in my head as I am in his house.

"Good for him," I say, to the confusion of Morgan and myself. I thumb to the door behind me. "Need to pee. Be right back."

Morgan has no chance to respond. I'm halfway down the hall, headed in the opposite direction of the bathroom, possessed by the spirit of Nancy Drew. A horny, age-appropriate Nancy with the urge to see another office and admire carpeting.

Normal Tuesday behavior.

I reach my destination after popping into the kitchen for water I don't need. No one is around to catch me snooping, but does that stop me from peeking around corners and ducking the cameras? Nope.

This is a bad idea. The hallway is silent but likely agrees with me. With my back against the door, I take another glance to the left and right and slip inside with the turn of a knob.

Morgan will kick my ass across every square foot of this floor if she finds me. What's my excuse anyway if I get caught? *My bad. I went down the wrong hall and helped myself into an office that wasn't the restroom. Total coincidence that it happens to be your brother's.*

The office is smaller than Morgan's, with a simple wooden desk and chair facing a worn leather loveseat the color of whiskey. Unlike the other offices dressed for show, Julian's is for comfort. Black and white photos of the city hang above a walnut sideboard half the length of the wall. A record player sits on top, next to a Wes Montgomery *Smokin' at the Half Note* album. There's no television, only two screens and a keyboard on the desk.

His office is an extension of his home. I inhale the cedar and sandalwood scent as my fingers run over the desk with a smile.

"Like it?"

I yelp at the deep voice behind me and squeeze the open water bottle in my hand, forcing out cold water that soaks my sleeveless blouse. Words stall in my throat when I face Julian. He's leaning against the doorway with his arms crossed and a wide grin.

His tailor deserves a raise and a forehead kiss for the light blue suit molded to his body. It's not tight enough to show a dick print, but it does force attention to his sculpted thighs, broad chest, and thick biceps, which are pulling at the delicate fabric.

Business Julian is a good look, an ebony Ken doll with a tight ass and muscles. His fade is fresh, like he stopped by a barber this morning before whatever meeting he had that required someone to focus on his words and not the gorgeous gladiator in a tailored suit. DC is in the middle of a heat wave, and there's a good chance the man in front of me is the culprit.

He offers me a white handkerchief. "You alright there?" His steps still at my nod. I follow his gaze down the buttons of my cream blouse to my breasts, which are now visible in my sheer bra. He swallows, his eyes committing the outline of my now hard nipples to memory.

I stare at him until he realizes he's eye-fucking my titties. "Sorry." He closes his eyes and shakes his head. With the flick of a button, he's out of his suit jacket. "Here."

A faint charge passes through our fingers when I take his jacket to drape it over my shoulders. "Thank you."

Julian rolls his tongue over his bottom lip. When our eyes meet, the corner of his mouth kicks up. Curse him and that dimple.

"This is the second time you've broken into my personal space," he says with a tsk and sits on the edge of his desk. His feet cross at the ankles like he has all day to entertain our interaction instead of client meetings and whatever else they do around here. Paperwork with a fancy thesaurus to rake in millions in billable hours.

I'm a hot-ass mess, in case that wasn't clear. Not because the temperature outside is a humid borderline inferno, but because of the man in front of me, whose dick print is now a part of this impromptu meeting. You'd think I'd never seen a penis the way I trace the outline against his thigh with my stare.

Get a grip.

I'd like to.

I take a breath and channel the almost-forty-year-old I am. I'm a card-carrying PTA mom for crying out loud. How does it look to gawk at a guy who's barely thirty—and my best friend's little brother? I revert back to school girl tendencies with Julian, and it stops today.

My chin lifts at his smirk. "It's not breaking and entering if the door is unlocked."

Laughter rumbles in his chest. "You sure about that?"

"Yes."

No.

He pushes off the desk and takes a step into my space. "Were you looking for me?"

PTA mom. "Nope. Your name isn't on the door, and I've never been down this hall." I stand straighter. "I was on a curiosity tour."

"A curiosity tour." He tries out the words and takes another step. "Didn't know we offered those here."

I make the mistake of sniffing the air filled with his scent. A hint of a moan and some pent-up sexual frustration slips out. Julian's nostrils flare. He closes the distance between us with a final step. He's only a couple of inches taller than me, but the power of his steady gaze reaches the ceiling. The intensity is at its highest setting.

Playful hickory eyes darken in an unspoken dare to test him. Luckily for Julian, I enjoy rising to the occasion.

His suit jacket lands on the loveseat with a soft thud. My chest lifts in a dare of my own. He smiles, his eyes dipping for a peek before returning to mine. We stand in place with knotted gazes until the door opens.

"I thought you went to the bathroom," Morgan says from behind me. "Did you get lost?" My blouse becomes her focus when I face her. She frowns. "What happened?"

Julian is the first to answer. "It's my fault. I was in a rush to get to my office and knocked into her when she was coming from the kitchen." He eyes me, possession long gone and replaced by a neutral expression.

My stomach growls with perfect timing. "Want to grab lunch, Morgan? I have ninety minutes before I get Haile."

Morgan considers me and Julian. My eyes are on her, and his are searing a hole through the side of my neck. See? Heatwave. "Sure, sounds good," she says. "We should get going."

I nod. "Yup." Julian is now in his chair in front of his computer. "Funny bumping into you. I'll see you Friday."

His focus is on the screen, but his dimple pops. "See you Friday, Ella."

Chapter 16

Julian

For two hours twice a week, the world evaporates under stadium lights. My calendar full of meetings disappears, along with the pressure to land new deals and the weight of my father's legacy embedded so deep I can't take a step without it.

When I get on my gear and head to the pitch, I'm Jules. Not one of DC's most eligible bachelors because of my bank account and ability to smile on a red carpet. Not the center of capital gossip turned think piece the family publicist says is good for our brand—as if we need one in the first place.

We're not royalty, but in Chocolate City, we might as well be.

Rugby is the steady constant that's survived time and distance. My team doesn't give a shit about pedigree, only how you show up for others and leave it on the field.

It became my first love after the Georgetown University Rugby Club went to the national championship. I was seventeen at the time, and I found my way to DC rugby soon after and haven't looked back. I play pick-up games in London when I have time, but nothing beats home.

As a flanker, it's my job to win the ball, be one of the first to a breakdown, and steal the ball from an opposing player. It's a responsibility I've shared with Antonio, the other flanker on my team, for years. Yet I was the only one putting guys on their ass tonight.

My muscles still ache from playing Whac-A-Mole on single-player mode after the third consecutive tackle. Confrontation comes with the territory, and clearly that means from the open-side flanker tonight.

The asshole in question smirks at me from across the table, just like he did on the field. He always does this shit at my first practice back from a long stretch abroad. It's tired, and so am I.

"How you been?" The question comes between bites of his burrito, the mix of chicken and purple rice visible with every chew. It's a miracle he's not stashing pieces in his beard to save for a snack later. You'd think he fasted for a week the way he's eating.

"Ask me tomorrow, after I recover from carrying your ass tonight." I reach for the sriracha, coat my spicy pork burrito, and eat half of it in one go.

Hunger is a guarantee after practice, and this Korean joint in Navy Yard always hits the spot. It's a short walk from the field, and this place always loads you up on veggies and proteins in house-made sauces.

You're full without the bubble guts.

"It's a bye week because of the holiday weekend. You'll survive," he says with an exasperated sigh, like I'm the one being annoying and not the other way around.

Antonio polishes off his plate and pats his stomach. The muscles in his arms flex when he stretches them back, past the big head holding up a tiny man bun. The bun has grown since the last time we saw each other, but it still looks like a turd in color and size.

"Speaking of the weekend, what are we doing Saturday?" His brown eyes remain glued on the laminated menu for the next item that won't satisfy his appetite.

Lucky for him, he inherited his father's metabolism, along with a well-paying position at his family's investment firm to support his never-ending food habit. His grocery bill would be obscene if he cooked himself.

I shrug. "Thought about staying in."

He pulls his attention from the menu with a lifted brow. "Another game night like last year?"

It's true. My game nights are unforgettable, even a year later. My basement is a playground for the grown and sexy—one that transforms into a playground for the tiny crew whenever Duke comes over.

Classic arcade games line a wall next to a Skee-Ball machine and a two-player basketball game. There's an air hockey table, a dartboard, and two rows of leather recliners in front of a large screen we use for karaoke, gaming, and watching movies. I added a small concession area with a bar, juice on tap for my nephew, and an old-school popcorn machine.

We get down in the basement, hence the soundproofing.

But Antonio isn't referring to a rowdy game of Uno, though slapping back-to-back Draw Fours like you're ready to throw hands isn't uncommon.

Anyone who saw me and Kierra circling each other last year didn't have to stretch their imaginations to guess we had sex. Lingering touches, shared fuck-me eyes, and a game of Twister was all it took to clear everyone out, and we spent the rest of the night in the back bedroom. Getting up early the next morning for work was the only bullshit excuse I could muster on a Friday night, but it did what it was supposed to do.

But before that, Kierra's roommate blew up her phone like she didn't have her own business to mind. She swung by to drive her home after the clubs closed and did not take kindly to idling outside for twenty minutes before we let her in. Whatever frustration she had stayed in the car. Once she came inside, she came again—under Kierra's tongue and on my dick.

I never told Antonio what went down, but I guess the stupid grin I had on my face during the barbecue at my parents' house the next day gave it away. He had his own to match after heading back to his Adams Morgan penthouse with a player from the ladies rugby team.

Thirty was a memorable birthday, full of unexpected turns and lots of positions. But what happened between me and Kierra was a one-time thing. I was back on a plane to our London office three days later.

Tonight's practice was the first time she and I have seen each other since then. Antonio assumes we'll run it back, but I'm not jumping to have people at my spot. Especially since I'm not living alone—or at least won't be once Ella and her kids move in.

Soft, full lips shatter my concentration and any thought of my birthday. Sure, I can have people over. She'd never hear anything, and the basement has a private entrance. Truth is, I haven't been able to concentrate since last weekend, much less on another woman.

Not since I tasted her mouth and the fiery determination to kick me out of my own house.

The same fire burned in her eyes when I caught her in my office on Tuesday. Neither of us wanted to back down from our standoff of will and unspoken desire. Ella left after Morgan popped in, and I spent the rest of the day keeping the urge to wrap my hand around my dick at bay. Her stubbornness still makes me laugh, which has Antonio wondering why the hell I'm smiling.

He stops mid-bite of another Korean-style burrito that somehow made its way to our table. "You good?"

Am I?

On the surface, nothing is out of place. Calm and detached is my default mode. But on the inside, I can't stop thinking about the woman in my bed whose lavender scent still coats the bedsheets I refuse to wash. Her memory traces an impulse I thought I'd buried far out of reach and sight.

There's something about Ella that's different but familiar. I've never had such a natural pull to someone. I want to know her better. Spend more time with her. For the life of me, I don't know why.

Antonio's stare pulls me back to our wooden high tables across from the bar. It mirrors the one his pops would give us every time we looked like we were up to no good—which was more often than not growing up.

Drawn brows.

Pursed lips.

Eyes scanning for guilt.

I clear my throat. "Never better."

He folds his arms over his bulky frame, currently wrapped in an athletic compression shirt, and waits.

A second passes.

Another.

By the fifth, his gaze dilutes to quick glances between me and the half-eaten burrito in front of him.

I flash a dimple at the flex in his forearms that would rather be on the table making work of his second dinner.

"You seeing someone?"

"Nope." It's not a lie. I've been single for years, and I plan to keep it that way.

"Kee looked happy to see you." The way he says it suggests more than what's there. Aside from a few random texts, I haven't spoken to or thought about her.

He's a second too late to snatch back the burrito I stole. If he's going to run his mouth, he doesn't need this. I cut off the part he gnawed, take an obnoxious bite, and throw in a moan for good measure at his scowl. Because I don't talk with food in my mouth, I make him wait, much to his annoyance.

"Where you going with this? It's barely been a week since I got back. If you want to play host so bad, tell people to pull up to your place."

The problem with knowing someone since you were kids is the ability to see through their bullshit. With anyone else, saying I'm staying in would be enough to drop the subject. But Antonio plans to press me for the answer he knows I'm hiding.

Persistent shit. Four years younger and forever in my business.

I exhale deep and roll my eyes. We'll be here all night, and I have an ice bath at home with my name on it. Our bodies must be over a hundred years old for each of the fourteen years we've played. "I kinda got someone staying with me."

The confusion twisting his face is understandable. How do I have someone in my house when I just returned from London? Why the hell did I allow it when I never have before? Each question scrolls across his face, which is stuck on WTF.

I'm still trying to wrap my head around the fact that the star of my fantasies every night since I met her is moving in with two kids. I've been waiting for the shock to roll through, but it hasn't happened yet.

Antonio knows better than anyone that I won't play house or make it official with a woman. I came close years ago, and that ain't happening again.

"You lying."

"Why would I?"

"So?"

"*So?*" My brow lifts in defiance. He's grating my last nerve. "All you need to know is I'm helping a family friend in a tough spot. It's temporary, and it's not a big deal." It's also none of his business, a reality that's yet to set in. "Can you respect that?"

He scoffs. "Of course." His shoulders, once tense from unanswered questions, finally relax, a sign the investigation is over. "We still on for Sunday?"

I shake my head and laugh. "He's already prepping your ribs."

Antonio earned his own container years ago, the way he flies through them. It's a testament to Langston Brooke's skills on the grill. They pull people from around the beltway to his backyard every Memorial Day weekend.

We walk back to the stadium to get our cars. I'm digging through my bag for my keys when my hand brushes against my phone. I open it to reread the text thread between me and Ella for the fifth time today.

We exchanged numbers through Morgan once she came back to the office after lunch. I hate texting as much as I hate talking on the phone, but I reached out to Ella for reasons I'm still trying to understand. Yesterday, she told me I was doing too much, like asking about your preferred loaf of bread was excessive.

Who wouldn't jump at the chance to not have to haul groceries into the house like a CrossFit workout? It's one less thing she'll have to worry about. I ended up getting them anyway after a call to Morgan. It took prodding and a verbal promise I wasn't sniffing gasoline for her to tell me.

The refrigerator and pantry now have her and her kids' favorite foods and snacks. Everything is ready for their arrival tomorrow night.

The question is, am I?

Chapter 17

Ella

The walk to the front door might as well be a mile. I stare at the black paneling with brass hardware I've come to love and sigh.

"Are we going in?" Jackson joins me in the middle of the sidewalk. I haven't left this spot since we pulled up six minutes ago.

Not that I'm counting.

"Yes, baby, we are." My fingers tickle the top of his curls.

Any minute now.

On a deep exhale, I pull the strap of my purse higher up on my shoulder and cut the distance. *Thump, thump* goes my heart on the slow climb to the locks.

Tonight determines if we're one step closer to a fresh start or back to square one. We're not staying here if my kids aren't comfortable sharing a roof with Julian, there's no question about that. I searched for apartments in my price range as an alternative, only to find units with unidentifiable stains, insufficient space, or a trek from the other end of the beltway that would add an extra forty-five minutes of cursing at stop-and-go traffic.

Morgan threatened to knock some sense into me with her "good Prada shoe" if I didn't stay put. I don't have enough saved up yet to land in an ideal spot, and I can't afford two moves within the year.

"Duke says his uncle is cool," I say to Jackson.

"You told me, Mom. Four times."

Of course my six-year-old doesn't need a pep talk. I'm the only one losing my shit.

His small hand brushes mine. "We can stay out here longer if you need more time."

My sweet boy.

Jackson and Haile know my mommy breakdowns by heart. Burning cookies for the bake sale. Reaching the baseball field only to remember I left Jackson's gear at home. They love me through it all and always give me the space to stumble—or gawk at doors while they put the chalk we keep in the car to good use.

I pull Jackson in and kiss his head. "I'm ready now."

A teasing smile lifts his cheeks. "If the food is awful, we can order pizza."

Wouldn't be the first time.

"Haile, you coming?" Her head is down to concentrate on her latest masterpiece: a frog in a cowboy hat. I keep a spare bucket of sidewalk chalk in the trunk she puts to good use.

"Yup!" She stands to brush off her hands on her pink pants. "Let's eat!"

"Okay then!" We climb the stairs. The lock clicks, and I open the door to soft jazz and the fragrant aroma of marinara sauce.

What the?

We drop our shoes in the hall cubby and head through the living room to the source of the divine scent. Julian is in front of the stove, swaying to the croon of trumpets in black slacks and an untucked light gray shirt rolled to his elbows. He's so caught up he doesn't register our presence until he turns to face the kitchen island.

He startles. "Oh, hey! Didn't hear you come in." He reaches for a dish towel to wipe his hand and walks around the marble slab. "And who do we have here?"

Haile is first to step forward. She grins when he crouches to her eye level. "I'm Haile. Good to meet you." She extends a hand.

Julian's smile reaches the corners of his eyes. Hello again, dimples. "It's good to meet you, too, Haile. I'm Julian." He turns to Jackson, who hasn't left my side. He matches Julian in light gray, only his shirt has Naruto on it. "You must be Jackson. I've heard a lot about you." He scans his tee and says, "Cool shirt."

Pink heats Jackson's cheeks. Unlike Haile, Jackson has to warm up to people he meets, especially men. Charles's inconsistent presence in his life is something I've compensated for time and time again. Jackson is old enough to pick up on who comes to his events, helps him with his school projects, and spends more than thirty minutes a day with him.

Julian's eyes flick to mine when Jackson doesn't speak. His perception tugs at my heart when he stands and says, "I heard you like pizza, and I hope you don't mind making your own tonight."

Jackson's eyes widen. "From scratch?"

Julian nods to the assortment of cheeses and toppings in bowls on the counter. "I made the dough, but I could use some help kneading it. You game?"

"Am I!" My six-year-old catches his enthusiasm and brings it down a notch. "Yeah, that works."

I turn to hide my smirk.

"The powder room is down the hall to the right," Julian says. "Why don't you two wash up, and we'll get these in the oven?"

"Sure." The word barely comes out before Jackson sets off for the bathroom, with Haile right behind him.

"No running!" Their sprint slows into a skip at my voice. Julian is back in front of the stove. "Someone made a good impression."

He looks over his shoulder with a tilted brow. "I aim to please."

I bite my lip to resist a grin. *I'm sure you do.*

We've texted nonstop since Tuesday. Questions about our living arrangement turned into random memes and video clips. The vibe was light, like friends catching up after time apart. Here, in the same space? Let's just say dinner isn't the only thing getting hot in the kitchen.

I threaten my hormones with a time-out and clear my throat. "What ya working on over there?"

"Come here and find out." The same timbre that commanded me last weekend licks the shell of my ear.

This was a bad idea.

So why does it feel so good?

It's shameful how quickly I comply. I'm now next to a skillet with a meal teasing my stomach and a man tempting my...stop it.

Julian gathers a small spoonful of sauce and blows. "Open." His gaze lowers to my mouth.

How the hell did we get from *Let's have dinner with my kids* to *You can eat dinner off me if you want*? Julian is a flirt, that much is obvious, but this sexual tension is about to sear the crotch right out of my panties.

This man isn't checking for me like that. That's my mantra, and I'm sticking to it.

I shake the after-dark *Lady and the Tramp* reenactment from my mind, swallow the sauce, and step back. There are no noodles in the skillet anyway, and fantasizing about my best friend's brother is just wrong. The problem is that the sauce is so delicious, I moan—against my better judgment.

Our eyes lock before Julian's rake over my body. They travel down my breasts in a simple white tee and drop from my hips in black ripped jeans to my lilac toes.

"It's amazing," I say through a breath. "What is it?"

His answer comes with a slight headshake, maybe to knock away the inappropriate back-and-forth we can't escape. "Skillet eggplant Parmesan." He glances at his creation and frowns. "A meeting ran late. I didn't have time to grab everything I wanted from the store."

"You do realize you're talking to a woman whose go-to dinner is dinosaur nuggets with macaroni and cheese?" I've mastered the art of comfort food. If it involves preheating and pouring a few ingredients into a pan, I'll make it.

"Is this—is all of this okay? For them?" There's a softness in his voice that's replaced the confident tone that dared me to suck on his spoon. Julian wants to make a good impression, and his effort goes above and beyond anything I imagined.

My hand reaches to cover his wrist. "It's perfect. Thank you."

We don't break apart until Jackson and Haile thunder down the hall. "We got our hands extra clean," Jackson says. "Washed them six times."

"You should be good," Julian says with a chuckle. "Are you into anime?" He points at Jackson's shirt. "*Naruto*. Do you watch?"

Jackson bites the side of his cheek and frowns. "Duke has this shirt. It looked cool, so I asked for one."

"He wanted it because of our Japanese lessons. I could teach you too and show you some anime if you want?"

"Really?"

Julian lifts a shoulder. "Yeah. If it's okay with your mom, we can start next week."

Leave it to this man to have my quiet child bouncing on his toes, waiting for my response. My smile deepens into laughter. "Fine with me. What do you say to Mr. Julian, Jackson?"

"Thank you!" he all but squeals.

"It's my pleasure, and please, call me Julian."

Jackson and Haile join Julian at the kitchen island to prepare their pizzas. The front door slams before Morgan and Duke appear through the living room. She drops onto a barstool with a huff. "Today can crawl back up wherever it came." The breath she blows out is long and comes with a quick look between me and Julian. "What'd I miss?"

Chapter 18

Julian

A soundproof basement comes in handy, and right now it's a barrier between my neighbors and the sore winner screaming her head off after she beat my ass twice in *Mortal Kombat*. My gut hurts from laughing so hard at Ella, who's now dancing a weird mix between a twerk and the funky chicken.

We came down here after the kids conked out and Morgan went home. El took one look at the bed I bought Haile and almost lost it. I wasn't sure if I overstepped until she turned to me with her sleeping daughter in her arms and tears in her eyes to say, "Thank you."

A thanks wasn't necessary. I've seen her stretch herself to maintain normalcy for her kids, even in the short time I've known her. A bed doesn't scratch the surface of all she's done and all she will do to ensure they have what they need.

The impulse to hug her won out over my need to kiss her. I ran my mouth about arcade games to pivot from her crying over a mattress and wooden frame. One simple challenge led to sore thumbs and a gloating woman who won every battle with the same character.

In fairness, Ella warned me not to talk shit. She spent hours inside her local arcade when she was younger. How was I supposed to know classic fighting games are like riding a bike for her?

"You done yet?" I'm messing with her. Ella's playful side comes out when she's not overwhelmed or in mom mode, constantly carrying the weight of two parents. Her eyes sparkle, and her mouth hasn't lost its grin.

She hops onto the L-shaped sectional with a giggle. "I guess you could use a break. Does that butt feel better after I handed it to you so many times?"

I snort. "Maybe I let you win."

"Right," she deadpans and reaches for the remote. "That's why you stood up to concentrate like you had to defuse a bomb. Step up your game and get back to me."

I shake my head with another laugh. "So damn vicious. Hey, let that play."

Full Force's "Ain't My Type of Hype" sets in motion one of the greatest dance-offs for the culture.

"What do *you* know about *House Party*?"

I lean back and shrug. "It's a classic."

"You weren't even born when it came out!"

"And that means what?" My eyes narrow. On cue, I stand and pick up the choreography on the screen. It's a muscle memory at this point. "Fix that bottom lip!"

Ella's gape becomes a shriek when I jump into a jazz split. Morgan clowned me for rewinding the VHS over and over again to learn the dance. It was a go-to during house parties (ha) in high school and undergrad. Outside of the Kid 'n Play kick step, no one matched my energy.

Until now.

It's my turn to stare as El dances Sydney and Sharane's part before picking up my steps. She doesn't glance once at the screen and smirks at my wide eyes. "What's the matter, junior? Can't keep up?"

The verbal jab and the nickname I loathe send me into overdrive. I hit a backflip on principle, not missing a beat with the choreography. We can take this from friendly to *Stomp the Yard* if she wants.

Our feet connect on the first kick step. She lines up her next sarcastic shot and fires. "Did you practice this when you were in diapers?"

Her feet leave the ground when I toss her over my shoulder and spin. She grips my slacks with a startled laugh. "Not another age joke from you, do you understand?" I smack the back of her jean-wrapped thighs and jog around the room.

"You'll make me sick!"

"Should've thought about that before you ran your mouth." I spin in another circle.

"Julian! I'll pee!"

Her grip pinches my skin. Does she really think I'll drop her? I stop to set her down but lose balance when she grabs the back of the sectional and pulls with a force that sends us flying over the edge. I flip to the ground with her on top.

To be honest, I'm not mad at this position, but I lift her hips so she's not on my dick, which is hard for the second time this evening.

Ella's pants become ragged breaths. Her palms flatten on the side of my face, her cleavage teasing me to peek inside the loose tee hovering in front of my face. Neither of us makes a move to get up. Our eyes lock.

The heat between us rises.

She pulls away and crawls to the coffee table to check her phone for the third time. The nanny cams from her old house are in her and Jackson's rooms. "It's late. I should go."

I stand and tuck my hands into my pockets. "I had fun tonight."

"Me too," she says with a smile. "Thank you again...for everything."

All I can do is nod.

Tonight was the most fun I've had on a Friday night in a long time. Not because Ella straddled me or we almost kissed. There's something different about her, and it tugs at my interest. She has layers, and I find myself wanting to peel each one back and learn more.

Chapter 19

Ella

"You two fucked."

The accusation cuts through Frankie Beverly and Maze to hit me square in the throat. I choke on the greens speaking to my taste buds in a seasoned love language and wipe my mouth with a white linen napkin, one that has no business being at a backyard barbecue.

Erica sits across from me with a plate of ribs she nearly wrestled from a guy with a man bun, her wrinkled brow hovering above turquoise-rimmed shades. She glances at the suspect in question, who's getting shoulder-bumped away from the grill. Julian's exuberant laugh tickles the hairs on my arms. I'm hyperaware of my heart hammering against my chest at his light-hearted tone and the way his Adam's apple bobs at his dad's jab.

An "Mm-hmm" brings me back to the nosy-ass friend in a jewel-toned summer dress, one I wouldn't mind stealing. Her lips curl into a smile, daring me to play in her face.

I grab my fork and study the collection of soul food blessing my plate to avoid her attempt at an FBI investigation. "Was that a question or a statement?" Rich potato salad slides off my fork and into my mouth.

"Play with your mama if you want, but y'all are fucking." She shakes her head and chuckles before grabbing a rib off her plate. "You two have tracked each other since you arrived with the kids. It's cute how he looks to see if you're okay and if Haile and Jackson are safe. But..." She curls a magenta thumb into her mouth to suck off sauce. "A man doesn't do all that out of the kindness of his heart."

"He...we..." The sun choose that moment to stretch beyond the trees and bore into my back. The literal hot seat. I fan myself and take a sip of ice water. "His family is like my family."

My living situation with Julian isn't public, and I'd like to keep it that way.

"I don't see him looking around for Morgan."

"Who's looking for me?"

I roll my eyes and groan. Morgan's gaze flits between me and Erica. She frowns but brushes it off, pulling out the chair next to me with one hand and putting her plate of rabbit food on the table with the other. Morgan never eats anything with dark sauces if she's wearing white or pastels. She has both on today, a spaghetti strap pink top and white linen pants.

At a barbecue.

Morgan crosses her nude sandals under her chair and assesses her plate of salad and fruit under a light drizzle of Greek dressing. "What are we talking about?" Her fork goes to work.

A sinister grin stretches Erica's face. "Julian and Ella," she says in an innocent tone, one that's as fake as her lashes.

Nope, not doing this. I stand and say, "I'm going to check on the kids." They're playing on the playground Langston installed a couple summers ago. Haile left my side to join Duke and Jackson after her brother promised not to cramp her style and treat her like a preschooler. She *is* a preschooler. The trio is visible from here. I wouldn't have sat at this table otherwise, and neither would Morgan. But Erica only has a few seconds before she gets reckless with her mouth, and I'm not sticking around for the aftermath.

Morgan frowns again. "We can see them from here, El. Sit. I haven't seen you since you got here, and I need a break from smiling at my parents' guests."

The Brooke family barbecue is the kickoff event of the summer, an invitation to enjoy seasoned meats in DC's Gold Coast. The traditional 1920s home upholds the history of Langston's father, as he and other Blacks moved into the Crestwood neighborhood. Edward Brooke passed down the brick colonial to Langston, who carried on the a legacy of attorneys who've changed the world in their own way. Minus Morgan, who took a different path.

Every window holds a story, and for as long as Morgan remembers, her home has been a place for Black joy. Now, friends and colleagues witness the power of her interior design prowess firsthand. Langston gave his daughter free rein to update the five-bedroom, four-and-a-half-bath home. The dining room is my favorite. It shares space with the open kitchen and has a wall of windows facing the backyard, the location of the annual holiday soiree. Today is my first, as I usually take the kids to visit my mom for Memorial Day.

The property next door eventually became part of the family portfolio, to accommodate out-of-town guests and expand the outdoor entertainment space. There's enough room for a dance floor, tables and chairs, cushioned loungers, and serving stations for the caterers. Langston cooks most of the meat, but he's intentional about hiring small, Black-owned catering companies and restaurants. At least fifty people are here, from partners at the firm to old college buddies.

And then there's Julian, prince of "the tingles," in an ivory polo and matching shorts. The tattoos on his right forearm flex every time he takes a sip from the cup nestled in his firm hand. His stance is wide, courtesy of thick thighs coated in muscle. With his shades on, the man looks like a professional athlete with a brand deal.

To say Julian is a people person would be an understatement. His easy-breezy aura draws people in, mesmerizing their senses until they don't know up from down. He mingles from person to person with ease and a megawatt smile—which is why I doubt any moment we've had has been anything more than harmless flirting on his end.

"What about Julian and Ella?" Morgan pierces a strawberry.

Erica laughs at her blank stare. "You don't see it, do you?"

At that, Morgan's perfectly waxed brows angle to her forehead. "Please." She Erica waves off. "They're both nice and friendly."

Erica's lip twitches. "I'm sure they have been nice...and friendly." She takes a sip of mango lemonade. "Haven't you noticed the looks they steal when they think no one is watching?" She turns to me. "You're not slick."

Morgan breaks into a fit of laughter. "Julian is a flirt. He's always looking at women, but that doesn't mean anything."

See? Nothing serious.

"He's not interested in anything heavy with anyone."

Exactly.

"He had a date last night."

Come again?

I reach for my phone to steady my expression and mask the frustration trying to claw its way to the surface. I have no right, to him or the pangs of jealousy constricting my lungs, but it's there.

After Friday's dance with temptation and Haile's bed surprise, which left me in a puddle of tears in the shower later that night, we had a good Saturday. We piled into Julian's car to watch Duke and Jackson's team win their baseball game. I told Julian we could drive separately so he could go wherever after, but he insisted. Morgan met us at the field, with Joseph arriving moments after.

Baseball turned into lunch and ice cream to celebrate the victory, Rose's email from earlier in the morning that said I got the job, and Julian's birthday. He looked so ridiculous in the polka dot birthday hat, but he was a good sport about our off-key "Happy Birthday" rendition. Julian even split his cake with me to commemorate my first job in over a decade. It was so sweet. It was—

Who am I kidding? The man gave daddy vibes in the V-neck tee stretched over his chest and khaki cargo pants.

We were back at the townhouse by three. Just when I thought he'd high-tail it to meet up with friends, he surprised me again by taking us for a walk around the neighborhood to check out nearby parks and good places to eat. Two hours later, we crowded around takeout lasagna and cannoli on the kitchen counter. I grabbed the kids right after and kept us upstairs for the rest of the night. We'd monopolized too much of his time as it was.

Julian is a thirty-one-year-old bachelor. He should be out enjoying the single life, and I guess he was at some point last night.

A date.

Was it a *date* date, or a meetup to throw someone's legs over his shoulders?

The woman is probably some up-and-coming professional, someone closer to his age with no kids and a tight ass. One of many he keeps on speed dial.

"That settles it." The smile I smear on is fake, but it gets the job done. Julian out with another woman shouldn't hurt, but it does.

Were the moments we shared this week a warm-up to last night's main event?

"The hell it does." Erica rolls her eyes and neck. "Do you know how many people I went on a *date* with who meant nothing more than dick? Him out with another woman doesn't mean shit. Your brother is into her." She says the last part with a finger directed at me. "Maybe it's for a good time. Maybe it's for a long time. But the vibe is there."

Erica mumbles to herself and assesses her nails. I catch *Mm-hmm* and *Tryna tell me what I saw* before her phone rings. She gets up to take the call, but not before pinning us with a stare. "He's looking over here again." She waves a hand in the air and says, "Told you!" leaving me and Morgan in a trail of warm shea butter and *Don't doubt me again.*

"The imagination on that one," my remaining friend at the table says through a giggle. "As if you and Julian would ever."

"Right?" I snort. "He's young, and my life—"

"Let me stop you right there." Morgan swivels in her chair to face me with a gaze only a best friend unwilling to entertain self-deprecation can give. "First of all, a year shy of forty is *not* old." She tosses hair, thickened from hours of humidity, over her shoulder. "I'm already forty, and no one will make me feel anything less than fine and fabulous.

"I gag at the idea of you and my brother because you're my sister. Not because you're eight years older. Julian might be a poster child for the bachelor life, but he's more mature than most men twice his age."

She cuts me off again. "And before you fix your lips to talk down about yourself and your situation, I'll stop you there too." She takes my hand. "You are priceless, El. Full of goodness that you pour into the people around you. Your circumstance is a blip in time, and it doesn't make you worth less or unworthy of love. Priceless, got me?"

Well, damn.

"Yeah." My voice shakes to push out the word.

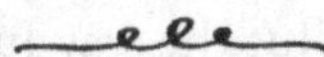

The sun relaxes its grip on the day as it fades to twilight. Cotton candy pink clouds stretch across a deepening blue sky. The string lights overhead cast a firefly glow on the remaining party guests, who are mingling and swaying to classic soul throwbacks.

My feet have yet to listen to the internal alarm that reminds it's Haile and Jackson's bedtime. I can't remember the last time they stayed up so late. Good thing tomorrow is a holiday.

The kids have been inside with Mrs. Brooke, Duke's grandmother, while I attempt to keep up with Uncle Skeeter on the dance floor. His sixty-four years haven't slowed him down. We hustled, two-stepped, turned, and dipped. Skeeter might be a balding banker, but Langston's line brother still has the energy of a teenager.

I'm ready to bow out when a familiar voice from behind startles my steps. "Mind if I cut in?" I still and remind myself to breathe.

Uncle Skeeter looks over my shoulder and nods. "Absolutely." He flashes me a smile and tips his head. "Ella, it's been a pleasure, sugar. You keep an old man young," he says in his Georgia twang. With a wink, he disappears into a small crowd near the bar.

Julian and I caught eyes too many times to count tonight. We kept our distance but stayed in each other's orbit, always a couple yards away, with secrets filling the void between us. One look turned into lingering stares that froze time and our ability to turn away.

My legs snap shut when his darkening gaze traces the lines of my curves. In no way am I showing enough skin to trigger a respectability critic. My sundress hits right above my ankles and only shows off my upper back and arms. But the way Julian's eyes sweep over my body has me ready to question if he has x-ray vision and knows I'm panty-free in his parents' backyard.

"You look incredible."

Not good or nice. *Incredible.*

My brain stalls at the compliment and the cedar and sandalwood cologne that once again short-circuits my ability to not be a blabbering idiot. It's at a two, and I'm already overheating.

"You look—" *Shoot, think.* "Ivory is nice on you." I clear my throat. "You look good too."

He steps into my personal space and reaches for my hand. Warmth travels through my fingertips and up my chest. "Still have one more in you?" His hand wraps around my waist to pull me closer and finds a home on my hip. The other guides my wrist to the back of his neck. His touch lingers on my pulse point and ignites goosebumps on the slow glide down my forearm.

Not once do his eyes leave mine. "This okay?" His question is a murmur that mimics the soothing circles his thumb traces on my hip.

My knees quiver, an internal warning that my legs are seconds from giving out. I mentally shake myself from his lure and wrap my other hand around his neck. The act chews away the little space between us. Just a few more inches, and our belly buttons won't be the only body parts rubbing together.

The intro to Marvin Gaye's "I Want You" builds as Julian guides us to the center of the dance floor. His hips sway to the sultry mix of bass and percussion, summoning mine. "Come here," he says against my ear.

Our bodies press and our breaths mix. My head finds a home on his shoulder, and I close my eyes and allow myself to get lost in the moment. A passing breeze catches the tips of my tendrils in a loose bun and blows warm air on the back of my neck.

The sigh I exhale releases a breath I've held for far too long. My separation has forced me to rely on others in a way I haven't before. When you aren't trying to save the day and be a superhero in someone else's story, you have room to pour into yourself. The pain of picking up the shards of my life doesn't compare to the love shared with friends by my side. With Julian.

"I got you, El." Julian presses his cheek to the side of my head and moves us around the dance floor like we're the only two people here.

The song ends, peeling away the fantasy for reality. Even if time and healing were on my side, divorcing a wealthy man for a young bachelor with an even bigger bank account and more women chasing after him is foolish. I already know how that story ends, and I refuse to put my children—or my heart—through another tragedy.

Julian searches my face, his gaze tracking the faded remnants of a smile. He frowns. "You okay?"

The invisible thread stretched between us tugs. How does a man I met a week ago recognize the self-doubt twisting my features? He sees all of me and makes me want things I shouldn't.

"Yeah." I take a step back and slap on a smile two sizes too small. "Thanks for the dance—and happy birthday again!" Damn my nerves for making my tone too chipper.

Julian rubs a brow and stares at me with a blank look. "Thanks."

"Did you have fun last night?"

"I got dinner and caught some jazz," he says with a cautious nod.

"Oh, fun." My excitement is complete bull.

Why am I giving him the third degree? He's not my man. I need to go in the house, grab my kids, and leave before I say something ridiculous.

"I hope your date went well."

Like that.

The smile I've been holding stumbles when his becomes a scowl. He draws a breath and releases it. "I went to JoJo's alone, and I came home alone."

A nervous laugh trips through my lips. "Forget I said anything. It's none of my business what you do. Or who."

Tension flares in his voice. "Michelle and her cousin happened to be waiting for a table. I had one, so they joined me." He sighs and shakes his head. "The next time my sister runs her mouth, come to me first. If you had, you'd know I went to see a band I like and eat lamb chops. I don't date, but since I can't breathe in this town without it tying me to a new girlfriend or my latest fuck, think what you want."

He leaves me on the dance floor, wishing I could take back the hurt I caused so we could sway in the breeze.

Chapter 20
Julian

The path to my exit is a maze of DC elite dressed in their summer finest. Politicians, CEOs, and other trust fund kids vying for more attention. I lower my head and weave through a swarm of back pats and lunch requests before my feet hit the steps to the porch.

Our house is off-limits to prying eyes and explorers desperate to shuffle around our private space. Only the few Claire Brooke deems worthy get an invitation to the in-house affairs she hosts, which are the talk of women's leagues across the DMV. The guest house is a different story. It's a place to escape humidity, where social climbers document your attendance. Most are in there now, sipping premium drinks and discussing business on imported furniture.

My fingers pound the passcode into the silver keypad. The first two attempts fail. I rub the back of my neck and force a hard smile at the person walking on the path behind me. Losing my shit in front of company would be a PR disaster my family can't afford. It doesn't matter that I'm in the backyard of my childhood home. I'd laugh if it wasn't so pathetic.

It took hours to fulfill my Brooke duties. I endured enough small talk and handshakes to last an eternity, and, to no one's surprise, questions about who I'm seeing were the hot topic of the night.

Did you reconcile with Camila? Is she the reason you came back?

When will you settle down?

Forget the deals I closed for the company, or my serving as an in-house translator on more than one occasion. That's not newsworthy. What is, however, is the player people assume I am, which brings celebrity status or shame to the Brooke name, depending on who you ask. I might not have paparazzi chasing me around, but the way I live in the heads of bloggers and the gossip-hungry is attention I never asked for.

Between elevator pitches and glances was a proposition or two to see my bedroom instead of the boardroom. One woman brought her niece to meet me who became a second shadow. I don't want to judge that family, but who parades around a twenty-two-year-old with emphasis on her "fertile" and "teachable" qualities? I mean, what the fuck?

Laura, the shy grad student, sat in the chair behind me for a good half-hour. She wouldn't answer any of my questions, except the one about wanting to be here. Her distant stare was enough for me to call a car to pick her up and take her back to the robotics lab. She didn't need to stick around, let alone have her aunt play matchmaker.

I'm an OG of well-intentioned ambushes. The level of gymnastics I perform to let people down gently and not disappoint my mother when I refuse a date with her friend's daughter makes Simone Biles look like an amateur.

My patience set with the sun. Was it too much to ask to go one night without a probe into my love life? Is that why I jumped at the chance to dance with Ella?

The truth is, I waited all day to spend time with her, and I sought her out the second I was free. The pull toward her is off the charts. She's always in my line of sight, so I can catch the height of her giggles or the edges of her smile.

Holding Ella felt like home. A place without judgment, obligation, or expectation. The soft curves pressed to my body rivaled the warmth of the summer day spread over my skin. Her blue and white dress swayed with her hips, daring for me to bow in worship. With the outdoor lights illuminating our steps, the urge to kiss her was too heavy to ignore.

Until she uttered an accusation folded in yet another question about whose legs I've been between.

I open the door when the keypad blinks green and find the cohost of the evening holding a glass of wine in the kitchen.

"Need a break?" The sarcasm in my voice hints at the running joke in our family. My mother keeps a tight ship to preserve every achievement she and my father amassed for this family. Pride flows through her veins, along with the desire to obtain the impossible and tower over adversaries with a gleam in her eye.

The same woman who commands the attention of every room she enters without raising her voice found hers learning the English language after she and her grandmother moved from Haiti.

She examines me with a raised chin and a practiced smile that will never stretch into a grin. "*Est-ce que tu t'amuses?*"

"Mwen byen."

A brow raises when I respond in her native tongue. English and French were the primary languages spoken in this house. The latter was to prepare us for the competitive private schools we attended and the world of international law. My mother stopped speaking the Creole she shared with Gran Grann who raised her and lived with us until she died. She's never mentioned why, but my guess is my mother misses her grandmother. We all do.

The tips of her manicured nails skim her intricate updo, trying to find a hair out of place, one we both know isn't there. "Are you leaving?"

I nod and walk around the white marble island, where she stands with perfect posture in a black gown more appropriate for a gala than a backyard barbecue. I learned from my father early on not to question her or Morgan's fashions.

Dark eyes examine the bitter smile engraved in my expression, a mask she knows and wears well herself. Her high-arched brows lower. "Tell me."

"It's nothing."

A quarter-life crisis six years late.

I step back and face the windows overlooking the backyard. Ella stands in the same spot on the dance floor. My feet angle toward the door to go to her until I force myself to reroute. "Goodnight, Mother."

Her nose wrinkles at my abrupt change in attitude, but I don't stick around for her to discover the source of my departure.

Claire Brooke would shit a dignified brick if the runway ever cleared to be with El. If I allowed myself to act on desires that have yet to fade. I have my own doubts about attaching myself to her life, which comes with two kids, but for different reasons than I expected.

Status isn't a prerequisite for me, but it is for my mother. Her shortlist for my future wife is a Tetris game of eligible women, all from refined families, and she moves them around until one lasts long enough to cancel the other out.

Nothing has happened yet, but if there's one thing my mother is, it's dedicated.

Two were here tonight, conveniently hours apart to hide any hint of competition. I couldn't remember them if I had to pick them out of a lineup. Ella kept my attention in her grasp without an ounce of effort.

A roar of laughter booms from the family room. I turn the corner to see my father on the rug with his head back, tears in his eyes, and not a care in the world. My mother will have his neck for the wrinkles in his Italian linen suit, but if Langston Brooke dies tonight, he'll die a happy man with three kids suffocating him in tickles.

Duke, Jackson, and Haile scream in delight before my father curls his arms around them with the voice of a swamp monster. What the press would pay to see him on his hands and knees crawling between the coffee table and sofa with children on his back.

Late-night card games to the soundtrack of his favorite jazz musicians were the extent of our interactions on the days he'd work late in his study, which was more often than not. My father loves me and Morgan, but all work and no play made him the success he is today.

Millions in the bank at the sacrifice of memories with his children.

What he lacked in our childhood, he makes up for with the affection he shows Duke and his bonus grandchildren.

"Hey, son!" When he's not in go mode, my father is the most chill person. "You heading out?"

"Yeah. Going to Swigs for a bit."

He nods with a smile. "Tell Nate we said hi. I'll see you in the office on Tuesday. Have a good night."

Duke peels himself off his grandfather and runs to me with his arms stretched behind him like Naruto. "Goodnight, Uncle," he says in Japanese.

I wrap a hand around his head to pull him in. "*Oyasumi.*" I press a kiss to his forehead.

Jackson's gaze shifts between us. He might be quiet around people he doesn't know, but he wears his emotions on his face. Right now, it's longing with a bit of curiosity.

"How about we practice Japanese on Thursday?" I ask Jackson. "Duke can teach you some phrases."

At that, my nephew runs back to his friend with an energy that incites a shy smile from my new house buddy. Jackson nods, and the two set off on their next adventure.

"Bye, Julie." My heart squeezes at Haile's words. She looks up at me with light brown eyes and a smile too big for her heart-shaped face.

I drop to my haunches and take in Ella's mini me. "If you call me Julie, it's only fair I give you a nickname. What about…" I touch my chin like I'm deep in thought. "Haile Bear?"

"Like a Care Bear!" She gives me a hug and yells, "Bye!" to take off after Duke and her brother.

I need to get out of here.

"So when's the big day?"

I focus on the glass in front of me and not my former friend about to laugh in my face for the third time tonight. Condensation drips down the tumbler to the concrete slab I helped pick out when he opened Swigs five years ago.

I sigh. "Have I told you to fuck off yet?"

Nate lifts a cuff on his gray cardigan to peek at his watch and grins. "Not in the last forty-seven minutes."

My visit started with me dropping off a plate of ribs since he missed the barbecue. That's what friends do for each other. Instead of a thank you, I got a Dr. Phil session after Nate took one look at my face. He should psychoanalyze why he's wearing a cardigan with a beanie in May. Not my life.

"Still in denial?" His hands move across his workstation to craft a complex mojito for a woman at the end of the bar. Muddled mint and strawberries rest in homemade simple syrup with fresh lime slices, club soda, rum, and crushed ice from a machine he spent a thousand on to give his cocktails the perfect texture. "Excuse me."

Nate grabs a straw and napkin to hand off his tastemaker master-piece to the auburn beauty. His chest puffs as her first pull touches her lips. Then he's off to tend to a beer refill.

Swigs is a place of pride with seasonal drinks, timeless classics, and craft beer selections from local breweries. The food menu is a love letter to the Filipino dishes that flavored his childhood. *Lechon manok*, *palabok*, and *okoy* are customer favorites, with recommend-ed drink pairings to match.

Every item is an experience Nate designed to unite his passion for mixology and taste of home. He pours in his attention to detail, lay-ers it with his mother's recipes, and serves it all up with his sociology degree for an upscale experience in a place that feels like a second home. The way he reads people's needs before they voice them is why he receives such high praise for his menu and customer service. The problem with his uncanny ability to mind-read is that he won't stay out of your business, especially when "bullshit" blinks in neon letters on your forehead.

"Where were we? Oh, yes. You were about to lie to me again about a woman you have feelings for and can't stop thinking about." Nate pops the top off a beer bottle and sends it down the counter with a push, straight into the hands of the intended recipient. "Is that why you're running back to London with your tail between your legs?"

That's part of it.

"No."

His gaze turns from mischievous to serious. "Did what she said piss you off that much?"

"Yes and no."

Ella never intended to hit me between the eyes with a reputation society expects me to uphold, but she did it with skilled precision.

I like to fuck. Plain and simple. But, contrary to public opinion, I'm not out here cruising through DC for a warm body and a fat ass. Not every woman I speak to ends up in my bed, and every woman I've had sex with understood what it was. They're acquaintances. Sometimes we pull pleasure from our bodies when the mood strikes.

Nothing more, nothing less.

That was before I tumbled into bed and found a woman I'd hang the stars for at the chance to stand in her light.

My reaction to her is frightening, but there's no denying the instinct to make her part of my life. It grows with every detail I unlock about her.

A relationship was the farthest thing from my mind until her. Ella is not a woman you taste for a night. She deserves a lifetime with someone dedicated to providing whatever brings her joy.

You want to attach yourself to her? To be a second dad?

The knee-jerk reaction to resurrect the barriers Ella shattered in a single week laces up my running shoes. My eyes shift from Nate to the floor at the thought of a promise I can't make.

It's clear Ella hasn't had a stable partner. From what I hear, her ex is an MIA dad and a fuckboy of a husband, which explains a lot. She's in a clusterfuck of a transition right now, and I'm not confident I'll navigate that field of landmines without blowing up in the process.

I don't do complicated. She doesn't trust me not to hurt her, and I won't put myself on trial to defend myself against crimes I never committed.

"Can I ask you a question?" Don't make me regret this.

"Shoot."

"When did you know Sadie was it?"

Nate stares at the counter, lost in a memory he blinks away with a smile. "The moment I saw her, I knew my life would never be the same."

They met during a statistics class their freshman year of college. Conversations before class turned into study sessions at the library. Sadie found out she was pregnant halfway through the semester, and it was a challenge to juggle a full course load and an unexpected membership into motherhood. Her high school sweetheart knocked her up a month before school started and then headed out west to play college ball. The promise of stardom and a roster of hookups left Sadie on read and him living his best life. He didn't come from a family with money, but they tapped into their savings with the quickness in order to "make the problem go away."

Sadie gave birth to her daughter, Jasmine, a week after spring semester ended. Nate was with her through it all, their friendship building into an unbreakable bond that would stand the test of time. They became roommates after Jasmine's arrival and staggered their school schedules to care for an infant.

Nate picked up shifts as a bartender at night and kept a sociology textbook next to an encyclopedia of drinks. His mother moved to the area during their junior year to watch Jasmine while he and

Sadie focused on their programs. They graduated a year later, with sociology and anthropology degrees between them.

Nate's gaze drops to an area behind the bar, the one that steals his attention every night he's behind it. It's become a mini exhibition of Jasmine's drawings over the years. They don't share DNA, but she's been his from the moment he held her. Sadie and Nate married right after college. Her wedding gift was adoption papers for the man who would love her and their daughter unconditionally until his last breath.

"You still with me, Rufio?" I dodge towel to the face he throws at his high school nickname.

Straight brows. Almond eyes. Thick nose. If you swapped out his beanie and cardigan for a mohawk and a sword, you'd think he was the stand-in leader of the Lost Boys in *Hook*.

"Fuck off," he says with a laugh. "To answer your question, Sadie and I didn't meet under ideal circumstances. But that didn't stop me from loving her any less. She's the love of my life and my best friend. The draw to her was my soul finding its other half."

Damn. "That's deep."

"That said, a woman with kids is nothing to mess with—and yours isn't even divorced yet. I get that you developed feelings after a week, but if you want my honest opinion...." I nod for him to continue. "There's too much shit going on right now to pursue anything. Let's start with the fact that you live together, with her *kids*. And that you don't know if she wants to hop from one relationship to another. And what about you?"

I grimace. "What about me?"

"You're amazing with Duke, but what happens if you go for it and things don't work out?"

What happens if they do?

Nate leans his forearms on the bar. There's no masking his deepening frown. It's the one Doctor Strange gave Tony Stark when there was no other option but one.

"I have to go back to London."

"It might not be a bad idea for a while, at least to get your head straight without your cohabitation complicating the situation even more."

"I'll miss you, bro."

"Same," Nate says. "But do what you gotta do to move with clarity."

Our conversation moves to shooting the shit before I head back home. Twenty minutes later, I'm packed and calling a car to the airport so I can hop on a red-eye.

Putting distance between us is for the best. Even if it's hard to say goodbye.

Chapter 21

Ella

"I need a warm bath and an IV of wine."

My head hits the back of my office chair for the first time since six this morning. These kids keep me on my toes.

Miss Greene!

Is it snack time?

Do I have to take a nap?

When is it time to go?

I stepped in for a teacher who's visiting her mom in the Dominican Republic on Monday, and between holding down the classroom and taking care of staff scheduling, program planning, and enrollments, I'm ready to use up all of my vacation time with an IOU.

"Bottom drawer on the left."

My cinder block eyelids lift to find Rose in the doorway. How her bun held up through the onslaught of toddlers and preschoolers testing boundaries is a miracle. Her five-two frame collapses into the chair in front of me. She points at the desk. "Give me a hit."

"You make this sound illegal."

Her head shifts from side to side. "It's for emergency situations." She checks her watch. "The center closed fifteen minutes ago. Give me a hit."

With a giggle, I pull out the biggest chocolate bar. It's peanut butter, an ingredient we don't allow around the kids in case one of them has a peanut allergy. Rose runs a tight ship, but everyone has a breaking point.

"I'm on my way to dinner, so I'll take a rain check." It takes a wide grip to hand her the thick-packaged dessert.

"Hot date?"

"The opposite. Meeting my ex."

She scoffs and raises her shot of sugar with two hands. "Good luck with that." Her head tips back to swallow the chocolate.

"Who are you telling?"

Charles reached out last week to wish me luck with my new job. It wouldn't surprise me if he had devil-worshippers chanting for my demise, but I took it at face value. Nothing with that man goes below the surface.

This is the first weekend he's taking the kids, and he wanted to have dinner to discuss logistics. Never mind the fact that our phones work. We settled on a place outside Falls Church, away from whisperers who would spread our business faster than TMZ.

"You should go on a date." Her brow lifts to hold me in a stare.

I scoff. "Did you forget I'm going through a divorce? I'm not looking for another disaster so soon."

She smacks her knees and stands. "You're right, it's still early. But don't assume life ends after divorce." Her phone pings, and her lips spread into a smile before she tucks her cell into her back pocket. "Louise is waiting for me outside."

Rose and her partner are the cutest. I've never seen someone dote on a person the way Louise does for the woman she loves. Anyone who has a fraction of the adoration these two share is lucky.

"I love your love. Please tell her I said hello."

"Will do." She pauses in the doorway. "You know, our stories aren't so different. One day I'll tell you about my ex and how Louise brought me back to life."

Tears prick my eyes. "There is life after divorce."

She grins. "Hell yes, there is. Have a great night, and order the most expensive item on the menu. You kicked ass this week, and I'm so grateful you're here. Fuck him!" She pauses. "But don't *fuck* him."

I shut off my laptop and pull my purse out the drawer. *Don't look.* Two weeks passed since Julian left, and not a day went by that I didn't think about him and the way we ended things. I hurt him, pinning an accusation on him that's none of my business. A note scribbled in neat cursive was on the kitchen counter when I woke up the next morning.

Headed to London. Enjoy your new job. You got this.

Julian

He went back because of me, but he still wished me luck with my job. The departure and kind words keep my stomach in a twist. Julian planned to come home, but I had him practically sprinting to the airport with his carry-on and swan-diving onto the security conveyor belt to get away.

My thumb hovers over the message I've wanted to send. *I'm sorry.* I miss our random texts about food, series we have no time to watch, and whatever random thought enters our minds. Even my kids ask when the man they call Julie with such casual familiarity is coming back.

The connection we've developed in a week is unnerving. I shouldn't get so attached to someone so fast—especially someone who will be around my kids—and I tell myself Julian staying in London is for the best. It's a lie.

I ignore another thought about Morgan's brother and head to the mirror to apply war paint in the form of red lipstick. *Blood* red.

Katharine picked up Haile after she got Jackson from school. They'll stay at her house until Charles gets them after our dinner. Bliss spread from crinkled eyelids to the wide smile that pulled at her mouth when I asked if the kids could come to her house. The criteria for sainthood models Katharine's kindness and unconditional love. Her son is a different story.

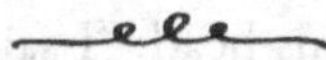

"Would you like another, miss?"

"Yes, please."

If I had the power to move objects with my mind, I'd fling Charles's ass into the Potomac from his Jag, which better be on the side of the road with a blow-out. There's no way in the hell that will become his eternal resting place he has me waiting for—*checks watch*—twenty-eight minutes. No courtesy call or text.

Nothing.

I take a long sip of my dark and stormy, the perfect drink to match tonight's forecast. Cloudy with a strong chance of ass-whooping. He has two minutes to walk through the door before I bill him and his attorney for wasting my time. Of all the things to do on a Friday night with no kids, waiting around for my ex in a Bethesda restaurant forty-five minutes from my house isn't anywhere on the list.

It's a quaint spot with floor-to-ceiling steel-framed windows and reclaimed wood flooring. A mix of circular marble and rectangular wooden tables surround the bar with emerald barstools that match the dining room seating. The restaurant is pretty, but no amount of decor will save Charles from my wrath.

"He's an idiot."

I turn toward the smooth voice and narrow my eyes. "Excuse me?"

Patrick Dempsey's twin widens his grin, setting off a dimple, and takes me in. He tilts his head. "I said"—his gaze drops to my mouth—"he's an idiot." His brow lifts when I don't respond.

I need to get laid. Not by McDimples here, but...forget it.

Don't think about him.

"He *is* an idiot." I stir my drink to avoid eye contact with the ice-blue eyes scanning the side of my face. "But I guess I'm one too since I married him." I take another sip.

He pushes off the bar, flexing the muscles in his forearm, and straightens. Two barstools separate us, and he moves closer. He stops in front of my stool, his legs inches from my thigh. There's no contact, but I'm close enough to feel the heat.

"My apologies." His eyes linger from above, forcing me to look up. I start at his square jaw covered in five-o'clock shadow and move up thin lips and a bulb nose to reach the hooded stare fixed on me.

"Not necessary. I'm in the middle of a divorce."

His hand goes to the bar, with another under my stool to turn me. He's now between my legs, his six-foot-something height lowered so our faces can be inches apart. "In that case, want to ditch your ex and go back to my place?" A mix of scruff and a halo of wavy brown strands frame his face.

McDimples is a beautiful man. But as handsome as he is, he's not the one I want.

"Tempting, but I'll pass."

Blue eyes flicker. "Okay," he says with a smile. "Not tonight. I'll see you around."

On his exit, I pluck a menu from the bar and order a Waldorf salad and scallops risotto. Charles makes his way to me when I'm halfway through the crème brûlée. "Thank you for waiting."

The nerve.

He unbuttons his gray suit jacket and sits on the stool next to me. "Scotch on the rocks," he says to a passing bartender, who peeks at me with a frown. "How are you, El?"

"Full." I pat my belly. "Then again, I did wait for close to an hour. Did your phone die with your manners?"

He sighs. "It's almost the end of the fiscal year at my organization. I lost track of time. Let it go."

"I did let you go, and your days of wasting my time are over." I smile at his glare. "Come late without a courtesy call again, and we'll speak through our lawyers. Am I clear?"

I spent years sitting in front of room-temperature dinners, questioning where my husband is and what excuse I'll give my kids. I'm done with being an afterthought. I'm the prize.

"I said—"

I lift a hand between us. "I heard your excuse, but not an apology."

His jaw tightens on a hard swallow of scotch. For someone who makes over half a million a year, he looks like crap. His suit, usually pressed to perfection, shows wrinkles, and the eyes currently annoyed with my existence carry heavy bags. "I'm sorry. It's been...difficult. I've made mistakes, but I do owe you an apology."

If I didn't have a season pass to this ride, I'd mistake his narcissistic tendencies for empathy. Charles only cares about himself. He has zero accountability and wears arrogance like it will never go out of style. Add up every "I'm sorry" he uttered over sixteen years, and it wouldn't amount to changed behavior.

"The only thing you should focus on is showing up for Haile and Jackson. They deserve another parent who will be there for them." Charles looks down and nods.

His father was never present in his life, and it shows in the way Charles buries himself in his work. But history will repeat itself over my dead body.

"I'll drop them off at your mother's by five on Fridays. Jackson's baseball ends in two weeks. I'll meet you and the kids at the games and pick them up on Sunday evenings. Don't look at me like I asked you to quit your job." I roll my eyes. "The least you can do is catch his final two games. We'll reassess the kids' schedule in July and go from there. Deal?"

Charles leans against the bar and considers me. The corner of his mouth twitches.

"Something funny?"

"No." He chuckles and raises his hands. "I've missed your feistiness."

"Don't start."

"I know." His laughter catches me off guard. It's been—goodness, I don't remember how long since this Charles made an appearance. I fell in love with this Charles, and I gave him chance after chance.

The memory steals a smile I had no intention of giving. "Just make sure you don't drop the ball again."

"I promise, El." His stare roams over my sleeveless white bodysuit and high-waisted linen pants. The olive cardigan meant to shield me from the steady blast of air conditioning stayed in the car. It's too damn hot, and I deserve to breathe easy.

Charles nods to the bar. "Ready for a nightcap?"

Did he forget in the ten minutes he's been here that he kept me waiting for close to an hour? Absolutely not.

"Knock yourself out," I say and stand. "Thanks for dinner, but I have other plans. See you tomorrow morning at Jackson's game."

A picture is worth a thousand words, and so is Charles's face when I leave him at the bar with my empty plates. The bartender passes him my bill and gives me a wink.

My heart races at the buzz of an incoming message. "I'm not looking," I mutter to myself. This isn't high school, and I'm not waiting by the phone for my friend to tell me if my crush thinks I'm cute. I'm a grown-ass woman.

Another ping.

A squeal slips, catching the attention of a man walking by in a black suit, who now has a smirk on his face. "We get like that too." He nods at the cell pressed against my heart. "You should answer."

I sigh and fish for my keys. "Get a grip."

What if it's Morgan asking about tomorrow's game? Or Erica showing off the latest friend with benefits who's working her over-time?

Julian is probably balls deep inside some supermodel, not think-ing about his sister's best friend who's occupying his house with her children. I need some action in my life too.

A glance at my messages confirms my theory. Morgan has a ques-tion about what snacks to bring tomorrow, and Erica wants me to go on a double date with her next week. I type back "orange slices and applesauce" to Morgan and tell Erica I'm game before my courage wears off.

Just because I'm not looking for another relationship doesn't mean I can't have fun, right?

Chapter 22

Julian

"Staring at your phone won't send the text for you."

"No shit." I peek at the time to play off the fact I've checked it at least twelve times. Nothing from Ella.

I fucked things up flying back to London without any communication outside the note I left. Work has been handing me my ass until after midnight, when I crawl from the shower to my bed and start the process over the next day. I've had no time for rugby, much less anything else. Meeting up with Preston was by chance based on our schedules, and I couldn't be more grateful for the distraction.

We're at a bar in a boutique hotel in the West End. It's crowded enough to rival a movie premiere. Flowers hang above an illuminated counter stretching eighty feet. Bartenders work around each other to satisfy the crowd pouring in, ready to indulge in the award-winning menu of cocktails and savory delicacies.

Like me, Preston is an heir to his family business. Unlike me, he's worth billions, thanks to a portfolio of hotels and resorts under the Donnelley brand. The interest he earns on his investments every quarter is more than my entire salary. We met last year during a business meeting and became mates, as they say. It's rare we're both in town at the same time, and even rarer to have left our offices to link up over old-fashioneds.

Five women have tried their luck at getting his attention in the half-hour we've been here. I'd laugh if I didn't know firsthand how annoying the wealthy playboy title can be. You're a magnet for unwanted attention and social climbers of all kinds willing to trade a night in bed for bragging rights, but Preston takes it in stride.

He removes a woman's hand from his navy suit with a subtle headshake to ward off embarrassment and future attempts. "Have a good night, love." The cognac eyes featured on the cover of countless trade magazines roam her body. His gaze is still on her ass when she leaves.

"Surprised you didn't want to take her home," I say over my tumbler. "She's your type."

Hickory hair. Light eyes. Curves for days. Shit, she's my type too—or was until a honey tan beauty entered my life and turned it upside down.

"I'm walking the straight and narrow these days. Doesn't mean I can't enjoy the view."

"She must be special to get you to settle down."

His head drops. "She is." He sighs. "One day, she'll be mine."

Preston Donnelley has many layers, but trepidation isn't one he shows. Tonight, it's front and center with the facial tics he tries to mask and the way he bites his lip like he's deep in thought. At least he looks like he's practicing for a spread in *GQ* and not on edge because of a woman who has him by the nuts.

"I see it now."

His brows pinch together. "What?"

"The whole"—I wave a hand in his direction—"brooding thing."

He runs his fingers through his dark curls and catches himself in another pose photographers would sell to the highest bidder. No wonder people lose their minds in his presence. Preston is a billionaire trapped in a model's body.

"Sod off." His London accent teases his vowels. He shakes off the trance of the woman who stole his heart and takes a pull of his drink. "I recently reconnected with someone after fifteen years." He nods with a sigh at my slow whistle. "Yeah, mate."

"So why aren't you two together?" A decade and a half apart is wild.

He tilts his head from side to side to weigh his response and takes another sip. "I'm all in, but she has reservations." His eyes meet mine with a sad smile. "A billionaire partner is good on paper until you start second-guessing if you're enough."

"Is she?"

"She's worth more than everything I have, including my life."

"How long will you wait for her to come around?"

He shrugs. "However long it takes. I lost her once, and I'm not losing her again. We're friends now, but she's it for me. She's my wife."

Wife.

I catch the thought and hurl it back where it came from.

It's not that I'm against marriage. My parents have a good one by society's standards, no matter how much it might come off as a situation of convenience. Loving one person for the rest of my life isn't the issue. The expense of my freedom is. I already sacrificed my independence maintaining the Brooke banner in a legacy job that cost me my sense of self. Expectations come with being Langston Brooke's son, and choosing a life partner based on my desires isn't one of them.

My fingers itch to grab my cell off the bar. "You should call her," Preston says.

I shake my head. "It's getting late back home."

"Who is she?"

Where the hell do I start?

Preston hits me with a glare that says, *Spare me the bullshit*. I peer into my glass for the right words. "She's my sister's best friend. Duke and her son go to school together. She also has a daughter in preschool."

"A single mom with two kids. Didn't see that coming."

I laugh at that. "Neither did I."

"Did you two meet at their school?"

"We actually woke up in my townhouse together. Morgan said she could stay there until the end of the year."

His mouth plunges open, and his eyes bulge. At least Preston has the decency to scoot closer and not shout my business across the West End. Morgan should take note.

"Let me get this straight. You like a woman going through a divorce with two kids who now lives with you? What else?"

"She's eight years older."

He brushes off our age gap with a wave of his hand. "I've been with older women. Men do that shit all the time, and no one bats an eye."

"Exactly."

Ella's age isn't an issue for me. I assumed *mine* would be a problem for her. Maybe it is, but she hasn't brought it up, which is a good sign.

"If you like her, why are you back in London?"

"We—I...it wouldn't work."

"Why not?"

My stare stalls. "She's still married. A cannonball from one relationship into another is a bad idea. El has kids; she doesn't need a distraction to add to her plate."

"Sounds like you got it figured out for her." He laughs at my middle finger pressed to my glass. "So then who are you fucking?"

The burn from snorting my drink singes my nostrils. "*What*?"

Preston lifts a shoulder. "You explained why it wouldn't work. She's coming out of a marriage and has kids. You left weeks ago, and you clearly dodge romantic relationships. Be grateful for frequent flier miles and go back to casual sex with people whose names you'll forget in the morning."

"Quit acting like a champ."

"I take it that's not a compliment?"

"It's not, you ass." I exhale and motion for the check. "Is it so bad to respect someone's boundaries and not want to make their life harder? I came back here because I'm tired of having my reputation thrown in my face, and to give El space without another man breathing down her neck. She's different. I can't explain it, and I don't understand it. I haven't had sex with anyone, or even thought about another woman since we met."

Time and distance have yet to pry off the chokehold this woman has on me. There are enough red flags to line the UN, enough reasons why whatever this is makes no fucking sense. I've had plenty of hookups, and I know this thing between us goes beyond the urge to fuck for a night.

"So what the hell are you doing here?"

What *am* I doing? Years ago, coming to London had brought an excitement that wore off as quickly as it came. I'm good at my job—damn good—but it feels like I've been biding my time, racking up success without purpose. I miss being close to my family and friends.

I miss...her.

"I don't want to fuck up her fresh start." The crowd threatens to drown out my confession, but Preston catches it.

His gaze drops to the rim of his glass. "Can I give you some advice?"

Tonight has been my *Fix My Life* episode. "Sure."

"Don't run. Time is priceless. It's the one thing we can't buy or get back. Get to know Ella better as a friend, but don't miss out." His stare dulls. "I'm getting my second chance fifteen years later. Don't make the same mistake."

The walk back to my suite takes twenty minutes. Hugh opens the wrought-iron door to the hotel with a nod. The elevator takes me to the fifth floor, a single bedroom with unobstructed views of Georgian townhomes and Hyde Park. Silence fills the suite, a place I've called home for the last few years. With all my hopping back and forth to DC, you'd think I'd bite the real estate bullet and purchase something out here that's my own.

I slide off my loafers, pull my wallet and keys out of my jacket to put in the foyer bowl, and pad across regal carpeting in a gray and black pattern to the bedroom. The black leather bed frame faces the best view of London in the area that's become the place I go when I need to clear my head.

Preston went back to his house in Knightsbridge after we left the bar. He's off on a three-city tour tomorrow for work, which somehow coincides with the city his lady is in.

Here he is running toward the woman he wants, and I crossed the Atlantic Ocean, Celtic Sea, and English Channel to put distance between me and mine. We don't share a roof, but Ella is here, anchored to my heart. I've fought to block it for weeks through work. The night is still young. I could find another way to redirect my attention and the weeks of pent-up energy I've had to take out at the gym or with my hand.

My phone dings.

Robyn reached out earlier in the week about dinner at her place. We always connect when I'm in town, exchanging more than discourse on contract negotiations.

I rub a hand over my face and reach inside my pants pocket. Me and my dick need to go to bed. I pull out my cell with every intention of charging it on the nightstand, but the name on the homescreen reanimates my exhausted body.

Ella.

Chapter 23

Ella

Two letters.

It was the best I could come up with after pacing back and forth in my bedroom for longer than I care to admit. I finally built up the nerve to send a text after a glass of wine, one I picked up at a nearby shop Julian showed me. I busted the bottle wide open—the same way he probably has some fancy Englishwoman spread right now.

My kids' first weekend with their father has been as eventful as someone roaming the grocery store after six because she didn't want to spend another night alone in the house. That someone is me: loveless in aisle four. Stocking up on unhealthy snacks I don't need in the house.

Last night, I slid across hardwood floors in knee-length socks, boy short undies, and an oversized tank to the tunes of Danity Kane. From "Damaged" to "Bad Girl," I belted out every lyric off-key until the small feast I ordered arrived. Dinner at the restaurant, courtesy of Charles's wallet, wasn't enough. I also didn't want to worry about a late snack and lunch today. Thus, two birds, one food order. I had every intention to stay up and binge *Buffy, the Vampire Slayer*, but I woke up after midnight with crusted drool on my mouth and a handful of white popcorn in my grasp.

Today's plan was simple: Make up for last night with an eventful day of well-earned laziness while resisting the urge to clean. Dodging Morgan's attempts to get me to another art event was easy, but losing track of time meant forgetting to cook dinner and a quick run to pick up food that didn't require assembly.

The quesadilla and nacho situation on the bed had me nice and cozy. Add in wine and a '90s movie marathon on the computer, and texting Julian sounded like a good idea.

Shoot, what time is it over there?

I race to send an apology when three dots appear.

Julian

Hey, how are you?

Not the kind of thing you ask if you're exploring the insides of someone's body. Then again, he is the type to multitask.

Sorry for the late-night text. I'm good. You?

Julian

I was up. Exhausted might be too mild of a word.

Relatable.

If Julian keeps hours like his father, he's working around the clock. I'll still take a room full of preschoolers over suits any day. At least my tiny crew takes naps and stays calm if snacks are in play.

Sounds rough. Julian, I'm sorry.

Is it too late for a call?

My skin tingles at the request. It's a call, not a date. We've texted before but never had a reason to hop on the phone. People make calls all the time. The President. Beyoncé. No need to act like a schoolgirl who finally got a note from her crush.

Maybe he's curious about the light bill, or if I'm putting out the recycling.

El? If it's too late, could we talk tomorrow?

Now works.

The phone buzzes in my hand. I expect to see the goofy photo of Julian in the birthday hat I took at the ice cream parlor, but it doesn't come.

"A *video*?" My scream reaches Julian's name written in white letters and not the man thousands of miles away who's hell-bent on staring at my oversized white tee and natural curls pineappled on top of my head.

Eff it.

I dive to the middle of the bed, careful not to tip over the bowl of tortilla chips and mini spread of salsa and queso. The call screen fades on a swipe right to a view that makes my thighs shake.

"There you are."

Julian leans back in a leather armchair, illuminated by the soft glow of the floor lamp that casts a crown over his silhouette. A king of temptation on his throne. The camera angle starts at a manspread of swole thighs in camel-colored plaid trousers and leads up to a long torso in a matching vest. His forearms rest on the chair, free from the white button-down rolled up to his elbow. My eyes travel from the maroon and blue tie up to the black goatee dusting his rich brown skin.

His plump lower lip dips behind pearly white teeth that accordion his mouth into a smile. He leans back against the chair and casts his hooded gaze on me.

"Hi." I shudder at the deep voice that seizes me by the throat. "You look...edible."

I should be ashamed of how fast this man has me panting from the same two letters I typed to him. A finger trails up my cheek to tuck a loose curl behind my ear and slides across a chunky texture.

Shit, my avocado mask.

Here I am overheating at wondering which part of my body Julian thinks is edible, and I'm the second coming of Jim Carrey from *The Mask*.

"Edible," I say with a groan. "Right."

His laughter rumbles through the phone he reaches to grab. "How are you?"

"A mess, apparently." I scoop a piece of the homemade avocado mix off my face with a chip.

This is me on a Saturday night. Stuffing my face, looking all sorts of unattractive in front of an international coochie connoisseur.

Julian's tongue darts between his lips. "Mask or not, I'd still eat you."

I choke on a tortilla chip. Is he—is he flirting with me? "I know you did not call my phone to act delusional. What time is it over there?"

"Close to three."

"Julian Michel!"

"We using government names now?" His smile spreads the amber light over his face. He is a beautiful man. "I'm a big boy."

I'm sure you are.

Stop it!

"I feel bad keeping you up." I sit back on the bed and take in his clothes again. "Those are some fancy pajamas."

He chuckles. "I just got in a little while ago from meeting up with a friend."

Ah.

"Your assumptions are screaming, El." His eyes roll. "Preston is handsome, but he's not my type."

"I didn't say anything."

Julian's voice softens. "You don't have to, sweetheart. Just do me a favor; get to know me for me. Not who everyone thinks I am."

The knot in my belly tightens at his plea—and *sweetheart*. "You're right. I'm sorry."

"Thank you, El."

Two weeks' worth of tension lifts with the two words I should've told him sooner. Julian might be a flirt—a delirious one, at that—but the man has more layers than the avocado concoction on my face. He's been nothing but kind and welcoming. I want to get to know him better, the person behind the bachelor label who has a room in his house for his nephew. The one who buys his sister's best friend a bed for her daughter.

The thread between us tugs. Our gazes linger through a comfortable silence, drawing our eyes from our mouths to our chests. The thread pulls again and brings out thoughts I'm in no place to entertain. "How's London?"

Julian's expression morphs. "Mostly cloudy, in the sixties."

"It must be a relief to be away. From the heat. From...everything." I laugh until it registers that I'm the only one. Okay, then.

His brows pinch. "Why do you do that?"

I frown. "Do what?"

He waits a beat and responds with a headshake. "Never mind."

"Well"—I clear my throat—"I should let you go." I wave a hand at his tailored suit. "I'm sure you want to get more comfortable."

His eyes hold mine. "I'm comfortable now."

Guess I'm the only one who needs to change their panties. "Okay!"

The corner of Julian's lip twitches. "Do I make you nervous, sweetheart?"

You make me want to ride on your London Bridge, especially if you keep calling me that.

"No," I say and mimic his headshake. But it's too animated to be believable.

Hickory-brown eyes keep me captive.

"Okay, fine." I throw up a hand. "You're...you and that manspread—"

He grins. "Manspread?"

"—are a lot. You're a flirt, I get it. But could you turn it down a notch? I feel the heat all the way over here."

Julian tilts his head back and laughs with a force that closes his eyes and jiggles his belly. It takes a full minute for him to come down. He wipes his eyes with a chuckle. "I missed you, El."

I resist the urge to fight back a smile. "Goodnight, Julian."

"Wait! What are your plans tomorrow?"

"Jackson and Haile are at their dad's until tomorrow evening." I shrug. "Order in, or make a pizza and watch a movie."

"Want company?" He snorts at my constipated look, because what the fuck? "I told you I'd like to get to know you better. Friends cook and watch movies. Plus..." He waggles his brows. "My pizza tastes better."

"Fine, but I pick the movie. Is one o'clock too late?"

"Nope," Julian says. "Lunch for you. Dinner for me. I'll text you what to get. And don't skimp on the ingredients, or it will taste like shit."

"I was wondering when you'd start to sound like Morgan."

"Hush. What are we watching?"

I bite my lip. "*Hot Fuzz.*"

Laughter erupts from his end. "And here I thought you'd pick *Notting Hill.*"

"Guess I'm full of surprises."

"That you are. Good night, Ella."

"Good morning, Julian."

Chapter 24

Julian

"Are you ready to order?"

I peek at my watch for the third time. "Maybe I should call Sebastian." It's not like him to be this late.

"No need. He's back at the office. Something came up." *At ten o'clock at night?* Robyn stares over her menu before they drop back down. "I'll have the beet salad. Hold the dressing."

The server takes her menu. "Excellent choice. And you, sir?"

"I'll have the duck breast, please." *With a side of ambush.* I hand him the menu with a tight smile. After a bow, he's off in his penguin suit.

When my assistant booked a late dinner, it was for a party of three, to discuss the contract currently under review with our Singapore client. Sebastian and Robyn work for the firm that represents the seller. Dinner never came up when I spoke with him today, which leads me to believe he didn't get an invite in the first place.

I've dodged Robyn's requests to meet up since I came back. Yet here we are, well past a respectable time to break bread—or roots, since she doesn't eat carbs. I've met clients early and late to accommodate their schedules. But this feels like a date.

Our small bistro table faces views of the terrace and the River Thames. It was another cloudy day, but the moon peeks over the Tower Bridge, illuminating Londoners and tourists who cross the neo-Gothic structure. Our section is quiet, minus two other couples at tables on opposite sides of the room.

I sip my scotch and keep my focus outside. Robyn lags in the periphery with a familiar hunger, one this five-star restaurant won't satisfy.

She leans on the table to rest her elbows, an act that widens the deep slit in her neckline and exposes the tops of her breasts. My eyes travel down her knee-length dress out of habit. It's in her signature red, and it molds to curves I've stroked on more than one occasion. I've praised her for wearing it during meetings that led to marathons between the sheets.

This dress and Sebastian's convenient absence are no coincidence.

"You're a hard man to reach." Robyn takes a long drink from her chardonnay, careful to sweep her thumb across her bottom lip.

"Same hustle, different day."

"Mmm. All work and no play makes for a dull Julian." Her eyes study me with a determined expression that makes it clear she's not talking about work schedules.

She's not wrong. I squeezed in a rugby practice last night after a ten-hour day. The temporary release loosened some pent-up stress and gave my left hand a break. I'll be lucky if I don't develop carpal tunnel or keep the skin on my dick.

I clear my throat. "Did you want to go over the Tan account?" I eye her. "The reason for this dinner?"

Her boldness was once a turn-on. Now, it's grating on my patience.

Robyn breaks eye contact and lifts a bitter smile. "I'd like to revisit the offer. I have compliance concerns."

A brow sinks. "There has been no previous apprehension voiced over the contractual terms," I say. "What are your expectations to amend?"

Her finger circles the rim of her wineglass. "The terms are implied from conduct, and I'll accept oral."

"Robyn." The strain in my voice cuts through the lust in the air from her side of the table. I sigh and sit back to make room for the server with our plates and nod in thanks.

A month ago, I would've done more than read between the lines. Robyn is a smart, the sharpest contract lawyer at her firm. She's gorgeous, a woman who takes what she wants and leaves people eating out of the palm of her hands.

We met eight months ago when she strutted into my office for a negotiation. Professional courtesies and late-night gatherings turned into laughs over nightcaps. Neither of us wanted anything serious and finally gave into the sexual attraction that intensified with each glance.

She's the only woman in London I've allowed to stay the night in my suite. We text on and off whenever we're in town, but that's been the extent of our communication.

No check-ins, lengthy conversations, or romantic gestures outside of dinner before sex. Our connection was purely physical to satisfy our urges without emotional attachment.

My thoughts drift back to Ella. Whereas Robyn is a path that's straight with no chaser, Ella is a road of speed bumps and detours under construction. The signals have been hard to read since we reconnected last week. It keeps me guessing. I'm hard-pressed to see her face each night, and I want to unravel more layers of the woman who enthralls me.

We've texted and video called almost every day since Saturday. Sunday's virtual movie morphed into binging random YouTube clips. I had my first Japanese session with Jackson on Monday, which became an hour-long conversation about the language and anime while El made dinner. Haile hopped on to give me a twenty-minute download on the life of a preschooler.

I video call Duke twice a week, and I look forward to adding space for Ella and her kids who've blended into my life so seamlessly it should terrify me. Except it doesn't.

The craving to connect in every sense destroys any impulse to gratify my drive with another woman. I want her—all of her—however she'll let me have her. For now, I'm Duke's fun uncle, but maybe there could be something more.

However long it takes.

I pull my cell from the silk lining of my suit jacket and thumb to our text thread. The last message came hours ago, when El told me a two-year-old asked for the *shits*. She ran the little girl bouncing on her feet to the bathroom, thinking she had to poop, only to find out she wanted Cheez-Its. I never laughed so hard in a meeting in my life.

The memory tugs at my cheeks.

"Everything alright?" Worry clings to Robyn's question and holds on for dear life.

"Peachy," I say, my eyes still on the screen. It's five o'clock in DC. Ella should be back home with the kids.

Ella

Remind me never to agree to a double date again.

I swallow hard and force my hand to loosen its grip on my phone.

This is the first I've heard of a double date, on a school night, with a man who isn't her ex. El isn't interested in dating. She made that clear with the shield she fortified to protect her and her kids from more heartbreak.

If she's on a double date, she's out with at least one person she's comfortable with. The question isn't who, but why now? She never said she was dating on any of our video calls.

With me.

Every night.

For hours.

"I'll be right back." I'm on my feet, headed to the restroom. And not for the *shits*.

Get to a bathroom. Now.

Ella

Okay...

I take the stairs to the lower level two at a time and follow signs for the toilets. My stride lengthens, the echo of my cap-toe shoes picking up speed over the slate-colored flooring. I reach an oak door and close it behind me.

Jealousy is a foreign emotion, one I dodge with ease for the simple fact I care, but not enough. My situation with acquaintances prevents me from developing the feelings necessary to stir such a reaction about the woman I'm with.

Until her.

My fingers fly to dial Ella's number on video call. She picks up on the third ring and rips the air from my lungs.

Curly black tendrils cascade down the sides of her face from a loose updo. Light pink dusts her cheekbones. It's the same color brushed with soft gold over her eyes. Plump lips seared in every fantasy hold a frown modeled in a lickable gloss.

Her brows dip. "Are you okay?"

Am I?

A slight growl in my throat catches us both off guard. I unclench my fist and jaw. *Pull yourself together*. "I should ask you the same question. With your...date." She squirms under my stare, and the flush in her cheeks deepens.

Ella short-circuits all sense of logic. Hence why I'm next to a public toilet. To do what, I don't know. Flush it in anger?

I let out a slow breath and reel in the impulse to claim her. I'm pretty laid-back, but this woman brings out a possessiveness I didn't know was there.

My eyes search hers; my voice lowers to extinguish the heat. "You good, sweetheart?"

She pulls her lower lip between her teeth and nods. El is feisty, quick with her wit, and sharp with her tongue. But tonight, she's nervous.

I stare in silence until she sighs. Her bare shoulders soften in her black crisscross top. A glimpse of a smile cracks. "I don't know what the hell I'm doing."

There she is.

"Why are you on a double date?" I lean against the pedestal sink. "Finally trying out hump day?"

She chuckles. "You're so nasty." *Only for you.* "Erica asked me to come, and I agreed out of frustration. I wanted to dress up for a night, for a change of pace from making chicken nuggets and answering to 'Mom' every two seconds."

"There's nothing wrong with that if you feel ready." *I'd grab the stars and pull down the moon for you.*

"Not for a double date," she says with an exhausted sigh. "It hasn't been two months since I left my ex, and I'm on my way to meet a man I don't know whose face I've never seen."

"So why did you agree?"

Her lip quirks. "I never turn down food."

That makes me laugh. Ella eats as much as the rugby team after back-to-back games. She says it all goes to her ass and thighs, and I say, keep eating. Her love of food and willingness to consume more than tiny salads and appetizers is refreshing. She doesn't hide herself, and it's one of the things I love about her.

Like.

I shake off the thought and smile. "How is the food?"

Her eyes widen. "Thirty-six dollars for a watercress salad. The weeds outside taste better for less."

Ella goes into a monologue about overpriced restaurants and unseasoned food. "The ancestors aren't pleased, Julie," she says in a huff.

My chest expands at her use of my nickname. I hated it the first time Antonio shouted it across the hall after school. The rugby team eventually remixed it to Jules, no thanks to him. Ella doesn't call me Julie much, which makes the times she does special. We've become more comfortable around each other, the awkwardness from our first encounter long gone.

The fact is she is more than a family friend. She's someone special who fits into my life without effort. "How's your date? Any chance it ends on a good note?" The word *date* leaves a weird aftertaste. Ella and *date* don't belong in the same thought, let alone room.

"Who, me and *Twilight*?" She laughs at my scrunched face. "His name is Carlisle. He's into finance and pauses after every sentence like he just said something profound. He probably sparkles in the sun the way he thinks he's God's gift to women."

My head tips back with the weight of laughter. "Go easy on the guy. Maybe he's nervous."

"I caught him swiping right on a dating app after I told him I'm going through a divorce and have two kids."

I frown. "I'm sorry, El."

She waves it off. "Don't be. I should've said I have the summer flu and canceled. You know daycare kids pass around diseases like Cheerios." Her groan is a shock to the dick. "I'll pull out the family photo album if it gets me out of here faster. I just want tacos and peace."

"You deserve both." I hesitate to say the next part. "You also deserve someone who appreciates all of you. Your children are a bonus, not a burden."

Eyes that have captivated me since our chance encounter glisten. Her chin wobbles, and she takes a moment to look away before facing me again. "Thank you." The words are soft, wrapped in the vulnerability she tries to hide.

I meant every word I said. Ella is extraordinary. Any man who doesn't comprehend that after a second in her presence isn't worthy of her.

Are you?

"I should let you go."

Her eyes meet mine. "Yeah." She nods. "Erica will send a search party. I'm going to call it a night."

It's my turn to nod. "Sounds good. Text me when you get home."

The smile that curls her lips is a direct hit to the heart. "Will do. Goodnight, Julie."

"'Night, sweetheart."

"Can I get you two anything else?"

The rest of dinner went as expected. If the sting from Robyn's glare doesn't take me out, hunger will. The server took my untouched food while I was in the bathroom, leaving me with a blank space and a woman who's demanding an explanation with unspoken words.

I lost track of time with El—twenty minutes, in this case. It wasn't my intention to keep Robyn waiting, even if she deceived me to come here. I apologized for my absence but gave no further detail.

"I'll take the check, please." I hit submit on my phone and stuff it back in my suit jacket.

"You're a busy man tonight." I don't miss the irritation in her tone.

My shrug is nonchalant. I take the billfold from the server with a smile. "That I am." I scribble in a thirty percent tip for food I never ate and sign the bill. "You'll have my full attention next time"—we lock eyes—"if it's business related." I stand and button my suit. "Shall we?"

Robyn gets up in a rush, her mouth pinched and her posture stiff. "I'm good with leaving it here." She'll have red marks on her shoulder from her fingers curling on her purse strap by the time she reaches her condo.

This is the end of the road for our romantic partnership. Our paths will cross again, but only in the boardroom. "See you around."

My phone chirps on my walk back to the office to wrap up for the night. The clouds lifted, offering a moonlit reprieve to a once bleak day. I pull out my phone and grin at the photo of Ella pressing her lips against the bag of tacos I ordered assuming she'd hightail it back home. Turns out I was right.

Ella

My hero! Thank you.

My pleasure. Enjoy.

Ella

Already ate two.

Three dots appear before they disappear. They pop up again.

Ella

Do you want to talk later? If you're not busy.

This is the first time she has initiated a video call. It might be because of the tacos, but I'll take it.

Never too busy for you. Call you soon.

Chapter 25

Ella

The vagina is a canal of wonders. It self-cleans, it's a passageway for babies, and, apparently, a place for home-improvement projects with sex toys that double as power tools. There's no way the dual-action vibrator in my hand won't remove screws and sandblast my pubic hairs if left at the highest setting. The thing has ten clitoral speeds and fourteen pulsing patterns.

Who's exorcising demons with all of this?

I have enough trouble preheating the fancy double oven in Julian's kitchen. Now I have to risk third-degree burns buzzing off the dust down below after a months-long hibernation?

"You'll see stars with that one," Janelle says in a whisper over my shoulder.

"And a gynecologist." I put the lilac contraption back on the black velvet display.

My relationship with sex toys is simple: I don't have one. Charles squawked at any threat to his "manhood," which included gadgets and gizmos to get me off in minutes instead of the exploration he undertook to discover my G-spot. He never found it, a testament to our years together and his dedication to one person coming instead of two.

The tiny vibrator I kept hidden in a drawer still had its new-car smell. When I'd remember I had it, I couldn't get my mind to focus on myself. It was a lost cause. But, unlike my ex, my friends are invested in my happy ending. As inappropriate as that might be.

"That will change your life." Erica pops a grape into her mouth and winks. Padded ankle straps dangle from her shoulders. She's double-fisting dildos and still reaches for the vibrator I just put down.

"Are those earrings?" Rhinestone chains hang from each lobe with gems at the bottom.

A grin spreads. "Nipple clamps."

Morgan walks up with a matching set on her ears. I do a double-take. "You too?"

She lifts a shoulder, like titty clamps as earrings are regular behavior for her, and proceeds to check out the pocket vibrators. "What? They match an outfit I have."

Today was a mixed bag of madness served in alcohol. From a rooftop brunch with bottomless mimosas to pedicures, we've been together since Erica banged on my door at eight this morning.

Juneteenth is tomorrow, a historic commemoration of Black liberation and, now, my own freedom. I officially fulfilled Charles's requirements in our separation agreement—out of Morgan's house within ninety days. One less hold he has over my life.

I take the seat next to Erica and toast my margarita glass with hers. "To dildos and divorce." A sex-toy slumber party isn't how I imagined my night without Haile and Jackson, but I wouldn't trade it for the world.

She mirrors my smile. "To dildos and divorce."

Janelle stands near the hallway like a mother who needs to remind her kids not to play with matches while she's gone. "Okay, ladies. The items on the table are new, and you can keep them as a thank-you for tonight. The orders you placed will arrive in three weeks in discreet packaging." She steps into her leopard-print pumps and casts her brown eyes on me. "The ladies got you a divorce gift. I left it on the kitchen counter. Happy hunching."

"To new beginnings and extra orgasms!" Erica's shout reaches the front door before she does. "I'll walk you out, Janelle. I need to ask you about a private party." There's no use reminding Erica that her silk robe barely covers her ass. She's on her fourth tequila shot, ready for bed with a bare face and wrapped hair.

"Bye!" I swing a hand in the air, one that misses the floor lamp next to the bookshelves by inches. *Oops!*

"See you!" I catch a glimpse of Janelle's sienna hand before she's gone.

The high from tonight fades to embers. We ordered in Greek to complement the Mediterranean masterpiece Morgan created on the spare charcuterie board she conveniently had in her car. A run to the nearby market for fancy olives and wine turned into a scavenger hunt for our favorite sweets.

Janelle came over with her box of pleasure around eight, and she spent the last two hours educating us on the importance of air pressure and mixing up textures. Well, she educated *me*, the only person who doesn't have a stash of adult goodies in her home.

Morgan, of all people, didn't bat an eye at Janelle's inventory, which included silicone anal beads I saw her eyeing more than once. Let me find out my best friend keeps it kinky. I'm light-years behind and need to catch up.

The closet freak in question pads across the floor in my fluffy pink slippers with a tray of dirty dishes. "Want another margarita while I'm in the kitchen?"

The last time I got shit-faced, I dry-humped your brother in bed.

Speaking of Julian, he's been quiet most of the day. We texted this morning, hours after another Saturday night watching a movie on a video call. He chose *You've Got Mail*, for his love of Tom Hanks and rom-coms. I thought the romantic comedy bit was a joke until he rattled off *Brown Sugar*, *The Best Man*, *The Holiday*, and *Something New*. There are many layers to Julian Brooke, and discovering them has become a daily adventure. If we're not texting, we're laughing on screen.

"Ella?"

"Hmm?"

Morgan's brow raises. "Want another margarita?" She scans me again. "On second thought, you might be good for the night."

"Yeah, just water, thanks." I clear my throat and all thoughts of riding her younger sibling's face, thoughts I'll blame on the alcohol, and move to join her in the kitchen. If you leave Morgan alone, she'll deep-clean your house.

She assesses me with a bemused smile. I need to work on my poker face. "Daydreaming about someone?"

Erica chooses that moment to walk back in and straight into my business. Her bare Naomi Campbell legs sashay into the kitchen, a move only she can serve three sheets to the wind. "Who's someone?"

"Yeah, who's someone?" Morgan asks.

I scoff. "No one. I was...thinking." *About your brother and why it's a terrible idea to get so close, because of the face-riding...and the galloping on other body parts.*

It makes sense for us not to be strangers. He's a family friend, and we get mail at the same house. But every time I tell myself we're friends who are getting to know each other as housemates, he calls me sweetheart and orders me tacos.

"Mm-hmm." Erica stands next to Morgan and crosses her arms. Terror twins in shades of pink, these two. "It's definitely a man."

My eyes can't roll any harder. "Y'all need to go to bed."

"And you need dick," Erica says.

She's not wrong.

Don't go there.

"I'm not paying you two any mind," I say.

Erica's head swivels, all attitude and fresh box braids. "We're not the ones having mental commercial breaks thinking about a man. Who. Is. He?"

They wait, fully expecting an answer. Morgan's focus eventually shifts over my shoulder to scan for a leftover mess to clean.

I huff out a laugh. "I don't have a man. As for dick, I'm not in the market for another headache." *Head*, maybe. But not the ache.

Morgan sips her glass of water with a nod. "Ella needs to stay away from dick until her divorce is final." Her eyes flit between me and the marble counter full of candies and sex toys. What a combo. "At least, real ones."

Erica's gaze finds a new target. "Don't be a cockblock."

"I'm not her attorney, but Grier told her penetrative sex during her separation is a no-no. If Charles's camp found out, he could take her to court for adultery." Morgan takes in Erica's sour face. "What? I pay attention, and I love legal dramas."

"That's fucked up," Erica says through a mumble.

Morgan nods. "It is. Honestly, it's best if you stay clear dating, El. At least until you're closer to finalizing."

Erica bites her lip and examines her canary yellow nails. "I kinda asked El to come on a date with me last week."

My best friend stiffens. "What date?"

"The kind that has 'double' in front of it."

If looks could kill, Morgan would would have Erica in the ground. Erica prattled on about the fancy dinner with Jovani and his cousin. There's no way in hell I'd give Carlisle or his ego the time of day again, but it's not enough for a certain art buyer.

The tension in her body matches her tone. "If Charles finds out you're going out on dates, he'll paint this like you're the unfaithful one who broke up your family." Morgan's head bows with a heavy sigh. "Promise me you all will tell me about your bright ideas *before* you do them. Is there anything else I should know?" Her stare widens.

Shit.

I tilt my head, finally catching on. *Double shit.*

This is different.

Does that matter?

"Are you two done yet?" Erica glances between us. "Your little back-and-forth isn't fooling anyone."

Morgan takes a deep breath. "You know how El had to find a place to live that wasn't my house?"

"Yeah."

She swallows and looks at me. "When I said Ella could live in this family home, technically, I never checked with its owner. Julian."

Erica speaks at the highest octave. "*Girl*, you live with *that* man?" She bounces with a squeal. "That fine Lance Gross look-alike eyeing you at the barbecue?" Her butt hits the counter with a graceless thud. "I knew you two were fucking."

I rush to cut Erica off. "I am *not* having sex with anyone. Julian lives in London. He came back the night of my divorce party, and it was a surprise. We agreed he would stay in the bedroom in the basement while he's here."

"Back up one second." Erica looks between me and Morgan. "You know I love you and good ding-a-ling, but won't it be a problem if your ex finds you're sharing a home with one of DC's most eligible bachelors?"

Morgan shifts onto a barstool. "If they don't publicize it, maybe could it work?"

"I asked Grier about it before I moved in. She's not thrilled, but since Julian is away and I'm leaving by the end of the year, she advised to be extra careful." The good news is he purchased the townhouse through an LLC to conceal his identity.

Erica pulls a strawberry off the remnants of the charcuterie board. "I'm no lawyer, but that might work if his fine ass stays in the basement. It would be like she's a tenant in his building. Only you share common areas, and you don't pay rent. How do the kids handle him when he's here?"

When I tell you what a battle it is to bite back a smile…I swallow the warmth rising in my chest, tempting my lips to curl. "They treat him like Duke's uncle when they see him. Jackson is getting in on the Japanese lessons."

My kids adore Julian and always ask when he's coming back. Their connection happened organically, but it gives me pause. I'd never introduce Jackson and Haile to another man—not so soon, at least.

You aren't together.

"Julian is on the other side of the ocean," I say. "He's graciously allowed me and my kids to stay here while he's away for the rest of the year. I have time to save for my own place, and he has someone to pick up his mail."

"We just have to be extra careful," Morgan says. "The spin if your ex finds—"

"He won't," I say. I pick up and drop off the kids at his parents' house. Neutral territory that keeps me from visiting the scene of his crime. "Who would believe that Julian would entertain a woman eight years older with two kids, and going through a divorce?"

Erica sizes me up. "I'd do you."

I roll my eyes and laugh. "Not helping. The point is, it doesn't make sense. There's nothing to worry about here."

When I glance at Morgan, I startle at her probing gaze. She opens her mouth to say something but thinks better of it.

"At least I can cross off a date, a sleepover, and a sex toy party from my divorce bucket list."

"True," Morgan says. "It's getting late. I should turn in." She wraps me in a hug and squeezes. "I love you."

"Love you back."

"Aww." Erica comes in for some love. "This was fun." She backs away toward the main hall. "Since El can't date, I think I'll sleep downstairs."

I frown. "There's no one down there."

She smirks. "I don't mind taking Junior's bed. Maybe I'll find something worth my while."

Morgan's big sister mode activates. "He's not a junior, and respect his shit. We're all upstairs."

"In his regular bed? Even better."

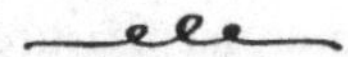

I spend the next thirty minutes cleaning up what's left of our night, which isn't much, thanks to Morgan and her *everything has its place* ways.

My mind won't stop racing with thoughts about my housing situation. It was a non-issue before, or so I assumed. Neither Charles nor his attorneys flagged who owns this home, which leads me to believe he hasn't looked. Or nothing turned up. My hope is option two. Jackson loves his room, and Haile adores her new bed.

I need more time to save and get on solid ground. A few weeks of work isn't enough—not in this economy, and not with my salary. Julian being away in London works in my favor. It's safer, for reasons beyond a roof over my family's head.

My fingers sweep over the kitchen island. The lighting underneath the cabinets on the wall casts a soft glow against the main floor's darkness. The house is quiet, minus the symphony of soft snores from upstairs. We confirmed Julian's bed is big enough to fit the three of us. There is only one reason someone without Nick Cannon's kids needs a bed that big, and it starts and ends with an orgy.

Janelle's black bag of goodies sits next to the prep sink. I never opened it, and I can only imagine what's waiting for me underneath the black and silver tissue.

Everyone is asleep.

My kids are with their father.

I'm alone, with new toys.

I stare at the source of potential pleasure with a newfound focus. I was never in the right headspace to take care of myself in the past, but maybe practice makes perfect? I bend over the gift bag for a closer look and pull out the decorative layers until my hand lands on a box I retrieve with raised brows.

A blue sticky note attached to the front grabs my attention.

I fully charged the battery in case you wanted a test drive tonight.

xo,

Janelle

My nose wrinkles as I squint at the letters that spell "G-spot vibrator." The light purple silicone has ridges underneath a curved, thick head. Seven vibration speeds promise satisfaction on a quiet setting.

I pull my bottom lip between my teeth and look around. Upstairs isn't an option to spread and moan. Those nosy heifers would wake up the second I changed a setting. The basement is soundproof, but I wouldn't dare get off in Julian's domain. I'm not trying to add to the collection of bodily fluids on the bottom floor. The sofa could work, but said bodily fluids could come into play if this thing turns out to be legit.

My eyes shift back to the counter, a bleachable surface. A good scrub and some disinfectant wipes would kill all germs and traces of play. Kitchen counter sex isn't uncommon. I never did it, but I can add it to my divorce bucket list. And then cross it off.

"I'm getting mine," I say in a shuffle. No one is awake in the house, and the neighbor's lights are off. The lighting in here is dim anyway. If there is a peeper, they're in for a show. Only my profile is visible. I'll survive.

I take my place in the middle of the all-white island. My legs hang over the edge, exposing the tops of my thighs underneath the black satin robe I bought myself last year for my birthday.

The stem of my wineglass feels light when I pull it toward me and let the herbal notes from the merlot coat my lips. My hands drag behind me, and I lean back to take in the shadows on the ceiling interlaced with ambient light. A faint moan escapes as my feet sway lazily through the air.

I focus on the gift of silence. The exchange of busyness for stillness, to center myself instead of others. It's a rare treat to indulge, but tonight, I give in.

The tips of my fingers glide across the side of my neck in a slow drag down my robe's edge to the swell of my breasts. My lips part at the heat of my skin against the fabric's friction. I close my eyes and pull open my robe, exposing a shoulder at the fall of the strap and hard nipple at my hand skating over my breast.

My breath quickens, matching the pulse hammering in my throat. I switch hands to anchor myself to the altar of self-play.

With legs splayed open and my nightgown pooled to my navel, my eyes skim the body that's loved me when I didn't love myself. My palms press against breasts that nursed my children. They're fuller and dip lower than they did years ago. I travel down my stomach and untie the robe binding my hips, which are wide with light stretch marks. My thighs carry extra cellulite and a thickness that makes them rub together.

Desire quivers in my body, demanding release.

I take one last sip before my bare back presses into cold marble, and I free myself completely of the robe.

Showtime.

The toy comes to life in a quiet vibration between my fingertips, and I let it roam my curves. My back arches at the heat inflaming my skin. Moisture builds between my legs, and my nipples tighten to diamonds at the kiss of the pulsating head. Lower my hand goes to the soft skin of my stomach, which houses a flurry of butterflies.

My vagina bucks in expectation and soaks the tip of the vibrator on impact.

My breath catches in my throat, and I arch again, rolling my hips into thick silicone. "Holy shit," I say between pants. Breathlessness takes over, and in a series of stifled moans, I come on my new best friend.

Morgan will have to understand.

Tension leaves my body in waves. I turn off the vibrator now coated in my essence and gaze back up at the light streaking the ceiling, astonished and embarrassed.

Nicolas Cage isn't the only one *Gone in 60 Seconds*. I only used the first setting before I erupted, and that was with the *tip*.

How in the hell do people last with that power drill buzzing up their insides?

I need to step up my game, and apparently my stamina.

My phone dances across the counter. It's on vibrate, a small miracle. I don't need the house to wake up and catch me in an X position on top of the counter we'll eat breakfast on with my titties and vagina out for all to see.

I lift my head to see the glow of the name that was on the edge of my lips before I came. A man who's quickly become a steady presence in my life, breaking through every barrier I put up to protect my heart.

The tug-of-war to answer after my test drive with a vibrator ends when the phone goes dark and illuminates with a photo of Julian's grin. It's a phone call tonight. Not a video chat I'd have to maneuver from the neck up.

"Hi." I huff and puff like a triathlon contestant attempting a swim in the ocean with floaties. This is ridiculous.

"You okay over there?" His voice can't hide his smile.

"Yes," I say through a breath and sit up.

"How was your day?" It's not lost on me that he's calling after ten. Maybe he had a bunch of meetings.

On a Sunday?

"Long but worth it." There's a faint shuffle that's hard to place without any background noises for clues. "I take it girls' night was a success?"

The tingles still prickling my vagina would agree.

"Yup. Lots of fun."

"Mmm." A deep breath travels through the phone. "Where is everyone?"

"Upstairs sleeping. I came down for some..." I eye my wineglass and vibrator. "Water. You're calling late. You okay?"

His breathlessness is a gentle stroke that works its way down my throat to lap my nipples. My thighs clench at the strange note in his tone. Julian's voice is usually deep with a playfulness to it, but that man isn't here tonight. Someone darker, with unmasked hunger, is in his place.

"I missed seeing you today," he says through an exhale. My hand skims the top of my breasts at his words.

I should feel shame or guilt, but neither comes. Julian and I have danced around long-distant dates we call hanging out and flirtatious remarks that are more foreplay than friendly banter.

I'm horny enough to leak over the floor, and right now I don't give a damn who knows about the forbidden relationship I have with my best friend's brother. I do care if one of my girls comes down for a midnight snack and catches me with my hand between my legs.

One thing at a time.

His voice turns thick with desperation. My hand traces my lower lips, and I bite back a groan. "I don't want to pretend anymore, Ella. You're so fucking beautiful, you know that?"

My mouth parts. This is the first time we're laying it out on the table. No more sidestepping the fact that he wants me as much as I want him.

He lowers his voice. "I want you to do something for me."

I'd smuggle diamonds in my ass if he asked. I'm kidding. I wouldn't do time for a man at the expense of my kids growing up without me. And back-door play isn't a road I've traveled, though I'm open with a partner I trust.

"Sweetheart?" His pet name is a tongue that glides up my neck and raises the hairs at the nape.

I should end the call after I put Julian back in the friend zone he broke out of. There are so many reasons why crossing the line with him is dangerous, beyond the simple fact he's Morgan's brother. I'm still married—on paper, at least. Charles broke our vows the moment he stuck his dick in a woman who wasn't his wife.

His sin is my reawakening.

The flutters over my body turn into a shiver. My tongue darts out to lick my lips. "Yes," I say with Jedi concentration to keep myself from humping the air.

When did I get this bold and carefree? I enjoy sex but have never been this forward.

His command comes in a slow drag. "Face the windows and spread for me."

It takes a second for it to register that this call isn't on video. Julian can't see me from London.

Which means...

"Oh my—" The hand exploring my heat hovers over my mouth. I hold the other in a strong grip on the phone against my ear and slowly turn to the window.

It's pitch-black outside. At least it was. Now the orange glow of a cigar outlines a seated figure facing me.

I switch the phone to my other hand, grasp the edge of the counter, and put distance between us. Only I miscalculate and meet the air, sending me and my topless body to the ground with a hard thump.

Chapter 26

Julian

I was six the first time I watched *True Lies*. A stack of Blockbuster videos, ginger ale, and crackers kept me company in my father's office while Langston Brooke held back-to-back meetings. It was a sick day from school, and my mother left a conference early to fly back, whip up some homemade onion syrup, and slick me in castor oil.

The elementary school me appreciated the big explosions and seeing someone ride a horse through a mall in my city. But the adult me, the man, appreciates Jamie Lee Curtis performing a striptease on a four-poster bed, all while her secret agent of a husband guides her—unbeknownst to his suburban wife.

Who knew life would bless me with the chance to reenact one of my favorite scenes in one of my favorite movies? I had no intention of smoking a cigar on my back patio when I got home, but how could I not with the show in front of me?

Watching Ella play out the desires in her mind has my dick straining against my zipper. It has to be a challenge for her to let go and put herself first. And my God, did she.

Like Arnold Schwarzenegger in the film, I was stunned into silence by the beauty before me, who has a body I yearn to worship in every way imaginable. And also like Arnold, I am on my feet the second seduction turns into an episode of *America's Funniest Home Videos.*

From outside the glass, I watch the kitchen counter, now clear of the woman who stars in my fantasies. I can't see her, but her groans are audible from the phone that took a tumble with her.

"You okay, sweetheart?"

"Yeah." Another grunt. "Just down here, slowly dying from embarrassment. You have gorgeous flooring, by the way."

Seconds pass until she resurfaces. Her top knot of curls leans to the left, and the robe that once exposed the most mouth-watering breasts is back in place. The hem hits the tops of her thick thighs, thighs I want wrapped on either side of my face. I match the step she takes to the window. "What are you doing here?"

Darkness conceals my shrug. "I live here, remember?" More silence. "I wanted to be here with you tomorrow."

Another step.

"Why?" The question hangs on the confirmation she wants, not her confusion about my actions.

We've dodged this conversation every night, only to spend hours talking to fill in the blank spaces between us. Time might not be our ally, but that motherfucker can have several seats if it tries to object to the force that draws us together.

"Because I care, El."

The truth of my confession steals her breath. I step into the light reflecting off the window and meet her smile. "Hi," she says.

"Hi." I point to the door on her left. "Can I come in?" Only a passcode separates us, but I won't pass the threshold unless she's comfortable. With a nod, she moves to the door, unlocks it, and steps back, leaving a stream of lavender that invades my senses when I enter.

The best video-call technology doesn't do Ella's beauty justice. I memorized the lines of her heart-shaped face and full lips. But seeing her in person now feels like the first time.

Our eyes lock, a mix of intrigue and sexual tension weighing heavy in the air. My restraint not to take her over the counter requires superhuman strength.

I lean in close and inhale her scent. "That was quite a show you put on."

Her eyes drop to my mouth. "I didn't do it for anyone else but me." She cuts her gaze back to mine with a lifted brow.

A chuckle rattles in my throat. *Tease.* "Fair enough." I slowly back her up against the counter and place my hands on either side of her. She draws in a sharp breath and leans back, leaving her neck exposed. I track the hard swallow that goes down her throat and drag my eyes to her cleavage pressed against the juncture of her robe.

The way I want to run my tongue across the peaked nipples taunting me and bury myself in her breasts is unholy.

Her legs part, an invitation to press myself against her heat. "Is playtime over, sweetheart?"

"It's been awhile since I did this." Her lip folds between her teeth with a downcast expression. "I'm out of practice, and shape. I didn't last long."

My eyes roam over her heavy breasts rising and falling with every breath, a soft stomach, hips for days, and those damn thighs. I lick my lips and meet her unsure stare. "Your shape looks perfect to me, but if you want to work on stamina"—I lean down— "practice makes perfect."

Temptation plays out in her dark chocolate eyes, which are now the size of saucers. A blush creeps up her neck as she glances at the staircase. No one is awake or around to pull us apart. She weighs the decision with pressed lips and a rub of a hand over the adorable nest on her head.

"I never got myself off before...with my hands."

My hand scrubs the scruff on my jaw. I'm at a loss for words. Ella stays busy with her kids, but if I looked like her, my fingers would be in my pussy at all times. My teeth grind at her bowed head and slumped shoulders. This woman is many things—fearless, confident, unapologetic—and I'll be damned if disappointment breaks her spirit.

I lift her chin. "Do you trust me?" At her nod, I say, "Good girl." Her pupils dilate. My dick throbs again.

She's into praise? Noted.

"You have everything you need." My other hand trails down a breast to her stomach and stops at the thin piece of satin covering her pussy. I press my palm against her mound and rub down, savoring the way she arches into me. "I could always help."

Ella grabs my hand, careful to break contact. Her words come out in a rush. "You can't. Penetrative sex during my separation is adultery."

Well, fuck me.

No, seriously. I might have to fuck my own hand for the third time today. It's become a daily ritual at this point. Penetrative sex could mean a number of things. My guess is my tongue and dick are off-limits.

And your fingers.

Fuck.

I've nutted imagining my first time inside El. That hasn't happened since puberty. They say good things come to those who wait, but damn.

Note to self: Stock up on boxer briefs and find out if we can expedite her divorce. Like tomorrow.

My grip shifts from her chin to her throat. I rub her pulse with my thumb and pull her close. "Guess you have the honor tonight."

Our stares collide in a clash of wills. There's nothing I'd love more than to possess her, but tonight isn't about me. She calls the shots.

Every thought leaves my body at the sight of her bare breasts. Caramel-tipped peaks move with her ragged breaths. She inhales deep and slides the fabric down to her elbows with a look that says, *Your move.*

My dick swells to the point of discomfort, but if I get a front-row seat to witness her in action again, it's worth it. Confidence eases back into her face, a reclamation of her pleasure independent of a partner to provide it for her. Her smile builds when she leans back on her elbows and widens her thighs. The act spreads the curtain of silk, putting her beautiful pussy on display. Her essence glistens on her lips.

The temptress laughs at my groan but yelps when I snatch her wrist. I lean over her, careful not to graze her with my erection, and come in my pants for the second time. "Open." I feed her her own pointer and middle fingers, and she swirls them in her mouth. "Coat your fingers good, sweetheart. That's it."

I drop her hand and press open her knees. "Scoot back for me. I want your feet on the counter." She does as she's told with her fingers still in her mouth. "Look at this pussy, wet and ready for me. Open wider, baby."

Don't touch her.

The chant rings in my ears. I clench my fist and swallow the urge to devour the feast in front of me. Ella pulls her feet back to spread her lips apart. Her clit is visible, pulsating on its own.

I close my eyes and take a breath. Tonight is about her. My gaze intertwines with hers, and my heart swells at the gift she offers.

Trust.

Ella has taken back her power every day since her separation. I don't need to have known her for years to see how much she pours into everyone she loves, to be what they need. If she had a partner who adored her, she would be able to breathe and indulge in what she wants—not as a mom, friend, family member, or wife. As Ella.

Tonight is her exhale.

My lips press soft kisses to her jaw. "You are amazing." I move to her throat. "Exquisite."

She leans into my touch with a moan. "Show me what to do."

I don't miss the request and place my hand over hers. We drag our middle and index fingers over her pussy with enough pressure to rock her hips. I move the fingers over her swollen clit. "Rub in slow circles." Her breath hitches. "Good girl."

Ella plays with the speed, moving faster until her toes curl, then she slows down. Her breath picks up, and she pumps into her hand while I move around the counter and stand behind her.

"Now insert two fingers. Remember, you're in control," I say against her ear.

She closes her eyes and nods, moving her fingers in and out at a relaxed pace. I continue the previous string of kisses, leaning over to pull my tongue along her neck. I shift to the side and stall at her breasts.

Is it penetration if I don't enter an orifice?

"Curl those fingers toward your belly button and guide them along the top of your wall." My breath is inches from a nipple, one I taste with a lick. Ella bucks off the island. "You like that, sweetheart?" I take the other nipple in my mouth and smile at her moan. "Now tell me to come hither with those fingers inside you."

Her voice trembles. "Julian," she says in a plea.

I rub her nipples between my fingers. "You're gorgeous, baby." Her hand flies up to grab a breast, and her pace increases.

"Oh God." Her heels dig into the marble as she thrusts into her pleasure with abandon.

Sweat prickles her brow, and her breasts bounce at the force of her finger exhibition. With her head back and her eyes still closed, she comes in a long moan, squeezing out the last drop of aftershock with a sigh.

"Oh...my." She looks up and searches my eyes. "Thank you."

I kiss the tip of her nose. "That was all you." I pull her fingers out and draw in a deep breath. With widened eyes, she watches the fingers that brought her to ecstasy enter my mouth. Her lip quivers at the swirl of my tongue. "I knew it."

Her brows draw together. "Knew what?"

"You taste incredible."

Whenever our time comes, once won't be enough.

Chapter 27

Ella

I always imagined the awkwardness that sets in right after a hookup, once the tingles wane. A handshake and a "thank you for your service" felt like poor taste after Julian and I…well, did what we did. He scrubbed the counter while I waxed on and off with disinfectant wipes before I pulled him in for half a hug and a dap.

A dap.

The man crossed an ocean and a time zone to spend one day with me, only to receive a send-off that made *me* question what the hell I was doing.

Last night's orgasm sent me straight to the moon. I saw stars there on top of the kitchen island, and maybe also that ancestral plane in *Black Panther*. There's no way I could form a thought, much less speak. So I said my goodbye, took a stealth shower upstairs, and joined the snores of an unknown melody from my bed.

The girls stayed until ten this morning before they dispersed back to their lives. I got called out on my "glow," one I chalked up to having tested out the new merch. If they only knew the source of inspiration for last night's release is in front of the stove in sweats and a sleeveless tee. His hands work at an expert pace between a pot, skillet, and saucepan. The movement flexes the slopes of his back muscles under the thin layer of white cotton, and his muscular ass is on display with each step he takes.

If the morning after comes with this view and a side of bacon, count me in.

Julian texted me around eleven to see if the coast was clear to come up from the basement. At least he got a good night's rest after the eight-hour flight it took to get here. He's back to the airport in four hours to head to London.

He didn't fly all the way here to cook eggs, which begs the question—

"Ready to talk about it?" He moves to the toaster and adds English muffins.

How can he cook so casually after he sucked on my nipples and helped me come in this very kitchen? Maybe he does that with guests on game nights, which is why he's not freaking out. A little cunnilingus and Connect Four.

The way my vagina sang last night, it deserves a record deal and world tour.

"El?" Julian assesses me with an unhurried gaze. He's the picture of peace with a smile to match.

Me? I'm on the edge of the scene of last night's performance with a million and four questions. "How are you so…" I motion to his gorgeous face, which now carries a smirk. "Nonchalant?" Like I didn't bare my body hours ago in a private after-dark special.

"Huh."

"Huh, what?"

He reaches for a cherry tomato, his focus still on me. Its journey to his mouth is slow. He drags the tips of his fingers through lips that are softer than cashmere, lips that coated my skin with kisses. Hickory eyes search mine as the steady crackle of turkey bacon scents the air. Light filters through the windows and catches the waves in his black hair lined to perfection.

"You're still wound tight. I would've thought we took care of that last night the way you levitated off the counter."

"Are you ever serious?" My cheeks burn from laughter. Also, I didn't miss the *we*.

"When I need to be."

"I'm not used to summoning orgasms through guided meditation. Excuse me if I need to process."

This is not my life. Married and comfortably miserable to a cheater one day, and discussing how to navigate the aftermath of an incredible night with a man I've known for a month the next. We might not have crossed the penetration line last night, but we sure did hopscotch the shit next to it.

"Your thoughts are in the clouds again," Julian says with a chuckle, his focus back on the stove.

I sigh. "Here's the thing."

"I'm listening."

"I don't do this."

"Eat a late breakfast after pretending to eat hours ago?"

"No, smartass!" I giggle into my coffee. "I—this. I don't masturbate in front of my best friend's brother. Or anyone." I've been the PTA mom and the committed wife who walks the straight and narrow without kinks. The one who takes her kids to swim practice and spends her week competing in the Olympic sport of laundry.

"Last night, I felt alive. I didn't think about errands to run, the kids' school needs, volunteer obligations, or the reality that all of this"—I point around the room—"goes away at the end of the year. I've been on autopilot these last two months, and I haven't stood still to take it all in. It's a lot. This is a lot."

The double take I give the plate he hands me is comical, like we're in the middle of a zombie apocalypse and he gave me the last Twinkie. Homemade eggs Benedict with turkey bacon and fresh fruit. He slides a mimosa in a champagne flute over and lifts his own for a toast. "To new beginnings."

I'm going to pinch myself and wake up because who the hell makes eggs Benedict from scratch, let alone without a recipe?

At the clink of our glasses, Julian scoots next to me with his plate. When he said he'd make breakfast with whatever I had in the refrigerator, I did not expect this. The hollandaise sauce is silky, and the yolk from the poached egg runs free with the slightest touch of my fork.

"Julian, this is amazing." *You're amazing.* I clear my throat and accidentally moan into another bite. "You might've missed your calling as a chef." If nothing else, I want him here to make breakfast, lunch, and dinner. The man can conjure orgasms from my body *and* knows his way around a kitchen.

He chuckles into his glass. "Thank you. Cooking is a way I de-stress. I'm not a baker, but I'm always happy to whip something up for you."

Don't tempt me with those hands again.

Stop.

"How has no one taken you off the market for your culinary talents alone? I bet women strap themselves to your chairs for their morning-after breakfast." I'm two seconds from dragging my tongue over this plate.

His laugh startles me. It's light, but his head tips back. "Well, these chairs don't come with straps, and I'm not in the habit of cooking for women." He laughs again. "Close your mouth, El. Outside of my mother and Morgan, it's just you."

I don't miss the emphasis on *just you*, or the way his eyes lock on mine as his words sink in. He studies me with unwavering attention, ready for me to redirect the subject I've been too nervous to discuss.

The breath I exhale takes with it years of driving myself into the ground to fulfill the duties I put before myself. My eyes well. "You see me as more than a mother or a woman going through a divorce. What happened yesterday was a reminder that I can pour into myself as much as I do for others.

"Do you know how that feels after sixteen years? My life is a mess right now. Every day is a leap into the unknown, one that terrifies me, but I'm doing it. On my own terms."

Julian reaches over to brush my cheek. The tenderness flutters my eyes closed, playing out a scenario that includes a lifetime of happiness. If only our circumstances were different.

"Your bravery is one of the things I love about you," he says. "Last night was special to me. *You're* special to me, Ella."

Love.

The man said *love*.

Focus.

"Julian." A smile flashes before I pull away from his hand. "You're special to me too, but this attraction between us will fade with time. We're at different stages in our lives, and we want different things."

My thoughts flit between our desire to give in to our deeply embedded connection and panic that it will cost me everything, including my heart.

"What do you want?" The softness in Julian's voice mirrors the warmth in his eyes.

My answer comes through a smile. "To never have to rely on a man for security again. When the time comes, I want a life partner who cherishes my kids and pursues me with a desire that won't stray with temptation. I want to laugh through the storms, dance in the rain, and enjoy new adventures beyond motherhood."

I take a hesitant bite of my food, careful to dodge his stare under long lashes. "Thank you again; this is really delicious. Where did you pick up cooking?"

Seconds pass through a small eternity until he speaks in a monotone, bored with my avoidance and another question about food. I dip my chin to hide behind the two-strand twists that create a barrier between us.

He lets out a heavy sigh. "A little bit here, a little bit there. I travel throughout the year, which means different cuisines and cultures. Though I do watch the Food Network during the week."

"Sounds tasty." A laugh surges from my belly, one we both know is crap. "Do you have a favorite—"

"Ella. Look at me." My breath catches at the request. Small movements add up to my fork back on my plate and me shifting in my seat to face Julian.

I swallow at his stiff posture. Frustration turns to amusement when he catches me studying the broad expanse of his chest. "You never asked me what I wanted."

That's because I already know that *Jeopardy* answer: What is a dangerous desire?

We need distance between us, or I'll set off the smoke detector with my vagina.

My inner good girl says to step back, physically and emotionally. My inner baddie says let's fuck around and find out.

I wet my lips to wrap around the words that come out in a throaty whisper: "What do you want, Julian?"

Thick hands wrap around my chair faster than my mind can process. The metal barstool drags across the hardwood floor on a slow journey deeper between his legs. His voice is husky when he says, "You, El. I want you."

There's no chance for me to soak in his words. Not when my heart pounds in my chest. Not when he's inches from my face.

"We can't," I say in a whisper. "I'm still married."

"You won't be next year."

"I have kids, and I don't want to confuse them. We live in the same house. We're close to your family."

He takes my hands, his fingertips gliding over my knuckles. "All I want is a chance. My attraction to you is more than physical. I respect your mind, and I adore your heart. I won't deny the timing is shit, but now that you're in my life, I have to try. We'll take it slow. Get to know each other, away from everyone. But I need you to give me the okay. Please?"

Our gazes mix with a connection that pulls us together. "My life is under construction, Julian. The most I could offer right now is friendship."

"I'll take whatever you're comfortable with."

A laugh slips free. "I'm eight years older than you with two kids."

His shoulder lifts. "My being younger means I have the stamina to keep up with your sexual awakening." He lifts my knuckles to his lips. "And in case you couldn't tell"—*Kiss*—"I care for Jackson and Haile." *Kiss.* "I want to get to know them better." *Kiss.* "But I respect their need for normalcy during this transition. They won't see or know me as anything other than Duke's uncle until you give your blessing."

Doesn't he have all the answers?

"We can't have sex."

A smile ghosts his lips. "That's where you're wrong, sweetheart." I yelp when his hands cup my ass in my pajama shorts to lift me out of the chair. Cold marble digs into my thighs, widening on this counter for the second time in twenty-four hours.

Déjà vu clearly isn't just a Beyoncé song.

He tips my chin and leans in, suffocating me with cedar and sandalwood in the best way. He eyes my nipples flashing an SOS through the silk material of my sleep shirt, craving for his mouth and attention. "I can't penetrate you for a year, but that doesn't mean we can't play." I shudder at the press of his lips to my neck. "We got creative last night, and there are many more ways to get your body to sing for me." His nose skates down my buttoned top to a peak. He circles it and follows up with his tongue.

I arch into his mouth when he tugs. "Julian."

"Say my name, baby."

The pressure of his chest pushes me back to the counter. My legs wrap around him on instinct, pulling out a deep exhale. "El?" He kisses the middle of my chest and moves south.

"Mmm?"

Lower he goes. "You know something else about me?"

"Yes?" The question comes out in a pant as his mouth hovers over my vagina.

I don't care if he tells me he shaves his dick hair on Saturdays or brushes his teeth with charcoal. The heat building between my legs is ready to explode.

My hips rock on their own. He chuckles, plants a close-mouthed kiss on top of my mound, and meets my eyes. "I don't have a problem with self-control." He stands with the biggest grin and pats my leg. "Any other questions I can answer, sweetheart?"

I.

Know.

He.

Didn't.

"Julian!"

He side steps a kick to the shin with a laugh. "You make it seem like I have to fuck everything in sight."

"So you're saying you'll wait until next year?"

All traces of sarcasm leave his features. "However long it takes. You're worth the wait."

Well, damn.

I raise up to my elbows and groan. "I might need to take care of myself later."

He grabs a piece of turkey bacon off his plate. "Can I watch again? Apparently, I'm good with guided meditation."

And, he's back.

Chapter 28

Ella

"You're here!" Amy breezes through the hall with a giant cardboard box and a grin just as big. A crowd of adults part, glancing at the next school project in her hands.

I pull a smile in place and dip my head for privacy from the curiosity she incited. But whatever questions might have been forming at the rare sighting of Charles's ex die under LED lighting. Amy moves with a determination to reach me like she won't see me at the next major school event.

"How have you been?" She shifts the box in her hands to brush the hair out of her face.

"Good. How was your summer?"

"Oh, you know! Camps and planning fall activities." The cheer in her voice dwindles to a level that no longer matches the tangerine radiating from her sundress. "It's good to see you. I'm glad you're here."

"It is back to school night."

Jackson's school always hosts the event during the first week. There are activities to say goodbye to summer and volunteers to watch the kids while the grown-ups have private conversations with teachers about the upcoming year. Ms. Rindheart took in the news of our family transition with warmth and the promise to maintain communication should school resources for socio-emotional support be necessary. Jackson doesn't jump to voice his feelings like Haile does. He's my quiet boy with a big heart, and I want him to feel supported and be able to express his thoughts.

Louise is a true gift. Rose's partner is a retired mental health counselor who worked with kids his age in DC public schools, and she is still certified to meet with families. We meet weekly on Fridays at Bright Spot so Haile and Jackson can have a safe space to talk about their feelings as we navigate our new normal.

It's not the easiest to grab my son from Virginia now that school started back up, but I would walk through traffic on the beltway to ensure my babies have what they need to thrive. The sibling duo is currently immersed in an ice cream social on the back lawn at the a mini carnival the mastermind in front of me planned.

"You really outdid yourself, Amy," I say. "This is a wonderful event."

She shoos away the compliment and smiles. "Thanks! We're wrapping up soon and are heading to Cara's for wine. You should come."

"I'm sure she has to get back to her side of the beltway."

Tiffany Hearst doesn't need a general election to win Queen B status—emphasis on the *B*. She wears it with pride and ice in her pale blue eyes.

Her nude pumps scrape across the floor until she's a foot away. I straighten my black framed glasses with my thumb and middle finger. The latter pops up first.

Every mean-girl school mom gives me the stink eye for breathing. And that was before I left my ex, back when I tried to play nice and they wondered what Charles ever saw in me, why I was ever granted access to their kingdom. It's one of the reasons I *do* stay on my side of the beltway.

"We should go if we don't want to be late," she says to Amy. Her eyes cut back to me, unable to hide the stench of her attitude.

"Don't let me keep you. I have plans myself." I look at my watch. "You should get going, Tiff, before someone conjures you up to star in their next nightmare."

Queen B spins on her heel with a *harrumph* and leaves her so-called friend behind, along with a layer of perfume that sears our nostrils. Amy might swing from ceilings, but her allegiance to Tiffany is why there's distance between us. Life is hard enough without looking over your shoulder to make sure someone in your corner isn't about to stab you.

Amy's pleading eyes lift to mine. "Talk to you later," I say. I'm not mad. It is what it is.

I also do have somewhere to be.

"Date night?" Katharine all but choked on her tea when I told her I was on my way to a date with myself. She had a million questions but held them in with a softness in her features for the woman before her reclaiming Friday nights.

A standing appointment at the end of every week is now on the color-coded calendar keeping my life in order. Uninterrupted me time while my kids are away for the weekend.

Summer was a shuffle between Jackson's camp and the one we ran at Bright Spot, along with our regular programming. Now that school is back in session, a full-time job has been an adjustment, but we're handling our business.

Today couldn't come soon enough, though.

The twenty-minute ride back to DC through the musk of humid air whipping my curls led me to a red brick building with a black awning on a street away from the thriving congestion of George-town nightlife. Every week, I choose a restaurant at random to try new dishes with a cocktail.

The verdict is in: I've fallen in love with a savory noodle soup.

Swigs is not what I expected. The dive bar setting had me skeptical at first, but the Filipino dishes are award-winning. Morgan and I have seen and tasted our fair share of gentrified cuisine—like the time we got generic pork rinds out a bag masquerading as *chicharrónes*.

Cooking might not be my ministry, but the tongue doesn't lie. My taste buds have shimmied since the first bite of an empanada I didn't expect to see on the menu. Karen better not put raisins in the potato salad, but they work as a filling alongside peas, ground meat, potatoes, and veggies.

Warm broth softens beef over noodles and slices of hard-boiled egg. Garlic and ginger blend with cinnamon notes, tempting me to slurp down the bowl and lick it clean.

"Room for dessert?" Tala, the server, drops a billfold into the black apron over her jeans.

My eyes are bigger than my stomach, but that's why the person who invented drawstring shorts has a special place in heaven. "As a matter of fact, yes. The banana cue, please."

Her eyes beam with the promise of caramelized goodness. "It's my favorite."

I smile and pass the menu I kept by my side all evening. "Then I have to try it."

Eating out by myself took time, but it got easier. I no longer hide behind my phone to distract from the fact that I'm out alone. Sometimes I bring a book. On other nights, I get lost in live music and people-watching.

Free time is a luxury I'm still acquainting myself with, and it doesn't require people to fill it now that I'm single. If I want company, I'll call up the girls, but I'm comfortable enjoying my own presence without buffers.

My phone buzzes with a text. Speaking of friends.

Morgan

> Girl, your little stunt with the mom exec is the talk of the town. Did you at least record it so I can watch Tiffany lose her shit in slo-mo?

Tonight, I reaffirmed boundaries to shed the weight of things that no longer serve me. My departure from school volunteer duties left the parent-teacher group aghast. Not one person cares about my well-being, only about the gossip they share and mold in their hands. My separation is still an official agenda item, with questions about why I left, how I can afford to live in DC, and whether I'm screwing up my children's lives—as if Charles screwing another woman didn't take first place for that.

The space my divorce is creating widened the gap between the image I felt obligated to maintain and people not worth pleasing. Amy and I still keep in touch, but with the first week of school officially done, she'll fill her days planning activities for the remainder of the year with people who talk behind my back while praising my organizing talents to my face.

It felt good to say no and even better to leave them in my rearview mirror for a date with a bistro table facing a black brick wall, amazing food, good ambiance, and myself.

> I didn't, but remember when Jody Sawyer turned down that uptight ballet company in Center Stage? Imagine that.

Morgan

> A queen remains undefeated. Enjoy your date night. Miss you.

> Miss you too.

"Banana cue and a mango mojito." Tala sets down a plate of skewered sweet plantains fried to perfection in a caramelized drizzle and a drink that tempts me to run away to the tropics.

My brows pinch. "I didn't order that."

"The guy at the bar did." She smiles and nods behind us.

I follow her gaze to a man with broad shoulders in a striped lapel neck shirt over khaki shorts. Thick lips curve into a relaxed grin.

Julian.

Our eyes meet with the same magnetic pull as when he walked through the kitchen door a few days ago. He texted to ask if it was okay since Jackson and Haile were with me, and they couldn't reach him fast enough with grins that stretched across their tiny faces. The tenderness he displayed for my children had me fighting to hold back tears. Until his dark lashes lifted from my entire world to me and sucked the air from the room. My skin prickled at his touch when he gathered me into his arms and whispered my name into my hair.

Julian spent most of the summer in London. He wanted to come back in July but had to finish work for a client.

"Um, you two know each other?" Tala's attention shifts between us.

My lips wrap around the paper straw for a pull of my favorite summer drink—another detail Julian locked away in his memory. I smile. "Something like that."

I never told Julian I was coming here tonight. Yet, here we are.

He shakes his head and mouths, *Date night*, to keep me from joining him at the bar.

I roll my eyes and reach for my phone.

What are you doing here? Also, thanks for the mojito.

He looks over his shoulder and reaches for his phone. Pursed lips and quick fingers respond.

Julian

Anytime, sweetheart. Here to grab a drink and catch up with my friend. He owns the

> bar. Put your phone away and get back to your date night.

Laughter bubbles through me. He picks the one day I dine alone to visit a friend and look all fine? "I didn't want to see you, anyway," I mumble to myself and swivel back to give these plantains my full attention.

Cue another shimmy. Between the mojito and this dessert, I'm soaring above the clouds with no plans to come down.

My phone dings again.

Julian

> You're cute when food turns you on.

> Uh-uh. You don't get to butter me up and ignore me. Tell your friend I said hi and the food is delicious.

I shoot Julian a quick smirk and focus on the dish that's about to send me to bed early.

Swigs.

Julian mentioned it in passing, but I didn't know this was the place his friend owned. I've never met him, or any of Julian's friends, but if Nate is anything like the meals coming out of his kitchen, he's top-tier in my book.

A deep chuckle pulls my focus back to the bar, where Julian carries a cheeky smile for the bartender, who's telling a story and wearing too many layers for late August. His olive-green cardigan rests over his lean frame as his hands stretch out, pulling a roar of laughter from Julian.

He looks younger than his thirty-one years when he's not nose-deep in the family's business. He's at peace here, away from the public eye and a reputation that never fit a man who prefers keeping a friend company on a Friday night over hitting up one of DC's many hot spots for eligible bachelors.

After another mojito and forty-six pages into my book, I jump at the hand on my shoulder and follow long fingers up to a face that was recently featured in a business magazine. It's now creased into a smile.

"Sorry I startled you," Julian says. "Mind if I join?"

"Done with the silent treatment already?"

He rolls his eyes and takes the seat across from me. Julian isn't a giant, but his muscular frame has to shift to squeeze into the space between the bistro table and chair. The tribal tattoo on his right forearm flexes. "Can't a man respect a lady's wishes? It's Friday. I know the deal."

Julian not only respects my boundaries, he encourages them. He won't call on Friday nights to honor the time I take for myself. I still get texts earlier in the day and one later at night to make sure I'm safe.

"Did it ever occur to you that I might break my date night for the one Friday you've been home in months?"

He leans forward, his bare knees brushing mine under the table. The touch is innocent, but it's enough for my heart to hammer inside my chest. "Did it ever occur to you why I came back?"

The answer rests between us in a haze of cedar and sandalwood. Julian makes no attempt to hide why he came home. It's for me. I know that, and he knows that I know.

"I missed you so much."

My eyes close as he leans closer...and eats the rest of my banana cue.

"Mmm. You don't get this in London." He takes in my glare with a laugh that vibrates the muscles in his chest.

Ass.

"Let me not disturb you."

"How are you after the first week of school?" The question comes over a bite.

I huff out a chuckle. "Ask me tomorrow after I sleep. Thank you for helping with dinner yesterday." It was a late one at Bright Spot. Morgan picked up Jackson when she got Duke from their after-school program. Did I mention how exhilarating it is driving from DC to Virginia and back in rush-hour traffic?

He shrugs. "It was the least I could do." His gaze turns serious. "How else can I help?"

My snort rivals a sneeze. "Have a million I can borrow without paying you back?"

"Want an honest answer?"

I drop my head into my hands and groan. "Be serious." I interrupt him when he starts to tell me he is. "You and Morgan have done more than I could ever express gratitude for or repay in my lifetime. Work hiccups aren't new, but they put it in perspective that I need to figure out my next move sooner rather than later."

"Have you and your ex spoken about Jackson going to school closer to the house since you have them during the week?"

Have we.

Jackson's elementary school is the final thread that ties us to Falls Church, and Charles is holding on for dear life. He's never home early enough to pick up our son, whose school is ten minutes away from his office. But hey, I can drive in from the city to get him. And by his logic, so can Morgan, who makes her own schedule. Jackson is a pawn that lets Charles maintain power.

"It's come up, but I won't push to change his school until I figure out where we'll land. DC is nice, but I'm not sure I can afford it and a charter school for two kids if it comes to it."

Falls Church is beautiful, but when I tell you never is too soon to see another cul-de-sac or sprawling lawn. Moving away created new challenges, but nothing beats the freedom we have away from the microscope that came with being Mrs. Charles Hudson II.

Julian's caress is gentle when his hand strokes my face. "I'm here for you, El. Always am."

I nod into his touch, a safe haven these last few months, which have passed in a blur. He'll never understand how much our friendship picked me up and helped repair the broken pieces of my life. It's now a blank page for me and my children to write our own ending.

"Is this a bad time to say hello?" Nate's glance shifts from me to Julian who blinks out of the trance that makes the rest of the world around us dissolve away.

"Of course. Ella, this is Nate. Nate, this is Ella." I don't miss the inflection in his tone at my name. It's full of care.

Nate strokes his goatee with a smile playing on his lips. "It's nice to meet you, Ella." He withholds "finally," but it's apparent in the way he takes me in. He and Julian are close, which means he knows a hell of a lot more than he's letting on.

"It's nice to meet you too. The place is beautiful." I motion to a mural of doodles that scales up the right side of the wall behind the bar. "Is that handmade?"

His smile broadens. "It is. My daughter, Jasmine, brought her sketches to life. It was a summer project she didn't finish before school started."

"Where does she go to college?"

"She's twelve," Julian says with a smile.

Nate and I share a knowing look, one that tugs on my heart: pride for our children and the accomplishments we have the privilege to witness.

We spend the next hour talking between laughs and Nate helping behind the bar. By nine, it's time for me to turn into a pumpkin. I say my goodbyes and step into the DC summer night, but not before Julian follows me out.

"Let me walk you to your car."

The soft glow of the moon filters through the canopy of trees overhead. Our steps slow to a lazy stroll. My car isn't far from Swigs, and I'm not sure I need a personal escort, but I'm not complaining.

"Did you have fun tonight?" A faint summer breeze carries my question through the rustle of leaves.

The corner of Julian's mouth pulls. "Always do. I spend most nights here when Nate is on."

"Shouldn't a bachelor like you be at the club?"

He tilts his head from side to side. "Clubs are overrated, in my opinion. I go out when I need to but stay in most of the time." His eyes roam my profile. "Did you have a good night?"

It was better with you here.

"Yeah. It was nice to get out."

We stop at the passenger side of my SUV. I lean against the door and look up at the trees with a sigh. It's a beautiful night. "Thank..." My gaze lowers to find him watching me. It catches my breath, but I press out the "you" and clear my throat.

He steps forward and lowers his voice. "The pleasure is mine, sweetheart." The pads of his thumb and forefinger lift up my chin. "Get home safe. I need to help Nate move a few shipments, but I'm right behind you."

"Okay." I swallow hard at the rapid pace of my heart. Another step, and he'll feel it on his chest.

Anyone on the street would assume we're seconds away from a goodnight kiss. It's hard to catch my breath around him, and I have no room to put distance between us.

I dig my fingers into my shorts to suppress the urge to reach over and touch him. To wind my arms around his neck and kiss him with all abandon. He's had his mouth on me, and he's guided me to ecstasy. Never a kiss to unseal the growing fire between us.

With Julian, intensity and intimacy weave together through an electric current that binds us regardless of time or distance. It's an equation I've yet to solve: how the desires I have for this man are foreign but also feel like home.

The air around us charges, jolting my skin with summer heat and unexplored passion.

He breaks us apart and steps back with a subtle headshake. "I, um, should..." He thumbs behind him.

"Yup," I say with a quick nod.

He takes retreating steps and settles his eyes back on me. "Goodnight."

"'Night."

Chapter 29

Julian

One more night like this, and I'm putting in for vacation. The week has been nonstop, chewing away at time to squeeze in a rugby practice or get home to see Ella and the kids before everyone goes to bed. Brooke Law International is expanding, but it doesn't get to take everything from me in the process.

My Audi shuts off with a purr in the garage. I grab my briefcase and close the door, headed for the back steps to the basement, when light from the living room catches my eye. The first floor is always pitch-black past eight o'clock on a school night. Ella is a fun mom, but she runs a tight ship through a routine I've now memorized. She usually turns in after nine thirty, and if there's a chance she's up at ten thirteen, I'm taking it.

I move around the assortment of summer planters to reach the kitchen door. My backyard is full of seasonal perennials and remnants of water toys from a summer of fun I witnessed through photos and video clips. I've never been one to feel like I was missing out, but seeing their laughter from thousands of miles away twisted something inside of me.

Ella Fitzgerald's "Summertime" is a low croon that pulls a smile. Ella and I sometimes listen to my jazz records with a nightcap after the kids go down. The slow drag of percussion instruments with an aged scotch was how I wound down after a long day. Now, I have company—company who happens to be passed out on my couch.

My briefcase hits the ground as I lean against the frame between the kitchen and the living room and take in the sleeping beauty. Ella's chest rises and falls in a steady rhythm. A silk wrap covers her natural curls in a loose bun on top of her head. Her lips part in a tiny snore. She's not big on dressing up, but the knee-length silk gown she's in is a stroke to the dick. I stifle a groan at the sight of her breasts under the fabric and drag my gaze down her soft stomach to her thick hips and the swell of her thighs.

Coming home to this every night would undo a day's worth of stress and unnecessary meetings.

My focus shifts when I step into the room and spot her divorce binder next to a half-full glass of white wine. Scattered around it are catalog clippings from home furnishing stores. I open the binder to the latest entry, a collage of decor and furniture with "Haile" written in her scribbly handwriting.

A folded paper with a series of numbers between the pages falls out. It's a wish list of items she wants for her new home and their estimated costs. Even with Charles's monthly child support, she needs a couple more months to save. She didn't take any furniture with her and has to replenish enough for an entire house on her own.

When I crouch down to brush the back of my hand against her cheek, I smile. The urge to protect and provide for her nuzzles itself deep between my rib cage. Ella doesn't need anyone to save her, but she doesn't need to do the hard parts alone.

My house is hers for as long as she wants. I take a picture of Haile's bedroom collage and text my assistant that I'm working from home tomorrow. Then I drain the wineglass, close her divorce binder, and pick up El, cradling her to my chest.

She stirs at first but settles with a kiss to the forehead. "I got you, sweetheart," I say against her hair as I make my way up to her bedroom.

My grip on her curves feels right. Her and her kids in my home feels right. I push away my desires to be more than the friend she needs and tuck her into bed.

Haile's voice is faint when she calls out. Mine is at a whisper so as not to wake her mother. "Hey, Haile Bear. Your mom fell asleep on the couch."

"Could you read me a story? I can't sleep."

That's new.

Ella is the one who does bath time, helps them brush their teeth, and handles stories at night. It's not my place, and I don't want to add more confusion to the four of us living under the same roof—or cross any lines and have to deal with El in mama-bear mode. That shit is terrifying. Yet, the schedule some might consider mundane becomes intriguing the more time I spend with this family.

I glance at my watch. Almost ten thirty. "I don't think—"

"Please, Julie? A short one."

Well, fuck.

Ella is still asleep. Maybe a quick one. "Okay," I say softly to Haile. "But if I get in trouble, your forehead is touching the wall too."

She giggles and hops out of bed. "Deal."

I meet her at the oversized chair next to a small bookcase and adjust the light from the floor lamp so it's not too bright. Haile hops into my lap with a book. "Here." Her little body nestles into the small space I create, and she waits for me to read *The Year We Learned to Fly*.

She falls asleep halfway through the story, her breathing evening out as she curls into me and wraps her tiny arms around my suit jacket. I sit with her cradled next to me and flip through the book of imagination and a grandmother's wisdom.

Ella and I didn't know each other when she was with her ex, but her children's resilience is a testament to her love. The evidence is in their laughter, the containers of crafts and toys neatly tucked away throughout the house, and the unbreakable bond they've created, one that thrives without the father figure Ella pushes to be present.

"Goodnight, little one." I put Haile in her bed and press a kiss to her hair.

If you'd asked me last year if I could picture myself with a woman with kids, I'd have laughed in your face. Settling down was the furthest thing from my mind. Yet here I am, trying to figure out how to shorten my next stretch in London.

I'm still sorting out what all of this means, but I do know one thing: It's making my life better.

Chapter 30

Ella

"**C**rouch. Bind. Set!"

There's a series of grunts as walls of muscle press their might into each other. The ball goes between them, and the teams shift in a way that mimics a dance—or would if they weren't trying to rip each other's heads off. There's a yell before someone on Julian's team shoots out with the ball, tossing it to another person in a blue and white uniform until the opposing team knocks him to the ground.

"Did he just unalive him?" I flinch in search of the blond who got swallowed whole. "There he is," I say, pointing to the pile further up the field just as Julian takes the ball and runs toward the other team's goal. "He's almost to the end zone. Go, Julie!"

"*Try* zone." Jackson shakes his head. "This isn't football, Mom."

"I knew that."

The side of his mouth lifts. "Yeah, okay."

Jackson watched hours of rugby footage on YouTube to keep up while schooling his mama in the process. He didn't want to miss Julian's first game of the season since he's been back, and he cheers every time he touches the ball.

Haile couldn't care less. She wants Julian to win but shows no interest in the game. She hasn't looked up from her books since she got here, just sits in silence next to Jackson and Duke, who are about to sprint down the sidelines to chase after the man who made me come in the tub during a phone call last week.

Julian wasn't kidding when he said he had self-control. Outside of a forehead kiss, he hasn't touched me since he's been back. He's still a flirt in person, but he doesn't cross the line. But when he's across the pond? All bets are off. The man has a nasty mouth and a filthy imagination.

Wind presses to Julian's uniform with every stride. Heavy thigh muscles lift the tiny white shorts clinging to his skin, which is fine by me. An amazing ass in athletic hoochie shorts gets zero complaints.

Three men from the visiting team rush him on his approach, but they come up short when Julian pulls off a no-look pass to his teammate wearing a number six jersey who slides in for the score. The crowd erupts, but my focus is still on Julian.

The hit was *hard*, but he shakes off the Mack truck collision to ruffle Number Six's man bun. The two share a shoulder check and jog to the middle of the field for the kicker to put more points on the board.

Julian's grin is contagious. This is the most relaxed I've seen him since he came back last week after another month away. Late hours with his father at the office have him home after eleven, but he still video calls Jackson after dinner to practice Japanese every other day. Exhausted eyes reflect on the screen, eyes that refuse to miss a chance to honor his time with my son, which always comes with a ten-minute bonus interlude from Haile about her day. Our time together, though separated by distance, has pulled us closer.

I broke down in his arms on Labor Day weekend over what he did for Haile. In one day, he brought her vision board to life, swapping out his home office for a bedroom she can call her own. Wisteria walls and new furniture to match her bed took over, with a light taupe sofa bed for my mom to use whenever she's able to make the trip down. The act was so selfless it caught me off guard—to the point I was ready to offer him my ass on a silver platter with a side of titties as an appetizer. It was a good thing he went back to London that Saturday. It's hard enough as it is to deny the man my kids adore. The man *I* adore.

I've learned there are three sides to DC's most eligible bachelor. The first is his public persona, the one he dresses in custom suits. That Julian is confident and all about the company brand. The second Julian is laid-back and free from the demands of the family empire. He's a brother, an uncle, and a friend whose loyalty knows no bounds. That Julian enjoys life to the fullest.

Then there's the Julian who's reserved for me. The one who watches rom-coms and teaches me about jazz. The guy who orders tacos for the house on Tuesdays because of the tough commute from my job to Jackson. A man whose face lights up when I order the savory chicken tikka masala from his favorite restaurant on the nights in the office when he forgets to eat.

In the space we've created for each other, he's free from external expectations and the internal need to fulfill them.

"What'd I miss?" Erica shuffles in from behind and kicks off her flats to join me on the quilt. She scans our makeshift VIP section. "Who the hell plans a romantic picnic at a rugby game? Is artisan bread and fancy jam really necessary?"

We share a look and break into laughter.

Morgan.

Who needs ten-dollar folding chairs when your best friend outfits a portion of the field with imported textiles, farm-to-table goodies, and homemade peach tea served in the reusable plastics flutes she just happened to have lying around her kitchen?

Erica sits cross-legged in her jeans and reaches for the container of assorted olives. "Where is Martha Stewart anyway?"

I lift a shoulder. "Haven't seen her in almost an hour. She missed most of the game."

"I saw her car on the way in," Erica says between bites of Manchego cheese. Here all of thirty seconds and already has a buffet in front of her. "Wait, here she comes."

Autumn winds kick up colorful foliage, splattering the grass in crimson and gold. Afternoon clouds crowd the cerulean sky, drowning out the stroke of warmth from the October sun. I pull the edges of my sweater over my cotton overalls at Morgan's approach.

Her mouth twists into a sneer that tightens the vein pulsing in her forehead. To any onlooker, Morgan is a runway model at a rugby game, wearing high fashion and the season's trendiest riding boots. She tries to mask the storm clouds brewing behind her eyes, but her Chanel shades aren't enough to hide her ice cold expression.

Morgan stepped away to give Joseph directions to the field. Nothing out of the ordinary, except the pain etched into his face speaks volumes about whatever conversation they had when he got there. One that clearly did not go well.

Erica opens her mouth but snaps it shut at Morgan's smile, which is tight enough to crack a tooth. She clears her throat. "I saw a food truck that has caramel popcorn. "I'll, um…yeah." With a final glance, she leaves, gripping a Caprese sandwich in one hand and a fistful of nuts in the other.

My eyes dart between Morgan and Joseph, who hasn't taken his off his ex-wife. I dip a brow at her. *He fucked up?*

Her arms fold over her off-the-shoulder sweater. *Yup.*

I tilt my head. *What he do?*

She sucks her teeth and looks away. *Girl, I can't.*

That bad, huh?

Our eyes drift back to the artist, wearing long sleeves and ripped jeans, who shakes out his hands. Joseph Catlett is a man of few words, but his silence alludes to the magnitude of whatever just happened between him and Morgan.

He clears his throat and says, "I don't have to go," low enough for only us to hear. It's directed at Morgan, but what kind of friend would I be if I didn't eavesdrop? They *are* right in front of me.

Morgan's stare is distant, trained on the steady ripples of the Potomac River and not Joseph's sidelong glances. She closes her eyes against the flood of golden rays breaking through the clouds and takes a deep inhale of the grassy field littered with damp leaves. "No." Her focus shifts down to her hands until she musters the strength to face him. "Go. Duke is fine with me this weekend. Enjoy your trip...with Sky."

Oh shit.

In the three years I've known her, Morgan hasn't dated or seen another man since her divorce. This is the first time a woman has come up, which begs the question of whether Sky is the first or the one who's serious enough to tell Morgan about. A weekend trip away signals more than just a friend.

"Morgan—"

"Just go." Her voice is slack. Tears well, and she looks away. "I'll bring Duke to you after school on Monday."

Joseph reaches for Morgan when she walks away, but he lets his hand fall. The contradicting instincts to console her and respect her boundaries play out in his gaze, which is tracking her down the sideline. He rubs the back of his neck. "I'm gonna head out."

My heart squeezes at his dejected tone. These two still love each other, that much is clear, but they never mended whatever broke between them. Sky might be Joseph's current interest, but the hooded brown eyes on his ex-wife cause him a world of pain.

"Do me a favor, El," he says, his attention on Morgan's back. Glassy eyes trail to mine. "Take care of her." *For me.* At my nod, Joseph heads to Duke and picks him up for a long hug. Then he high-fives Jackson and drops to his haunches, never letting go of his son.

"Hey." I jump at Julian's voice and clutch my chest. He raises his hands and laughs. "You alright?"

The weightlessness of his tone pulls a grin to my mouth, one that matches his. A brow lifts. "Did you win, or are you normally this cheerful after a game?"

His laughter is melodic. "Yes to the former." His eyes crinkle. "I'm happy you came." He scans the field. "Where's your ex?"

"Extended his work trip after I asked to keep the kids until today. I'll drop them off at his mother's after this."

"A work trip?" We share a look.

"He never cared about breaking the no-penetration rule with other women during our marriage." I shrug. "Why start now?"

Julian steps closer and lowers his voice. "Does that mean you're up for a few rounds of poke and play?" His fingers dance across the knotted belt at my waist and tug me closer. "For a game night?"

"Game night? Bro, you back to those?" The man bun in the number six jersey scratches at his broad chest and stands between us. "Please tell me it's tonight."

"What's tonight?" Another teammate appears next to Julian. Brown eyes examine me under slightly raised thick brows. He leans forward to extend a hand. "I'm Viru, by the way."

"Ella."

"Nice to meet you," he says with a slow smile.

Man bun's eyes ping-pong between Julian and me like he's solved a murder mystery. "You're Ella? You're the friend? The—"

"Antonio." The clip in Julian's tone leaves no room for discussion.

"My apologies." He exchanges a look with the man whose hand is now at the small of my back. *Possessive much?* "Heard a lot about you. It's good to put a face with a name." He studies the curves of my hips and smirks at Julian. "What a beauty you are, *Ella*."

Julian shoves him away. "Enough. Go out if you want. I'm good."

"El, we're going out," Morgan says in a huff. She takes in the half-circle of rugby players. Antonio is a few inches taller than Julian and has a bulkier frame. Viru, whose quiet appraisal of my relationship with his teammate plays out in his gaze, is smaller but not lacking in muscles. If thick thighs save lives, consider these three my life insurance.

Morgan fidgets and touches her forehead. "Sorry to interrupt." She turns to me and leans in. "I really need to go out tonight."

I drop my face to hers and whisper. "They can still hear you. I'm down, though."

She grimaces and swallows against the flush creeping up her neck. "Why don't we meet at my place around five?" I say. "We'll eat dinner, go to the bar for drinks, and you can flirt your ass off with whoever you deem worthy."

"That'll work." She hooks a thumb behind her. "Let me get this one to my parents'. Thank you," she says with a sad smile.

I squeeze her hand. "We got you."

At her exit, Antonio moves to get a better view and damn near twists his neck. "You know, if Morgan needs attention, she doesn't need to go out. I volunteer as tribute."

Julian's slap lands on the back of his head with a *thwap*. "That's my sister."

He tilts his head, his eyes still on the woman scorned who's about to bring DC to its knees. "And I could be your brother-in-law."

Viru's hands land on Antonio's shoulders. "We should go before you end up in the Potomac."

Antonio pouts. "Ella, when will we see each other again?"

"Weren't you just trying to pick up my friend?"

He raises a lazy shoulder. "Can't blame a man for trying. Why don't we make tonight a group event?" He dodges the punch Julian throws with a laugh and jogs backward. "My boys with your girls. Pick the place, and we'll be there."

"You're on, Man Bun!"

Viru lifts a hand and trots off with Antonio, leaving me with a pinched-lipped Julian. He shoves his hands under his armpits and clenches his jaw, pissed off at the world.

It's cute, the overprotective brother part, but Julian is far from cute. The man is fine at the most disrespectful level. Muscles in his wide biceps flex against his chest.

I pinch his cheek. "What's wrong, Julie? Can't handle a night out with two single moms on the loose?" The teasing smile tugging at my lips fades at the first swipe of his tongue over my finger. "Julian." My body shudders under the brief connection.

Four months. Four long months since he commanded my orgasm on top of the kitchen counter. Heat from his touch strokes the tip of my finger and works its way down through my nipples to my toes.

We've been so careful not to cross any lines that would require legal counsel and thousands of dollars inside a courtroom. Yet here I am, about to come, feet away from my children and on the side of a field for everyone to see.

He tightens his grip on my hand when I try to step away. I wet my lips. "Julian, please." It's a plead through a hard swallow.

His groan is low in his throat. "I like my name on your lips. Look at me, Ella."

I suck in a breath at the tightness in my stomach and peel my gaze off the thighs that are taunting me in small rugby shorts. Quick glances across the field show the world as it should be. Haile and Jackson dash with Duke and the other players' kids. Erica squeals at her phone next to another woman, the source of their laughter likely inappropriate for a Saturday afternoon. Even Morgan is all smiles, with Antonio staring her down with a look that would make Julian lose his shit if he wasn't staring at me.

"Tonight. Give us tonight."

The thread between us pulls, unraveling what little resolve I have left. "We can't. People—"

"I don't give a fuck about people." He steps so close I have to put a hand on his chest. "Let me have you. Please."

No one, not even Charles, has wanted me with such longing. It's like he physically aches.

"My separation. I can't have sex." The words are small, a reminder that this distance from my ex is a temporary freedom. Not permanent liberation.

He presses a hand to my cheek. "Do you trust me, sweetheart?"

Without question.

"Yes."

His exhale is deep and comes with a single nod. "Tonight. No penetration." He cuts off my question. "Trust me to take care of you, okay?"

"Okay."

"I'll text you a place. Meet us there at seven."

I frown. "Why don't we all ride together?"

"Because." He takes a step back. "If I get you alone before I calm my dick down, I'm penetrating you on every surface of our house."

Our house.

My vagina roars to life. Don't tempt me with a good time.

He winks and turns just as Duke pummels him, with my kids hot on his heels. Julian falls back and barks out a laugh. Corded forearm muscles flex as he wraps his nephew and Jackson and Haile in a hug.

In a different life, I would run head-first into the arms he extends to me and my kids. A supportive partner by my side who pursues me relentlessly.

I have that with Julian. A trust molded in adoration taking up residence in my life.

He's everything worth fighting for—and the very thing to derail my divorce if I get too careless. I'm so close yet so far, which is why we can only have tonight.

Chapter 31

Ella

"Question."

"Yes, loading up on carbs after contorting ourselves into tiny dresses is dumb but delicious." Fresh mozzarella blends with meat and homemade sauce on my fork. It's Julian's lasagna recipe, one of many we've practiced together over video calls.

Morgan and I got dressed to go out in record speed. Peeling ourselves away from the counter will be a different story.

"Did you rob a craft store?" White leaves dangle between Morgan's fingertips. Her brows pinch. "What is this?"

As if it's not obvious.

"Ghost leaves, duh." I flip over the hand-painted foliage to reveal three dots, two for the eyes and one for the nose.

She takes in the runner of leaves and mini pumpkins on the marble island, the faux sunflower bushels around the kitchen. "We decorated a little for fall."

She zeroes in on the leaf art in a kaleidoscope of autumn hues on the once bare cabinets. "I can see that."

Our house is the official destination for the season, complete with construction-paper apple place cards on the dining table we never use, paper-plate animals, suncatchers, and swag we picked up from the latest trip to the pumpkin patch. We went three times this month and spent two hours each visit taking tractor rides, solving corn maze puzzles, and launching pumpkins into the sky.

Charles would rather pass a kidney stone than compliment any decoration we dared to put up in the house. It was a battle to get a *fake* Christmas tree in November, much less hang more than two of Jackson and Haile's creations on the refrigerator.

So, yeah, we overdid it on the crafts.

"Julian didn't lose it when he saw all of this?" She motions around the first floor, which looks like a tornado of pinecones blew through and brought every leaf in the metropolitan area with it.

My lips twitch above my wineglass. "Who do you think picked out the hay on the front steps?"

I was on my tippy-toes in the living room with another home-made leaf garland when firm hands wrapped around my middle and pulled me off the step stool. Julian encased me with his cedar and sandalwood scent to the soundtrack of a Brian Settles record I found on the shelf. We swayed in low lighting while Jackson and Haile slept. I was nervous that our overindulgence in crafts would trigger his inner neat freak when he came home from London last week, but he pressed his lips to my hair and whispered, "I missed you."

Julian appreciates order, but he doesn't treat his home like a showroom.

"He left early last Wednesday to join us at the farm," I say to my friend's cartoon eyes. "We had our fill of apple cider donuts and pumpkin painting." Our creations are in the backyard next to the makeshift scarecrow Julian built with Jackson while they practiced Japanese.

Morgan chokes on her lasagna. "*My brother*, the neat freak?"

I nod.

"Did you drug him?"

"No!" I laugh.

The decision to tell Morgan about me and Julian weighs heavy. I've wanted to, but he and I haven't defined *what* we're doing. Would she be upset if we became more than friends? Am I ready to be more?"

Getting a divorce and falling for my best friend's brother wasn't on my vision board this year. Did I second-guess responding to his calls and texts while he was away? Of course. But I couldn't come up with an excuse to shut out the man who has been nothing but kind and attentive to my needs.

To my children's needs.

"You're good for him."

Now I'm the one who chokes. "What?"

"He's happier." Morgan eyes me. "Julian. He's less stressed than I've seen him in a long time." She cuts into her lasagna. "You look happier too, El."

Where is she going with this?

It takes work to push down my grin, but I do. "I am."

My smile is no longer forced, to keep up appearances for the kids. It's one I wear daily in gratitude of the life I'm building with my babies and the people who fill it with joy.

"How are you holding up?"

"Better than expected. Haile and Jackson are doing great. My job is amazing, and I—" A tear falls. Morgan reaches for my hand. "He didn't break me."

"Look at us," Morgan says through sniffles. "Divorced moms crying before we go out. I mean, really." She dabs her eyes with a napkin.

"At least we look good." Our glasses clink.

"About today." I take a sip. There's no way to dance around the topic. "Are you okay...with Joseph?"

Her body stiffens at his name. She lifts her glass to her lips, but not before I catch the tremble in her chin. "We couldn't get it right." Her shoulder lifts. "Sky is an artist. She's good for him."

Silence tugs itself into place with unspoken self-doubt and regret. I'd endure another five months in divorce limbo if it meant I could ease the pain in her eyes. Staying in a relationship with the wrong person is a walking hemorrhoid, but losing time with the one you love is an ache that time doesn't always heal.

"Do you want to stay in?"

"And order wings and watch *Living Single* reruns again? No. We're going out." Morgan's red bottoms hit the floor with a *clack*.

Never mind then.

She thrusts a finger in my face. Okay, this is serious. Note to self: remember to schedule a manicure.

"Let's dance, drink, and cut up. We have no kids tonight, and I don't want to think about my ex railing an abstract painter."

I reach for the dishes and rinse them off in the sink as Morgan continues her monologue. I add in the occasional "That's right" in solidarity. There's no bringing her down when she's this worked up.

That's a lie. Alcohol does wonders.

A loaded dishwasher and two whiskey shots later, we call up a car and are out the door with no mom duties or fucks to give.

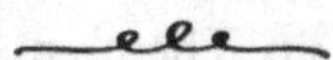

"Are we at the right spot?"

Music flows through ebony speakers against lacquered walls in the same hue. Clusters of people in hushed conversations gather in front of a mahogany bar under industrial pendant lamps on a pulley.

I double-check my phone to the steady beat of jazz fusion and nod. "This is the place."

Julian and his teammates aren't among the silhouettes of collared dress shirts and slacks. He and his crew have enough muscles for a *Magic Mike* cabaret, and then some.

Morgan checks her champagne-colored watch, which matches the metallic silk draped over her body. "It's seven. Want to get a drink at the bar?"

"I didn't put this dress on for nothing."

It takes a special occasion or a dare to get me in a skirt. Both are true tonight, as I'm out celebrating my best friend not thinking about her ex. Morgan dared me to slip on a few pieces of fabric, hence the black asymmetrical dress gripping my ass and keeping my mom pouch in place.

Panty-free, might I add.

Our strappy heels click across the wood floor. At the corner of the bar, two men approach.

"Who do we have here?" Thin lips curve to reveal pointy teeth. Beady green eyes move up my thighs to study my face. "I'm Edwin."

Tonight isn't going to end well for Edwin—at least, not with me. He's not unattractive, though his bushy eyebrows could use a wax. Still, I've seen his type before.

Clean-shaven.

Ash-blond hair slicked back.

Navy blue tie flopped over his shoulder.

White shirt rolled to his elbows.

"Hi, Edwin. Which brokerage do you work for?"

He stops mid-chew of the chicken wing brushing his lips. "Have we met?" I might be out of touch with dating, but hitting on someone while snacking is a bold choice.

"No. You're wearing the uniform of someone who deals with Wall Street or Capitol Hill." It could also be a completely different industry, but my guess is one of the two.

His eyes narrow at my assumption. "I'm an investment advisor." The tone is cautious, questioning whether he's that easy to read or I'm psychic.

Years with Charles made it easy to spot people in finance. My radar about his faithfulness was shit, but I'd win a game show about who speaks mutual funds and 401(k)s.

I glance over at Morgan who's lost in conversation with Edwin's friend. He's a brunette with a broad frame tucked under a gray

Mister Rogers sweater. It's a questionable choice for a Saturday night in the city. He gives Henry Cavill vibes, with blue eyes of steel and a strong jawline.

Their stares say they want to do something other than talk.

"So, what's your name?"

My attention shifts back to Edwin, who's now inches from dropping a wing on my dress. The music isn't that loud, and he doesn't need to acquaint himself with my shadow. My lips part to tell him I'm waiting for someone, but then Julian says, "Taken."

Edwin whips around and comes face to face with a thick chest under a fitted button-down, a chest I've had the pleasure of seeing bare on more than one occasion. He eyes me for confirmation, but I can't take mine off of Julian and the neatly trimmed goatee outlining his smile.

Julian steps closer once Edwin and his chicken wings leave. "Sorry I'm late." He presses his lips to the back of my hand. "Cell reception gets dicey in the back room, but it's set up now." His eyes slip from my mouth to the outline of my breasts and down my crossed legs. "You're gorgeous, sweetheart."

My cheeks heat. "Your sister is right next to me," I say in a whisper loud enough for him to hear.

"Is it a crime to tell a friend she's beautiful?"

"Maybe, when you're staring at me like you want to fuck me."

"I do want to fuck you."

"*Julian!*"

His lips twitch. "Fair enough." He extends a hand to help me off the stool. It finds a home just above my ass and pulls me close in front of him. "Are you wearing panties?"

"You tell me." I wiggle my cheeks and laugh at his groan. That is, until the bulge poking my butt hardens.

I shiver at his breath to my neck. "Don't play games you can't win, sweetheart." With a quick peck, he adjusts himself and calls over to his sister, who's still talking to Sweater Guy. "Hey, Mac, you coming?"

She peers around the torso blocking her from our view. "Can Eric come?"

Julian sighs but gives in. "If he checks his phone with security."

At that, Julian takes my hand and guides us through the small crowd to a black door between two bookcases. It looks painted, but to my surprise it opens to a hulk-sized bouncer who's all muscles and no neck. With a quick dip of his head to Julian, he steps aside, and we enter a private room the length of the lounge we just left. Tufted leather booths outline the perimeter of a dance floor that half a dozen of his teammates and some women are putting to use.

"Hold up!" Erica tries to pass but gets stonewalled. "Listen here, Dave Bautista, I'm with them." She points at us.

"She's good, Joe," Julian says over the arm wrapped around my shoulder.

Joe steps aside with a grunt and lets Erica pass. She gives him a playful elbow to his black muscle tee and a booty graze that hits its target. "I'll see you later. I like 'em big." The sequins in her sapphire dress catch the light and the bald bouncer's attention, which instantly shifts to her ass.

Bangs and a high ponytail sway toward us. "You are *wearing* this dress! Doesn't she look amazing, Julian?"

He doesn't miss a beat, nor the chance to rake his eyes down my body for the second time tonight. I arch toward him when his thumb draws circles on my back and bite my lip to keep the color out of my cheeks. "That she does."

"Ella!" In jeans and a white polo, Antonio walks over with open arms and a grin that deflates when Julian steps between us. "What, I can't say hi now?"

"You're fine from there," Julian says.

He scoffs. "You see how he treats me, Ella Bella? Some childhood friend." Erica's dress catches his eye and pulls him toward her with heart eyes and his tongue hanging out of his mouth. "Naomi Campbell."

"'Erica' is fine."

"Yes, you are." His eyes stall on the tops of her thighs.

The tip of her silver nail lifts his chin. "How old are you?"

"However old you need me to be." He shudders under her gaze and says, "Twenty-six."

Erica's face splits into a wide grin. "This will be fun."

She sashays over to a small bar, leaving Antonio in a pool of drool. Without another word, he spins on his heel and practically sprints to join Erica next to a group of women. One in particular stares at Julian, who turns to face me.

"Friends of yours?"

She's a knockout, with long black hair, sharp cheekbones, and almond eyes. She looks like she never misses a day at the gym.

Julian's nod is brief. "She's on the women's rugby team. Antonio ran his mouth and invited everyone at the drink-up."

That explains the toned Tinker Bell shape. She hasn't taken her eyes off Julian and casts us another curious glance.

"I take it you two have history?"

The muscles in his jaw flex. "We hooked up last year. It was a one-time thing that meant nothing."

"You sure about that? She hasn't stopped tracing your shadow since you walked in." If Julian is as good with his dick as he is with his hands and mouth, I can't say I blame her.

I lift a hand when he rushes to speak. "I'm not judging, and you don't owe me an explanation." I dip my chin at her. "But maybe you two should talk. It's clear she still has feelings."

Julian spends so much time with me and the kids, I forget about his playboy label until it taps me on the shoulder. First it was whispers about company during his birthday. Now a rugby player. An international roster isn't far-fetched, but it doesn't match the man I know. Plus, his work schedule keeps him wiped to rotate lovers.

We never discussed exclusivity. How can we when I'm technically still married? No sex for a year would be hard on anyone. Well, maybe not a nun. Julian's past hints at a man who kept active between women's legs, and I'm not sure he can wait that long. Would it be fair to ask him to try?

He's young, unattached, and has options.

"I'm going to find Morgan. Talk to her." I give his arm a squeeze and set off in search of my friend.

Chapter 32

Julian

Tonight, I'd planned to lay my cards on the table. I wanted to talk to Ella about us and working toward whatever kind of relationship she's comfortable with, one that doesn't jeopardize her or the kids' well-being. Another five months don't need to pass for me to be sure of what I already know—what I've known since the day we landed in bed together.

I want her and only her.

It's been years since I committed myself to one person, and back then it was someone I thought I'd spend the rest of my life with out of duty to my family. Ella is different. I yearn for her, whether I'm thousands of miles away or stuck in meetings downtown. She's not just a bright spot in my life; she's become my source of my peace and joy. My love.

I'll admit the connection was damn near instant, which gave me pause. I've been physically attracted to women before, but not like this.

Ella, Jackson, and Haile are part of the future I'm writing, the one I want to live for me. At least, that's my hope, but all of that could go to shit if she doesn't take a chance on me because of my reputation.

She's cautious, and rightfully so. Last time she trusted a man she loved it blew up in her face in one of the worst ways imaginable. In a twisted way, it brought us together, and it intertwined our lives in ways I never expected or knew possible.

I want more, without an ocean between us, and I intended to tell her once we got home.

That was the plan. I didn't want to have the conversation here, in the private room of a lounge, surrounded by my team, the women they brought, and a reminder of the past I've been dodging. If there's one ounce of suspicion that I'll put El through the same shit her ex did, she won't jump, and I need her to know I'll catch her.

The swish of her hips moves her ass from side to side as she glides across the wood floor. The little black dress she's wearing dips in the back, held up by two thin strips I want removed. Preferably with my teeth.

She looks exquisite tonight—that wasn't a lie. My dick has been standing at half-mast since that guy with the wings fucked off and she circled the ass I can't take my eyes off of over my erection. I can't have her the way I want, but that won't stop us from discovering new loopholes to the no-penetration rule.

"Julian."

Kierra's voice registers, but my focus is still on Ella, who's laughing next to Morgan and a guy I need to ask my sister about later. Her private life is her business, but she can't be reckless trying to get over Joseph who obviously isn't over her.

"Julian."

"Hey." I keep my expression indifferent but soften when I see Kierra's disappointment.

Her gaze darts over my shoulder. Kierra isn't mean-spirited, but it's clear she's sizing Ella up. "I haven't seen much of you since you came back. Are you here for good?"

"Working on it."

She nods. "Maybe we can catch up." Her eyes flicker to Ella. "When you aren't busy."

"Kee," I say with a sigh. "That's not necessary. I'd like for us to be friendly when we see each other in passing, but I'm with someone."

"Yeah, okay." She squares her shoulders and takes an abrupt step back.

I reach the other end of the circular bar to order a scotch, and I catch Antonio tracking Kierra and her friends, who are heading for the door. "You should go after her." I nod her way, but when I follow his gaze, it clicks. His focus is on someone else. "Miriam?" The name of a woman who's his exact opposite wedges in my throat.

"She doesn't want me." He glances sideways before his eyes land back on Kierra's best friend, who's in textured black leggings and a loose blouse. She adjusts her wide-rimmed glasses and giggles at something her friend said, shaking her long black curls.

Antonio has never been hard up for women, but the way his eyes cling to Miriam suggests something different than a casual hookup. There's a quiet calculation, like he's counting the steps between them and might leap off his barstool at any minute. His chin lowers at her departure, bringing his attention back to the bar with a low sigh.

I take a sip of my scotch. "Do I have to watch you sulk at this party I didn't ask for all night?"

"It's about time you showed your face. You never go out anymore. Aren't you tired of playing house yet?"

"Who says I'm playing?"

His eyes grow three sizes. "What happened to the in-house sex situation? I thought it was just a casual thing, not that you'd become a stepdad to her kids."

I cut my eyes at him, silently telling him to knock it off. Whatever crawled up his ass and pissed him off is not a license to act reckless with his words. "It was never casual," I say with emphasis. "If you knew half of the shit Ella went through, you'd watch your mouth. The truth is, I got tired. All of this"—I wave a hand around the room—"got tired fast."

I took a break from the nightlife when I left for London last year because I'm sick of being the center of attention. Who I'm dating. Who I slept with. I didn't expect to come back and fall for my sister's best friend, but the more we got to know each other, the more I wanted to be around her and her kids.

We turn our heads toward the laughter from across the room at the start of "O.P.P.," and I do a double take as Morgan raps the lyrics like she's at a cypher. My sister. In couture. The guy she's with peers down at her with fixed intrigue. His hands clench at his sides before he draws her to his front. It's good to see my sister let loose, but I don't want regret to be waiting for her in the morning.

My eyes shift to Ella, who knocks me breathless. I've seen her dance around the house and on camera countless times. But not in an almost backless dress that's inching up her thighs, and not face down ass up, waving her cheeks like a flag.

"Forget I said anything. With that ass, I'd adopt her kids." Antonio stands next to me and zeroes in on Erica twerking on her friends.

When exactly I left my barstool remains a mystery. My booty-bouncing housemate has my undivided attention, with every ounce of blood in my body headed straight for my dick. Ella isn't the only one on the dance floor, but she's the only woman I want to devour.

I'm halfway to her when Antonio shouts, "Good chat!" She's so focused on throwing it back that it doesn't register I'm behind her until her back presses against my bulge. Tension eases at the circles I rub into her hips before moving us to the beat.

"Hey." The innocence in her voice is a front for the temptress who summoned me without so much as a glance. As a single mom with a demanding job, Ella doesn't get many chances to let loose, and I cherish these moments that don't require a device and high-speed internet.

With heels on, she's a few inches taller than me. I don't respond. I let my actions speak louder than my words by turning her to face me and draping her arms around my neck. The song is too fast to slow dance to, but I don't care.

She swallows and takes in the calm that masks the beast I'm ready to unleash.

I make a mental note to ask Antonio to escort Morgan to her car and take Ella's face in my hands. She releases a sharp breath when my thumb grazes her bottom lip. In the middle of a crowd oblivious to the connection pulling us together, I do what I've wanted to do since we danced under the stars Memorial Day weekend. I kiss her and whisper in her ear, "Let's go home."

Chapter 33

Ella

My text to Morgan on the ride home is the last contact we have with the outside world.

Home.

The shiver that four-letter word sent down my spine required one of those "Slippery when wet" signs above my vagina. Of all the days to not wear panties.

That word should terrify me, but it doesn't. Julian's townhouse feels like home with Jackson and Haile. With *him*. The memories we've made have so much love that I no longer question it. I embrace it with open arms instead of criticizing the perfect timeline that never existed.

Cool air presses to my skin when Julian opens my door. His firm grip is a reminder of the way he held me in place tonight. He hasn't said a word since we left the bar, but based on the way his eyes sweep over my body, I'm in for a long night.

He anchors his hand to my back as we walk the short distance from his car to the door off the kitchen. His fingers shuffle over the keypad. At the click, he guides me with soft pressure from his hand that never leaves my back. Memories linger around every edge of the counter as he removes my jacket to hang in the foyer with his. The absence of his touch and my lightheadedness from the tension that explodes between us hardens my nipples.

The soft steps of Julian's bare feet and the heat radiating from the entryway alert me to his presence. He didn't mince words when he said, "Let me have you," on the field today. The man is here to collect.

Part of me wants to sprint around the side of the island and make a run for it. The hunger in his eyes is suffocating, but running is pointless. Between his rugby reflexes and the way he's monitoring my movement, I don't stand a chance.

Why would I run anyway? I've done enough of that, and I can't suppress my feelings for him. I'm over fighting it and questioning why I deserve someone to treat me right.

So I take the first step toward him and smile when he closes the distance.

We stand in each other's arms, our heads pressed together and our eyes closed. I bury my face against his throat and inhale.

"You look beautiful tonight, sweetheart." The softness in his tone is as tender as the forehead kiss that follows. "You're always beautiful to me." Another kiss.

His fingers slide over my shoulders, removing the straps of my dress in the process. Gentle eyes study my face and move down the swell of my breasts. He cups my bare cleavage and massages my nipples, releasing my hiss at the burst of pleasure. I tip my head back with a moan.

"Let me take care of you," he says before his mouth covers a sensitive peak. My knees buckle at the flicker of his tongue.

"Julian."

My breath is ragged when he takes the other nipple into his mouth. There's no trace of restraint when he comes up for air and lifts me around his waist. Thick lips crush mine as he deepens our kiss. He takes the stairs two at a time, his fingers digging into my flesh.

Not only can the man kiss, he can climb steps with me in his arms and his eyes closed.

My heart kicks up speed when we cross the threshold to the bedroom. The small nightlight next to the former location of Haile's bed bathes the oversized duvet in a soft glow. Julian eases me to the center of the bed. His exploration of my thighs is a slow procession toward the swell of my hips.

"No penetration." A tender kiss connects with my inner thigh as he removes my heels. He cups my sex, careful not to enter me with his fingers but with enough pressure to edge me closer to an orgasm.

I've never wanted to yodel in my life, but the way my legs part readies the tremor in my vocal chords. An unsteady shout charges out of my throat and catches us both off guard.

"Don't judge me; it's been awhile," I say, like my breathlessness isn't a sign.

"No worries, baby." A trace of laughter is in his voice. "I got you." Julian's mouth dips down to coax mine into a kiss.

"Why are you still dressed?" My tongue traces the outline of his lips.

He pulls back with a groan. "You ready for me?"

"Please." He might've humped half of DC, but I have eight years on him. Not that I've been super active. Okay, I've only slept with two people, the first being a high school boyfriend who turned out to be an ass. Charles needs no explanation.

The point is, I can handle Julian. At least, that's what I tell myself—until he's head-to-toe naked.

You miss a lot of details when you don't see a person in their full glory. Julian's wide chest and broad shoulders draped in muscles are no secret. Neither are the hard lines in his abdomen that trail down to his sculpted thighs. What squeezes the air from my chest is the rod between his legs and the hardware glinting in the moonlight.

A metal barbell impales the head of his penis from top to bottom. It looks angry against the engorged flesh and has me second-guessing whether or not I'll tear up my coochie rubbing on that thing.

"When—?" I sit up and scrub a hand over my face. Apparently, I forget how to breathe and process thoughts when I see a dick with a spike through it.

Julian's laugh is strong enough to vibrate his six-pack. His length bobs in response, the edge of the silver ball hovering just below his belly button.

"Got it a few years ago. What's the matter?" He gives himself a tug. "Scared?"

He can kindly go fuck himself and let me know how it goes. Julian thinks I'm playing, but I need a pep talk. Possibly a numbing cream.

"How come—"

"You didn't see it the night we met?" His lips curl. "Airport security screenings are evasive enough without alerting them to my dick."

And what a dick it is.

He strolls the rest of the way over and settles between my legs. The bottom of his piercing skims over my clit in a lazy thrust. *Oh, this is nice.*

"Stay put, baby." His words are a murmur on my lips. "We'll break the law if I poke you."

Laughter bubbles between us. Adultery is still a Class 4 misdemeanor in Virginia, and penetrative sex earns me a scarlet letter until my divorce is final. Unless I want to roll the dice in court with a judge who might side with Charles and rule that his dick inside another woman was simply exercise.

I melt into the duvet and run my fingers up the forearms on either side of my face. I smile at the man who's watching me like I'm enough and reach for his neck to capture his lips. He curls into me, igniting a passion that takes my breath away.

"You did not!"

My head falls back in a roar of laughter. Tears flow at the image of Julian hopping over a balcony and splitting his pants to evade another social event.

He grimaces with a deep chuckle. "A security guard tackled me on the back lawn. He thought I was there to crash the party." His laugh is full. "I had on a tux, El."

"Poor baby." My teasing laughter becomes a shriek at his grab. "Stop! I'm ticklish!"

Julian's fingers wiggle over my body in an assault that ends with a hand to my chin to take my mouth. I moan and wrap my arms around his athletic frame tangled in bedsheets.

We slept together. Not sexually, but in each other's arms. Last night, I had more orgasms than I could count, and without sexual intercourse. Julian put the power drill between his legs to good use, sliding it back and forth over my clit until it cried out for release. Between the toys he used on every inch of my body and me making him nut with my hand, we both got a happy ending and a good night's sleep.

Dog barks mix with neighbors greeting each other outside the bay window. It's the perfect Sunday morning to stay under the covers.

The tips of our fingers thread our hands together as we lose time laughing, talking about our lives, and staying present in the moment. We already know a lot about each other, but we use every opportunity to dig below the surface.

"Do you like it?" My eyes follow the lines on his forearm that are dusted with black hair. "All that status, I mean." I lift my gaze to find his on me.

Julian kisses our joined hands and lays them over his heart. His breath is slow when he stares at the ceiling. "No. It was cool at first, the privileges that come with the Brooke name. Access to the best

DC has to offer and more money than I'll spend in a lifetime. But," he sighs, "it comes with a price. People prying into my personal life. Dictating my calendar. Rugby is the one thing that's mine. As Langston Brooke's son, I have responsibilities that require certain sacrifices."

"Camila."

He nods.

Julian has spoken about their relationship before, but he never alluded to it being an obligation. His eyes drift, lost somewhere between determination to please his family and the cost of forfeiting his desires because of it.

"We met my first year of law school. She was in graduate school for public relations, and we kept running into each other at the same events. Camila comes from a similar upbringing, which made it easy to relate to her. She understands the stress of trying to keep up with your family name.

"Once our families caught on that we were seeing each other, they wanted us to make appearances and move faster toward a more desirable commitment. I ended the relationship after I graduated and spent five years dodging another one. I'd had enough of my mother's attempts and asked to take over the London office."

"Then you came home and found a woman in your bed who had taken over your home with her kids."

A smile spreads. "That I did."

I snuggle into his warmth. "Itching to run again?"

He kisses the top of my head and pulls me to his chest. "Never. It's been hard to stay away as long as I have. Nothing about you, about this," he says with another kiss, "feels forced."

"Have you ever dated an older woman with kids?"

"I am now."

A blush heats my skin. Are we really doing this? Us?

Julian's eyes search mine. "Could you ever love again, after divorce?"

The sheets rustle as I straddle his length, the metal barbell prodding my entrance. I lean down to kiss his smile. "I am now."

Our kiss electrifies every nerve ending. My hips roll into his erection, pulling out a deep groan from Julian. With a punishing grip on my love handles, he slides me back and forth over his piercing and pulls a nipple into his mouth.

We're panting so much that we miss the front door opening and the heels echoing up the stairs. When Morgan barrels into the bedroom, I'm on top of her brother.

We all scream, and out of habit, I toss whatever is next to me at the perceived threat. A dildo, in this case.

She stumbles back, grabs the doorframe for support with one hand, and uses the other to shield her eyes. "What the—" She rubs her forehead and looks down in horror. "Did you just launch a dick at me?" Her eyes trace an invisible line from the clothes scattered on the floor and up the bed, to me and Julian. "No! *No!*"

I roll off Julian and pull the covers up to my neck. "What the hell are you doing here? Ever heard of calling first?"

Last we checked, Morgan was sleeping off plans of revenge sex in her hotel room. Alone.

Henry Cavill didn't accompany her to her bed, which is where she should be. In the softest sheets an overpriced night in a suite could buy, with a mimosa in hand and surrounded by room service. Not at the foot of my bed, shaking a yellow and pink dildo at us like we need a sex education lecture.

Morgan's tone is high on shocked and appalled. "When did this"—the silicone phallus waves from side to side—"start? Don't tell me?" She steps away to take a breath but boomerangs right back. "I—this wasn't the arrangement. Housing. Hospitality. Not..." She shakes the dildo she's yet to drop, recharging her frustration in the process. "This!"

My sigh is heavy. "Are you almost done, Viola Davis? I'd appreciate it if you'd stop waving the dick around so we can go downstairs and talk." If she's going to invade my bedroom before nine, I need a cup of coffee.

Her eyes shoot daggers, as if she finally registers that it's Julian next to me and not an illusion from the corners of a nightmare. He's yet to utter a word since his sister stormed in wearing a make-up-free face and a forest green sweater dress. He's completely at peace, bare-chested, with tattoos and a smug smile on full display. How often does she pop in for him to be this calm?

Morgan redirects her ire at her brother, who now sits straighter. "*You.*"

Never mind.

Julian's eyes go wide. "Mac." His hands shoot up in surrender, but it's too late. Morgan reaches him in three steps and pulls him out of bed by the ear. "Wait, Mac—ow! What the fuck?!"

Skin I've kissed and sucked struggles to stay upright as Morgan heads back to the bedroom door, leaving Julian to use both hands to cover himself while shouting at his sister to let him go. He trips over his jeans but is able to get a foot through one of the legs. It takes a few hops for him to get the other one through and stand to his full height, but he does.

"Enough!" he barks. "You're worse than our mother."

A lacquered pink nail wags in his face. "You better be thankful it's me here and not her to see all of"—her hand waves in disgust—"this." She scoffs. "Of all the women in DC."

"Hey!" I take offense at that.

Morgan peeks back at me in apology. "Sorry, girl. You know I love you. My mother does too, but she's had plans for this one"—her index finger flicks Julian dead in his forehead—"for some time. A fling isn't worth all that drama."

"It's not a fling!" We both say to the intruder who's fucking up our Sunday.

Julian spins her to face the hall and pushes her out. "Go downstairs and give us a minute."

Morgan's shouts fade to a pestering buzz as sunlight hits Julian's body and dances off the hard muscles he wrapped around me last night. I watch the crease between his thick pecs and the lines in his abs as he zips up. A barefoot Julian in jeans is a sight to see.

He wets his bottom lip. "Take your time getting ready. I'll make us breakfast." His eyes crawl up my curves draped in the white sheet I let pool in my lap. "I know what I want to eat."

Then Morgan appears in the doorway. The dildo she throws connects with the back of Julian's head, knocking him forward. "Quit being nasty with Ella and get down here, Julian Michel!"

Julian rushes out the door. "Throw another thing in my house, and I'll hang this dick outside yours like a door knocker!"

The sibling banter carries through the bathroom like surround sound as I wash my face, brush my teeth, and get ready to stand in front of Morgan's one-woman firing squad. This wasn't how I pictured my life five months into my separation, or telling my best friend about me and her brother, but I welcome the chaos of Julian shouting, "Do you want eggs or not?" and Morgan yelling back, "Yes!" with the goofiest grin on my face.

Chapter 34

Ella

"Another one from the 1900s?" Haile has the nerve to scrunch her face in disappointment as she sinks into the sectional with folded arms and a pout.

"Excuse me, little girl, but the '90s wasn't *that* long ago." I grab the Twizzlers from her hand and make a face. So much for our basement movie marathon. "Jackson, back me up."

He leans back on the chaise with his hands behind his head and crosses his ankles, shifting the blue robe over his Minecraft pajamas like a man who pays the mortgage. He smirks. "It was over thirty years ago."

I look between the two children who came from my womb. *The audacity.* "Have I steered y'all wrong today?"

"No," they say in unison and with as much enthusiasm as someone counting carpet fibers.

I point to the screen. "This is a classic. You'll both thank me later."

And thank me they did. *3 Ninjas* is the shit, and I'll hear no slander about it. By the end of the movie, we're chanting about Rocky and Emily and ordering pizza, ready to throw hands if the delivery person turns out to be a robber.

The day has been a cleansing breath, a reset from the hustle of work, school, Katharine's, and the commute we sprint week after week on the hamster wheel of routine. I don't have Haile and Jackson on the weekends anymore, and I soak up every second with them between long days at Bright Spot and making dinner.

School is out today and tomorrow, which was the perfect opportunity for me to call off, spend all day in pj's, and order in. Jackson opted for his Minecraft pajamas, and Haile and I refuse to change out of our matching unicorn onesies.

We've gathered around the kitchen island, our central place in the townhouse since we've moved in. Our transition hasn't always been smooth or perfect, but we've got each other. And lots of carbs.

"Can I have a playdate with Duke tomorrow?" Jackson's question comes between chews of his jumbo pizza slice. The thing is bigger than his head, but he also has a stack of veggies on his plate. Balance.

"If he's not with his dad and Aunt Morgan is okay with it, sure. I'll text her to ask."

Haile groans and reaches for her water. "Can we do something else, Mommy? I'm sick of boys; they eat boogers."

I choke mid-chew and fight to swallow the soft dough melding with cheese and sauce. "They're not the only ones who do it, sweetie."

She scoffs. "They do at school."

Holding back my laugh is a lost cause. Haile is too grown for her age. "What about a picnic near the Potomac? We could pack sandwiches and lemonade."

"Could we come too? I want to stay in DC if it's okay with Aunt Morgan." Jackson peeks from under his thick lashes, his eyes heavy with worry.

"That's fine with me, sweetie," I say with a frown. "You okay?"

"Yeah." He fiddles with his napkin and looks up with a shy smile ghosting his lips. "This is home. I like DC."

I gulp hard to keep my tears in check. If I had a wig on, I would've shaken it off by now with all this nodding. "Okay. We'll make it a group event."

"With our own picnic," Haile adds.

"Yes." I snort. "We'll pick a place big enough for everyone to have fun."

I slip out the kitchen to the powder room while Jackson and Haile recap *Beethoven* and *Homeward Bound*, two movies that reignited pleas for a dog I've tried to avoid at all costs.

The brass lock clicks into place, and I turn on the exhaust so the imprisoned sob in my chest can break free. My back slides down the charcoal wall to tiled flooring where I tuck my head and let every tear fall. I cry for the times I thought my children would resent me for uprooting our lives and my endless fear that my shortcomings will cost them their joy.

Weekly family therapy fortifies the affirmation that we're building a life that's whole and healing. One that doesn't need to fit into a box of expectations, because it's the perfect size for us.

A knock beats on the door. "Mom, Julian is video calling for our Japanese lesson. Can we watch *The Sandlot* right after?"

"Sounds good, Jackson!"

Better than good. Perfect.

Chapter 35

Ella

"So, what do you think?"

"I *think* you should quit being so damn stubborn and take your man up on his offer."

I close my laptop with a frustrated sigh and turn away from the counter and my friend, who's about to get kicked out of the house she so desperately wants me to claim. "At least look at the photos. In DC, a three-bedroom apartment under $2,300 a month is rare." I lift the hot cocoa mug with the perfect mix of red and green sprinkles and marshmallows. "That's with heat and air conditioning included. It's a great deal."

Erica swings her hand around the kitchen in dramatic fashion. "And what the hell is this?"

I smile at her challenge. "Christmas decorations." Holiday garlands with white lights line the tops of the cabinets and windows.

When Morgan offered me the townhouse, it was only until the end of the year. Now, I'm getting side-eye for keeping our agreement?

My declaration for independence turns into a group intervention when Erica calls Morgan. She picks up in a huff, annoyed that I won't concede after weeks of back-and-forth. "Are we still on this?" Her tone slices through speakerphone.

Erica sucks her teeth. "Destiny's Child over here wants to be Ms. Independent, even at her own expense."

Is no one listening?! I throw up my hands. "It has *three* bedrooms and an in-unit washer and dryer!" Not to mention it's close to Bright Spot and within my price range.

Erica's stare reaches me over her glazed donut doused in holiday sprinkles. She takes an obnoxious bite. "Mm-hmm."

"Why pay rent when you can stay in a townhouse and save *more* money?"

The economics professor with fresh pressed hair lifts a shoulder. "Those dollars don't make sense."

"Hello? Julian and I can't live together anymore. Not after—"

"I caught you two rubbing private parts?" Erica's mouth twists into a sinister smile at Morgan's words.

Oh, screw them both.

It's funny now, but two months ago I had to stop Morgan from laying into Julian. He might play rugby, but he'll hop over furniture to dodge a blow from his big sister. The way she cleared the kitchen island in a dress and heels had me ready to call *America Ninja Warrior* about their next competitor.

In her fit of shock that morphed into rage, she missed the open door of the home office Julian turned into a bedroom for my baby girl. Morgan took one look at Haile's room and lost it. We got her approval that day—and her promise to keep whatever is between us quiet until the time is right.

As for Erica, what can I say other than she's thrown her *told you so*'s in my face since she caught Julian calling me "sweetheart" on video call during Friendsgiving. How was I supposed to know I didn't shut my bedroom door all the way? Apparently, I need a deadbolt to keep my nosy friends at bay.

I haven't told Grier about the change in development, not that there's much to say. She and her family have been in and out of the area, getting Zora situated at college and visiting family in Mexico for mini getaways. She and Mateo are empty nesters now. I don't blame them one bit for taking time for themselves.

It's not like Julian and I have a title, anyway. We're getting to know each other better, and that might involve heavy petting, my nipples in his mouth, or a virtual peep show while he's back in London. We're still friends without flirting in public.

And do you know what would help our situation? Me moving out.

I'll get the apartment, hold a funeral for my savings after all of the deposits, and move us in during Jackson's winter break in February. The plan makes sense. I just need Tweedle dee and Tweedle dum off my back. It's a quick walk around the kitchen island to pop Erica in the head and grab the phone. It's playful, but she hops off the barstool and mumbles, "Bitch," but backs down when I grab the spatula.

Try me.

"I need my own place, Morgan. I don't want to confuse the kids or give Charles ammo to come after me in court."

"So let Julian move out," she says, the edge in her voice replaced with affection. "Stay where you're at. The kids love it, and you don't need to move somewhere temporary to prove a point. You're saving for a house, and you'll be able to buy one next year—if you don't waste money on rent you don't need to pay."

"Or you can let his fine ass buy you a house." Erica lifts her chin before she bites into another donut.

"I already learned my lesson with one wealthy man. Not happening." Julian wouldn't lose sleep or interest in his bank account if I asked him for a new home. He'd happily buy one for me, but that's not the point. I don't want to rely on a man to provide for me or my kids, which is why I have to do this myself.

"Does she still look gassy?"

Erica nods at my eye roll. "Mm-hmm."

Morgan's sigh is deep. "The townhouse is yours for as long as you need it. Julian already moved into the apartment above Swigs. *Stay*."

He did what?

I stare at the phone like her brother will magically appear to confirm a truth he never told me. He said he was busy this weekend, but I took it as to mean *I'm running around*, not *I moved without telling you*.

He flew back the day after Christmas, came straight to my job, and took me in his arms behind the privacy of my office door. He whispered, "Merry Christmas, baby," before sealing his mouth to mine. The kiss was a homecoming after months apart, and, my, was it worth the wait.

Rose fanned herself the second she laid eyes on him in a long camel wool coat and heather gray slacks, and he and I snuck off for a quick lunch at a nearby soul food restaurant. The kids didn't see him until later, after they weeded through the stacks of presents waiting for them under the tree. It was perfect. My favorite people together under one roof, surrounded by twinkling lights and the fresh scent of pine from our first real Christmas tree.

"I'll talk to him."

Morgan lets out a breath and "Thank you, baby Jesus" at Erica's cheer. "Now that we settled that, get your ass over here."

I can't groan loud enough. "Pajamas and junk food on the couch are calling me."

"I refuse to let you ring in another year with pantry snacks and Ryan Seacrest. El, this is the last year you'll be married to that ogre."

"Technically, I'll still be his wife tomorrow," I say.

"You know what I mean! I promised I'd make an appearance at this gala, and I need a plus-one. I have dresses and a stylist on the way to do hair and makeup. Bring yourself."

"Don't look at me," Erica says, reaching for her purse. "I have a date. See you next year!"

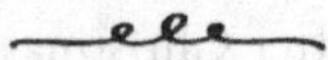

"You owe me a proper meal and an apology."

Morgan laughs at my frustration as I try to piecemeal a dinner of two tiny sliders and a skewered chicken strip. Between the sample-size portions and lack of seasoning, I'm over it.

She leans in to whisper with a smile. "I could go for a milkshake myself." Her eyes widen at a man in a tuxedo who could star in Blair Underwood's biopic. "Senator Douglass," she grins. "It's great to see you!" The hug they share is one of familiarity.

"Morgan, always wonderful to see you. Is your father here?" Warmth ripples through the rich timbre of his voice.

"Couldn't make it. How's Emma doing?"

A grin plays across his lips. "Good. Always on the go. It's hard to keep up with my daughter." He laughs. "I'll tell her you said hi."

"Please do. Have a good night." Morgan's stomach gurgles after his exit. "Twenty more minutes, and we'll see if a drive-thru is open."

"Deal."

I break out of our huddle in couture and head to the bar while Morgan gets swept up in another conversation. Minus her, everyone is a stranger here. Except for the server who always has the good food on her tray. Amber, I think.

We've been at this black-tie event for two hours, and I'm ready to swap out this A-line dress for flannel pj's and turn in. It's off-the-shoulder, and I can't lift my hands without fabric drooping against my pits.

Morgan is gunning for first place as Ms. New Year's Eve. Her asymmetrical maxi dress hugs her hourglass curves. Green is always good color on her, but this particular shade in velvet attracts every eye in the room.

A spot opens near the bar. It's a small trek across a sea of plush burgundy carpeting. Small high-top tables draped in ivory linens create a maze of DC elite and servers carrying trays that should have more than finger foods for two thousand a ticket—not that I paid.

I'm still clueless about the who and why of the evening. Morgan is making the rounds with her Brooke smile plastered on like a billboard as I grab a glass of champagne and make eye contact with a person carrying a sushi platter.

Now you're talking my language.

The band plays a slow medley, drawing guests into the dim pink lighting that cascades across the parquet floor and vaulted ceilings. Movement near the entrance has photographers crowding around a step-and-repeat behind a strip of red carpet. I reach for another piece of sushi and watch cameras flash as a small entourage poses for photos. A path clears, and Julian steps front and center with his hand pressed to a woman's back.

My mouth tumbles open on its own. I'm unable to control my shock, because what in the entire eff? I blink slowly to make sense of the camera shutters that are snapping Julian's every move like he's the damn prince of Zamunda.

His steps are slow with practiced precision. The corner of his mouth lifts into a smirk, like he's a bachelor on the prowl in a tailor-made tuxedo. Photographers point to the woman next to him in winter white feathers. Ms. Peacock effortlessly mirrors his poses. It's like she graduated top of her etiquette class the way she sucks in her cheekbones and smiles with her eyes. Julian stands closer to her and lowers his head to whisper in her ear.

Is that what this is, the DC version of *Coming to Americad,* only Julian returns home to sow his royal oats before his parents force him to marry a woman of their choosing? Ms. Peacock has golden brown hair in loose waves and flawless skin. Does she hop on one foot on command like the woman did in the movie?

I turn back to the granite counter to drain the rest of my champagne. I've seen enough.

When Julian said he'd be busy this weekend, I didn't take that to mean a red-carpet appearance with a caramel beauty. Or maybe that's exactly what he meant, and I've been Boo-Boo the Fool? I don't pay attention to blogs or follow DC gossip. How am I supposed to know the six degrees of love connections and hookups?

The glance over my shoulder is my last one, or so I tell myself. They're off the red carpet, holding separate discussions with the small groups gathered around them. I snort at the pretentiousness of it all. Who waits around to see how far they can stick their nose up someone's ass for a sniff?

Morgan's eyes lock on mine from the other side of the room. She steals a look at her brother and the woman who's found her way back to his side. She now has a hand to his chest.

Morgan's gaze turns to me. *Who the hell is that?*

I scoff. *These are your people.*

She dips a brow. *Want me to say something?*

That gets a headshake. *Nope.*

If Julian wanted to tell me he was going out, he would've. My date with a New Year's Eve special and a homemade dessert bar was no secret. *His* date was, and I refuse to play out every what-if scenario.

"Want another one?"

I stare speechless at blue eyes on a face I never expected to see again. McDimples? "What are you doing here?"

He lifts a glass of amber liquid to his mouth and smiles. "Running into you again." His throat works over a long pull of his drink, and his eyes never leave mine. "You look amazing."

My tour of his all-black suit and wavy brown hair leads to a trimmed goatee over a square jaw. Looks like he replaced his five-o' clock shadow. "You clean up nice yourself."

"I don't think I introduced myself last time." He reaches for my hand. "Asher Campbell."

"Ella Greene."

His eyes flash with an expression I can't place, but he recovers with a smile. "So, Ella. Is that ex of yours here?"

"Don't you have a good memory? No, he's not."

I had the kids Christmas Eve, and I dropped them off at Katharine's after breakfast the next day. Seven hours is the amount of time they had with their dad. Then I picked them up and kept them for the week. You'd think the holiday spirit and weeks of unused vacation time would inspire him to be less of a Grinch and spend more time with his children. Father of the year he is not.

Asher leans closer, introducing me to a musk of tobacco notes that rivals the cedar and sandalwood currently wrapped up in feathers. "Are you seeing anyone?"

The word "Yes" almost tumbles out, but I catch it. I thought I was, until tonight's display. "Nope," I say. "Just getting through my divorce."

For a second, I expect Asher to call BS. The way he studies me is unsettling, like he sees through my attempt to mask the fact that I might be in love with a man who's out with another woman—or that there might be a stash of California roll pieces in my purse I'll ration for the rest of the evening.

What should I say? *I'm seeing a confirmed bachelor during my separation?* There'd be no way to dodge headlines and not put my family's future in jeopardy if Charles accused me of adultery.

Asher steps closer. "Dance with me."

The absence of a "please" or a question mark warrants laughter. Why waste the dress and shoes? It's only a dance. "Do you always get what you want?"

His gaze sharpens. "Yes."

Two songs later, the band slows to a ballad of horns. Asher's hand is firm against my back with the other around mine in a controlled grasp. We've laughed with questions in between about what brought us to DC. He told me that tonight is an event for lawyers in the area to raise money for charity, which explains why Julian is here.

My black dress flares on a spin. "Do you practice law in the city?"

He shakes his head. "I'm not a lawyer."

"So what are you doing here?"

"I came for the free food—or lack thereof," he says with a slow grin that turns into a laugh to match my own. A fellow freeloader. "I didn't grow up with money."

"Same. This all gets overwhelming at times."

"Speaking of overwhelming." His eyes lift to a spot above my head. "Is he a friend of yours?"

I crane my neck to see Julian standing against a wall with a drink in hand and a glare at Asher. The tic in his jaw is visible from here.

"A friend, yes." The words come out even, a small achievement based on the possessiveness in Julian's eyes. How long has he been standing there? I clear my throat and smile. "Our families are close."

Asher nods. "Well, it seems like your friend wants to take you around the dance floor." He steps back, his eyes still on Julian until they return to mine with a smirk. "It was nice running into you. I look forward to doing it again."

There's no chance to process Julian taking me by the wrist to spin me into his chest. The momentum threatens my balance, but he steadies me against his muscular frame.

"I did not expect to see you here." His eyes take an appreciative tour down my dress before they snap back to mine. "Or with another man."

The laugh in my throat is a slow rumble until it folds into a full-on body jiggle. His bow tie must be too tight. "Need I remind you, I wasn't the one who did a slow stroll down a red carpet to pose with another woman. Where is Ms. Feather Duster anyway?"

"Gabrielle left," he says with a chuckle.

"You still have time to catch her. Wouldn't want to mess up those weekend plans." I give his chest a pat and step out of his hold. I need another glass of champagne to wash down the jealousy changing lanes to make a U-turn. That bitch needs to go home and get a good night's sleep.

Julian tugs me back to his middle with a force that steals my breath. I'd be lying if I said my thighs didn't clench.

"What?" His stare is so intense, I look away.

"Do you think I would do that to you? Disrespect you?" He tilts my chin with a soft command to look him in the eyes. "I'm not him, sweetheart."

"I know." My voice is low.

His thumb brushes the corner of my lip. "My father asked me to make an appearance tonight since he couldn't do it. Gabrielle is the daughter of my mother's friend. The photo was a courtesy to her. I came alone, and that's how I planned to leave. I'm sorry for not telling you. I didn't plan to stay long." He steps back to take me in. "But then I saw you across the room. You are divine perfection."

Check, please!

"Thank you." *For making me feel safe when insecurities surface.*

Julian and Charles are not the same. I know that, but it doesn't shield me from the thoughts racing to make sense of what my heart holds as truth and what plays out in front of me.

If it were my ex, I would send him packing the way I did when I caught him screwing another woman. I mean, technically, I left, but I didn't hesitate. Truth be told, our marriage was past its expiration date. I was too busy keeping our family together to smell the stench until it smacked me in the face.

Charles could screw the entire parent volunteer roster and I wouldn't give a shit. I wouldn't have the urge to claim him as mine, the way I do with Julian.

"El?" His smile fades, and his brows draw together. "Are you okay?"

I'm starving for something more than that damn California roll in my purse. My heart pounds in an erratic rhythm. My jealousy subsides as a sudden flush of heat spreads from my thighs outward and seizes my neck with a squeeze.

I've been good these last eight months—damn good, considering. I did what I needed to do to provide for my family, and I upheld my end of the separation agreement. I've blocked the desire to express my love for the man in front of me, who hasn't wavered in his adoration, for as long as I could. I might toe the line, but I always play by the rules others set in place.

Tonight, I'm playing by mine.

"I'm ready to go."

"Okay," Julian says. He thumbs over at the double French doors. "If you have your coat check tag, I'll get our things..." The rest tapers off in a groan at my hand on his crotch. I tighten my grip on the bulge pressing into my fingers.

With his back to the other guests, we look like we're slow dancing. Hooded eyes study mine. Julian doesn't say anything, but he doesn't have to. His physical reaction says a thousand words, and the brother is locked and loaded.

I lean closer so my lips can tickle his ear. "I'm ready to go, but not home. I won't make it." My hand slides up to his hard chest, which quivers under my touch. "Can we get a room here?"

For a long moment, he looks at me. I would too, because who am I? Call it liquid courage or fatigue due to a lack of protein, but I want what I want, and I want it now. This is the first time I'm asking him to spend money on me, and it happens to be the only time I initiated anything beyond a kiss, nevermind the implied sex.

"Are you sure?" Huskiness lingers in his tone, and he watches me for any tells that I've had too much to drink or lost my mind.

Maybe I have lost my mind. Julian isn't going anywhere, and getting a room will raise speculation, whether we unite our bodies or not. There's no way everyone won't think we slept together. So let them think what they want.

I nod. "Text me the floor and room number. I'll meet you up there."

With a deep inhale, he speed walks past the black-tie attendees hoping to get his attention and disappears into the hall.

Morgan steals another peek at the door Julian high-tailed out of on her approach. "Did he eat something bad?"

He's about to eat something good the minute we get upstairs.

"He went to get a room."

It doesn't register at first, but when it does, her eyes balloon and her mouth falls open. I close it with a hand. She paces with hers on her hip in a struggle to either cuss me out like his big sister or support me like my best friend. The two converge when she folds her arms and faces me.

Tears glitter her eyes. This is more than a New Year's Eve hookup, and she knows it. "Okay," she says. "He can drive you to my house to get your car tomorrow, after you two..." She throws her hand over her face. "I can't think about it."

"I hope you don't," I say back with a laugh that gets her guard down. While she supports us, anything hinting at our physical intimacy gives her the bubble guts.

Her smile fades. "Be careful, El. People get curious about who he's with. If anyone sees him get a room, that curiosity will follow you two upstairs."

I frown. "It's not that serious."

"To some gossip sites, it is. They're not paparazzi who follow him home, but when he's out, it's fair game." She sighs. "On second thought, I'll come back in the morning with your overnight bag. No one will think anything if we leave together."

The hug we share is a testament to our friendship, an bond that's become a sisterhood. We've had each other's backs through it all, and now we'll add me and her brother swapping fluids to the list.

"You two be safe. For once, I don't want any details," she says. "I might vomit in the poinsettias thinking about it."

I smack her arm. "Don't act like you never met one of his partners before."

She huffs a soft laugh and motions for me to head out. "None I ever liked. In case you can't tell, you're different. I've never seen him this caring and invested in someone, the way he is with you and Jackson and Haile."

My phone buzzes with a text from Julian that sucks the air from my lungs.

We're doing this. Okay.

Morgan looks down at the screen with an eye roll. There's nothing vulgar there, just a room number, but if I had a brother she was going to ride for most of the night, I might get grossed out too.

"See you tomorrow." It's a struggle to hide my smile.

"Yeah, yeah. Have a good night."

"I plan to."

She covers her ears and shoulder checks me. "Too soon!"

Chapter 36

Julian

I should get an award for the round of Red Light, Green Light it took to get up here. Haile taught me how to play once after dinner, and a week's worth of pizza and juice boxes for her class are on me.

My life is the DC version of *Squid Game*, only I dodge attempts to pry into my private life instead of deadly bouts for a cash prize.

Speed walk through the suits waiting for their next photo op. Green light.

Play twenty questions with the front desk attendant who's scanning the lobby for whoever is about to join me. I dodge the blogger next to the elevator pretending not to pay attention. Red light.

Who the fuck cares why I'm getting a room for the night or if I'm alone? Assumptions fuel gossip, and I'll be damned if I enter a new year with my face plastered across articles about reality show wives.

Which means...

Fake a stomachache from one too many spring rolls and get a suite for the rest of the night. Green light.

That will clear the entire floor and stop gossip-chasers in search of their next scandal, one that doesn't involve bad gas or a toilet. My stomach is just fine, except I could use a real meal.

Who thought appetizers on a holiday we spend *hours* celebrating was the move?

Between the finger snacks and dodging investigations about who I'm dating, I'm over the galas.

I wouldn't be panting this hard from rushing down the hall if I was still overseas. No one over there cares about the "fame" I get from my father's company. With London comes anonymity, but the distance between me and Ella is no longer an option.

A few weeks here and a month and a half away was doable in the beginning, when we were navigating the friendship lane. Now that we're merging onto the next level, I need more. I need *her*. If that means searching for hidden cameras with a phone flashlight in the dark like a special agent, call me 007.

It takes me ten minutes to sweep the 1,800-square-foot suite that screams gaudy in high definition. At $7,000 a night, there are enough drapes to clothe the naked and hold a fashion show to pat yourself on the back about it in front of the press.

I send Ella a text. She would lose her shit if she found out the price, but I didn't think twice. Just like when I bought the building Swigs is in and moved into the apartment upstairs. It uncomplicated our living situation and put my best friend's rent money back in his pocket. Win-win.

Ella should know I'd drop enough to hole up here for a year if it meant I could see the flash in her eyes when she stepped into her power with confidence. The more she takes back her independence, the less she puts her own needs on the backburner to care for others. She can have it all on her own terms, and witnessing her metamorphosis in real time is an honor as much as it is a turn-on. Morgan can talk all the shit she wants, but I'm Ella's biggest fan, ready to help if she needs it and cheering her on every step of the way.

Especially if it comes with a dick grab. That caught me off guard, but he and I are both here to be of service however she needs tonight.

Sex is a bonus to the intimacy we've nurtured through a friendship that set itself ablaze over time. I want her truths as much as I want her moans. Her joy and well-being come before my desire to be inside of her.

A delicate knock taps against the door. "Housekeeping." The sing-song carries through oak with a giggle at the end.

I smile at the trace of laughter and press my hands to the ivory barrier that stands between me and the woman whose mischief rivals my own. "And what do you have for me? I didn't ask for towels." I turn the deadbolt.

The door opens to reveal the most beautiful woman, who's unaware that the grin she wields would bring any man to his knees. She chews the inside of her cheek and says, "Just myself. Is that enough?"

Her breath hitches when my fingers wrap around one of her wrists, and I pull her into the room and push her against the door. In her heels, she's a couple inches taller than me. I run my nose over the blush creeping up the soft column of her neck and inhale. "You're more than enough. You're everything missing from my life."

Ella's shoulders relax on a sigh. She leans into my touch and tips her head to the foyer light casting a mosaic of shades on her face. I take my time sweeping over the thick natural curls pinned above her nape, then move to the swell of her breasts behind lace and satin.

The urge to rip the fabric and suck on her nipples until I feast on her pussy into the new year takes effort to smother.

This is her night to do what she wants, when she wants, and how she wants.

My eyes move from her red lips to her hooded gaze. She glances at my mouth and meets my stare with an invitation. Her legs part, the high slit in her dress giving way to accommodate my size. My dick probes between her thighs through my slacks, searching for the heat it wants. If there's one thing we've mastered, it's the art of dry humping.

I press my lips to hers and swoop down to lift her. Her legs wrap around me and hold on for dear life as our bodies pummel into each other. I widen my stance and dig my fingers into the soft flesh holding up a thong I plan to tear with my teeth.

A series of long kisses turns desperate with each thrust. The force of my hips pumping into her center rattles the door. My balls tighten, and I pull us apart. Not yet.

"Take me out." I lick the bottom lip Ella snatches between her teeth and wait.

She fumbles with the belt and unbuttons my pants. The zipper whines in a slow hiss. I hold back a moan and take a small step to give her space to pull out my dick, tracing the shell of her lips and rocking into her hand as it caresses my head. She spreads precum up and down my length, cautious around my piercing, like I won't dick her down into the mattress with it later. My mouth rejoins hers for a slow kiss, our tongues exploring

I've wanted Ella since the moment she showed up in my house and scared the living shit out of me. I never expected for our living situation to be more than a favor to Morgan, but somewhere along the way, I fell in love.

The reality of having her in real life, beyond my dreams, sends me to my knees. Literally.

I set her down on the ground and kneel. We could stand here all night, but my mouth has other plans.

"Can I taste you, sweetheart?" At her nod, I run my fingers up the dress that hugs her curves and expose thick, honey-tan thighs.

The scent of her essence coats the air. I'm a patient man. I've been patient because of the complexities that come with her separation. Tonight, that patience is gone.

"Keep your back against the wall and lift this leg." She hesitates, but then her right leg settles on my shoulder. "Good girl," I say with a kiss to her thigh. "Hold on to the wall for me, baby."

Her body quivers at the first swipe of my tongue over her lacy black thong coated in her juices. I hook a hand under the leg on my shoulder to steady her, pull the fabric to the side, and drag my tongue from the sensitive skin above her ass to her lips. She releases a shaky moan when I open her for deep strokes to taste her. The tip of my tongue flicks to her clit before I devour her whole.

"Julian." Her hips buck forward as I edge her closer to her breaking point.

My hand wraps around my dick, the way it has many nights as I imagined the scene in front of me. I quicken my pace at the force of her fingers pulling my head deeper between her legs. Her voice is a raspy plea between thrusts. "Don't. You. Dare. Stop."

Thick ropes of my cum hit the door. I make a mental note to clean up before check-out and stand. Ella sucks in several breaths in the aftershock of her orgasm. "That was—"

I swallow her gasp with my tongue and plunge two fingers inside her pussy. Her skin is fire on my lips as I sear a path of open-mouthed kisses down her neck. My teeth scrape over the black fabric of her dress and capture a nipple with a hard tug.

"We're not done yet," I say at her throaty whimper. My fingers curl inside her to stroke her G-spot, and I hold her steady and press a kiss to her lips. "You're stunning when you come, El. Let go, baby."

Her brows crease, and her mouth hangs open at my summon for another orgasm. Dark chocolate eyes glaze over with years of repressed desire. Her head falls back, and she unleashes a moan that hardens my dick back to life.

Ella collapses over me, spent from the pleasure I've drawn from her body. I press soft kisses to her forehead and pull her to my middle. My arms wrap around her soft frame, and I bury my nose in her neck and soak in the lavender scent that etched itself deep into my memories months ago. I can't get enough, and I never will.

"Julian?"

She takes my face in her hands and leans forward to recapture my lips, her kiss brushing across my skin like a whisper before she thrusts her tongue inside. My mouth leaves from hers to admire her. I could spend the rest of the night kissing her, but she has my dick between her hands, and it's hard to think.

"*Ella*." Her name tangles with a moan at the firm strokes over my shaft. I got my first release out the way, and I'm ready to go again, but I don't want to push her. Judging by the heat in her eyes, that won't be a problem.

"I want to feel good." She dips her tongue into my mouth and says, "Again."

It takes two attempts to clear my throat. *Fuck yes.* "Whatever you want, sweetheart." *Use my dick like a game controller. I don't care.*

A brow lifts. She tugs me closer with another hard stroke and licks the shell of my ear. "Take your clothes off and sit on that dining room chair." She nods to the one closest to the window.

"Yes, baby." My voice is thick and unsteady, because holy fuck. I don't know what button I pushed to activate this version of Ella, but I'd stick my dick in a light socket if she asked.

My clothes are off in record time, and I add a shimmy as I stride to the chair, for good measure.

"Sit back and spread for me." Not a problem. "Stroke yourself, slowly."

Fuck.

I part my legs and move my hand up and down my length. The movement stutters as she steps out of her dress and reaches down to remove her thong. My hand stills as she walks toward me in nothing but black heels and a confidence that steals my breath.

Ella stands between my legs and peers down at me, her breasts teasing me to take them into my mouth. I lick my lips and stay put so as not to disrupt her or this sudden change in demeanor. I always sensed her sexual prowess. She just needed the right partner to nurture it and watch her bloom.

My attention shifts from the beauty with endless curves in front of me to my wallet on the table and the condom I keep in the back. I never even thought about using it since we met, but I'm glad I didn't take it out.

"El, baby. I need to take out my piercing and put on a condom."

Her eyes drop to my erection and back up to mine. "Have you been with anyone else since we met?"

My brows sink in a frown. "You know I haven't. I had my annual physical last month, with all negative results. It's in an email on my phone if you need to see."

She shakes her head with a smile. "I trust you, Julian. I'm on the pill, and I'd rather not have anything between us."

My hand covers my dick, which bobs in a *yes*. I try to blink away my shock, but I'm not sure it's possible. I've always used protection with every partner, even Camila. I never trusted anyone. Until now.

I pull her to straddle me and take her mouth. Her hands find a home around my neck, and she rocks into me, fully aroused. She writhes when I lift her up and enter her in a slow glide. My lips brush her nipples, and I drag my tongue over her peaks.

"You okay, sweetheart?" Her quiet moans ignite movement. Fuck, she feels good.

We find a tempo to bind our bodies in an explosion of pleasure. Ella is magnificent in every way imaginable. I root her with a hand on her hip and one on her back as she leans away, unable to control her cries.

I rock back and forth to stimulate her clit and stare in awe as she grinds against me. Light from the window filters through, contouring her breasts and stomach with a series of shadows.

My hands anchor her hips to me as I pump into her with forceful thrusts that draw sweat from my brow.

"Julian!" She sits up and proceeds to fuck the life out of me. Her head tilts into my caress, pulling my thumb into her mouth to suck.

Every muscle in my body tenses at once in a burst of sensations and the clap of our bodies colliding. Our eyes connect, and I wipe a single tear from Ella's cheek. A ripple of emotions overwhelms me, and the growing need to protect her and love her the way she's always deserved takes over.

My lips slowly ascend to meet hers. "I love you." The confession triggers her release, to let go of the past and forge ahead. She cries out, succumbing to the orgasm before she melts against me.

Her name is a proclamation as I spill inside her on the final thrust. Our pants melt into slow strokes of our tongues as we kiss through a whirl of emotions.

Fireworks sound outside to indicate the new year. Ella settles into the crook of my neck, our arms curled around each other, and lets out a long breath. "I love you too."

Chapter 37

Ella

You'd never know Julian Brooke is thirty-one unless you searched online or caught him on a day off. He never takes one, which is why the successful attorney who wears suits like nobody's business sitting in the center of the bed with a bowl bigger than his face and cartoons on the TV is a sight. His feet swing back and forth under plush white sheets with the biggest grin. He nods at his bowl and spoons in another mouthful of cereal.

"Comfortable?" Judging by the view from the bathroom door, the answer is yes.

"Very," he says between another bite. His focus is still on the screen, until he tracks the white towel covering the bits he sucked and pleasured out of the corner of his eye. A tent forms between his wide thighs. It's impressive and terrifying.

"Don't let me ruin your breakfast and your Monday morning cartoons. You want a glass of milk with that?"

He snorts at my smug smile. "Is that your attempt at an age joke? I'm disappointed, sweetheart." The glance he cuts me comes with a wink. "Just remember who cooks your breakfast before you lose your privileges." He nods at the metal dome on the nightstand.

"Your eggs Benedict and side of fruit came while you were in the shower."

I blow a kiss, grab my breakfast, and join him in bed. He scoots over to make room, and my head tips back with laughter at a closer look into his bowl. "Is that...bran? Who's the elder in this relationship?"

"This"—he points to the bowl with his spoon—"is how my younger ass keeps up with you." Another bite reaches his lips. "Breakfast of cham—"

"Don't you dare!" My cackle is more of a wheeze at Julian eating Wheaties to recharge.

"I'm not the one who kept us up half the night with a sex marathon in forty-six positions," he says. "Don't judge my Wheaties or my Gatorade."

"What ab—"

"Not one word about *The Powerpuff Girls*." My lips do yoga to suppress a giggle, and I dig into my food.

Last night was the perfect ending to a chaotic year. I left behind a woman who settled for good enough, who took what was given and was never satisfied. I spent more time loving myself in the last eight months than I did in the last sixteen years.

Have I fully healed? Of course not, but I'm on my way.

Am I freshly fucked? You bet your mattress.

Julian took me forward, backward, and sideways. It's a miracle I can sit on my ass, the way he pounded me into the new year. Housekeeping will need a blacklight to clean the bodily fluids hiding in plain sight. One shower wasn't enough.

Things changed for us. We broke the no-penetration rule in every sense of the word, and I have no regrets. The sex was amazing, but what's developing between us is incredible. We not only shared our bodies, we declared our love out loud. During the course of finding my footing, I found a friend who became a partner for the simple fact that he wanted to be present and remains a constant in my life. Letting go and allowing myself to feel required trust. Julian will catch me if I fall, but I can save myself.

"Julie?"

He tears his attention away from the TV. It takes four chews to swallow. "Should I order more Wheaties?"

I huff a laugh and push him with my shoulder. "No."

How do I put into words how alive I feel?

The answer is in the way my pulse catches at his affection and his promise to care for my heart.

"I love you."

He kisses my temple, and my eyes flutter closed. "I love you too, sweetheart."

"So, we're doing this?"

"Whatever you're comfortable with, baby. I'm not going any-where." He interlaces our fingers and kisses my hand. "Last night doesn't change anything—with the kids, I mean."

I nod. "You're still a family friend, we'll keep it that way until the time is right."

"I won't rush this, sweetheart."

My throat works to rein in the emotions expanding my chest. "You always know what to say."

The corners of his mouth tip into a smile. It's timid for such a confident man. "When you love someone, you pay attention. You and the kids are my priority. I want to do right by you, and I'll show you through my actions what I say with my words."

"Good." I put my plate back on the nightstand and nestle into the hard planes of his chest. "Because I don't want this to end. April isn't that far away. We've been good so far and haven't drawn attention."

Minus Morgan who caught us in bed, and Erica, who sniffed out a love connection before we did. We can keep this up for a few more months, until it's safe to step into the light.

Together.

The silver twin bell alarm clock I almost murdered with a pillow earlier blares so loud it pulls my smile into a frown. "I'm not ready to leave," I say in a grumble and peek at the time. "Where is your sister? I texted her four times. She has my clothes, and she needs to get back here."

Julian shrugs. "Maybe she's sleeping."

I face him with *You can't be serious* set in my expression. "Have you ever known Morgan to sleep past ten? She was probably up at seven and already halfway through her itemized to-do list."

"I'll drive you to her when it's time to check out."

My jaw drops. "And leave here together?"

"You plan on running next to my car?" His chuckle is light, unbothered by thoughts of her in a ditch or someone's basement with a ball gag and no heat. "She probably forgot. Maybe she's busy. I don't keep tabs on her."

"It's not like her, Julian. We should go, just to check." We'll figure out the logistics of leaving separately later. "My friend might need me."

I fold my arms and stare until he gives in. It may or may not have come with a nip slip.

Oops!

He throws up his hands. "Okay, fine. Get dressed."

A plan I can get behind. "I'll take the stairs and meet you in the alley."

Julian laughs his toned ass off. It takes three tries for him to calm down and wipe the tears from his eyes. "I love you, El."

I giggle and smack his arm. "I'm serious!" Great, now I'm laughing. "We have to be discreet."

His brow quirks "*Now* you care about discretion, Dora the Exhibitionist? You begged me to bend you over the balcony this morning, but walking through the lobby together is too much?" He swings his legs over the bed and stands, his morning wood mirroring his arms stretched over his head. The piercing I rode and licked winks in the light on his way to the bathroom.

I move to grab my dress but stop at his warning. "Don't even think about leaving the bed! I'm eating your pussy before we go."

On second thought, Morgan will be just fine for another half hour.

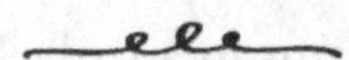

Julian's SUV rolls to a stop in front of Morgan's driveway. His tongue sorcery turned into me riding him like I had to jumpstart a car. I regained my sexual appetite last night and will now keep a lifetime supply of Wheaties in my pantry—not that the man needs it. His recovery period is ridiculous.

He nods and scans the lawn. "Alright, Secret Agent Greene. How do you suggest we breach the perimeter?"

"With a key?" I hold up my keyring.

Julian deadpans, "You plan to walk through the front door when I had to scoop you out of a hotel alley?"

I wave him off and unbuckle my seat belt. It made sense at the time. "There are no bloggers here. Don't act like you weren't impressed."

"Oh, yeah. You get a gold medal for hiding behind flower arrangements in the lobby and ducking behind dumpsters outside." A deep chuckle rumbles through him. "Let me get the door for you, Carmen Sandiego."

The house is quiet when we enter. "Morgan?"

"Mac?" The bass in Julian's tone carries up the stairs.

Nothing.

My brow wrinkles. Her car is out front. Where is she?

"Check upstairs," Julian says. "I'll go outside." He leaves out the back, headed to who knows where.

I'm making coffee—for investigation purposes—when the white French door opens and slams in a rush. Julian's natural shade is a rich chocolate brown, but right now it's gray, and there's sweat over his brow like he saw a ghost.

I stare at his flat gaze. "Did you find her?"

He blinks slowly and moves his eyes toward the direction he came. "Time to go." He grabs my coffee, gulps half of it in one go, and ushers me to the front door.

"Hey—what...Stop!" I dig my heels in the hardwood floor. Morgan would have my head if she was here, but she's not. "Did you find her or not?"

Julian nods, his eyes distant. I've never seen him so shook. In his suit and bow tie, it's kind of adorable.

"*Okay*. Let me go say hi and give her the business for ignoring us." She's barged into my house one too many times. No way I'm not returning the favor.

I leave Julian standing in front of the main door. The coffee cup is still in his hand, and his terrified look is reflecting in the glass. I might have to drive him home.

My heels shuffle along the stone pavers through the backyard. For January, the day is unseasonably mild. Morgan isn't near the outside kitchen or the playground. Muffled sounds from the shed weave into Miguel's "All I Want Is You." Is she working on a school craft?

That answer is live and in living color.

I cover my mouth and push down a gasp. Morgan is visible through the window panels next to the sliding door. Her hair and face are covered in a splatter of rainbow hues, which would be shocking if she wasn't naked. Her legs intertwine with Joseph's as they rock into each other in a seated position on the floor. They share a kiss before he rolls her over and hammers inside her.

The walk around the house and to my car is as graceful as catching your best friend in a paint-by-orgasms session. Good for them. I'll wait for her to bring it up once she's ready. People are in my business enough as is, and I won't return the favor.

My laugh bellows at Julian who's still traumatized. At least he made progress moving from the house to the front porch. "Do I need to drive you home?"

That gets me a glare. "Now is not the time. I'm going to bleach my eyes." He shakes his head and reaches for his keys. "See you tomorrow for tacos?"

Our Taco Tuesdays are my favorite day of the week, outside of my me time on Fridays. It's tough for me to cook after shuffling from Bright Spot to pick up Jackson, and the kids love the mini feast he brings.

"Sounds good." He pulls me in for a deep kiss and pins me to my car. My fingers tease his scalp as I moan into his mouth.

His forehead dips to touch mine. "I love you."

"Love you too, Julie."

Chapter 38

Ella

If it wasn't for my current sugar high, someone would find my body curled up in a deep sleep. The thought crossed my mind to sneak up to my room and toss the week's worth of laundry I've yet to tackle over me for a nap. It'd be musty but worth it.

Jackson speed walks by with a half grin and quick glance. I told him three times not to treat this house like a running track, and I won't repeat myself again. He and his friends sound like the herd that stomped Mufasa to death in *The Lion King*, assuming the fall didn't take him out.

Textured brown curls bounce under his blue party hat as he and two buddies head to the basement. Between the arcade games, air hockey table, and gaming consoles, they have more than enough to keep them entertained.

"Thank you again for the invite. Javen was more than happy to attend." Phaedra, his mom, takes a sip of fruit punch through a silly straw. Her three-year-old daughter, Divine, attends Bright Spot and is the cutest little girl. She and Haile are hosting a formal tea party in the dining room, complete with tiaras and boas, far away from their brothers.

I pull out two cupcake stands to load up the baked goods next to the cake. "Jackson hasn't stopped talking about Javen or Tyrell since they met. We should set up a playdate soon."

"I'll run it by Keisha, but it sounds good. You sure I can't help with anything?"

"Nope." I shake my head. "Make yourself comfortable."

Phaedra and Keisha are cousins. They grew up together in DC and watch each other's kids when they have to work. Phaedra is on double duty while Keisha works at the navy hospital.

The front door opens, and a wave of guests enters, with Duke in the lead. "Did I miss it?" He frantically scans for the party underway.

"They're downstairs playing games," I say through a smile.

The exhale he releases is too grown for a seven-year-old. "It took too long to get here." He directs his pinched expression at Morgan, who lifts a brow. Duke quickly averts his attention to Noah, who's standing behind his mom. He's a quiet one, but he peeks his head out. "You play Pokémon?"

Brown doe eyes widen. He nods.

Duke lifts two card carriers from his jacket. "Let's go. I'm Duke, by the way."

The kids, including Elijah and Xavier, who shuffled in behind Duke, toss off their coats and shoes and race to the basement in an assortment of melanated hues and fresh barber cuts. "Walk Duke!" His socks skid on the wood floor at his mother's command.

Haile and Divine hear the commotion and take off after them but slow their pace at Haile's hand. "We run after no man," she says. Off they walk with their tiaras held high.

Jackson isn't open to big gatherings, so I expected his request for an at-home birthday party. What I didn't anticipate was that Duke was the only invite from his school. Everyone else is one of the new friends he made over winter break at Bright Spot. They all go to DC schools, sparking a campaign for him to change his. A few parents have raved about a charter school not too far from my job with small-group instruction and after-school STEM programming. Two of the kids play intramural sports, which was the final push for me to download an application. I still need to talk to Charles, but I support our children in spaces where they feel seen.

"Hey, lady. Where's my party hat?"

I pass Morgan, Ashley, and Leah paper cones and introduce them to Phaedra. Within five minutes, we're laughing around the kitchen island with hot cocoa.

"Girl, this place is *nice*," Leah says, her eyes fixed on the garlands twinkling with white lights from the kitchen to the living room. I always wanted a winter wonderland during the colder months. Now, I have it. There wasn't a holly wreath spared. Tiny circles of festive cheer hang on each of the interior doors, because why not?

"I lucked out. The owner heard about my separation and did me a solid." I take another sip from my snowflake mug. "There's no way I could afford to dream here, let alone pay the taxes on a place like this."

"No lies told," Phaedra says over her own mug.

"Is your ex coming today?" The slight frown Ashley casts reminds me of Noah. They're both anxious, and they hate drama.

"Yeah, where is he?" All eyes shift to Julian and the maroon Henley hugged to his frame. In jeans and white socks, he strides to the refrigerator to pull out a reusable water bottle like he's right at home.

The room is now a few degrees warmer with the moms ogling him like a packet of chicken at the store that's five cents cheaper than the rest. Can't say I blame them, because my vagina is a sauna in his presence.

Julian pauses mid-gulp to take in the lust-filled eyes on him. A flush creeps up his neck, and his gaze shifts to me. For such a playboy, he gets shy easily. I know he's not his image, but it's still cute.

"Should be here soon," I say.

The ding of the doorbell has Julian in action. "I'll get it." He scurries off to the foyer with a tail of horny women staring at his ass. Minus his sister.

Phaedra is the first to say what we're all thinking. "That man is *fine*." She stares at me like she just saw an angel and has to close her mouth by hand.

"Yes, he is." Leah touches her neck and swallows hard. "He could open my door any day."

Morgan grimaces. "I'm going downstairs to help watch the kids." Julian volunteered to oversee the game play. He probably wanted to dodge the attention, but I appreciate the gesture nonetheless.

It's hard not to laugh. I don't know how I'd react to people eye-fucking my brother if I had one. She only got comfortable with me fucking him recently, and that's still a work in progress.

Ashley's eyes go wide. She snaps. "That's Julian Brooke. The lawyer who's always in the blogs."

Leah tilts her head to the side. "Wasn't he in England somewhere? I'd let him have me from sea to shining freaking sea, okay?" She high-fives Phaedra, who giggles with her tongue out.

I open my mouth to end the conversation, but my voice gets caught in my throat at the sight of my mother. In my living room.

The brown eyes I inherited look back at me and move to Julian, who's standing next to her with a smile, before falling on me again. "My baby."

Her voice is a balm. I choke back tears and run to her. "Mama." The word lands against her soft curls. There are more gray streaks since I saw her last April. She rubs circles on my back and squeezes me tighter.

Oh, how I've missed her. We talk multiple times a week, and we video call now that she grasps the concept, but it's not enough. I planned to bring her down for the holidays, but it didn't work out with her schedule as a home health aide.

"H-how long are you here? *How* did you get here?" Every question is rapid fire. My mother is finally here.

Thick lips pull her face into a grin. "Seems somebody sent me a plane ticket to celebrate my grandbaby's birthday and a car from the airport. Is Julie here? I want to thank her."

At that moment, I want to risk court action and public scrutiny for kissing Julian. I mentioned how disappointed I was that my mom couldn't be here for the holidays days ago, in passing. Never did I imagine he'd fly her here to surprise us.

I stare at the man who continues to take my breath away and love me and my family in a way we've never experienced. His eyes sweep over my face and soften at the tear streaking down my cheek. "This is Julian, Mama," I say without breaking his gaze.

"Oh." Her tone matches the gentleness of her glances between us. Her eyes settle on Julian with a warmth that pulls out his dimples. "Thank you for the sweet gift. I didn't realize you were Julie."

He bends down to reach her hug and engulfs her in his frame. "It was my pleasure, ma'am," he says softly.

"How did you get her information?" I never told him my childhood address or her phone number.

A small smile touches his lips. "Morgan helped steer me in the right direction."

I introduce my mother to the other moms before she goes with Julian to the basement hand in hand. The three sets of eyes that were once on my man are now on me. "What?" I clear my throat and gather the mugs to wash in the sink.

"I did not come here for you to test my lash glue." Phaedra fans her face. "If you don't marry that man, I will."

"Can I be a sister wife?" Leah chimes in.

"Would you two stop?" My laugh is light, a far cry from the drama I just starred in. "Julian is a family friend and Morgan's brother. We're"—I snort at the three of them leaning in—"friends!" I tip my head back and let out another laugh at their groans. "My divorce isn't final yet, and I don't want to confuse the kids, you know?"

"You mean the kids playing downstairs with your man, who's entertaining all of ours so we can have peace and quiet? Who just flew your mother in?" Leah winks.

"We get it," Ashley says.

"And we hope you do too," Phaedra adds with a chuckle. I cannot wait for them to meet Erica. The world isn't ready.

"That's the thing." I shrug. "Dating and *et cetera* could jeopardize my divorce. In Virginia"—I push my index finger through the circle I make with my other hand—"while separated is technically adultery. The accusation alone would have me knee-deep in attorney's fees and battling about my business in court."

Leah wraps an arm around me. "Say less. We didn't see a thing. Just do me a favor?"

"What's that?"

"Send him over to my house if you don't want him after your divorce. I'll fix him a plate and help him start the healing process."

I bounce her away with my hip. "Get out."

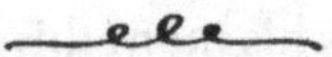

The music is so loud, I miss the doorbell. Charles appears in the backyard, wearing a scowl like he walked over hot coals to get here. He squints at the chaos in the kitchen.

As luck would have it, Beyoncé's "Break My Soul" pipes through the speaker system. Erica and the girls provide background vocals as I sing into the rolling pin. Julian is voguing next to Joseph, who came after an art installation. Mama and Ms. Thelma are off to the side, chatting, and the kids are busy stuffing their faces with the pizzas they made. Haile gives me a thumbs-up and a wink, so that's a plus.

Charles points to the back door to let him in. I'm a little out of breath, which draws his brows together when I open it. "Hey," I say to his clenched jaw.

He scans me from head to toe, taking in the gray fuzzy socks the kids got me for Christmas, my black leggings, and a Jimi Hendrix tee. "Aren't you going to let me in?" His gaze flicks to the party over my shoulder.

I match his glare but add in an eye roll and step aside. "Check your Grinch at the door. This is our son's party."

Rustling behind him has both of us turning to see Katharine navigating the walkway with wrapped gifts up to her nose. "Hi, dear!" The boxes muffle her voice but not her enthusiasm.

My eyes snap back to her worthless son. "You left your mother with all those boxes?" Just when I think he can't sink any lower. "Move." I push him out the way and take the four steps to relieve Katharine.

What kind of son treats his mom this way? I'd pop Jackson if he dared. His dad is six three, so it's only a matter of time before I'll need the chair to reach him.

Exhausted blue eyes meet mine with an appreciative smile. "Thank you."

Charles is already inside. Heads turn as he ignores everyone and goes straight to the dining room. He squats down and stretches out his arms, his gray peacoat engulfing our children. All eyes are on him, except for Morgan, who sneaks a shot of liquor into her hot cocoa from a flask in her gold clutch. She's the only friend here who's had the displeasure of experiencing Charles Hudson up close and personal.

Mama's eyes dart to me from the other side of the kitchen island. It's big, but not *that* big for Charles to ignore her. He already left his own mother outside to deal with the gifts and winter cold. I guess he's on brand.

"This is a beautiful home, Ella." Katharine unbuttons her long beige coat and takes in the winter decor and homemade crafts. "It has your touch." Her smile lands on Mama, and she touches her pearls. "Is that Mary Lee?" A wisp of her southern accent tickles her tone as she rushes to my mother for an eager hug.

"Oh my word! It's so good to see you!" Mama is half a second from squealing in her face. She gets giddy seeing people the same way I do at the sight of a restocked pantry.

"Grandma!" Jackson pulls away from Charles to rush to Katharine, only this time he's cautious not to tackle her.

Haile chases behind with an infectious grin. "Come see our rooms!" She and Jackson reach for their grandmothers' hands to guide them up the stairs, their chatter disappearing as they go.

It's a rare occasion for both grandmas to be under the same roof. I'm thankful I don't have a monster-in-law, even if the monster is her Gucci-wearing son.

"You landed on your feet."

Speaking of which.

I save myself the trouble of asking why he's wearing a three-piece suit to his son's birthday party.

His gaze tips up the stairs. "Don't even think about it," I say to his profile. His ass will hit the sidewalk before his Italian leather shoe clears the first step.

He seers at my command and squares his shoulders, earning Julian's attention. My headshake lets him know I got it, but Charles's lips twitch at my defiance. "You're still cute when you're angry."

"It's sad that you still think this a game. If you want to play any more today"—I nod at the basement door—"go downstairs."

The grin he gives me curdles my stomach. Charles is an attractive man on the surface, but I know better. He steps around me to tour the living room. "You've done well for yourself, El. New job." He picks up a vinyl record. "New house. A furnished one in Georgetown, at that." His gaze slides back to me with a scowl, and he steps closer. "The child support I allow you would be a few thousand short of what you'd need to stay here."

I fold my arms over my chest and narrow my eyes. "What are you getting at?"

We're close enough for me to inhale the cologne that once drove me wild. Now it burns my nose hairs. He leans forward to cut the remaining distance between us. "If you wanted to be a kept woman, you should've stayed at home. All of this"—he motions around the living room—"for what? To say you can live without me while I still foot the bill?"

Heat explodes through my body at the sudden urge to push his head through a brick wall. This spineless, arrogant, heartless man thinks he can walk into my house and make *me* feel bad about it?

I flex my fingers to keep them from tightening into a fist. "The child support you *owe* me, for taking care of our children, goes toward them."

His brows shoot up in surprise, and my slip-up tips his lips into a smile. *Shoot.*

I've gracefully dodged this conversation. He never asked, and I never told. It's not his business how much I pay in rent. The answer is zero, but that's for me to know and him to never find out. As long as I provide our children with stable housing, clothe them, and keep food in their bellies, my finances are my finances.

"Your luck just doesn't run out, does it?" Charles's expression is heavy on the resentment. It's not like I was his wife for over a decade or the mother of his kids.

My chin lifts to meet his icy stare. "Don't mask your hope that I'll fall on my face on my account."

"I want you home where you belong. Enough with this independence bullshit. You think you can cut it in a city like this on an educator's pay? Be real, El. Your annual salary is my quarterly bonus after tax."

The sting of his insult stuns me to silence. Charles never saw me as his equal. Only a vessel to birth his heirs, a nanny, and a maid to maintain the illusion of his picturesque family.

Everything I fought for over the last nine months has been cut down in nine seconds.

Charles's smile widens. He is just like his father, down to the glower and flared nostrils. I have always been a thorn in his side for daring to be seen and heard. It's a miracle Jackson and Haile didn't inherit his spitefulness, but I'd be damned if they did.

I draw a deep breath and release it. I added yoga to my newfound free time on the weekends, and namaste in my peace for the sake of my babies.

"She looks good from where I'm standing." Charles straightens to his full height and swivels to face Julian.

The muscles in Julian's shoulders coil, and his stance widens. He assesses me with concern before his eyes move to my ex. Two deep lines take residence between his brows above hardened hickory eyes.

Julian is always upbeat, whether he's stressed at work or running through an opponent on the rugby pitch. His temper flaring draws my lip between my teeth. It's a rare sight, and I'd be lying if I said it didn't make my pulse race for other reasons.

"Julian Brooke." Charles slips a hand into his pocket. "Trading in the single life for cake and ice cream?" The sarcastic quip doesn't reach its mark.

Julian's eyebrow lifts. His eyes never leave my face when he says, "I show up for family." He steps around Charles to stand next to me. I can hold my own, but him by my side is a calming presence. "Did you come all this way to disrupt your son's party and disrespect his mother? Or does the ire you still hold for Ella leaving you only flare when she reminds you she can live without you?"

"This is none of your business."

"It is now." Julian steps in front of Charles to block his view of me. "What would the board think of its CFO terrorizing a wife he cheated on and belittled? Not even Daddy could save you from that PR nightmare."

"Son." Katharine's clipped tone takes us all by surprise. She stands at the edge of the kitchen in a cream couture dress and with her last nerve plucked. "I think it's best we go."

Charles steals one last glance at me. "This isn't over."

"It is for today. Here"—Julian nods toward the kitchen—"I'll see you out."

My eyes dart to his. "The front door—"

"I got it." Julian's face splits into a grin. "Would you get me another cup of hot chocolate please? Thanks, El."

I join the ladies at the kitchen island, unsure how we got from the showdown in the living room to me fetching Julian a drink. He was ready to rip Charles's head off a minute ago, but now he wants cocoa?

Movement catches my eye out the window. Julian is in step with Charles one minute and ducking behind the house the next. It's too quiet. I step closer to the window. "Where are the kids?"

As if he hears me, Julian jumps to his feet and yells in Japanese. Charles's steps falter as he peers over his shoulder, trying to figure out what's going on, when Duke and Jackson respond in Japanese from the side of the garage. Their matching Joker grins are in 3D as they unleash an assault of snowballs Julian's way. Only Julian ducked behind the patio, which means—

"Make it rain!" Joseph stands with Haile, Divine, and Noah across from the garage with their own arsenal of snowballs they release into the air. Charles will have to go through them to get to back to the front of the house, unless he hops the fence.

Phaedra rushes to the window at the sound of our children's screams. Javen, Tyrell, Xavier, and Elijah roll out from their hiding places. "Leah! Get over here and look at these kids assembling!"

Laughter drowns out Charles's muffled screams as he runs in circles to get to safety. "For Wakanda!" a child yells. It comes with a direct hit to the face. "And the Southeast!" another adds with a snowball zipping by.

Charles grabs the lid of the trash can to shield himself from the snowball fight he's now in the middle of, but not before tripping over the hose. An Italian shoe launches in the air as his ass hits the pavement.

"I hope he gets a hole in the big toe," Leah snickers as Charles army crawls in a sock, one shoe, and a ruined suit and coat. There's so much chaos around him with the kids ducking and diving shots, Haile and Jackson miss his departure.

"That's my cue." I turn to Katharine, who's fastening her jacket. She hugs Mama. "Please come see me before you leave." Her eyes lift to mine with a smile. "Enjoy your night, Ella."

"Get home safe."

She takes one look out the window and laughs. "I'll go out the front. Goodbye, ladies."

Morgan stands by my side and hands me a mug of hot cocoa. "How are they having a snowball fight with no snow on the ground?" It must be fifty degrees outside.

I catch her smirk before she takes a sip. "Julian bought a snow-maker and has been sneaking out the basement to get it ready."

Jackson hoped it would snow in time to have a snowball fight for his birthday. It didn't happen, so Julian brought the snow to him.

We clink our mugs together and take in the battle of Georgetown in the backyard. Charles is long gone, and the kids are pelting the remaining snowballs at Julian and Joseph. The latter lifts Duke as a human shield and takes off behind the garage. Julian isn't so lucky.

Jackson leads a high-speed chase after Julian, who's now jumping over backyard debris. He finally surrenders, but that doesn't save him from a snowball to the chest. He falls gloriously, and my son's grin is infectious as his friends and sister surround him and cheer. Julian scoops him onto his shoulders and jogs around the backyard.

My quiet child who reserves his emotions is living out loud in vibrant color. His joy is uncontained as he smiles down at Julian, who looks up at Jackson with a smile of his own. His birthday was perfect. A reminder that when life throws a curve ball, have a snowball fight.

The guilt of my kids having an asshole for a father is not for me to carry, but it's a weight that presses down on me. This moment, and the smile on my beautiful boy's face, proves the power of uncondi-tional love and chosen family.

Chapter 39

Julian

"I'm glad you finally called."

That makes one of us.

Camila considers the paper menu written in fancy cursive, oblivious that I haven't responded. Or maybe she just doesn't care. Her focus drops to the section of entrées guaranteed to be as unseasoned as this reunion.

I check my phone. Maybe there's an email about a work fire I have to put out or an emergency that will get me out of here faster. Nothing.

"Excuse me." I catch our server on his way to the kitchen. "Could I please get one of those giant pretzels with the dipping sauces? Get whatever you want, Camila."

"I'll have a dish of olives," she says, confirming only one of us will suffer from trying to be cute in a restaurant. I've seen her take down a full rack of ribs and a half a pound of potato salad. She eats when she's not keeping up appearances.

"Right away." The server nods and disappears into a small group of colleagues in black and white. They're zigzagging between mahogany booths and round tables draped in white linen.

District Bakehouse is a top spot for business lunches. The bakery alone tempts you into a carb coma, but the restaurant offers upscale dining without any romantic ambiance or undertones. Valentine's Day was a month ago. Save the hearts and flowers and bring the bread.

Camila pulls her napkin into her lap and adjusts her cream blouse. "Your mother was at the benefit luncheon last week. She was thrilled to hear we're meeting today."

"I'm sure she was." Pleased I obliged her request to see Camila after months and bribery attempts in the form of homecooked meals. A man can only take in so much *soup joumou* and *poul ak nwa* before he caves.

"You look good." Heat flashes in her eyes as they roam over my charcoal suit and canary tie. "What's new?"

Everything worth protecting.

My head tips from side to side as I decide how best to respond. Camila thrives on gossip like the rest of the DC socialites who never learned to mind their business. I trusted her at one point, but that was years ago and under different circumstances.

"Work." A given. "I'm coaching kids' rugby. Our first game is coming up."

"Fitting." She nods with disinterest. If it doesn't involve an exclusive guest list, it doesn't register as important. "Are you seeing anyone?"

Straight to the point.

Camila peers around the server dropping off our appetizers who looks between us and smiles. *Please don't encourage her.*

It was a risk asking her to lunch. She hasn't stopped texting since she came back from whatever trip she was on last, and I don't want her or anyone else to get the wrong idea. Ella agreed that Camila's constant *Hey, what are you up to?* messages breached excessive. The fact that she didn't string me from the ceiling by my dick or kick me to the curb for drama with my ex is a testament to how incredible she is after everything she's been through.

Am I appeasing my mother today? Yes, but there's another reason this reunion needed to happen—not counting this tasty-ass pretzel.

I straighten and push away the tiny spicy mayo container. "My personal life is no one's business. It hasn't concerned you for years."

She flinches but reaches for my hand. "I didn't mean to upset you. I just...Don't you miss this? Us? You finally moved back home after years away."

The server returns holding a tiny vase with a single red rose and drops it between us with a wink.

Great.

"Cam—"

Her hand darts up. Not the one that's still holding mine in a death grip. *Shit, does she lift?*

"Hear me out. We both had other relationships—flings—that didn't matter or come close to what we had. We couldn't get our timing right then, but we can now."

"Ayo, we don't need another thing on this table." I stare down the server, who's hell-bent on making a love connection that isn't here. He really came back with some tea lights and matches.

I shake my head. "Camila, we weren't a fit then, and we aren't now. I hope we can coexist, but that's the extent of it. A 'hello' in passing if we ever run into each other. No more calls. No more texts. Let's move on."

The fire in her eyes triggers her glare, which tells me this conversation is far from over and it's one I'll need to repeat. She and my mother share a determination that would be admirable if it wasn't a pain in my ass.

She rises from her chair and pulls her purse to her shoulder. "I lost my appetite."

Surprising since you only ate four olives.

"Have a good day, Camila."

"One way or another, you will come to your senses." She storms past the table in a flurry of expensive perfume and ego more bruised by my rejection than the fact we were never a match.

The server tracks Camila pushing her way to the entrance. His face drops. "Was it the candles?"

"Nope. I'm ready to order."

Chapter 40

Ella

"**G**ood evening, Ms. Greene."

"Hi, Otis."

"I'll buzz you up." Otis walks the short distance to the elevator. His stride is efficient, modeling his years in the Secret Service. Puppy-dog eyes shift to the bag in my hand. "He hasn't eaten since lunch."

"We'll have to fix that." I step onto the elevator.

Otis always packs the same meal for his shift. Avocado chicken salad with a side of pretzels. The man enjoys routines and doesn't veer away from them or the black suit he wears to work. He leans in to swipe his key card, his jet-black hair dusted in silver glinting in the light. "Enjoy your evening, and thanks for the birthday gift."

I caught him watching the Home Edit ladies doing a makeover, and I ordered him some organizing supplies to use throughout his house. The perfect present for a man who loves order with style.

Julian didn't choose to work late tonight, but he does at least once a week so he can see Otis. The security guard has been with the company for twenty years, and he's family, even if he doesn't like hugs or socializing. Julian makes a point to see him regularly ever since his wife died two years ago. Otis is a hard shell to crack, but he's a teddy bear inside.

"It was my pleasure, O. See you soon."

The climb to the fourth floor is quick. There's no time to calm the butterflies in my stomach. I've visited this office enough; it's not like it's the first time. I was here days ago, when I popped in after his "lunch" with an ex.

Was I thrilled he was meeting someone who's likely a knockout with no gray hairs? Of course not.

Did I fold over with laughter at Julian asking Morgan to sage him down in his office and when said sage lighting ceremony almost set off the sprinklers? Absolutely.

The poor guy was traumatized, begging for mercy between a fit of coughs.

I trust Julian, and I trust what we have.

Metal doors widen to an empty office floor draped in darkness. Three recessed lights illuminate a pathway I follow to a second hall around the corner. Julian's voice weaves through a tenor of soft syllables. His throaty laughter ignites a flashback to New Year's Eve, when he nearly licked me into a coma.

I stop at the doorframe to take him in. His back is to me, which is an all-access pass to his ass and muscular thighs in black pants. A light brown leather belt holds a white button-down in place. He dips his head and chuckles with his hands firm in his pockets.

My man is wearing that suit.

As if he hears my thoughts, Julian turns mid-sentence of what I now register as Japanese. We haven't seen each other since my

Tuesday drop-in, and we have no plans to get out of bed this weekend—except to shower and replenish our fluids.

He's still talking through his earpiece when I reach him for a hug. Cedar and sandalwood roll through my body at his kiss to my temple before he unzips my coat to hang next to his. When he registers the bag in my hand, he taps his earpiece. "For me?" My smile is stupid big at the joy on his face for the takeout from Suegra's. "Thank you, sweetheart." I get a quick kiss before he points to his desk and hits the earpiece again.

He and the bag make their way to the loveseat next to the coffee table. He pulls out the container of *sancocho de gallina* and has to bite his lip to stop a moan. His eyes lift, and he mouths *I love you* before he's back to his call.

I pull out the laptop from my messenger bag and set up shop at his desk. Grant work chews up a lot of time during the day. Two deadlines are approaching, and we need money to sustain our services. Julian started weekly donations to cover the kids' lunches for us, so we can use funding elsewhere, but I won't rely on him or anyone else to carry our expenses. Financial freedom is independence.

Childcare in DC is some of the most expensive in the country, which creates barriers for families who can't afford to invest in high-quality early education and development. Legislation to appropriate funding to the most vulnerable isn't moving fast enough. Bright Spot is steady and thriving because of our angel donor, but how many facilities can say the same? For our kids to soar, it takes all centers around the area. A grant or two is not enough.

An hour passes before Julian ends his call, his dinner and tie gone.

Firm fingers press into the tense muscles in my shoulders. I close my eyes and moan. "That feels amazing."

My head falls to my forearms as Julian scoots out the office chair for better access. He lifts my gray sweater and glides his hands down my back, targeting knots to rub loose. "Your ass is amazing." He grabs a handful and squeezes. "So are these breasts." His hands skate up my front to cup my bra. At this angle, the lace fabric over my nipples is holding on for dear life to keep said breasts from spilling over with a sensation that sends me over the edge. I pierced them for Valentine's Day, as part of my divorce checklist and a gift to myself. Morgan couldn't believe it, and honestly neither could I.

"Julian." The hormones this man excites are currently playing double Dutch.

My butt lifts from the seat in his grasp. He kicks the chair out of the way and spins me around to face him. Desire darkens his eyes as he holds my face and takes my mouth. I soften at the probe of his tongue and lean back on the desk, closing my laptop and all thoughts about grants.

"We should stop, sweetheart," he whispers over my lips. "It's late, and you haven't finished your grant application."

If there are two things mothers excel at, it's handling business on limited sleep and tackling multiple to-dos at once. We can walk and chew gum, and I can finish grant work and get this dick.

I sit up and pull his mouth to mine with my teeth. His groan deepens when I reach for his length and squeeze. "I appreciate your chivalry, but you need to finish what you started."

A knock at the door startles me out of my nap. I haven't taken one since Haile was younger, but I have zero shame admitting I needed it. Julian put me straight to bed after three orgasms. He had to cover my mouth for Otis not to hear me howling after midnight.

Another knock.

I flip off the loveseat and fall ass-up on my knees with no underwear on or common sense. Julian ripped through the lace with his teeth and locked them in his drawer before he contorted my legs like I graduated from Cirque du Soleil.

Hence the need for a nap.

I cover myself with Julian's navy blazer, the one I used as a blanket while he took his final call, and bolt to my feet, trying to find a good hiding spot. Otis has to know we're together, but he can't see me like this. *Stall him*, I mouth.

Julian rolls his lips to hold in a laugh. "Just a minute, O."

"Is Ms. Greene hiding?" Otis's amused tone filters through the other side of the door. "It's unnecessary, sir; we know not to say anything."

My eyes balloon while Julian cracks up.

Here I am trying to blend in with an office plant that barely reaches my shoulders. I swear I'm usually more dignified than this, but the man currently wiping tears from his eyes brings out the nasty part of me, and that heifer clearly has no home training.

Julian stands to round the wooden desk we tested for quality assurance less than an hour ago. "Relax, sweetheart. We're safe here." He winks before pulling the door open, but not wide enough for Otis to walk in and find me covering my coochie.

"Stop with the 'sir.' I've only asked for a decade," Julian says with no bite in his tone.

"Sorry to interrupt." Otis clears his throat like he didn't catch us acting like two teenagers sneaking around. Technically, he didn't, but he's in for an eyeful if he steps inside this office. "You good back there, Ms. Greene? I hope the door isn't crushing you."

How—

A deep chuckle vibrates in the former Secret Service agent's chest. "Part of the job, Ms. Greene, which is why I'm here." He sighs. "I saw someone lingering out front. I think it's best if you two leave through the back. Just to be safe."

I glance at Julian, who's staring at the longtime security guard. "Does this happen?"

"Once, after I called it off with Camila," he says, his fingers digging deeper into the door.

My brows rise. "Lady Prim and Proper is outside playing catch a stalker?" I never searched for Camila online, but from what I've heard, activity that requires flats over heels and all black isn't her style.

Otis snorts, a break from his usually stoic character. "Two bloggers hid in the bushes across the street after spotting this one with a pageant queen, a model, and...what was the other one?" He snaps his finger. "A chemical engineer."

I pop my head out. "A chemical engineer?"

He nods.

Julian lets out a deep sigh and looks down at the floor. The tip of his shoe scrapes against an imaginary scuff mark. "A very different time. Moving on." He eyes me. "Where did you park?"

"In the private lot out back." I got a pass for when I visit.

"Thank you, baby." He and Otis continue talking, but I can't hear a word after that velvet "baby." We could be under siege, caught up in some Jordan Peele situation with aliens and us staring up at the night sky with a collective "Nope," and I would still be here, staring at this man who's worried about our safety, with vagina tremors from playing naked Twister on his desk.

I've never felt this, these tingles or the freedom to enjoy pleasure without feeling guilty for prioritizing my needs. Ella Greene is a damn good mother who loves tacos and happens to enjoy weekly doses of sex. Safety is also at the top of the list.

"I wouldn't worry yet. It could be nothing, just someone hoping to catch a glimpse of you," Otis says to Julian. "I called Luis at Suegra's and told him to keep an eye out, and I'll do another sweep before I walk you two out."

Julian nods. "Appreciate you, Otis."

"No problem. I'll be back up in five."

A peeper the same week Julian meets with Camila? Maybe it's nothing, but I don't like it.

Chapter 41

Ella

"We're going to be late!"

Small feet stomp to the top of the staircase. "Julian isn't here yet, Mom. We're fine!" Annoyance simmers in Jackson's tone, just enough for me to hear it without it being disrespectful. I'm hovering, but I can't put away my parental license to helicopter until I know he packed his cleats and ate enough.

Baseball was easy. Hit the ball, run the bases, and make it home. No one chases you down, and the odds of you ending up at the bottom of a human pile are slim to none. I'm not opposed to Jackson playing rugby, but Julian gives me a heart attack at his games. It's a miracle he hasn't ended up in the ER with broken bones, stitches, or a concussion. *I* might need medical attention by the end of the day.

The skillet sirens with a loud pop. "Shit." I flip over the layer of egg and lower the heat.

"Still freaking out?" Haile hops down the steps with a knowing grin. My daughter turned five last month and wastes no opportunity to remind me I'm overreacting. Her soft curls bounce in purple barrette pigtails on her way to the kitchen island. She pulls herself onto a barstool and folds her hands on the marble counter.

I clear my throat and turn back to the stove, unwilling to allow a preschooler in a lilac unicorns and pizza tee to read me to filth before nine a.m. "I'm fine, Haile. Eggs?" I snort at her tiny hand cupping her face. "Do you want eggs or not?"

A series of taps on the patio door pulls my focus. I turn and freeze, all thoughts crashing into the sculpted chest cloaked in blue and white. Track suits aren't anything out of the ordinary, but the way the material molds to Julian's body is a sight that never gets old.

"Hi." My jerky welcome sparks a relaxed smile.

"Hi, sweetheart." The words lull me into stillness. Julian's presence has a way of soothing my nerves while riling up the sexual appetite we resurrected months ago.

Eggs.

Shit.

"Come in." I rush back to the abandoned skillet with a silent prayer that breakfast isn't a casualty of the dick magic that left me dumb and speechless at the door.

"Haile Bear." Julian slides his rugby bag off his shoulder to join her at the island. They share the handshake they've been practicing with Jackson for weeks.

"Can you please tell my mom Jackson will survive today?"

"She's still nervous about the game."

"Uh-huh."

"*She* is standing right here," I say with a laugh. "Haile, please get your brother and tell him breakfast is ready."

"Yes, Mommy." She takes off for the stairs and yells for her brother halfway up. "Jackson! Get off the game and come eat!"

I scoop pillowy eggs onto two plates with a satisfied nod. I might have burned toast on more than one occasion, but I am good with scrambled eggs. "Want some?"

"No, thanks. I usually keep pregame meals to a protein bar. What's going on today?"

I slide the plates over the island and avoid his stare. Can't a woman worry in peace? "It's fine." I wave a hand and put the skillet in the sink. "I'm fine, really. Just being silly."

Julian rounds the island, pulls me to his chest, and buries his face in my neck. His voice is a velvet murmur. "How can I put your mind at ease?" Soft lips brush the hollow of my throat. "Need me to take care of you downstairs?"

I bump him with my butt and giggle. "If you don't back up!" He leans against the counter to mirror my stance. "I know it's safe."

He nods for me to continue.

"I don't want him to get hurt. What if some kids forget it's flag rugby and tackle him? There's no protection." I bite my lip at how foolish this must sound to Julian. Here I am freaking out about flags when he and Antonio send men on their asses every game.

"There's a risk of accident or injury with any contact sport, but we make flag rugby as safe as possible," Julian says. "We emphasize on- and off-pitch safety and encourage an environment of respect and safe play. Jackson has natural instincts, and he's building the awareness of a great player. Plus, he has a good coach."

I roll my eyes and huff out a laugh. "Says the one coaching him."

Julian started up a youth rugby team in February with a former player who now coaches at a nearby university. He takes Jackson with him to practice every Tuesday and Thursday before he hits the pitch for himself. I put the ninety minutes to good use by taking Haile to the jiujitsu classes I no longer need to figure out how to squeeze in on Saturdays. Her MMA gym—yes, that's still wild to say about my five-year-old—isn't far from Jackson and Julian's practice pitch, which makes for a smooth pick-up.

Everything fits, and where I once had to shuffle solo, I now have someone who willingly puts in the effort. I don't rely on Julian because I have to. God knows enough mothers have proven time and time again that when our backs gets pushed against the wall, we'll find a way to get it handled.

The past eleven months have taught me that time is priceless. I discounted myself for a man who never recognized my value, and I won't make the same mistake again. I'm a rare commodity, and the price went up.

I stare at the one who enchants my heart, caresses my imperfections, and helped nurture me back to life. My steps are quick to close the distance for a kiss. He meets my lips, capturing every emotion whirring through me with a soul-reaching tenderness.

"I love you." He reclaims my mouth at the declaration, lifting my face into his hands with a gentle possession.

The rumbling from upstairs breaks us apart as Jackson and Haile barrel down the steps. Our glances linger while the kids sit in front of their plates and proceed to scarf their food.

Jackson and Julian clown me for the snacks I packed for them, which make Costco samples look like crumbs. We throw the bags and the kids' suitcases in the trunk and head to the pitch belting songs from the *Aladdin* soundtrack.

"He sure is fast. Look at him go!" Ms. Thelma sticks two fingers in her mouth to whistle at Jackson. I would do double take at the gesture if my son wasn't speeding down the turf.

Julian is jogging along the sideline with a clipboard in one hand and a raised fist. Jackson's opponent gets within reach of his flag, but at the last minute, my son cuts left to score.

"Woo!" Our little cheering section is small but mighty. Ms. Thelma is on her feet, whistling. Katharine narrows her hands into a makeshift megaphone. I'd never heard my mother-in-law raise her voice, let alone show up so casually dressed. She's in high-waisted khakis and navy heels, but at least it's not a suit or a blouse.

Even Haile is taking in her brother's big moment.

Julian and Jackson share a look before Julian ruffles Jackson's curls and calls him and the rest of the team in for a huddle. He's in his element as coach, laughing with the kids and using his knowledge to build up the next generation of players. A natural educator, and quite the mom magnet.

More than one has come up to offer him everything from a Capri Sun and fruit snacks to a neck massage. He's been sending bunny-eyed SOS signals from the field, but what does he expect me to do? Brawl in the stands? Go off on someone willing to give up their pretzels when he's been snacking on my trail mix?

We can't draw attention to ourselves, and no one has crossed the line—though DJ's mom does look a little sus with a paper airplane in her hand, one that I bet contains her number.

Ms. Thelma leans over and nods at the formation of mothers on the first row behind Julian. "That poor boy will have to fight them off with a stick. Can't say I blame them. You could bounce a quarter off that butt."

My jaw drops. "Ms. Thelma!"

"I'm old, baby, not blind." She pats my jeans with a warm smile, one I now know masks devious thoughts, and leans back on her elbows to stretch out her legs. She's wearing a peach sweat suit and black and white high-tops that are too cute for words.

Katharine scoots closer. "Are you talking about Julian?" His butt is delicious."

Who *are* these two?

Haile is off to the right, four rows in front of us with the sibling of another player. Out of earshot from her grandmother and Grier's mama thirsting over my man.

"He's very good with Jackson," Katharine says, her focus now on the top half of Julian's tracksuit where it belongs.

"Doesn't he teach him Japanese? And Duke?" Ms. Thelma adds in the last part to play down why Jackson and Julian are close. She's been to the townhouse a few times, but she remains a trusted vault of secrets. When she's not throwing shade.

Katharine's eyes grow three sizes. "Wonderful and impressive! Learning another language so young will benefit him when he gets older."

Right now the benefits include him watching anime with a mixing bowl full of cereal, but sure. I add a "Yup" and take a bite of the blueberry muffin I packed in my basket of excessive goodies. Morgan and Duke had a scheduling conflict since his baseball season has started, but her spirit is here in the snacks I lugged. Minus the figs and soft cheese.

A play on the field ignites Julian's cheer, but his fan club I'm wedged between isn't done singing his praises.

Katharine leans in front of me to speak to Ms. Thelma. "I'm surprised he's not courting anyone." I keep my chuckle low at her choice of words, like we're in a *Bridgerton* episode. "Successful lawyer. Great with kids. Multilingual."

He is *good with his tongue.*

"Who knew he was such a the family man?"

The bitter breeze of winter rolls its head through the fresh cut grass and buds of flowers perfuming the air. Rows of eyes shift from the pitch to the tall figure in a lightweight black peacoat and fitted gray pants.

Charles hovers next to his mother, his green eyes piercing the distance between us, before he takes a seat in the row in front to face me. Wisps of jet-black hair tapered neatly at his collar flutter in the faint breeze.

"What are you doing here?" Our standoff is a trade of icy glares. There's an edge to my voice that leaves no doubt I am not here for any of his bullshit.

His mouth thins with displeasure he forces into a smile. "I'm here to watch *our son* during his first rugby game."

You'd think he'd watch Jackson play instead of scowling at me with the time he magically found in his schedule to attend the only sporting activity since we separated. He only cares about others when it benefits him, which begs the question: why today?

Charles's sharp gaze wanes when Katharine clears her throat. He leans over to kiss her cheek. "Mother."

"You remember Ms. Thelma." She nods to the now empty space next to me. Katharine's brows dip. "Where did she go?"

Good question. I didn't hear her get up, but then again, I am facing off with evil.

"Keep going, Jackson!" Julian's energetic call swivels Charles's focus to the field, where our son runs feet from the try zone before an opponent snags his flag. His claps reach the bleachers with a grin to match, until he sees my ex. Julian glances from him to me with a stone expression. Our eyes land on Haile, who left the bleachers to run around with Arabelle.

"Interesting." A chill hangs on the edge of Charles's words and coils his back. He turns just enough to give me his profile, which is lit up with rage.

Katharine casts me a sad glance and squeezes my knee. "It's wonderful you could make Jackson's game. I'm sure he'll appreciate it," she says to her son's back.

Charles digs into his pocket for his ringing phone and stands, but not before his cold eyes slip over the screen to me. "We are a family. Nothing will change that." With the phone raised to his ear, he heads off to take the call.

Here all of ten minutes before work calls him away. Or another woman. The distraction is irrelevant. What matters are the two humans we created when we could stomach each other for more than three seconds at a time.

I scan the field to find Jackson high-fiving a teammate. He's getting older, and he'll remember who was present and who wasn't. Charles deserves whatever comes from his actions, but not at the expense of my son's emotions.

Ms. Thelma shimmies up the stairs with a switch of her hips and plops back in her seat. "Did I miss anything?"

I snort. Charles and I will need to figure out how to coparent without shooting daggers at each other. I *want* that, but his controlling antics have worsened since I left.

A soft hand lands on my leg. "Don't you give that man an ounce more of your energy," Ms. Thelma says. "A hit dog will always holler, especially the ones who mess up their home." Her eyes soften above her plump cheeks, which stretch into a smile. "You turned pain into power. For yourself and those babies."

I brush away a tear and keep my head high. "Yes, ma'am, I did."

She shakes her head and chuckles. "You were a sobbing little thing when I found you in that tent. But look at you now. Mm-hmm!" Her eyes close, and she swings her head from side to side like the card-carrying, devil-stomping Pentecostal woman she is. "Cherish the unexpected blessings in your life. The people who bring goodness and peace. Everything will work itself out. Keep the faith, and keep pressing on." She offers up a "Glory!" to which a woman behind us shouts, "Hallelujah!"

There are fairy godmothers, and then there's Ms. Thelma. A praying grandmother who picks you up, dusts you off, and breathes life back into you.

She stands at the call of a fellow churchgoer and climbs the bleachers to meet her kindred spirit in the Lord. Katharine wrings her hands with a pained stare.

"I didn't know." Her lips tremble as she works up the courage to face me, and her eyes brim with tears. "Charles told me you left him. I didn't know things were that bad."

I take a deep breath and finally tell her why I packed my bags and took our children.

Leaving was already an awkward transition, and part of me feared she'd back up her son no matter what. She had the outline of the demise but never the details.

Katharine takes in everything—me catching Charles with another woman and the IKEA run-in with Ms. Thelma that kicked off my separation. She sighs and hangs her head at the thought that the son she raised could be so vengeful against his wife, who upheld her vows until he broke them.

Shaky hands wipe the tears dampening her face. "I'm so sorry, Ella." She reaches for me but pauses. "There are no excuses or words to make up for what he did. Please know I care for you deeply. You never have to suffer in silence. Far too many of us do."

I take her hand in mine. "Thank you, Katharine. I'm better now. Stronger."

"If you don't mind me asking, how did you find a home after my son demanded you move out of Morgan's?"

A smile finds its way through a haze of painful memories. "A certain Japanese tutor opened up his while he was away, to give me the chance to find solid ground."

Katharine follows my gaze to Julian. He's walking backward, watching the game, but slides his focus to me when he senses my eyes on him. He glances between me and Katharine and mouths, *Are you okay?*

I nod with confidence and a gleam in my eye.

"Well then." Katharine smooths out her beige trench coat. "I'd say Ms. Thelma was right. When you come across an unexpected blessing, hold onto it with everything you got. I just hope there's still room in your life for me?"

"Of course."

We lean against each other and watch Jackson score again. The whistle sounds, and the team erupts in shouts and claps at their first win.

Julian rushes the field to meet Jackson, who jumps into his open arms. They exchange a smile before my son seeks me out in the stands. He waves and shouts, "I did it!"

Yes, baby, you did.

Chapter 42

Julian

Electricity explodes through every cell in my body. "*Fuck.*" I cup Ella's ass as she slides up and down my length.

She surrenders completely, her lips parting as the thrill of arousal ignites a scream. She rises to her feet to swallow my dick inch by inch with slow circular motions that pick up speed when she bottoms out.

I kiss the nipple rings teasing me through the sheer fabric of her bra, bouncing in my face, and hold her hips in place as I meet her thrust for thrust.

"My. Knees. Sound. Like. Glow. Sticks," Ella says through an unsteady pant. She yelps at my smack to her ass.

"Less talking, more fucking." I sit up straighter against the headboard and spread my thighs wider, careful not to agitate my knee as I drive into her.

"Ah! I can't hold it, Julie!"

"Yes, you can!"

"My—!" Ella screams. It's the same pitch as Marv from *Home Alone* being electrocuted. It lasts so long, my brow creases at the possibility that my piercing hurt her. Then she leans back, moving through a ripple of motion that draws my balls up—until her hand slams into my injured knee. *Hard*.

"Fuck!"

She parrots my outburst when her performance gets cut short with a leg cramp.

"My knees!"

"My knee!" I close my eyes and clench my leg, which is outfitted in a cryo knee wrap. It takes a second for the throbbing to subside. *Shit, that hurt*. "Are you okay?" I ask through labored breaths.

"Yeah." She crawls off to the other end of the bed and glances back at my knee. "Sorry about that."

"Don't worry about it." I move off the bed to test the pressure. "Come here." She looks at me with a blank expression, so I help her by grabbing her foot and pulling her to me. This bed is a king, but it's not as big as the one in the townhouse. "Come here means *here*. Get on your knees."

She scoots away. "Julian, your knee—"

"Is fine. Yours is snap, crackle, and popping." A smile slips through her lips and presses into a straight line. "Don't get tight because you couldn't finish what you started. No one told you to hold a squat for that long."

We agreed to come back to my place after the game and have a quiet night in with Chinese takeout after a long day and an unexpected visit from her ex. He didn't cause a scene and stayed through most of the match to watch Jackson and spend time with Haile before he left. El was visibly shaken at first, but she powered through like she always does.

Acrobatics weren't on the menu, which means matching knee wraps tonight.

Ella crawls over to me with a tight mouth and a go-fuck-yourself glare for not calling it quits. I'll take care of my knee after I take care of her. "Wet me." My lips twitch at the fire in her stare.

Since you want to gawk, put that mouth to work.

I expect a lazy swipe of her tongue, but El surprises me when she grips my dick and takes me to the back of her throat. Her head bobs with vacuum force suction, buckling my good and bad knee. It takes extreme focus to dislodge her and not come on her face. *Jesus.*

She spins around to give me her back, lifts her ass, and casts a challenge over her shoulder. Two can play this game.

I fist my head and tap the barbell against her seam. She pushes back and gets just enough of the tip to incite a whimper that becomes a groan at my shallow strokes.

"*Julian.*" She rocks into me with a whine. When she looks back to see the smirk on my face, she pleads with a frustrated moan.

My next command is a whisper. "Forearms on the bed. Knees on my chest." I lift her legs to my shoulders and feast.

I've eaten Ella from the back plenty of times, but never with her pussy in the air like this. My grip tightens at her attempt to wheelbarrow away.

Nope.

"Ride my face, baby." I savor her with long licks. She wants to be more adventurous, and this position won't force her to do the work with her knees.

"Oh my." She spreads wider to throw her ass back. It puts her yoga classes to the test, and my lady is passing with flying colors. I flatten my tongue at each body roll and apply more pressure. "God yes!"

At her orgasm, I put her back on her knees and drive into the warmth between her legs. Her walls thicken, squeezing me like a finger trap. The heat from our skin slapping together turns her thick globes crimson.

Her body vibrates, and I tremor inside her at my release. She collapses onto her side and scoots to make room for me to join her. "That was..." Ella swallows. "*Shit.*"

I pull her in for a kiss and chuckle. "Not bad for an injured man, huh?"

She frowns. "We need to elevate your knee."

My lips seal her to me before she goes full mom mode. "I know, sweetheart. Thank you for caring for me." I reach for the toilet paper we keep under the pillow, put some between her legs, and hobble to the bathroom, where I turn on the shower. "Come get in, baby."

It's our second shower after a day on the pitch. Washington held it down, winning the youth game and the A- and B-side matches. I only played in the first after my old injury flared up. I'll be fine, but nothing could stop me from getting to Jackson, who ran onto the field from the bleachers to congratulate me and the team. He asked his grandmother if he could stay to watch my game before they left to wherever their father was.

I love that kid. Haile too, even though she couldn't care less about rugby. Her pint-sized screams for her brother every time he scored or had a good play were all that mattered. Coaching has brought new purpose into my life, and I'm grateful to watch Jackson flourish and come into his own.

There was a point I didn't think we'd be able to pull enough kids together for a spring league, but to my surprise, the summer coaches knew some kids who were itching to get back on the pitch. Jackson heard I was coaching, and the rest is history.

He's come into his own since the first time I met him almost a year ago. Still a quiet kid but no longer shrinks himself. He takes up space with a growing confidence and shines as bright as his mother, who pours into him and his sister.

Dating a woman with kids is new territory. It's not my intention or place to replace their father—the thought of being someone's parent still terrifies me, like I'll fuck up in some way—but I can be a positive image to balance his disappearing acts. I pride myself on being the man my parents raised me to be, one who provides peace and security.

Haile and Jackson are an extension of the woman I love. They don't know me as more than Duke's uncle yet, but they see my adoration for their mother through my praise and, more importantly, my presence. I can't undo the relationship they witnessed between her and their father, but I can show them something better to model as they grow. A partner who protects, uplifts, comforts, and steps back to anchor the ground while their lover flies.

I'm out of my depth, but I'm in this a hundred and fifty percent.

Ella pads into the bathroom in a light jog that makes her booty jiggle. I soap up as her foot taps out to whatever song is in her head while she pees.

Loving her is the easiest decision I ever made.

She steps through the frameless shower door with a nest of hair in a messy side bun and reaches around me for her exfoliating gloves hanging on the caddy.

"You're staring again." Her hooded eyes flicker as she lathers her body in the scent that drives me wild. It's impossible to not get lost in her.

"You sure you're okay?" We spoke about her ex on the phone before she came over.

"Yeah," she says quietly. The beginning of a smile tips up the corners of her mouth. "We'll be okay."

"That's right." I kiss her forehead and pull her close. "Know something else?"

"Hmm?"

"I love you."

"The feeling is mutual," she says with a playful grin that morphs into laughter at a smack to her ass. "I love you, Julie."

"You better."

Soft curves mold to the contours of my body under the spray of the showerhead. She drops her cheek to my chest with an exhale.

We settle into each other to the melody of water echoing off the subway tiles. My hand glides down the lines of her back. "Someone has a birthday coming up," I murmur against her shoulder with a kiss.

She groans. "I need no reminders I'm turning forty, please and thank you."

My chuckle vibrates off her collarbone. "You act like your AARP card is in the mail." Her nails dig into the flesh of my ass. I nip at her earlobe. "Don't start that freaky shit." My erection juts between us for emphasis. "Let me take you away."

Her wiggles to get out of my arms are a sign this vacation will be an unnecessary battle. She's also in for another round in this shower if she keeps squirming.

"Can't we do something small at the house?"

"I promise to spend $19.99 for a cake and a bottle of wine." Why is it always a fight to do something just for her? "You deserve a vacation, and you're always reminding me that I need to take time off. Let's take it together. You, me, a quiet weekend getaway."

"Julian." She releases a long sigh. "As amazing as not waking up at six and shuffling to pack lunches sounds, I have a bad feeling."

"Did you eat those old nachos in the refrigerator? I told you to throw them out." She flicks my nipple. "Ouch!"

"I'm serious!" She snorts. "Your ex. A creeper at the office."

"*Maybe* creeper," I clarify. Otis never confirmed that the person he saw was an actual threat.

"Charles popping up at Jackson's game for the first time ever? I—it's all too much of a coincidence for me. What if something happens?"

"What if nothing happens? Tell you what." I kiss her neck. "Think about what would make you comfortable enough to say yes. If you're honestly not," I shrug, "we stay here with cake and cheese."

Ella's lips quiver at the hard length in search of her heat. She swallows hard. "You never play fair."

I press her into the wall and whisper, "Where's the fun in that?"

Chapter 43

Ella

"Thank you for the trip. It was amazing." I snuggle into Julian's parka and rest against his chest. Green looks good on him. So does every color, but this olive on his skin has my mouth watering. I'm a sucker for beanies and goatees. I'm a sucker for him.

Raindrops patter against the car, a lullaby that would coax me to sleep if we weren't seven minutes from my house.

His lips touch the tops of my curls. "Thank you for coming with me."

Julian's definition of a "small" birthday celebration was renting a farmhouse in Wintergreen, Virginia, during spring break, which happened to coincide with Mama's visit.

Taco Tuesday turned into a three-hour road trip with Mama, the kids, and directions Julian gave my mother that had me scratching my head. We ended up at a gorgeous property that had a carriage house on the grounds and enough space for Morgan and Duke, who arrived with Joseph twenty minutes after us. Erica, Grier, and Mateo eventually joined us for three nights away to celebrate my fortieth birthday. Rose laughed me off the phone when I called about missing work, like Julian didn't already check in to square away my time off.

Thursday night came with champagne and rose petals on the balcony. Friday, we all drove back, and Julian surprised me yet again with an hour-and-forty-five-minute nonstop flight to Montreal for the weekend. Less than two hours away and home by Sunday afternoon were my stipulations for our private trip, and he met them with ease.

Time stood still once we were away from our phones and weekly demands. We got lost in each other and indulged in every temptation. When Julian wasn't feasting on my body, he was my personal tour guide, weaving in and out of French and Haitian Creole during our time in Saint-Michel.

Otis is driving us back from the airport. I suspected it was a way to keep our privacy, and for him and Julian to see each other since they hadn't in the office. At least, that's what I thought, until he took one look at my mother in the doorway on Friday and tripped over the curb to introduce himself. Mama already picked up the kids from Katharine's today, and she's working on dinner. Judging by the tie Otis is fiddling with, someone is hoping to score another look.

Julian raises the partition and leans me back to lay on the black leather seat. My pulse skitters under his appraisal, and I move toward him and brush my lips against his. The touch of his mouth prickles my skin under my turtleneck and utility jacket. For a long moment, we get lost in each other.

He grazes his nose over mine. "Do you forgive me for spending more than $19.99 this week?"

Laughter floats up my throat. "It was too good to stay mad." The phone buzzing in my pocket pulls us apart. This weekend was magical, but come tomorrow, it's back to a life of chauffeuring kids across state lines and heating up spaghetti and meatballs.

Julian leans back over me to bury his face against my throat with a groan as the car comes to a stop. "I don't want to go back."

Same. Also, I've never been more thankful for an SUV with large back seats. The man would crush me with his full body weight if he didn't have the room to pout half-draped over my body.

He really is sad.

I kiss his neck and smile. "Want to run away?"

His head lifts. "Don't tempt me. Otis!" He lowers the partition while still covering me like a weighted blanket. "We need a private plane. We're running away."

My cackling shakes the car. "What about the kids?"

"I'll homeschool them myself on the beach."

I snicker and push him to sit up. "Right." My phone buzzes again. "You might want to turn your phone back on unless you want to spend all day responding to messages across different time zones."

Morgan and Erica are blowing up my phone, but one notification leaves me at a loss for words.

April 1 was the date I left Charles, the start of the yearlong separation requirement to officially file for divorce. That time is here. Tomorrow.

"I made it." I show Julian the calendar reminder. "Grier can file the divorce papers."

Every sleepless night.

Every fear, every step into the unknown brought me to this moment.

Julian cups my face and seals his lips to mine. Through this journey, I unlocked my heart. I rediscovered myself, and I found love.

His phone vibrates in rapid succession. "Sure you don't want to run away?" The words tickle my lips in a whisper.

Buzz.

Buzz.

He curses under his breath, kisses my nose, and reaches for his phone. I don't check the rest of my notifications. How can I when tension is twisting Julian's features? His thick lips purse, and his brows dip.

"What's wrong?"

Julian swallows hard, his eyes still fixed on the screen.

"What is it, Julie?"

"Me and Camila." Come again? "A blog posted photos of our lunch at the District Bakehouse."

"Did they write an exposé on her swallowing olives after rejection?" I shrug. "Not exactly newsworthy." The smile playing at my lips and trying to pull one from him dies when his gaze snaps to me.

Whatever it is can't be that bad.

Can it?

That's what I tell myself...until I pull the phone from his fingertips and stare into hazel eyes I haven't seen in a year. Nausea floods the adrenaline shooting through my system. Now I want to pack up my kids and run away for real.

Just when I thought my divorce wouldn't bend me over more than it already has, irony spreads my cheeks and tells me to take a deep breath.

Camila, my husband's mistress, is Julian's ex.

It's a struggle to suck in air and regain control, to push through the dizziness dotting the corners of my eyes. I'm on edge, desperately trying to cling to something—anything—to make sense of the senseless. The DMV is small, but holy shit.

Julian gently reaches for me to soothe what he must assume is my insecurity at seeing him with his ex-fiancée. If only. "Don't give this your tears, sweetheart." His thumbs brush away the streams falling to my cheeks.

"Camila"—I sniff—"is Charles's mistress. Did you know?" I say the last part so low, I don't think Julian heard it until he blinks rapidly.

Hurt slices through him in deep strokes.

The woman he once loved slept with my husband.

"Are you—" He shakes off the question. I don't need to remind him about her descending the stairs with guilty eyes and a just-fucked glow—the latter I've worn often since ditching my ex for hers.

We sit in lonely silence, inches from each other but worlds apart. "I'll never get away from this, will I?" My whisper is a shaky breath layered with the burden of pretending to be fine when I'm not.

I bury myself into Julian at his kiss to my shoulder. He drops his chin with a heavy sigh and tightens the grip around my waist. "Tell me what to do, El." The timbre in his voice is sad but firm.

"I love you." The words are smothered on his lips. Time sprints by in a haze until I pull us apart. "I have to go." I'll be okay, I always am, but I need to lick my wounds and process.

It takes a few seconds, but he scoots away. "I love you, sweetheart."

"I'll call soon." My smile is faint but it holds. I leave him in the back of the car with his head bowed.

Otis is already out of the car with my suitcase and a wry smile wedged between his salt-and-pepper whiskers. "Here you go, Ms. Greene."

"Thank you, O." He nods with a side glance to the townhouse, which makes me smile. "Want to help me with my bag?"

"Sure—yes." Otis runs a hand over his freshly cut gray hair and smooths down his navy fitted shirt under his open gray coat. The man is giving Shaft today with his outfit and a side of bashfulness too adorable for words.

I pull out a manila folder addressed to me from the mailbox next to the front door.

Otis sniffs the scent flowing into the entryway and looks around as if the cook herself will manifest.

"Want to say hi?" Mama is a woman of many talents, but her cornbread is top tier.

"I want to"—his eyes fall to me—"but I should get Mr. Brooke home." *Someone is shy.* The sheepish tone in his voice lowers. "Take care, and keep your head up, Ms. Greene. It will blow over soon enough."

I smile. "Thank you, O. Have a good day."

Mama grins when I enter the kitchen. "Hi, sweetie! Was that Julian?"

"Otis. He helped me with my suitcase but had to get Julian home."

"Oh." She wipes the counter with a nod and zero game at hiding her crush. "That was nice of him." She clears her throat. "Did you have a good time?"

Up until I found out his ex-fiancée and I had been trading dick. "Yeah, it was nice to get away. Montreal is beautiful. How were the kids?"

"The same as when you asked me before you boarded the plane." She chuckles. "They're upstairs watching other kids play games on YouTube. Since when is that entertaining?"

My lips curl. "Where have you been?"

"Clearly in the wilderness. What's that?" Mama nods at the long envelope in my hand.

"I don't know." I turn it over for a hint at the source. "Maybe Grier dropped it off since she knew I was coming back today. I fulfill my separation requirement tomorrow to file for divorce."

Warm brown eyes light up. "How quickly a year goes when you're happy." She turns back to the stove with her palette of spices and starts talking about Easter service with the kids and Ms. Thelma today. She rattles off something about Katharine almost catching the holy ghost when the choir sang "Melodies From Heaven" before the dizziness returns.

My lungs heave. I clutch my throat and fasten a hand on the counter to support my shaky knees, which are ready to collapse. A letter-size photo that shouldn't be in the world, let alone this envelope, floats to the ground.

How?

Chapter 44

Julian

Something is wrong.

I gave Ella space on Monday, texting once to tell her I love her and how sorry I am about everything. Camila's decisions are hers and hers alone, but it doesn't remove the sting of someone I once cared for hurting the woman I love.

Yesterday morning, I tried to brush off the prickling suspicion that something more than photos of me with Camila was causing her silence. Work gets busy for both of us, and wrangling kids solo is no walk in the park. Then last night came, and I knew her rain check on Taco Tuesday was a red flag. I'm attuned to her needs, and El would chew off her own arm before turning down two al pastors with extra *pico de gallo*.

Every worst-case scenario ran laps through my head.

Was there a problem with the paperwork Grier submitted to the court?

Is there a push for a hearing?

Do we have to wait months until a judge signs the final divorce decree?

The last one is an inconvenience but not the end of the world. I'd wait a lifetime for her.

Ella said she'd be in touch, and she asked for space to take care of a few things, which wouldn't be a problem if I didn't know in my gut that something is wrong. Just like I do now heading into this meeting.

I open the door to the conference room the same way I do every day: with a silent prayer that this won't be a waste of time. Every day, I see the same oak table I crawled under with my toys as a kid when my dad was on calls. But the air is thicker now, heavy with a pressing weight that shows in Chanda's expression. Our PR consultant staring back at me with her band of merry fixers isn't new territory, but my mother dressed in a black suit at eight in the morning and wearing a glare of her own is.

"Hi."

It's the only response that comes to mind at the Dora Milaje who are looking at me like I offed a congressperson and asked them to hide the body. Chanda's all-women team might as well be the special forces. They won't let any threat penetrate my family's business or good name. If my mother's here, something summoned the queen.

I take the seat next to her and wait for Chanda to reveal how it is I fucked up. I ditched a ballet fundraiser last week to go away for Ella's birthday, soaking in her smiles and reveling in the warmth between her thighs. She needed a trip away, and I was happy to oblige.

Whoever is mad can stay that way. But a plié and flesh-toned stockings wouldn't cause Claire Brooke to unwrap her hair before nine, so what did?

Chanda picks up the remote for the flat-screen TV we use for presentations and takes a breath. "My soror at The Capitol Tea

Report gave me a heads-up late last night about a story running today."

And?

My mouth doesn't say it, but my face sure as hell does. This is the reason we came into the office an hour early in DC traffic? A blog? It's one of the biggest in the region and a leading thorn in my ass, sure, but still.

We could've kept this *New Jack City* reenactment for another day—or a justifiable reason. You'd think we were hosting a funeral with all these in memoriam outfits.

Did someone die?

Chanda's copper tips whip back to the screen. She points the remote and clicks to a photo of me in a restaurant with Camila. It's a long-lens image, based on the grainy quality and invasion of privacy. The photo itself isn't incriminating, unless you consider a large pretzel with dipping sauces vulgar. I had a taste for carbs and hot cheese. Sue me.

I lean into the leather chair and fold my ankle over my knee. "My mother asked me to take Camila out to catch up. I did. How is this news?"

"This is the first photo taken of you two alone since your split. Or so we thought. There's speculation that you two reconciled and have secretly been together for some time."

"That's not true," I say. "Cam and I had lunch recently, but I haven't seen her—"

"Since she came to your London hotel last spring." Chanda clicks to another photo. "Sarayah also received this one of Camila leaving early in the morning."

Fuck.

My thoughts filter back to a year ago, to her tear-filled eyes pleading with me through puffy lids. It had been erased from memory until now.

I'll admit her unexpected visit was a moment of weakness. We fell back into old habits, and the night was what it was. *One* night.

Have we had sex since I called off our short-lived engagement? Once or twice. But I haven't spoken to her since our assistants set up lunch back in March.

Communication turned nonexistent once I met Ella.

"How much to make that go away?" The first is already out in the world. The second can't see the light of day.

"I wouldn't have called this meeting if a check would solve the problem. What and who you do on your personal time isn't my concern." Chanda's eyes hold an unspoken apology. "Unless it creates a scandal." I swallow hard at the next image on the screen.

Ella and I are in front of Swigs one of the mornings after she spent the night. Wild black curls that were splayed on my pillow hours before are hidden under a faux fur-lined hood that conceals the blush in her cheeks from the cold. I have the biggest grin on my face as I pull the edges of her hood to me. She looked like a kid buttoned up to the neck in that big ass winter jacket that reached her calves and hid the honey-tan skin I worshipped inch by inch. The picture only catches a glimpse of her thick, kissable lips poking out, but it's clear she's not Cam. I would never light up with anyone else the way I do with her.

"There's reason to believe the woman in this photo is married, and you're sleeping with her." Chanda sighs. "We've dodged salacious stories in the past about your...activities. But this is too big to kill, even for us."

The knot in my throat churns until it plummets to my stomach. *Protect Ella*. "Are there more photos?"

"No." The breath I've been holding finally dislodges. "The pictures came in anonymously, but these are the only ones so far. The Capitol Tea Report plans to run the rest soon. Reporters haven't been able to confirm who the woman in the coat is, only that she's married. Per a source."

The question hangs from Chanda's lips. She wants to know if it's true, if I'm messing around with another man's wife. Technically, I am, but it's more than that. *We're* more than that.

I've never wanted anyone more than I want Ella, and I will never love another woman the same way.

"She's finalizing her divorce," I say, without adding that it's no one's business. "Do everything you can to keep her identity a secret."

"If you tell me who she is—"

"Leave us."

Mother's sharp command doesn't raise her voice, but it has enough bite to straighten every spine in the room. Chairs shuffle in a medley of screeches before Chanda and her five associates pour out of the room in a synchronized movement of red-bottom heels.

Her frown anchors deeper into a stony expression full of high cheekbones and disappointment. French-tipped hands clasp in her lap. She's coiled to strike—at the threat of family shame or my forehead remains a mystery.

It's pointless to pretend my mother doesn't know the woman is Ella.

"She stays out of this. I don't care how much it costs."

Three million. Sixty. My whole fucking trust fund. I'll rip myself in half and take on the whole city. "I'll draw up the cease and desist myself."

Considering a level-three PR meltdown has just assembled Chanda's entire team, Claire Brooke remains unbothered by the threat of a blog launching the woman I love into the spotlight.

There's a long pause before she responds. "Do you love her?"

"Yes." Without a doubt.

"If you want to protect her, give them something that will help overlook her." Her tone is unhurried, like she's picking lint off her custom suit.

I shake my head. "You always wanted me and Camila together." The question is, how much?

The woman inspecting me with a measured gaze is a far cry from the one who read me bedtime stories.

The kiss to my mother's cheek is as swift as my departure from the conference room. I take the rest of the day off to figure out the best course of action. I need to keep Ella and the kids safe in a way that won't fuck up her divorce or our future.

Chapter 45

Ella

If I didn't say it before, I'll say it now:

I hate galas.

Okay, *hate* is a bit harsh. I tell my kids not to hurl four-letter words and choose something less potent. Like *despise with a strong passion*, which sums up how I feel about gala season and black-tie events.

On the surface, they're opportunities to gather in the name of a righteous cause and put an ironing board to good use. But they mostly prove that even the best surgeons couldn't separate ego from what should be a selfless act. The ass-kicking in costumes that cost more than most people's rent and extravagance on 'roids in the name of charity are too much. What isn't enough are the Easy Bake Oven samples that pass for a meal on good china.

To be fair, tonight is a regional fundraiser dinner to benefit prospective college students who wouldn't be able to afford tuition otherwise. I'll pull myself out of comfy pants for that. So long as the lurking cameras stay far away.

I've kept to myself since the day we flew back from Montreal and landed straight in a Netflix drama. Between work and the mental images of a man in the bushes snapping our every move, I couldn't chance anyone photographing me and Julian together in public.

Julian is still apologizing like he bears responsibility for the tear in what was healed heartbreak. The temptation to pull up the image online scratched at my curiosity, but I didn't give in. Unlike Morgan, I don't spend my days on social media, and I only have a Facebook account, one that collects more dust than likes.

Hearing him tell me he had sex with Camila after she country-hopped just hours after sleeping with my husband hurt, I'll admit. But how could I get mad when we didn't know each other at the time? Plus, I still have a whole husband on paper. Add in someone flexing their paparazzi kink, and there are bigger issues at hand.

Another envelope arrived yesterday, with a photo like the ones you see in the movies, before government agents conduct a raid or pin you with a murder. I'm no Will Smith, but I have one more fuck left to give before I sprint down the streets of Washington in a fluffy robe to chase my own enemy of the state.

The candid shot of Julian's beautiful face mid-laugh may or may not be under one of my bedroom pillows, which is unrighteous behavior at its finest. Yes, it was an invasion of privacy, but the close-up of his goatee stretching to straight teeth and a side of dimples lured me. I'm still pissed someone took it, but I'm not ashamed to admit I'm not perfect, either.

The photo is one of us walking next to a small park in our neighborhood. It's far from newsworthy, with no kissing or holding hands to set off romance rumors. Yet, here were are, tip-toeing around threats to plaster us all over a blog like they caught Beyoncé giving a performance in front of the National Gallery.

"Eat this before you pass out or cut someone." Erica slaps a roll into my hand. "How are you doing?"

"Better now." My next bite stalls at her you-know-good-and-well-what-I-mean glare. I brush my upper lip for crumbs. "What?"

The dinner bell rings, herding a throng of sequins and suits to decorated tables under the winking chandeliers. Erica plasters on a smile for a short, balding man who's pushing through the forming line in a gray suit two sizes too big.

"Little bastard," she mumbles under her breath.

"What was that?" His breath reaches us before he turns around to reveal a sheen of moisture on his forehead and a glistening, hairy wart.

Her hand soothes her throat over a chuckle. "I said *a little faster* if you want to be the first one in." The smile covering her thick lips in deep plum dissolves the moment he's through the double doors to the banquet hall and out of earshot.

I snort. "You're a mess!"

"Oh, please." She pulls the midnight ponytail cascading down her back. "Professor Epstein is a halitosis monster from an era when women were seen and not heard. He thinks his students of color are the byproduct of affirmative action." Her inhale tugs at her frustration and her gelled edges. "The college I worked at gave him tenure even though I had enough research published in academic journals to papier-mâché his office and that comb-over. So, yes, that little misogynistic bastard can kiss my whole ass." She pauses. "I mean no disrespect to men under five-six. I'll be the first to testify that shorter men are excellent lovers. Katt Williams didn't tell a single lie."

I pinch my cheeks together—because what else is there to say?—and follow her into the room with a cloud of crystals and cascading ivory fabric down the walls.

Erica is many things. Loud. Uncensored. But one thing she does not play about is her career. Smiles and quick conversations capture her peers in our procession to one of three tables reserved for economics departments. I'm proud to say Professor Epstein and his breath didn't make the cut.

She slides into a gold Chivari chair and crosses her legs, creating a slit to match the lines of her single-shoulder asymmetrical dress. "Back to my question. How are you holding up?"

"The best someone can be after seeing their man plastered all over the blogs with his ex-fiancée, raising questions about when they're tying the knot, while someone drops off photos that threaten my pending divorce." I flop into the seat next to her with a sigh. "Just peachy."

"Shit." Erica blows out a long breath.

I tip my head back and stare at the chandelier glittering shadows across my robin's-egg blue and ivory blouse. "Yup." The word emphasizes the extent of my exhaustion. "I just want this all to be over."

She nods and reaches for me. "You're almost there."

"Twenty-five more days to freedom," I say. Uncontested divorces in Virginia are quicker without the back-and-forth and court hearings. They only take weeks to process and review before a judge signs the final divorce order.

May 6 needs to get here soon.

"No fucking way."

The air shifts, and my skin prickles at Charles walking through the door. His father flanks his side with the same jade-green eyes scanning the room. Charles Sr. is a vintage version of his son. Same square jaw and straight brows to furrow at people beneath their social status, same small lips to twist at threats. They're all set on me once he registers I'm here. He leans over to whisper in Charles's ear and sharpens his disdain on me with a scowl that has to earn a new world record.

I fill my wineglass from one of the bottles at the table. If they're here, it will be a long night.

By my second glass, Charles is invading my space.

"Ella." Bitterness spills over his vowels.

I take in the hovering figure, who's wearing a tailored black suit to match his soul. "Charles. Now that we got that out the way"—I nod to his empty table—"feel free to take your seat and ignore me for the rest of the evening."

Erica slides closer to speak behind the smile she's wearing to keep from glowering at my ex. "Do you need me to get security?"

I turn to her dangling diamond earrings. "No," I whisper. "Thank you, but Mt. Corbel Health recruits from this university, and you don't need to jeopardize your tenure track."

She pats my slacks and drops her head to mimic my tone. "I was talking about the stun gun in my purse. Say the word, and Silkk the Shocker will *zzt zzt* his ass in a dark hallway."

I slam my eyes shut and clench my lips. Every muscle tenses trying not to howl at this fancy dinner. Erica slaps my leg and stomps her foot to keep from falling out her chair. "It ain't my fault!" I grip my napkin and cover my face after a snort escapes.

Charles clears his throat to break up our stand-up routine, reaches for my glass, and takes a sip. "Your little friend is quite the local celebrity." That gets my attention. "The question is, are you ready for your close-up, Ella?"

I'm on my feet. At six three, Charles is eye level, courtesy of these heels that will find a home in his ass before Erica gets to Silkk the Shocker. My eyes narrow at how low he'd stoop he all but confirms with a smug grin.

"You're the one behind all of this. The blog, the pictures of Julian and his ex. The ones sent to my house, where your *children* live." I shake my head at the man I once vowed to love until death. "Why?"

It's a dumb question because I already know the answer. Adultery rumors don't have to be true to do damage. What judge would look at those photos and not assume we penetrated the no-penetration rule—whether we waited or not?

"Friday nights out. Galas. Sleepovers." He grinds the last word between his teeth. "Quite the busy woman since you broke up our family."

"*Excuse—*"

"Don't forget the grocery store. I have a new appreciation for fresh mozzarella."

A bitter tang burns my throat at the familiar voice creeping into our conversation. Ice-blue eyes crinkle at the corners, pulling thin lips into a smile. When did he get here? *Why* is he here?

"Asher."

"Told you I'd see you again. Where are my manners?" He shakes himself out of a thought. "This one got the private schools." His hand extends. "Asher Campbell. Charles's brother."

Katharine only had one child, which means Asher is the son of a mistress. Charles Sr.'s frequent trips to Florida now makes sense, but a whole second family? How many more are there? On second thought, I don't want to know.

The voice inside warns me to run as fast as Asher creeped up, but where would I go? Charles knows where I live, and he has a brother tailing me around town. No wonder we kept running into each other. "You've been *following* me?"

Another dumb question with an obvious answer.

Pleasure melts into the hard jaw he shares with his brother. The two of them side-by-side, the straight brows and sharp eyes that match their father's are more prominent.

Asher tilts his head in a nod. "You and Julian were very careful. I tried to catch you both at his office, but that old man was fast." His chuckle is dark. "Those overnights at his apartment? Dead giveaway to anyone paying attention. I have to give it to you, El—can I call you that? He's a bold choice after this one."

Fear blends into outrage and shifts into a glare at this family reunion. "I don't give a damn if you have photos of me tap-dancing naked in my kitchen. You have no right. This divorce *is* happening. The time to come to terms with it was last year"—I point to Charles—"when I caught *you* cheating."

Asher folds his arms over his black suit and smiles. He wags a finger at me and looks to Charles. "I like her. It's a shame things didn't work." His hand runs over his Patrick Dempsey scruff. "But that could be a good thing since Charles here never wanted to share you."

"You're both disgusting." I jerk away at the suggestion of women they tag-teamed.

"Call off the divorce." The edge in Charles's tone scrapes the bottom of the barrel he must be in to pull such a stunt. "I would hate to see photos of you end up in the news. There's still time for us, El."

"You son of a—"

A flash of ebony moves out the corner of my eye in time for me to catch Erica before she puts hands on him. "Keep Silkk in the bag."

She sneers. "That's blackmail."

Vengeful eyes the color of envy pierce into mine. "Want to go to the police?" He shrugs. "Good luck keeping a low profile when I take it to court. The blogs will eat up my wife cozying up to Julian Brooke after he reconciled with his former fiancée. Is that what you want?" I dodge the hand he raises to stroke my cheek, triggering a thunderous glare over a heavy sigh. "You were always difficult. Final warning, Ella. Call off the divorce and come home where you belong."

Charles turns on his heel and heads for the main door in a series of long strides. If Julian had his way, he would've unleashed enough fury on Charles to bury him for three eternities the second his assumptions proved true. He wanted to protect me with legal action and knocking out a few of Charles's teeth, but those options would lead to a very public battle, one I refuse to drag my kids through. They've been through enough.

"See you around," Asher says with a wink before taking off after his brother.

"Girl, what in the entire fuck?" Erica searches for a plausible explanation, but it's simply not there. Charles is out for blood, and he doesn't care how deep he has to cut to get what he wants.

His misery is a steel weight that buckles every muscle I have to fight against it. This is bigger than Julian.

Charles won't stop until he wins, even if it breaks me in the process.

Chapter 46

Julian

"Would you please look at me?"

Coming into the office was a mistake. The smart thing to do would've been to call off or work from Antonio's penthouse. Risking a secondhand STI in a home in need of a black light and year's supply of disinfectant wipes was a better option than facing the curious frowns that have been tipping over cubicles.

I'd have also avoided the woman I've dodged since someone fed The Capitol Tea Report photos of us. For all I know, she was the one who gave the blogs the photos.

The blog released the photo of Camila leaving my London hotel last year. It spread across social media and has yet to extinguish.

Are we back together?

Will we walk down the aisle soon?

The attention is unlike anything before. My home was always off-limits, tucked behind the shield of an LLC, but now it's for public consumption. Would-be reporters took turns creeping around Swigs after an "anonymous tip" so often I swapped houses with Antonio to keep them off my scent. They haven't discovered the townhouse with Ella and the kids a few blocks down, and I'll do what's necessary to keep it that way.

Ella is a fantasy, an answered prayer wrapped in hips and thighs. She's my place of peace, and I'll protect her with everything I got.

"I never meant for this to happen."

"Were you involved?"

Camila steps back when I finally look up from my computer screens. If she expected sympathy, she's in the wrong office. My mother's name isn't etched on a door plate, but she'll be here soon for her standing lunch date with my father. Camila can cry to her.

I didn't put two and two together—that my ex was the other woman in Ella's marriage, or at least one of them—until El dropped the bombshell. How could I? Camila has been Director of Philanthropy at Mt. Corbel Health since her father created the position for her after grad school. That was five years ago, around the time we broke up and well before Ella and her ex relocated to the area. I barely travel to Virginia as is, and I wouldn't remember the clean-shaven Wolverine knockoff from an assembly line of suits clawing their way to status.

Executives. Politicians. They're all the same.

Now that our paths have crossed, I won't forget the snarl on his vindictive face or the hatred for the woman I love in his green eyes.

It took everything I had to stay inside and not rush over to beat the shit out of him after Ella's call last night. Hugh Jackman will wish he had superpowers if he steps to her again. He already crossed the line, and it's a struggle to let El handle him as she sees fit when all I want is to speed up the karma headed his way—accomplices included, like this one, who hasn't stopped her soap opera performance while doing backbends to dodge accountability.

"Were. You. Involved?"

Charles made good on his promise. The Capitol Tea Room also published the photo of me and El in front of Swigs today, igniting questions about the relationship I don't have with Camila and whether or not I've changed my "playboy" ways. Threats of legal action were enough to omit "the other woman" is still married, but the photo is out there for all to fixate on until her identity comes to light.

Camila shifts in heels and twists manicured fingers in front of her black knee-length dress. My arched brow doesn't move no matter how many times she peeks to see if I'm still pissed.

Spoiler alert: fuck yes, I am.

Hearing the despair in Ella's voice was all it took. She's regaining her strength for a battle. But I want a war.

Camila's fixation on the imported rug I asked Morgan six times not to order is all the confirmation I need. "Leave." Neither time nor patience are on my calendar today. It's threat enough for her to be in my office. Bloggers might manufacture yet another story.

"I can explain." Her words spill out in a jumble. She wants me to hear her out, a privilege she'll never have again. She scurries to the side of my desk to audition for my forgiveness, the stack of paperwork in front of me be damned. "I agreed to stay quiet about the photos—"

"Let me guess. You thought media attention would pull us back together, the same way you thought a married man would leave his wife if you spread your legs enough?"

Her chin trembles, the promise of new tears clinging to hazel eyes. "I never meant to hurt you, Julian. Charles was a mistake. I love you."

Love.

I turn back to an open email.

"Please don't ignore me. We can be together," she says with an awakened sense of self-assurance, one that leans on ignorance instead of reality. The truth is, nothing stopped us from reconciling before.

"Do you have an ounce of regret for your part in this whole thing?" I shake my head, loosening memories of her selfishness, which I overlooked for a partner in crime on the social scene and good sex.

Camila steels her voice. "Of course I do. I felt awful the first time."

"But not awful enough to stop having sex with a man whose wife caught you in their bed?"

Camila is no better than the Montgomery name she denounces behind closed doors. Practiced smiles and performative empathy were talents inherited from a family who prioritized their needs at the expense of others. Glimpses of her indoctrination made cameos, but this is different. She really doesn't give a shit.

"He said they were separated!" She spins with a glare like *I* repulsed *her*. Last I checked, I'm not the one begging. "I got caught up, and now you are too. It's not odd to you that she moved herself into your house, the ex-fiancé of the woman who slept with her husband?" Wavy blonde hair fans in a head tilt at the question. She scoffs. "Wake up, Julian. She's not like us. She's using you to get back at me. I'm willing to give you space to get whatever is going on out of your system, but you need to come back to your senses."

Camila and I had an open relationship before we broke up. Work replaced intimacy, so we sought it elsewhere at times and with shared consent. What I feel for Ella isn't temporary or a placeholder. If anything, it's a reminder that my time with Camila was out of convenience and lacked depth.

I stand, straighten the tie behind my camel vest, and do what I should've done twenty minutes ago: walk her to the door.

If I have to school her about not playing in my face about my lady, consider class in session. "Get out." I point to the empty hallway she's about to fill with her departure and stare at her ashen face to expedite the trip.

"You can't be serious! *Her?* She's old, and she has kids!"

"There is no end to how low you'll go, is there? Ella is the best thing that's ever happened to me, and I won't tolerate disrespect. You stand here and judge her when the catalyst for her leaving her ex was catching you two fucking." *A man twenty-one years your senior, but go off about her age.*

"It was a mistake! We worked on a project together, and long nights turned into dinner and drinks. Don't throw away what we have for...her. It's not worth the media backlash; you know you can't recover from rumors that you're sleeping with a married woman with a family."

Camila doesn't corner the market on casual sex—my Mt. Rushmore of regret came in first place years ago—but to not hear "I'm sorry" or "Damn, that was kinda fucked up" is as wild as her desire to reconcile while she attempts to bury me in the blogs.

"Piece of free legal advice? Lose my number and lawyer up."

"You have two minutes to leave our building before security tosses you outside." Morgan keeps her eyes trained on Camila as she steps through the door. "And, just so you know, a forty-year-old woman knows what she wants and won't settle for less. Ella never went after Julian; he pursued *her*. While you're conspiring with her ex—who still wants her—she's living happily and free. The only thing *old* around here is your desperation. Lay it to rest and move on."

Morgan isn't confrontational unless it comes to El and the proximity of my penis to her. Right now, she'd catch a case in my honor.

Camila sidesteps her scowl and damn near runs into the doorframe rushing out, possibly to the nearest airport, for another disappearing act.

"I'm scared of you, Mac. Ouch!" I dodge another swat to the chest.

Morgan squares her shoulders and grins. Her hands fall on her hips belted in gold above black slacks. "No one messes with my brother except me. Camila needs to stay away, for good this time."

"Tell that to our mother."

"Give her time, JuJu," Morgan says with a sad smile. "She only wants what's best."

What's best is to leave me alone and let me live my life how *I* see fit.

I check her shoulder. "Easy for you to say. Our parents don't monitor your love interests."

She folds over in a roar of laughter that lasts so long, I question if her sanity ran out with Camila. "I needed that." The tip of her finger catches a stray tear swaying from her cheek. "Me marrying an artist brought zero pride to the family. You engaged to the daughter of the CEO of one of the largest health systems in the region?" Her whistle is slow. "You're the golden child."

I roll my eyes and pull my blazer off the coat rack. "Stop." Our parents never stop asking when I'll marry and give them another grandchild. "They love Joseph."

Morgan and Joseph had every odd stacked against them, but they found a way to make it work until it didn't. Pressure from our parents was never a factor, go figure. They had their doubts about Morgan marrying an artist, but she'd already shut down their syllabus for her life, studying art history instead of law or medicine and marrying a man she'd been dating for a few months, a man she met on a two-week trip to New Orleans.

I always looked up to my big sister because of it. Still do.

"How is he?"

The edge of her mouth tips up. "Good. Really good. We're working with a couple's counselor and a family therapist to get us ready to live under the same roof again. Come on, Goldie." She wipes another tear with a shy smile. "I'm buying lunch."

The top of the wooden fence catches on my jeans, propelling me head-first over it and into a knee-high stack of chopped wood left over from winter. I groan at the pain cutting through my face as the kitchen light turns on.

Ella flies out the house in silent fury, wearing an oversized t-shirt and holding a rolling pin raised to the night sky. Her sprint comes to a screeching halt when she trips over Haile's jiujitsu dummy on the grass and lands in a hard somersault.

It's pitch-black out here, but I've never been more grateful that Chad and his wife in the townhouse behind us are still in Florida. With the house on the other side for sale, no one should hear or see us acting a mess in the dark.

"Are you okay, baby?" I wince and roll onto my side.

"*Julian*?" Ella's confused whisper is rough after busting her ass. "What are you doing out here?"

"I came to see you."

"Did you climb over the fence?"

I stand to brush the dirt off my jacket and go to help her off the grass. "I didn't want to come around front in case anyone followed me."

Her snort calls me an idiot. "So you hopped a *fence*?"

"Seemed like a good idea at the time." In hindsight, it was dumb. Me and fences don't exactly have a good track record.

Her laughter ripples through the mild night that promises warmer days, and she pulls me in by the shirt. "I missed you, Julie. So much." Our kiss sings through my veins, a reminder that the intimacy we've shared was pulled apart by exes who can't let go. Her nose brushes mine. "I hate being away from you."

"Me too, baby," I whisper.

She hooks a thumb at the house casting a glow over the backyard. "I was going to run a bath, if you want to join." *More than you know.* "The kids are away for the weekend."

My fingers slide over her bare arms. "I want to, but I can't stay. Otis is a few blocks away. I'm leaving, sweetheart." I take her face into my palms, stroking soft flesh I haven't caressed in weeks, and swallow the stab of guilt. "You, Jackson, and Haile are my priority. I can't protect you here, not with your ex and mine conspiring together. I can keep the blogs away if I go back to London, at least until your divorce is final."

Leaving won't stop Charles from hurting Ella. We *will* deal with him in court, but I won't jeopardize her freedom. Not when she's so close.

Even if it hurts like hell to say goodbye.

Her sigh drops her lashes to hide hurt she fights to conceal. She hesitates but eventually nods. "It's fine. It has to be this way, right? I'm just..." Another sigh. "I'm tired, Julie." Her head tips back to the moonlight clearing from a formation of clouds. A tear streaks down her cheek. "I'm tired."

I lift her trembling body to mine, trying to absorb the despair that's been weighing on her for far too long. Her legs wrap around me, and she buries her face in the crook of my neck and sobs. I hold her closer. She bears the cross of every emotion by herself, and

I'll always remind her they're no longer hers to carry alone. Her vulnerability is a gift for me to cherish and keep safe.

She lifts her head, unable to tear her eyes from mine. I kiss the tip of her nose, which triggers a response of her own. Ella smothers my lips with a fiery possession soaked in passion and anger. Her tongue captures mine on a moan, savoring every moment—for the time we've had together, and the time we have to spend apart.

My legs move on their own to the garage, which took me moving out for the woman in my arms to finally use. With her anchored to me, I reach around, twist the brass knob, and step into the small structure with light gray board and batten walls. The new organizing system stands proud, a project I helped her finish a month ago so she could store the kids' bikes and seasonal toys.

Maintaining our kiss is as challenging as it is rewarding for the simple fact I have my heart in my hands and it's blocking my view. I check the temperature of her SUV's hood before sitting her on top. My hands explore the perfection of her honey-tan thighs and glide up under her New Edition T-shirt.

Ella's lashes flutter closed when my thumbs drag across the base of her breasts. She leans back and bites her lip, dropping her gaze to my hand as it trails back down her belly to the heat between her legs. She arches when my fingers delve into her pussy and bucks her hips to match my speed.

"Julian," she says through a hitched breath.

"Let me take care of you." I reach down and pull a nipple into my mouth.

She lifts to brace her hands on the shiny black hood and rocks into my fingers. The soft pouch of her stomach rolls as we watch her juices coat my fingers. The squelch of her wetness slices through the air, and a rush of pink stains her cheeks. Ella comes in a cry for release I'm happy to give her.

Her lips part at the fingers I used to bring her to orgasm swirling in my mouth. I'll spend a lifetime savoring her taste and will never get enough.

Ella grabs my long sleeve tee and tugs the white fabric to pull my lips back to hers for a slow, savory kiss. Her hands fly across my belt to unbuckle the leather and then my jeans, pulling the zipper in a rushed hiss. She reaches inside to free the engorged flesh pulsing against my boxer briefs and excites a groan from me.

I grip her ass to drag her closer, push my pants and briefs further down my hips, and bottom out inside her. Her cries are smothered by my mouth at every thrust, and the turbulence radiating from our joined bodies rocks the car underneath us. A burst of sensations vibrates through me like liquid fire.

Rage for the ex who's making her life hell.

Hurt for the pain I can't take away.

Sorrow for leaving her, because it's the only way to keep her safe.

My back tightens, and I fall onto the hood, covering my body with hers. I'd give my life to see this woman happy without having to look over her shoulder or wonder how long it will last.

We seal our last moments together with an endless kiss until Otis texts me it's time to go.

Chapter 47

Ella

"Asher Campbell is headed back to Palm Beach." Grier holds back a laugh to take a bite of her sandwich that has more pickles than turkey. "Remind me not to piss *you* off."

I blame Angela Bassett. Her pursed lips and narrowed eyes are why I woke up and chose violence after a long weekend of sulking. Thursday night's Scooby Doo reveal confirmed what I knew, sans half brother. But Julian leaving was the final straw. Our separation, while temporary and because of an ex who refuses to let go, is too much. Even the strongest person would crack. Anyone exhausted from holding it together would lose it, so I buried my face inside a tub of cookie dough ice cream on Saturday, contemplating who I pissed off in a past life to have ended up the object of a narcissistic cheater's obsession.

Sunday was a different story.

After church with Ms. Thelma (and two hours of wishing I'd stashed snacks in my bag for the late morning service), I put the Lifetime movies away for a Terry McMillan classic, one that had me marching to my closet to prep for a showdown with fancy suits. It's why I headed west this morning instead of driving back to DC after dropping off Jackson at school.

I wanted to reclaim my power without lighting a cigarette next to my ex's burning car. It worked in *Waiting to Exhale*, but I won't risk a case. Or these eyebrows.

My shoulder lifts. "Can't go wrong with Angela."

I parked my car in the main lot of Mt. Corbel Health headquarters and straightened my sunglasses for the stroll between low-rise buildings shackled in metal and glass. Each step I took was slow and cautious—not because I was second-guessing my decision to poke the bear, but because of my choice of heels. Sleek patent leather pumps are a look, but that linebacker strut was not.

The benefit of my pending divorce is that I'm still Charles's wife on paper, with a key that unlocked access to the executive suite. Gloria, Charles's longtime assistant, was one hug away from tears at my unexpected visit but none the wiser about my ulterior motives. Her ability to see only the best in others through her rose-colored bifocals is a gift and a curse. I'm not in the habit of breaking grandmothers' hearts, but I paid my respect in smiles and hugs to a woman who's been nothing but kind. Then I began the long walk down the carpeted corridor to the C-suite conference room.

Fifty shades of gray-haired men swiveled in their overpriced chairs watching my figure through the wall of glass panels. I smile into my coffee cup at the memory. "Papa Charles wasn't happy with my drop-in." Understatement of the year. If the man could have sniped me when I stepped through the door, he'd have taken the shot without blinking.

Grier's lifted chin exposes her neck, which is garnished in the crisscross of two thin gold chains over a light gray blazer.

"But you came dressed for the occasion," she says, her Annalise Keating brow rising with pride at my black pants and ivory blouse."

I extend my nude pumps. "I even brought the toe cleavage."

"The cleavage is a must." She sips her coffee and wiggles a black stiletto.

"Charles Sr. didn't take too kindly to the Board of Trustees finding out about his extra son. But what's the mother of his grandchildren to do when a man who claims to be his only son's half brother pops up on security cameras? He could be a con artist."

Grier's head falls back with a cackle. "I know he was beet red when you passed around the receipts. Exhibit A, your other son showing his ass." Our heads bump on a snort.

Nate came through with the footage that showed dear Asher in a black Acura outside of Swigs on six separate occasions. Anyone could brush it off as circumstantial until he popped up in front of the townhouse. Once? A coincidence...maybe. Three times? True crime territory.

I left Charles to explain why he was at a company event with a stalker and came to meet the attorney next to me, who's laughing her curly bob loose, at the courthouse. The mission: secure a temporary protection order. The verdict: victory.

At no point did my ex consider that calling his brother to keep tabs on me would mean a far bigger scandal than photos that didn't show my face. The protection order guarantees that Asher is out of commission. I don't know how many he has in reserves, but I had to cut off his supplier. There hasn't been one of me and Julian since last week, but I won't hold my breath that more aren't on the way.

"All jokes aside." Grier blots her face. "It's good you took action. Men like Charles won't stop once the divorce is final."

Whereas Charles Sr. cleared the room to rip his son a new one for calling up his Florida secret, my father-in-law-for-now won't endanger his image just to bury someone he holds in little regard. But judging by the flash in Charles's eyes, he'd risk it all on a solo mission to make me pay. Now he'll have to do it without Daddy.

"I want to look into pressing charges once the divorce is final." Charles would have to shell out thousands and maybe face a small sentence behind bars if a judge found him guilty of blackmail. His privilege would likely buy him a get out of jail free card, but he crossed a line and needs to learn his lesson. "He should've put his kids before his ego, and this Tubi-level drama he's causing is too much."

Grier wipes her mouth and stands. "It might take some effort to prove in court that he's the architect behind the photo leaks, outside of the confession he'll likely deny, but the case is there. Think Camila would talk?"

"Julian threatened her with legal action after he and Morgan kicked her out of their office. Doubtful."

"Damn." Grier laughs. "And the brother won't do us any favors after we sent him back to Florida. Knowing your ex, the trail leads away from him being the anonymous source. He'll cover his ass."

A damn mess.

"Are we still good for May 6?" I want this to be over, to not have to wonder if today will be the day Charles turns my life into another *Scandal* episode.

Sunlight from the afternoon sky presses to my face on our walk back to Grier's office, a sign of brighter days and the chance to swap out these heels for sneakers on the way. Toe cleavage might look sexy, but it bruised the shit out of my pinkie toes.

"The court has the paperwork, and Charles signed all the documents for an uncontested divorce earlier this month," she says. "His tantrum will earn him a case on his hands, but we're getting that final decree."

I pull her in for a side hug. "I'll miss plotting and scheming with you."

"You're back early."

Sophia stirs in my arms but settles when my nose brushes her curls in daffodil barrettes. Rose catches me in the nursery during naptime at least twice a week. New-baby smell still stirs my ovaries into a two-step.

"It was a quick one," I say at the softest setting. The sleeping angels become screeching gremlins if they don't get their full rest. I place Sophia back into her crib and crack the door on the way to the hall.

Bright Spot is shining. Admissions are up. Renovations are underway, and Rose couldn't be happier...which would explain the grin on her face, but not why she's staring at me like I won the lottery. Did she play my numbers?

"What? Do I have spinach in my teeth?" I do a cautionary swipe.

"Nothing." Her ponytail sways with a headshake. Warm brown eyes crease at another glance my way. "Happiness looks good on you."

I nod but don't miss her eyes flitting back to me. What is she up to?

"I never told you about how I acquired Bright Spot," she says as we slow to the entrance. She sifts through the basket of mail and hands me an envelope. It's white and letter-sized, thank God. "I was once married to a banker. He was the breadwinner, and I was a nineteen-year-old in love. I spent ten years caring for the house and upholding my duties as the perfect wife.

"I got pregnant at twenty-nine, and by thirty, I was a single mom." Her face clouds as she relives a memory. "He came to the hospital after Christopher's birth to inform me that he'd met someone else and was leaving. Boom. Done. I had no work experience, a newborn, and no home."

A lump forms in my throat. "How did you do it, get to the other side?" To look at Rose is to see joy and experience a strength forged in fire. She wears happiness over her heart, a testament to the quiet battles she's fought on her own.

Her chin lifts with a watery smile. "My Aunt Birdie, my bright spot. I moved into the attic here and worked my way up and out when I could afford an apartment. She passed away when I was thirty-nine, and I inherited the center, which I'm now passing on to you, the new executive director."

Come again?

All I can do is stare as wave after wave of shock and confusion slap into me. A year ago, I was living in my best friend's house, unsure how my knee-jerk reaction to leave Charles would pan out. Never in my wildest dreams did I imagine that Haile's preschool tour would turn into this.

Rose's laugh is hearty as she watches the emotions play out on my face. "The board approved your promotion last week." Tears shine in her eyes. "I've been waiting for you for so long. It's time."

"Y-you're leaving right now...for good?"

"Heavens, no!" Her lighthearted chuckle tips her cheeks. "I'm taking the rest of the day off. Louise and I are going to look at RVs." Her smile stretches into a grin. "It's been our dream to travel across the country. Now we can. Thanks to you."

She pulls me into her canary sweater and wraps her arms around me with a squeeze. "Thank you, Rose." The crack in my voice holds back a tsunami of tears.

"This is your next chapter. Life can start again at forty. That was the year I met my Louise, and we're only getting started twenty years later. You've got yourself a good man. Don't forget your own needs while you take care of everyone else."

I'm a bumbling mess, but I get myself together while she grabs her coat. "I don't know how I'll ever repay you."

Her smile widens. "Pay it forward, and keep it going when the time comes. I'll see you tomorrow."

The rest of the day is a mix of happy tears and ugly crying at the most inconvenient times. Two instructors asked if someone died, and one parent promised to add me to the prayer card.

Not even Charles could steal my vibe. He texted not too long after Rose left with the threat that I'd pay for my stunt today. I expected him to unleash an explosion of photos across the internet, photos of Julian and me that didn't obscure my face. Or maybe he'd repay my visit to his office with one of his own and show up here.

By four, I was off with Haile to pick up Jackson for the stop-and-go journey back home.

After dinnertime, I went to the streets—technically, the end of the block, but I was outside. The only suspicious activity was me about to reenact *I Know What You Did Last Summer*, screaming in a circle in the middle of the road asking an absent killer how much longer until he appeared. But I refrained, in the name of basic decency and preventing a CPS visit.

By ten, I drifted to sleep with the surveillance photo of Julian tucked under the pillow next to me.

Chapter 48
Ella

If the FBI tries to recruit Haile before she starts kindergarten in the fall, it wouldn't surprise me at all. Behind those brown eyes and big brown curls is a five-year-old too young to be interrogating me like I stole her lunch money and took off to Vegas on a gambling spree. Is it too much to pee in peace without her running to call Aunt Morgan to say she hears a sniffle?

The truth is, I've kept up smiles and thrown myself into work since Julian left for London three weeks ago. Distance is no stranger to us, but we're not the same two people who stumbled into each other's lives last year. I *love* him, something I never thought I'd say—about anyone—again, least of all during a divorce. I've never felt as safe and seen as I do now. And that's frightening but worth the risk.

Julian didn't leave because of work, though a project across the pond is taking up most of his time. So, yes, I sulk. For the time apart forced on us by an ex who plays more games than MTV's *The Challenge*.

"It's okay."

"Sorry?" My eyes lift to the rearview mirror. Haile stares back in her lilac jacket with a knowing smile.

"To be sad and not hide it," she says, like the answer is obvious. Maybe it is.

I might have to call the FBI myself. "I'm fine, baby."

"We got here five minutes ago. Your hands are still on the wheel."

Well, damn.

My back straightens, and I chance a glance at my future profiler daughter's full-on grin. Jackson sits next to his nosy sister, in a Minecraft trance on his tablet. We could be in this parking space for another half hour without a peep from him as long as the Wi-Fi works.

"Can't I have a long week, Miss Ma'am?" The center has kept me on my toes. Between onboarding new hires, fundraising, and filling in whenever someone gets a spring cold, Haile should thank every star in the sky I'm not staring into space for hours.

She giggles. "That's fine. Grandma has cucumbers for stress. You should try them."

I choke out a laugh and smooth the edges of my ponytail. "Anything else?"

"It's okay to miss him," she says quietly. "I do."

What the heck do I say to that?

Julian and I saw each other in secret almost daily. Outside of a dinner or two and Jackson's rugby, he's not around the kids enough to look like more than a family friend, even though he's much more. He's the steady presence—patient, kind, and devoted. It's foolish to expect my kids won't feel his absence. With the time difference and our hectic schedules, we barely speak.

I miss him.

I need him.

"Me too, baby," I whisper back. "Ready to go in?"

I grab the small suitcase with their weekend clothes out of the trunk and tap the window for Jackson to quit his game and make the short trek across the gravel path to the front door.

Katharine and I have weekly drop-offs down to a science. I head over with Haile and Jackson after our weekly therapy session. Katharine greets us and takes me to the kitchen for tea before I head back, and Charles comes whenever he does. We do this every Friday, but tonight is different.

My skin needles when Charles Sr. answers, wearing a stony glare he doesn't hide from my children. I manage to smile enough for my kids to see it from my profile but without giving the man in front of me any indication that I'm happy to see him.

"Well, isn't this a surprise? Where is Katharine?"

"She's out," he says in a clipped tone.

On a Friday at six in the evening? Did the ladies who lunch finally let loose?

I peer around his narrow, clean-shaven face into an empty marble foyer lit by the edges of light filtering in from the study. Katharine would be squeezing the kids to within an inch of their lives instead of keeping us on the doorstep like we're trying to sell him a cable package.

"Shame." I force another smile and turn to see Jackson and Haile's eyes dancing between me and their grandfather. I might not mind if a bus made it over to this side of Falls Church and ran his ass over, but I won't be the person to turn my kids against family. "Why don't you two see if Ms. Beverly has those scones you love in the kitchen?"

Haile is the first to hug me at the promise of a frosting-covered snack. "Love you, Mommy."

I kiss the top of her head and squeeze her little body wrapped around my legs. "Love you too, sweet girl."

Jackson is not as trusting. He lingers under the decorative porch light with me. He glances up at his grandfather and back to me before speaking in a whisper that hits my heart. "Need me to stay out here with you?"

"I'm okay, baby." I meet Charles Sr.'s glare to show him I mean it. "Better than okay." I squeeze Jackson in a hug. "Love you."

He squeezes tighter. "Love you too."

"See ya Sunday. Have fun."

Jackson walks by his grandfather but stops to look over his shoulder. At my nod, he tucks his hands into his gray jacket and disappears into the maze of crown molding and gilded frames.

"I'll call Katharine later," I say to the man still foaming at the mouth.

"I don't know who you think you are, little girl, but you're about to learn an important lesson."

"And what's that?" I spin to face the father-in-law I wish I never had. Charles Sr. has always been cold, but it looks like the gloves are finally coming off.

"Don't fuck with my family."

"Then tell your son not to fuck with me. I wanted out of this marriage after *he* was unfaithful. *He* is the one holding on for dear life"—*like those struggle strands you call a comb-over*—"having me followed and making threats if I don't call off the divorce. Speak to your son."

"Oh, I have." He steps closer, smacking me with his cologne and rising temper. "Had to send him down to Florida after your stunt in the conference room. My son is the least of your worries now. You never deserved the Hudson name, so I'll grant you a divorce."

"How *kind* of you. If you'll excuse me."

"You think I don't know what's going on? Who you've been sneaking off to when you think no one is watching? Charles could never control you, but the photos he has will show the world what an adulterous whore you are, one who broke her family for a younger man with a trust fund." He dips his head to take in my frown and smiles. Charles Sr. is a few inches shorter than his son, but from the doorstep, he's a giant.

My throat tightens to the point of pain. "I never—"

"Was unfaithful? Doesn't matter." He grips the door, his eyes blazing fire. "Women should know their place, and you, Ella, will get an education soon enough. Enjoy your weekend. It will be your last before I take everything from your worthless life."

The wrought-iron door slams in my face, leaving me speechless surrounded by imported stone and a manicured lawn. I suck in a breath at yet another threat by a man named Charles Hudson. Every time I step forward and fight for the life and joy my kids and I deserve, I get knocked back down on my ass.

No amount of distance between me and Julian will fix this. I'm not sure *anything* will allow me to leave unscathed and away from the public eye.

It's been too quiet, and now I know why.

Chapter 49

Ella

Morning comes in eerie silence until my phone blares on the nightstand. I peek an eye open to see Morgan's name flashing on the screen, too brightly in the nearly pitch-black room, and swipe right on the incoming call with a groan.

"Did they cancel school?" I croak. It's the only reason why she'd be on my phone at such an hour. We're past any real threats of snow, but I keep the hope alive that today is not a day I have to make the trek to Falls Church.

"Turn on the TV!" she shouts through the other end, ringing my eardrums. I wince and check the time: 5:42. Why does this woman sound like a human dog whistle?

It doesn't take long for dread to resettle in my stomach. The threat from Charles's father. The promise to paint me as a cheater in the media.

"Did you turn it on?"

"I don't—there's no TV up here."

The call ends.

Is it a photo of me and Julian? A video of us together? A blog is bad enough, but the *news*?

The phone rings again, on video call this time.

"Morgan, I'm not—"

"Shh! Look."

She turns the camera to face the television over the small fireplace she added in her bedroom after watching a Hallmark movie. My screen fills with a morning news show that people with too much energy before six watch. I cover my mouth to hold back the bile threatening to erupt at whatever media spin is about to play out. A red "Breaking News" box appears to the right of the anchor.

My stomach lurches again. He really did it.

I need a miracle, Jesus...

"I can't watch," I say from the little black void that's my side of the video call. A void I'd very much like to make my permanent residence if the mortgage is affordable.

"Look."

The volume increases as a primped woman in a royal blue blazer speaks to whoever else is up at this ungodly hour with practiced diction and hints of etiquette classes. I'm mid-yawn when I catch "Hudson" and move the phone closer to my face.

Katharine Hudson files for divorce from her longtime husband, Charles Hudson Sr., Chairman of the Mt. Corbel Health System Board of Trustees. The couple, married over forty years, have been a prominent fixture in the Falls Church community. Katharine Hudson, who now prefers her maiden name, Katharine Bennett, filed court documents alleging her husband has a second family he kept secret for the length of their union. Bennett released the following statement through her attorney:

"After much consideration, I have chosen to end my marriage and move forward with my life. It is a new day and a new chapter."

The attorney representing Mr. Hudson declined to comment.

We will follow this story closely as it develops.

Morgan and I sit in silence as the news program switches to a segment about last-minute spring-cleaning tips.

"Did you have any idea?"

"No." My fingertips graze the silk head wrap covering my forehead. "I haven't seen her recently."

The camera flips to my friend, who's fully dressed and looking radiant without an ounce of makeup. I have crust in my eyes and around my mouth, but Ms. Tika Sumpter over here is ready for her close-up. How is this fair?

I check my phone again. No new messages. The last one came from Julian yesterday.

Julian

Thinking of you, sweetheart. Do your stretches before I come back. Wouldn't want you to pull another muscle.

My snort is groggy with sleep. I don't know when I'll squeeze in a yoga class before the man bends me in two whenever he gets home.

Morgan pulls me out of my nasty thoughts about her brother. "Anything Charles tries with those photos won't touch this story. His parents are practically town royalty. They'll string out a timeline to piece together the other family for *at least* two weeks' worth of coverage."

"Handed on a silver platter."

I never told Katharine about her son's blackmail attempts or Asher. The second is no secret, based on the broadcast, but does she know about the first?

"I'm keeping Jackson home today, just to be safe." Kids are relentless. They make gossip sites look like amateurs with what they yell. They repeat discussions from home without nuance or consideration of the sting it will cause the receiving end. Not my child, and not today, of all days.

She nods. "Smart. You took the day off?"

"Yup." It's not every day a woman's divorce becomes final. I have a small cake tucked in the back of the refrigerator with my name on it. I'm not lying. It says "Ella gets the D"—with D for divorce, of course. The other *D* isn't here. "I should go." There are a million calls to make. Grier. Julian. Mama. *Katharine.*

"Text me once it's done. Officially Greene!" Morgan waves spirit fingers in the air with her mouth open and her eyes closed. "We should have another party."

The yolk of the sun's glow lifts the sky out of darkness, stretching vibrant orange hues with golden tips. Today, one Mrs. Hudson quietly sheds her title while another publicly calls attention to the end of hers.

What a way to start the day.

"Tacos!"

"Tacos!" The small crowd in my living room parrots back.

Tonight is a celebration, but not one to advertise with neon letters and a dartboard with my ex's face plastered in the middle. Clinking cocktails to chants of "Fuck him!"—the junior and the senior—is good for a night in with my girls. My kids are a different story. They know I'm no longer with their father, but I'll fight the urge to do high kicks in front of them.

Thus, Taco Monday. A commemoration of hand-sized tortillas stuffed with tasty meats and toppings. The margaritas and collective side-eyes are the silent eff to my ex.

Akua Allrich's Kennedy Center performance croons through the speaker system in a succession of smooth melodies. Currently playing is "Take My Time," a wonderful song in concept, but not for the three kids circling the kitchen island for their food.

"Here you go, vultures."

Haile and Duke take off to the dining room with all their tacos and their tablets. Jackson is the only one who reaches on his toes for a kiss to the cheek. "Thank you, Mom. Love you."

That's my baby.

He's been extra affectionate, hugging a little longer and sticking by my side. They miss Julian; we all do. The dinners. Games. Random sing-a-longs.

"Do you need to call your man?" Morgan bumps my shoulder on her way to the taco station.

"I'm fine," I say through a breath and add more ground beef to the large serving platter. These kids will eat their weight tonight.

"Mm-hmm," Erica says with a margarita in hand and no good intentions in her eyes. "What will you two do now that you're officially a single woman? Besides each other."

"Don't start." I point a serving spoon at Grier, who's coughing to hold back a laugh. She better not act up, either.

Have I thought about this day since Julian and I decided to blur the lines of friendship ? Abso-freaking-lutely. Do I know what this means for us, for bringing things into the light? No, but that's where I want to stand. In the open with him.

The doorbell rings.

"I'll get it!" I call over my shoulder to the women scarfing down tacos like they deep-throat dick. I wipe my hands on the half apron covering my jeans and open the front door with a frown.

Claire and Katharine exchange a look void of smiles or any hint at a pleasant visit. *What happened now?* "Hi, dear. Can we come in?" My former mother-in-law's kind eyes sweep over me. Charles and I might be over, but I refuse to lose her in the divorce.

"Sure, of course." I step aside for the duo I didn't think knew each other and hang their jackets as they step out of their heels. *Camila's father is president and CEO of Mt. Corbel Health, and Charles Sr is chairman of the Board of Trustees, remember?* That does check out.

Claire heads into the living room and assesses the space like it's the first time she's seen it. The foundation is still Julian, but my family has weaved in seamlessly. She takes in the kids' craft storage neatly off to the side and the spring decorations that accent the bookcase of vinyl records. If my mind isn't playing tricks, there's a tip of a smile. "It looks good in here."

"Thank you," I say. "How are you, Katharine?" Our texts this morning were brief—expected when you break the news you're filing for divorce because of a secret family.

"Better." Her tone is strong, resilient. "You?"

"Free."

Katharine's eyes shine. "I'm glad you are, dear." She takes a breath. "We don't mean to disturb, but we wanted to tell you in person." She glances left and right. "Where are the children?"

"In the dining room, eating dinner." My gaze hops between them. "What's going on?"

"I think you should sit," Claire says with a nod to the sofa behind me.

God, please don't let it be Julian.

"I'll stand."

The two share another look before Katharine steps forward. "Charles is getting arrested."

My ass hits the leather sofa with a thud, but not loud enough to alert the house. "*What?*" I must've misheard her.

"I hired a private investigator after photos of Julian and Camila started turning up," Claire says. "I assumed it was him, but I also discovered certain...habits that signaled something else." She pulls out her phone from her cranberry sheath dress—with fabulous pockets, by the way—and scrolls. "Do you know this woman?"

The hell?

"Tiffany Hearst." I nod at the image of the parent volunteer Queen B and Charles huddled together in the corner of a restaurant. "Was that here?"

"Santa Barbara."

What?

"There's strong evidence he used money from the organization for personal gain. He'd expense business trips to conferences he wasn't present for and travel to destinations that did not benefit the organization. Tiffany popped up twice this month. There is also reason to believe he used Mt. Corbel money to help finance a property in Florida."

"Misappropriation of funds is serious," Katharine adds.

"Don't forget embezzlement," Claire throws in.

"Yes." Katharine tears her eyes away to steady her chin. "Because my son crossed state lines"—she sucks in a shaky breath—"he could face federal charges." *Shit.* "I can't undo the harm he's caused, but I can make sure he doesn't hurt you again." Her trembling hand reaches for mine. "You are my family, Ella."

"And we protect the ones we love. Always have, and always will," Claire says. "I'm sorry I didn't catch Asher in time." Her gaze shifts to Katharine. "We didn't know, and Charles was careful to not meet him in person. The only time they did was at that scholarship dinner. I was ready to go after him, but you beat me to it." She considers me with a gentle stare that eases into a smile. "Whether you and my son make it official or not, which I hope you do at some point," she laughs, "you will always be my daughter."

All I can do is gawk. Julian's mom hasn't been unkind to me, but I wouldn't expect her to root for us, either.

"What about Camila?"

"What about her?" She scoffs and sucks her teeth. "I only entertained that girl to see if she was the one feeding those photos to the blog. They came from your ex, but she will answer for her part. Trust me on that."

Claire's words hit me at full force. They would knock me on my ass again if I wasn't already sitting. I'm baffled and dumbfounded, which might be the look of the day. A nervous smile peeks out. "I didn't think you'd approve of us."

Claire tips her head back and laughs. *Laughs.* "I see the way my son lights up when he sees you or speaks about you. The boy is sprung, and I couldn't think of a better person for him to be with. Just don't tell anyone. I do have a reputation." She winks.

"Grandma!" Haile drops her plate on the counter to rush into Katharine's arms. Her small hands wrap around her cream trousers. "*Bonswa*," she says to Claire, whose eyes grow at the familiar greeting.

She looks to me for an explanation. "Her class is learning about cultures." I smile. "Julian is teaching her some Haitian Creole phrases."

"Maybe you could come one day?" Haile peeps.

Claire's eyes shine. I've never seen her cry. Ever. She wipes a stray tear and nods. "I'd love to."

Haile leads them into the den of laughter known as our dining room. Charles's pending prosecution is another fight for another day. He'll need to figure that out with his attorneys. For now, our kids are happy, and they have everything they need to heal.

I take the opportunity to grab my jacket and shoes and head out into the night air.

The moon is full, bathing the neighborhood in a luminous glow. The kaleidoscope of tulips and primroses in full bloom sway in a tender breeze. The kids and I made the flower bed last summer, a lifetime ago, when I dug through hard ground to scatter seeds I would nourish and grow.

I tip my head back, close my eyes, and repeat Grier's words from earlier today in the courthouse:

"It's done."

Finished.

Complete.

"Excuse me? Sorry to bother you, but I'm looking for a recently single woman." A grin stretches across my face as I turn to the deep voice, which is strolling slowly up the sidewalk.

Julian's dimples wink in a smile. His hands are behind his back in a black leather bomber jacket with a matching hoodie. A thin gold chain peeks above his white undershirt. My gaze moves from his fresh fade and down the broad thighs wrapped in dark denim over black and white high tops.

I restrain the urge to maul him and his fine ass and walk down the steps to reach him. "I might know a person. Is she important?"

"*Very*. She fell into my life unexpectedly." He grins to himself. "More like my bed, but that's semantics. I thought she would rob me blind, but she turned out to be the best thing that ever happened to me."

Moonlight conceals my blush. "She sounds pretty special." I bite my lip. "I'm sure she thinks the same of the man who's looking for her."

"I sure fucking hope so."

I giggle.

We reach the last few steps and stand toe to toe. "Hi," he says through a ripple of cedar and sandalwood.

"Hi. So, what are your intentions with this woman?"

His eyes capture mine with a longing we can put away with his passport. "I want to be her anchor, to laugh through the storms, dance in the rain, and take new adventures together. I want to love her and her kids for the rest of my life and"—he pulls a hand from behind his back—"I want to give her this."

I snort through tears at the bag of tacos. He never misses a word I say or the chance to feed my bottomless stomach. "I missed you, and I love you so much."

"I love you too, sweetheart."

We lean forward, and I grab the bag and take off in a sprint to a trail of his laughter. "Oh, how I missed you!" I wave the brown paper sack holding my al pastor tacos in my hand.

"That's cold as shit!"

I squeal at the heavy footsteps behind me and cut behind a black Jeep to run across the street. There's no way I can outrun him, and he proves that when he wraps an arm around my waist, lifts me off the ground in the middle of the street, and spins me in a circle.

My head falls back in a howl when he pins me to his front and tickles me over my windbreaker. "My tacos!" I cry through a cackle at the bag on the ground.

"Nah, don't sniff me after you threw my ass to the side for some food." His nose nudges up my chin as a smile curves his mouth.

We stare at each other as our breaths come in unison, our gazes roaming over each other in slow appraisal.

"No more waiting," I whisper.

"No more waiting."

We inch closer.

"Kiss her already!" I startle at Haile, who's hanging halfway out the door with the biggest grin.

"Gross." Duke takes one look, shakes his head, and walks back inside. Jackson stands next to his sister for a beat before he follows him in, but not before I catch his smile.

"It appears all systems are go," I chuckle.

Julian shifts me in his arms with a smirk. "Well, in that case." He leans down and presses his lips to mine in a slow, drugging kiss.

"Woo!"

"Haile, come on in this house and leave the grown folks to their business." Erica's voice does a lap around the street before we're left in silence.

I give myself over to the passion flowing between us. In the middle of the road. For all to see.

Epilogue

Julian

Three years later

Watching an eight-year-old lay out a grown man would be concerning if it wasn't regular Friday behavior. Haile hooks a leg over his neck as she leans back perpendicular to the burly frame under her with his stretched arm in tow. She is a shining star under the hanging halogen lights on blue mats among her counterparts here for open practice. A shark in the deepest end of the ocean.

With the pressure from her leg blocking his airway and the threat of hyperextending his arm, Levi taps the mat with his free hand. Haile rolls away in a flash of fuchsia shorts and a lilac rash guard. Strands from the jumbled nest of curls on her head stick to her skin. She kneels in wait for her coach to slow down the sharp inhales clutching his chest—the aftermath of contending with a ball of energy.

I've been on the receiving end of an arm bar, and I would take five in a puddle of my own sweat too. That shit hurts, though Haile reminds me that "it's not meant to be comfortable."

"Haile Bear, wrap it up. We gotta go."

"Okay!" She turns back to Levi, who gives her a wide grin and a fist bump before standing to his full height. He towers over her by more than a foot and a half but trains her with a gentleness that contrasts the broad muscles etched into his body from years of fighting.

He lifts his chin to the cluster of chairs that have become my front-row seat to their one-on-one and pulls Haile in for a side hug. "Tempted to call my old manager about this one."

"I need her out of high school first."

Ella would beat my ass inside an octagon. She still gets nervous that Haile will hurt herself but doesn't want to discourage her daughter's passion. I offered to take her to Friday open mat so Ella wouldn't see her training with older kids and adults. Haile is really good, the result of hard work and a coach who saw raw talent the moment they met.

Levi retired as a professional MMA fighter years ago and started his own gym, Ground and Pound, to teach the next generation. It's a southeast gym in the same neighborhood that raised him. He's a cool dude with what Erica calls "the Morris Chestnut appeal." He's been with Haile since she was five and works with her and other kids in her age group on their ground game and striking throughout the week. What started as a few jiujitsu classes soon morphed into boxing and kickboxing. My girl will have the UFC knocking before middle school if she keeps up this pace.

"There better be some ribs when we get there," Jackson says loud enough for his sister to roll her eyes. "At this rate, we'll have to fight Aunt Morgan for one of her salads."

At ten, the kid comes to my shoulder and shovels down as much food as I do. We're a house of athletes, which keeps me at the stove whipping up three meals a week.

A text buzzes my phone in my slacks. I check the smartwatch on my wrist and smile.

Ella

You have ten minutes to bring my babies. All of them.

"Looks like your mother left Bright Spot. Time to go."

Jackson snorts, his face morphing between the little boy he was and the young man he's becoming. He glances at his sister asleep in my wrap carrier with a grin. "Told you to stop breaking her out. Mom doesn't play about Anite."

The smirk touching my lips hopes she isn't. El tackled me the last time I took our six-month-old from the center and kept her with me for the day. Our baby girl played, ate, and conked out, just like she did today in the office. It's Take Your Daughter to Work Day at least once a week, and I have a mini fridge in my office with Anite's baby foods and the pumped milk I bring in for the day.

My father gets extra time with his granddaughter when Morgan doesn't steal her, and I'm on the receiving end of Ella fucking out her frustration.

A win-win.

"Some battles are worth the fight." *Like your mother turning feral in the basement once you all go to sleep.* "Come on before she hunts me down."

We pull up to my parents' house in record time, but we're a few minutes past her ten-minute warning. I park the car in the garage and grab the wrap carrier. Anite is wide awake in her rear-facing car seat, babbling next to Jackson. She squeals when I reach for her, moving her little mouth at warp speed.

"Da-da-da-da-da-da?" Hickory-brown eyes stare back at me from under thick lashes. That's all Anite got from me. Everything else, from her heart-shaped face to her full lips, is her mother.

"*Vin jwenn, Papa,*" I say to my baby girl.

She jumps in my arms and tugs on my goatee with squishy mahogany hands. We're a blended family in a house full of languages. Japanese and Creole flavor many conversations.

Haile darts to the door and enters the passcode in a rush to get to the shower. "Say hi to your grandparents!" I yell to the petite frame and yellow backpack. She throws back a "*Wi!*" before rounding the corner.

Jackson pulls his bag out of the trunk, circles back to kiss Anite on the head, and goes in. The kids are spending the weekend here while Katharine is away on a cruise around the Mediterranean.

Life settled into place after the divorce heard around the DMV. Katharine's bombshell dominated headlines and sparked investigations after several women came forward with sexual harassment allegations against her husband.

Charles Sr. dodged accountability with his wallet and got a slap on the wrist, through a reduced charge and a six-figure fee he didn't blink to pay. His fall from grace was swift. It came with professional exile and a judge awarding Katharine half of every asset he owns.

His sons are a different story.

Charles pled guilty to federal embezzlement charges after officials and an internal audit confirmed he'd misused Mt. Corbel funds and altered statements to cover his tracks. Financing a personal property in Florida was the last straw before a judge sentenced him to eight years in federal prison and six years of unsupervised release. He's serving his time in a low-security correctional facility in Pennsylvania three hours away, and he paid restitution for the privacy intrusion and blackmail charges he caught trying to force Ella to call off the divorce.

Asher served a couple years behind bars for stalking, harassment, and complicity. Last we heard, he's somewhere in Vegas after his father cut off all financial support for him and his brother.

Ella doubled down on family therapy to build a wider network of support for Jackson and Haile. They meet with a new therapist now that Louise retired and is on her RV tour with Rose. She also hired a mental health specialist who helps children navigate having an incarcerated parent. The kids communicate with Charles through email. Ella now has sole custody, and she left the door open for in-person visits but won't force them. Jackson struggled to forgive his father for the harm he caused his mother, but he did it for his own healing.

Amidst all the pain, my family lives life to the fullest. El and I kept our relationship under wraps after her divorce was final. We didn't fool anyone, but with Charles heading off to prison, we didn't want to add our love into the mix. That was until Haile and Jackson asked why I wasn't taking their mother out on proper dates. I courted

Ella for a year and a half. We married six months later, in a private ceremony at a small Virginia vineyard with the kids and ten of our closest family and friends.

Loving her and our children is a gift I'll never take for granted. Even if it comes with her ready to square up on the side of my parents' house.

My wife stands with a hip jutted out in a black pencil skirt I want to peel off, a striped blouse cuffed at the sleeves, and an attitude that's seconds from knocking me on my ass. Her gold hoops chime at her head tilt, the spirals from her curly updo fluttering in the breeze. "What did I tell you?"

Her tone arouses me and Anite for two very different reasons. Our baby smacks at my chest at her mother's voice. My dick hardens against my zipper at the promise of her fury. "Hi, sweetheart." I keep my tone even and close the distance to kiss her cheek.

She softens but catches herself. "Don't hi me. I had meetings with funders all day, and I missed my baby."

That explains the outfit. Ella dresses casually most days, when she helps to wrangle kids or work on programming in the office.

I shower her with light kisses along her jaw and move to her neck. "You look beautiful today." My hand cups her ass, which spills over, and I groan at the peek of toe cleavage from her pumps. "I promise to make it up to you tonight if you wear those shoes."

She leans into my hug and kisses Anite, who all but slobbers on her. "What do you think?"

"She thinks it's worth your while," I supply.

"Mmm." Her fingers trail down my thighs. "Tempting."

A little to the right and you'll get it.

The desire in her eyes sends tingles up my body until she douses them with an eye roll and takes her daughter. Anite fiddles with the gold chains hanging from Ella's neck with an animated giggle. "You're in the doghouse."

"Oh, come on! I do it every week."

"And you can suffer every week."

Her playful laugh screeches to a halt when Morgan swoops in to grab her niece. "Thank you," she says without stopping.

Ella whines, "Get back here with my baby!"

"No! This one had her all day," Morgan says to me, walking backward to the party. "You two have her all the time. You need to share."

"Good luck keeping her from our mother, Mac!" That's a showdown I'd pay to see.

"Who's scared of her?"

Joseph sticks his head out from the corner of the house with a raised brow. "You're on your own if she comes for Anite. I love you, but I would rather fight a bear than face off with Claire."

Morgan huffs but turns the corner while chatting to my baby about husbands and their lack of loyalty.

Joseph moved back in with Morgan after they remarried months after Ella's divorce, only to help pack up and move his family to DC. With his studio and our law office in the city, it made sense to cut down the commute. When they told us we'd be neighbors, they meant it, literally. They purchased the house next door. The kids go to the same charter school and shuffle between houses on any given day.

Ella reaches for me and wraps her arms around my waist. "So you forgive me now, Madam Hold-a-Grudge?"

Her lips press into the skin above my collar. "You know I can't stay mad at you. You're an amazing father, Julian."

"Thank you, baby." I lean against the brick wall and brush my lips against one of her nipples. She arches her back, exposing a pathway up the column of her neck, one I follow with my tongue. "Let's make another."

Her head falls back with closed eyes and a tormented groan when my hands fall to the swell of her hips. "We just had a baby. That's three kids, Julie."

I kiss her chin and crush her to my chest. "We have room for four." We finished the upstairs renovation before I moved back in after the wedding. Jackson's old room became Anite's nursery after he took the main bedroom.

Her moan catches when I take her mouth, smothering her to my body and the depths of my soul. Kissing Ella always feels like the first time. It's explosive, shocking every nerve in my body with a bright flare of desire.

"I'mma need you to unhand her, Russell Wilson." We chuckle at Erica's new nickname for me and put space between us. "You're finally baby-free, and I want my friend." She pulls Ella by the wrist so they can make their exit. "Fuck her later!"

Plan to.

The blaze from the May sun dips below the skyline of trees and rooftops to bathe the city in dusk's glow. My parents' annual Memorial Day party got a major revamp years ago. It's now only accessible to trusted friends and family and no longer a destination for the masses.

"Your dad's ribs always hit the spot." Nate leans back in his chair to stretch his legs and tap his stomach. He's finally cardigan-free but refuses to give up the beanie. He clears his throat with a quick glance. "Sadie saw Camila on one of those reality dating shows. She's competing for a grand prize."

I take a sip of the local craft beer he supplied. "Sounds like her."

Camila never shied away from the limelight. She embraced it until her social status got revoked for her part in the Charles drama. She wasn't aware of his blackmail efforts—so she said—but she did answer questions from blogs about our past. Always ready for her close-up. Her charm scored her footage of us leaving my London hotel, footage she supplied to Charles as proof we were together right before I met El. How that didn't trigger more than community service and a fine is beyond my understanding.

Her father cut her off at the threat of my mother's lawsuit, leaving her homeless and without a car or job. A dramatic battle for someone else's affection seems like a game she could win.

Nate hits me with a double pat. "Everything worked out for the better."

"Yes it did."

He checks his watch and stands. "Gonna run by Swigs on the way home. See you and El this weekend."

"Bet. Tell Sadie and Jasmine I said hi."

I relax into the chirp of crickets, but then a bang pulls my attention to the grill. Antonio squats to peek underneath my father's station, which he cleaned hours ago. "Kitchen's closed, Mo!" I bark out a laugh at his hands on his hip.

"I flew down here for my ribs." He glares. "Your kids conned me."

"How so?"

His hands fly up to flex the muscles on display in his aqua cut-off shirt. "Haile and Jackson challenged me to *Mario Kart*. The rounds lasted so long, your dad gave away all my ribs. I'm never having kids!"

My laughter trumpets through the empty backyard. The man is pouting, at his big age. He has enough money to buy a company that will hand-feed him for the rest of his life. I wipe my eyes and bring my cackling down to a chuckle. "What time is your flight back to Buffalo?"

"Four hours."

I nod to the back door. "If you stop your whining and look in the refrigerator, you'll find the plate he saved you."

Antonio punches the air. "I always loved your family!" I swat away the kiss he tries to drop on my forehead as he sprints to the door. "I'll come out before I leave. Come and visit me soon, prick!" The screen door slams behind him.

In an unexpected twist, my childhood friend signed with a new professional rugby team two years ago. He packed up to relocate to the tundra and has been kicking ass as a starting flanker on the Buffalo Steel. I'm so proud of him after all our years on the pitch together. He's earned his spot.

The screen door opens again, and I bite back a groan. The hairs on my neck prickle, and my chest warms. My eyes are closed, but I still register Ella's presence and smile. I open them to see my wife padding down the stairs barefoot with two tumblers of what looks like scotch.

"Hey." The breeze picks up her lavender scent.

"Hi."

I stop her when she moves toward the chair next to me and widen my legs for her to sit. On me. She bites her lip but finds a seat on my lap, pressing her curves into my chest and her head in the crook of my neck. My arms reach around her, and we take in the peace and quiet as the outdoor lights strung overhead illuminate a space that's carried a lifetime of memories I get to add to with the woman in my arms.

My heart.

My wife.

The mother of our children.

There was a point when I could never imagine myself tied down. Now, I can't imagine my life without Ella, Jackson, Haile, or Anite. Maybe a fourth if she gives the okay.

The tip of my nose brushes her neck. "The kids okay?"

"Yeah," she says while toying with the buttons on my shirt. "Morgan and Joseph left Duke here for the weekend. Him, Jackson, and Haile are teaching your mother how to play *Mario Kart*." We crack up. "Haile ratted her out for cussing in Creole."

My mother loves all of her grandkids, but she shares the bond of language with Haile, who gets private lessons in her grann's native tongue. She and Jackson might not be my blood, but they are my family.

"Where's my father?"

"Out cold on the sofa in the family room with Anite on his chest."

We laugh again.

"When are Mama and Otis leaving to catch up with Katharine?"

"Tuesday," Ella confirms. Mary Lee and Otis's love connection blossomed the second our former security guard laid eyes on her mother. The month after Ella got her divorce decree, Mary Lee sold her house and moved into the townhouse. That only lasted for three months before Otis retired and the two bought a condo in College Park near Ms. Thelma. They enjoy the retired life and take trips in and out the country when they're not loving on our kids. Mary Lee and Ms. Thelma often take girls' trips with Katharine, who stepped into the single life and hasn't looked back.

Everything is perfect, except one thing.

I nudge El to stand and take her by the hand to the dance floor. "Wait here."

"What are you doing?"

"You'll see." I plug my phone into the sound system, find the song, and hit play. The bass and percussion of Marvin Gaye's "I Want You" start, pulling a smile from Ella at the memory of our first dance cut short. "Come here."

Our bodies press when she steps into my arms and I guide her wrist to hold the back of my neck. Her sigh is similar to the one she released years ago, only this one has the promise of peace and forever. She closes her eyes and rests her head on my chest.

I move us around the dance floor with the press of my cheek to the side of her neck, now and always. "I got you, El."

THE END

Acknowledgments

Ah, yes. The awkward part of the book for me (lol). Writing *Ella Gets the D* was easy. Putting "the D" in the title didn't take much thought. But this is where you'll see me flounder, so I promise not to take up too much of your time. (I'm long-winded, so this is likely a lie.)

Whether you found me from my debut, *The Seven Month Itch*, or stumbled across this book, thank you for indulging in my shenanigans. *Ella Gets the D* was a story that popped into my mind—as all of them randomly do—about uncoupling from a spouse.

(Calm down, Mom and Dad. No one is thinking about divorce over here.)

What would happen if you chose to walk away?

What if your spouse forced your hand?

For some reason, my mind drifted back to where I grew up (I'm a Baltimore girl, but the DMV was a former stomping ground). I thought about the women's leagues I was once a part of when I worked in DC in my early twenties. Infidelity isn't exclusive to a particular tax bracket. But the dynamics of someone leaving a partner who's the primary breadwinner—and hearing horror stories through the rumor mill about said breadwinner acting a complete fool—kept coming back to me.

So I kept asking what if and found myself looking up how to get a divorce in Virginia. I had questions about the no-waiting period for adultery and ended up speaking to a family attorney who entertained my hypothetical questions. From there, *Ella Gets the D* had its timeline and restrictions, as penetrative sex *is* considered adultery—even while separated on the road to divorce. Sidenote: Adultery really is a Class 4 misdemeanor in Virginia.

It goes without saying that *Ella Gets the D* is fiction woven with real-life inspiration. Bellaire, Ohio, is a place of family ties, and *Suegra's* is a restaurant idea I once told my Panamanian mother-in-law (Maritza) about years ago. There are other little nuggets sprinkled throughout the book, but I'll save those for myself for now and the people who know.

In an ideal world, every parent and caretaker would have strong support to navigate their new normal without struggling. In real life, you have a higher chance of tripping over a curb than you do winding up in a bachelor's townhouse who eventually becomes your next husband. But we read romance for escape—at least I do—and gas and eggs are too damn high for me to stick Ella in a motel. I also wanted to portray Black wealth as mainstream media often threads our depictions through stereotypes.

This story is about life coming back together to form the unimaginable when it feels like everything has fallen apart. It's also for those of us entering the 40 club—or who've been part of it—as a reminder your next chapters are only the beginning.

I didn't write *Ella Gets the D* to be your typical rom-com, but I hope it made you laugh and enjoy the unexpected love, spicy moments, and found family. Though its own standalone (this one won't be a series), all of my books are in the same universe. I've been itching to write a sports romance, and as the rugby wife of a flanker, I'm looking forward to Antonio kicking off the Buffalo Steel era. My newsletter followers get a special shout-out as they voted on the team name.

Okay, this is getting long. (Told ya I lied.)

Thank you to everyone who was part of this wide ride—the beta readers, the editors, the cover designer (Ashley blessed us again!), and all of you who picked up a copy. A special thank you to my real-life cinnamon roll. My husband keeps me going when I second-guess myself, and I appreciate it more than he knows.

I'm still finding my footing and look forward to connecting more in the community we're building.

Until the next shenanigans.

© Frenchy Press LLC

Tanvier Peart is a future bestselling romance author with a healthy obsession for snacks and happily ever afters. She is a good girl with kinks who spends her days working on policy and enjoys the wild life of being a wife and PTA mom. By night, she writes and reads romance books with steamy scenes. When she's not lost in the land of smut, Tanvier enjoys long walks in Target and the chorus of grunts at the gym.

Want to stay up to date on all of Tanvier's bookish news? Sign up for her newsletter:

https://tanvierwrites.substack.com/

Connect with Tanvier online:

@tanvierwrites

(Instagram, TikTok, Threads, Facebook)